THUNDER CANYON HOMECOMING

BY
BRENDA HARLEN

All the characters in this book have no existence outside the imagination of the author, and have no relation whatsoever to anyone bearing the same name or names. They are not even distantly inspired by any individual known or unknown to the author, and all the incidents are pure invention.

First published in Great Britain 2011
by Mills & Boon, an imprint of Harlequin (UK) Limited,
Eton House, 18-24 Paradise Road, Richmond, Surrey TW9 1SR

© Harlequin Books S.A. 2010

Special thanks and acknowledgement to Brenda Harlen for her contribution to MONTANA MAVERICKS: THUNDER CANYON COWBOYS.

ISBN: 978 0 263 88925 3

23-1111

Harlequin (UK) policy is to use papers that are natural, renewable and recyclable products and made from wood grown in sustainable forests. The logging and manufacturing processes conform to the legal environmental regulations of the country of origin.

Printed and bound in Spain
by Blackprint CPI, Barcelona

Brenda Harlen grew up in a small town surrounded by books and imaginary friends. Although she always dreamed of being a writer, she chose to follow a more traditional career path first. After two years of practicing as an attorney (including an appearance in front of the Supreme Court of Canada), she gave up her "real" job to be a mom and to try her hand at writing books. Three years, five manuscripts and another baby later, she sold her first book—an RWA Golden Heart winner—to Silhouette Books.

Brenda lives in southern Ontario with her real-life husband/hero, two heroes-in-training and two neurotic dogs. She is still surrounded by books (too many books, according to her children) and imaginary friends, but she also enjoys communicating with "real" people. Readers can contact Brenda by e-mail at brendaharlen@yahoo.com.

For two of my most loyal readers:

Marjorie Gennings,
a wonderful aunt who has been there for me
through every stage in my life;

and

Marilyn Bellfontaine,
a true friend who has supported my career
not only from the beginning but
"above and beyond."

And with sincere appreciation to the other authors in
this series for sharing histories, brainstorming details,
answering last-minute questions, and making this
project such an enjoyable one.

Chapter One

Erin Castro stood at the front of the church and tried not to fidget.

It was Erika and Dillon's wedding day and she knew that the attention of all of the guests was focused on the bride and groom, but since she'd arrived in Thunder Canyon, she'd worked hard to blend in and couldn't help but feel uncomfortable with so many eyes turned in her direction.

Her fidgeting fingers found the wide ribbon that bound her bouquet. The satin was smooth and cool, and the rhythmic winding and unwinding of it gave her something to concentrate on rather than the crowd of onlookers.

When she'd come to town a few months earlier, she'd had two suitcases in the trunk of her secondhand Kia, a newspaper clipping in the pocket of her faded jeans and absolutely no clue how to begin the quest she had set herself upon. Then she'd seen the "Help Wanted" sign in the front window of The Hitching Post and had taken the first step in her journey.

She'd worked with Haley Anderson at the restaurant and when Erin mentioned that she didn't want to live at the Big Sky Motel forever, Haley had helped her find an apartment. With both her job and housing concerns alleviated, Erin had believed that she was meant to stay. A few weeks later, she learned of a position available at the Thunder Canyon Resort. Realizing that the more people she encountered, the more likely she was to find someone who might have answers to the questions that prompted her trip from San Diego, Erin willingly took on the second job. When she started working a lot of overtime at the resort, she'd had to give up the waitressing job, but she had no regrets. It was at the resort that she'd met Erika Rodriguez, who was now exchanging vows with Dillon Traub.

She was happy that her friend was marrying the man of her dreams, but she couldn't help wishing that she was watching the nuptials from somewhere in the back of the church rather than the front. She wound the ribbon around her finger again as her eyes moved restlessly over the assembled crowd, focusing more on the stunning white décor of the winter wonderland setting than on any of the guests.

Her thoughts and her gaze continued to wander, until caught by the hot, intense stare of Corey Traub—the groom's brother.

Her breath stalled, and her heart pounded.

She'd met Corey the night before at the rehearsal. And her response to his presence had been just as powerful then as now—and just as unwelcome.

Her reasons for coming to Thunder Canyon hadn't included any thoughts of romantic entanglements. Especially not so closely on the heels of the end of another relationship.

She knew that her mother had harbored great expectations for the future of her almost-twenty-six-year-old (read "virtually unmarriageable") daughter and the man she'd already envisioned as the perfect (read "willing to marry her daughter") son-in-law. And while it shouldn't have been so difficult to end a relationship that meant more to Betty than it did to her, it had been tough. More so than she'd expected. She'd always felt as if she hovered on the periphery of her family. She couldn't have said why she felt that way—it wasn't anything specific anyone had said or done, it was just a sense that she didn't quite belong, and she desperately wanted to belong. And perhaps on some level, she'd thought—hoped—that a good marriage would give her the gold star she'd longed for.

As the youngest child and the only daughter, her parents didn't have the same expectations of her that they had of their sons. One of the few things they expected was that she would meet a nice man and start a family. After only a few weeks of dating, Trevor had told her that he wanted to get married.

He'd laughed at the shocked expression on her face, then explained that he wasn't actually proposing to her. He was just putting it out there, he said, so she understood what he was looking for and so that she could let him know if she didn't want the same thing.

She *wanted* to want the same thing. She tried to make herself feel more for him than she did because she knew that her parents would approve of Trevor and she really wanted to be approved of. But in the end, she couldn't stay with a man whose kisses left her unmoved. She couldn't plan a future with a man whose touch made her want to pull away rather than press closer. She knew that physical attraction was only one aspect of a relationship, but she couldn't imagine building a long-term relationship with a man without ever feeling that little quiver in the pit of her belly.

As she looked into Corey Traub's espresso-colored eyes, she felt that quiver—and a whole lot more. There was a crackle and sizzle in the air that assured her his kisses would not leave her unmoved.

When his gaze drifted to her mouth and his own lips curved, she knew that his thoughts were following a similar path to her own. Her body's response was strong and swift, and she was shocked by the purely visceral reaction.

She wasn't the type of woman who got swept away by passion. She wasn't sure she even believed in the kind of all-consuming passion that could sweep a woman away. She'd certainly never experienced anything like it before. And what was wrong with her that she was having such thoughts about a man she barely knew—and during her friend's wedding, no less?

She resisted the urge to lift the bouquet of flowers to her face and use it as a fan to cool the heat that had suddenly infused her cheeks.

"…I now pronounce you husband and wife."

The minister's voice broke through Erin's reverie and refocused her attention.

"You may kiss your bride," he told the groom.

She watched Dillon as he lowered his head toward Erika's, and the obvious love and happiness in his eyes brought tears to Erin's. Standing behind Erika, she couldn't see the expression on her friend's face, but she knew Erika's eyes would reflect the same emotion and joy. Erika had been floating on cloud nine since she'd finally accepted that Dillon loved her and admitted that she felt the same way about him. This wedding was just the icing on the cake—a public ceremony to affirm the love they shared and formalize the commitment they'd already made to one another.

Erin was surprised to realize that she envied her friend. Surprised to realize that getting married and starting a family might not be as far down on her list of priorities as she'd suspected. Of course, she'd have to fall in love first, and she wasn't looking for any kind of personal involvement right now.

She'd never been all the way in love before. Sure, she'd experienced attraction and infatuation and there had even been a time or two when she'd thought what she was feeling might be love. But when those relationships had ended and she'd felt more relief than regret, she'd known it wasn't. And the relief had given way to doubt as she wondered if she would ever know the intensity of emotion that was supposed to be love.

Her parents had it—she recognized it in the looks that passed between them, the casual touches they exchanged, the secret smiles they shared. Even after more than thirty years of marriage, there was an enduring bond of both attraction and affection between them that Erin someday hoped to find with someone.

Of course, her life was too unsettled right now to be making any kind of long-term plans, but…someday.

She glanced at Corey again and found his eyes still on her. Her future might be uncertain, but she wasn't immune to the attraction of a handsome man.

And she found herself wondering what it would be like to be held by him, kissed by him. She wanted him to take her in his arms and hold her tight against his hard body until she was breathless. Which would take all of about half a second considering that just the *thought* of kissing him stole all the air from her lungs.

She tore her gaze from his and forced the treacherously enticing thoughts from her mind.

Because she had no doubt that the six-foot-tall oil heir

had kissed more than his fair share of women and she had no intention of joining the undoubtedly long line of willing women he had left behind. And he would be leaving—he might have family in Thunder Canyon, but his home was in Texas and her home was…well, she hadn't quite figured that out yet.

Which was just one more reason that any kind of involvement with Corey Traub would be both foolish and reckless.

When the bride and groom's kiss finally ended, even the minister was smiling his approval. Then he turned to the assembly and said, "Ladies and gentlemen, it is my pleasure to introduce to you Dr. and Mrs. Dillon Traub."

The guests all rose to their feet and applauded.

Dillon took Erika's hand with one of his and held out the other to Emilia, his two-year-old stepdaughter. The little girl's bright, happy smile made Erin smile, too. Her friend had harbored doubts about Dillon's willingness to be a father to someone else's child, but the sexy doctor had proved that he wasn't just ready to step up but was eager to do so, and it was obvious to everyone present that the bride and groom and tiny flower girl were already a family.

Erin felt an ache in her heart as she thought of her own family and the questions that had brought her to Thunder Canyon. Questions that remained, after more than three months in town, unanswered.

Her parents still didn't understand what had precipitated her sudden decision to pack up and head to Montana. She'd claimed dissatisfaction with her job and the relationship with Trevor, but she knew they were worried, that they felt she should have tried to change the situation rather than run away from it. But after her last meeting with Aunt Erma, only hours before the elderly woman passed away, she'd realized that she needed answers her parents couldn't—or wouldn't—give her. Answers that might finally explain why she'd always felt a little out of place in her own family.

You need to find your family. Her aunt's words echoed in her mind. *They're in Thunder Canyon.*

Erin had been as stunned as she was skeptical, especially when Erma didn't provide any more information. As for the newspaper clipping the elderly woman had given to her, Erin still didn't know what to make of that. She didn't have a clue which of the families in the photo—if any—might be able to help her find the answers she sought, and Erma hadn't steered her in a specific direction.

She hadn't shown the clipping to her parents—a decision that she continued to wrestle with. But both Jack and Betty had been dismissive of Erma's claims. When Erin had asked if she'd been adopted, her mother had offered to show off the stretch marks and unsightly veins that were her reward for the nine months that she'd carried her daughter.

But there was something about Erma's words that haunted Erin in a way she didn't understand and couldn't disregard.

If she wasn't adopted, maybe her parents had gone through a rough patch in their marriage and her mother had been involved with someone else. It had taken a lot more courage to ask Betty about *that* possibility, but her mother had actually laughed, assuring Erin that there had never been anyone before her father and never anyone since.

Still, she couldn't help but feel that there had to be some kind of foundation for Erma's conviction. Unfortunately, her aunt's death had left Erin with a lot of doubts and uncertainties, countered only by her determination to find the truth once and for all.

"Shall we?"

The question jolted her out of her reverie and made her realize that the bride and groom had already started down the aisle. She forgot about Erma and all of her reasons for coming to Thunder Canyon when she settled her hand in the crook of Corey's elbow.

She concentrated on putting one foot in front of the other as she followed Dillon and Erika and Emilia, refusing to look at the groom's brother. But as they approached the doorway, Corey pulled her a little closer to negotiate the narrow opening, and she shivered.

Thankfully, the cool November afternoon gave her a ready excuse for the goose bumps on her flesh, even if she knew they were more a response to the man at her side than the chilly weather. But she had no intention of being distracted from her fact-finding mission by anything or anyone—not even the groom's far-too-sexy brother.

It was torture, riding beside him in the limousine on the way to the resort for the reception. Although there were only five of them in a ten-passenger limo—and one of those five a child buckled into a car seat—the interior of the vehicle felt small to Erin. Or maybe it was that Corey was so big.

She shifted on the seat so that she was pressed against the side of the car. But she could still feel the heat of his body and smell a hint of his aftershave, and she couldn't help but watch the smooth, efficient movements of his hands as they peeled the foil off of a chilled bottle of champagne.

He unfastened the wire and popped the cork while Dillon struggled to unwrap the straw on a juice box for his new daughter. Erika reached for the drink, obviously trying to help, but her groom was determined to master the task. The bride shrugged and settled back against the cushy leather seat, content to let him.

Erin felt a little tug of envy again but pushed it aside. Maybe Erika did have it all, but getting it hadn't been easy for her. She'd had her heart broken when Emilia's father walked out on her, and then she'd had to tackle the trials and tribulations of single parenthood. From Erin's perspective, her friend had done a wonderful job, and if she'd lucked out when she'd fallen in love with Dillon Traub, well, no one deserved it more.

Corey had finished pouring the champagne and passed the crystal flutes around to the adults.

"To the bride and groom," he said, lifting his glass.

Erin joined in the toast but only took the tiniest sip. Although she was sure the bubbly wouldn't be nearly as potent as Corey's proximity, she didn't want to take the chance of alcohol further compromising her judgment.

"To Erika," Dillon said. "Not only the most beautiful bride I've ever seen and the most amazing woman I've ever known, but also the one who has given me the greatest gift I could ever hope for by becoming my wife today."

Erika's eyes were misty with tears when her new husband brushed his lips against hers.

"To my daughter," the groom said, tapping his glass against Emilia's juice box. "One of those greatest gifts."

The little girl beamed at him and slurped down more juice.

"And to my brother," Dillon continued. "For always being there for me when it mattered, and especially today because it mattered most of all."

Corey grinned. "I'll remind you of those words the next time you grumble about me being underfoot."

His brother smiled back before he shifted his attention. "And to Erin—"

"Wait," Erika interrupted.

Dillon's brows rose.

"As the bride, I should get to toast my maid of honor," she said.

Her husband gestured for her to continue.

Erin's fingers tightened around the stem of her glass as she felt the attention focus on her.

"To Erin. I know you were surprised when I asked you to stand up with me at my wedding, and more than a little reluctant, and I want to thank you for saying 'yes' because although we've only known each other for a few months, I feel closer to you than all of the people that I grew up with here in Thunder Canyon. More, I feel accepted by you and appreciated for who I am rather than judged by what I've done, and I will always be grateful for your unwavering support and your unconditional friendship."

"Hey, can you say something about me?" Corey asked his new sister-in-law. "Because that was a lot more eloquent than what Dillon came up with."

Everyone was laughing as the limo pulled up in front of the resort.

Erin slipped away from Corey's side soon after they entered the ballroom.

The bride and groom had opted for a champagne reception rather than a formal meal, so there was no seating plan and guests mingled freely while waiters circulated with trays of hot and cold hors d'oeuvres. Erin decided it was wise to do her mingling as far away as possible from the best man.

It was a strategic retreat. She simply didn't know how to deal with the feelings that stirred inside of her when she was near Corey. During the brief time that she'd dated Trevor, she'd been aware that something was missing. She'd liked him well enough and they'd shared some common interests, but there was no spark between them.

When Corey Traub had walked into the rehearsal the night before, she could hardly see for the sparks. She'd always thought she should feel *more,* but she had never guessed how much more there could be—or how unsettled the more could make her feel.

She had no experience with this kind of immediate and intense attraction. But she was certain that Corey did. That he had this effect on women all of the time and no doubt knew exactly how to handle it. How to handle *her*. And as intrigued as she was by the idea of being handled by the sexy groomsman, she was even more wary.

She didn't do a lot of mingling, but she made a point of chatting with the people she knew and spent several minutes talking with Haley Anderson and Marlon Cates, Haley's now-fiancé. When she turned away from the couple, she found herself face-to-face with Corey.

Actually, it was more face-to-chest because, even in heels, she was several inches shorter than he. And it was quite a chest, the breadth and strength of it evident even through the shirt and jacket he wore. She forced her gaze to lift to an even more impressive face.

Was it any wonder the man took her breath away? He had a look that could sell…anything, she decided, and managed to hold back a sigh.

He had a strong forehead, sharp cheekbones, a slightly square jaw. His brows arched over dark eyes surrounded by thick lashes, his lusciously curved mouth was quick to smile, and when he did, her knees simply went weak. The slight bump in his nose was the only imperfection, but it didn't detract from the overall effect.

But he was somehow more than the sum of all of those parts, and the devilish charm that sparkled in his eyes and winked in his smile was just one more weapon in his over-stocked arsenal.

"You've been avoiding me," Corey said, sounding more curious than offended.

"I have not," she denied, though not very convincingly.

"Prove it," he challenged.

She eyed him warily over the top of her glass. "How?"

"Dance with me."

Erin took another tiny sip of her champagne as she considered how to respond. She knew she should refuse, that getting closer to the groom's brother was not a good idea when he could make the nerves in her belly quiver from clear across the room. But how could she refuse? What excuse could she give for declining a seemingly innocent request? Especially when he'd already guessed that she was avoiding him.

Thankfully, before she could say anything, another woman approached from the other side and latched on to him, deliberately rubbing the curve of her breast against his arm as she leaned close. "Hey, cowboy, you promised me a dance."

When she'd been waitressing at the Hitching Post, Erin had gotten to know Trina as one of the Friday night regulars. Trina frequently came in with a group of girlfriends and often left with a man—and not usually the same one as the week before.

At the resort, Erin frequently worked at check-in with Trina, as had Erika. No doubt it was their working relationship that had compelled the bride to invite the other woman to her wedding despite the fact that Trina had been instrumental in churning the gossip mill when Erika started dating Dillon.

Erin didn't know whether Trina had attended the event with a date, although she knew the presence of an escort wouldn't inhibit Trina from flirting with anyone else who caught her eye—as the groom's brother had obviously done.

To his credit, Corey didn't roll his eyes, though Erin

didn't miss the quick desperate plea in them before he shifted his gaze from her to the other woman.

"But I already promised this particular dance to Erin, didn't I, darlin'?"

She had the power to save him. She simply had to agree that he had promised this dance to her. But she sensed that saving Corey from the she-wolf at his side would somehow end up with her becoming a sacrificial lamb, and that was a risk she wasn't willing to take. Because the way he said "darlin'"—the subtle Texas twang in his voice combined with the unmistakable heat in his eyes—sent a delicious shiver over her skin and stirred desire in her body and reminded her that what she needed to do was keep a good, safe distance between herself and the far-too-sexy Texas oil heir.

"Actually, I really wouldn't mind sitting this one out," she said.

"I'll be right back," Corey said to her, and his narrowed gaze told her that the words were more a threat than a promise.

Trina's satisfied smile, however, warned Erin not to count on his prompt return.

She watched him move around the dance floor with the other woman in his arms and tried to convince herself that the sensation overtaking her was relief and not regret.

Corey knew when he was being brushed off. Though it was something of a new experience for him, he had no trouble interpreting the message in Erin's polite words—she wasn't interested.

The woman in his arms, however, definitely was. Unfortunately, Corey couldn't even remember her name.

Catrina? Tina? Trina! At least, he thought that was it. He admittedly hadn't been paying much attention when she'd introduced herself earlier. He hadn't paid much attention to any of their conversation, having been thoroughly captivated by the sexy bridesmaid in the frosty blue gown.

The one who claimed she wasn't interested.

His gaze drifted across the room to where Erin stood with a glass of champagne in her hand, and his gaze locked with hers again.

And he knew that, although she might feign disinterest, the look in her eyes contradicted her words.

So what was the story there? Why was she pretending to be immune to the chemistry between them?

After meeting her at the rehearsal the night before, he'd made some discreet inquiries and learned that she didn't have a steady boyfriend. In fact, by all accounts, she hadn't dated anyone since moving to Thunder Canyon a few months earlier. Which made him wonder if she'd made the move because she needed to get away from someone who had broken her heart.

The thought was strangely unsettling. He didn't even know her, so he didn't understand why he would feel protective of her. But there was something that had struck him from the first—maybe it was the hint of vulnerability in those deep-blue eyes, or the wistfulness in her smile, or maybe it was just the feeling, irrational though he knew it was, that Erin was the woman he'd been waiting for.

He smiled at the thought, recognizing it as not just irrational but ridiculous in light of the fact that he couldn't even get her to agree to dance with him. Then again, Corey had never been one to back down from a challenge.

More and more couples were joining those already on the dance floor and soon the space was so crowded with bodies that he lost sight of her. When the song finally ended and he released Trina, she pouted prettily.

"Are you really going to let me go so soon?"

"Yes, I am, darlin'," he told her, but softened the rejection with a smile.

She tucked something into his pocket. "My number—in case you change your mind."

Because his mother had raised him to be a gentleman, he didn't tell her that he'd had her number from the start, but he also didn't give her another thought as he walked away.

He was too busy searching the crowd for a certain blue-eyed girl in a familiar blue dress.

Chapter Two

Erin had let down her guard. It was the only excuse she had for being caught so unaware. But when Corey had followed Trina onto the dance floor, Erin had been certain her coworker would keep him thoroughly occupied. She hadn't expected that he would walk away from an obviously willing woman and come looking for her.

But she'd barely started to nibble on the hors d'oeuvres she'd put on her plate when he lowered himself into the empty chair beside her. She popped a coconut shrimp in her mouth, slowly chewing then swallowing.

"I believe you owe me a dance," he said, choosing a stuffed mushroom from her plate.

She lifted a brow. "Do I?"

"At the very least."

"Why don't I share my dinner and we'll call it even?" she suggested.

He grinned, and she felt the now-familiar weakness in

her knees again. "I'll get you some more mushrooms as long as I get the dance."

She nudged her plate toward him. "I'm really not that hungry."

"What are you afraid of?" He bit into a petite quiche.

"That you'll stomp all over my toes with your cowboy boots."

She'd meant to insult him, hoped the affront would dissuade him. Instead, he laughed.

"I'm sure you'll survive," he told her. "My previous dance partner was barely limping when she walked away."

"She was plastered so close, you wouldn't have been able to step on her toes if you tried."

Too late she realized what she'd said—that her response proved that she'd watched him with Trina.

Corey's smile confirmed that he'd caught her slip, but thankfully, he didn't call her on it.

"What do you say?" he prompted.

Erin knew that to refuse again would only succeed in making a big deal out of something that shouldn't be. After all, it was just a dance.

So she took the hand he offered and let him lead her away from the table. Though her heart was hammering furiously against her ribs, she decided that there really wasn't any danger in spending time with Corey on a crowded dance floor.

The minute he put his arms around her, she realized she was wrong. Because every fiber of her being was acutely aware of his nearness and every nerve ending in her body was suddenly humming.

She should have guessed that he'd be a good dancer. Contrary to her earlier teasing remark that she feared for her feet, he moved smoothly and confidently around the dance floor. No doubt he knew all the right moves in any situation, but despite that warning to herself, it required no effort on Erin's part to follow his lead, nor was it a hardship to be held in his arms.

She saw Erika and Dillon dance by and was grateful for the distraction. "They look so perfect together," she murmured.

"I've never seen my brother so happy," Corey admitted to her. "It almost makes me forgive him for pulling up stakes and moving to Montana."

She tipped her head back. "Almost?"

He shrugged. "A Texan is always a Texan, regardless of where he parks his horse."

The mental image of a horse tethered outside of the medical clinic made her lips curve.

His gaze dropped to her mouth, lingered. Her breath caught.

"You have a beautiful smile," he told her.

Immediately, her smile faded.

"Why do I make you so nervous?"

She couldn't—wouldn't—tell him that it was her own response to him that made him nervous. Instead, she said, "Because I don't know what you want from me."

"Right now, just a dance."

"And later?"

His smile was slow and filled with sensual promise. "Why don't we figure that out later?"

"If you're looking for a good time while you're in Thunder Canyon, you should be looking in Trina's direction," she told him.

"You don't think we could have a good time together, darlin'?" The challenge was issued in that same lazy tone that skimmed over her like a caress.

"I'm sure we could," she replied honestly. "But I'm

not the type of woman to go home with a smooth-talking stranger."

He pulled her closer so that her thighs were aligned with his. They were more swaying than dancing now, and the light brushes of his body against hers felt disturbingly like foreplay.

"I'm hardly a stranger," he said.

"I just met you yesterday."

"And I haven't been able to stop thinking about you since then."

She wasn't entirely sure she could trust what he was saying. Because while he sounded sincere and the look in his eyes confirmed that he felt at least a hint of the same attraction that had her whole system tied up in knots, she couldn't help but feel that Corey Traub was the type of man who had a line for every occasion—and a woman in every town he'd ever visited. She'd be a fool to fall under his spell, and she was already halfway there.

He dipped his head toward her, his dark eyes sparkling with a hint of playfulness. "So tell me, are your toes black and blue yet?"

"You know they're not," she said.

He grinned, and again her breath caught. *Damn.* The man's smile was a seriously dangerous weapon.

"So why do you sound annoyed?" he teased.

"I'm not annoyed," she denied.

But she was wary.

Corey could see that in her eyes. And he couldn't blame her. She was probably used to being hit on by guys who wanted nothing more than to get naked with her, and although Corey wouldn't deny that idea appealed to him, he was trying not to objectify the woman who was obviously a close friend of his new sister-in-law.

Sister-in-law.

The word echoed in his mind, made him shake his head. Erin raised a brow.

"I was just thinking about the fact that I'm dancing with the most beautiful woman at my brother's wedding," he answered the unspoken query, "which made me realize that Dillon is actually married."

"Is he one of those guys who swore it would never happen?"

"I don't know if I'd say that, but he and his first wife divorced after their son died and he never gave any indication that he was looking to settle down ever again. And certainly no one expected that, when he came to Thunder Canyon to fill in for Marshall at the resort, he would fall in love and become a husband and a father only a few short months later."

"Especially not Erika," Erin noted.

He chuckled. "Yeah, I think she fought against falling in love again even more than he did."

"She had reason to be wary."

"I guess she did," he agreed. "And so did he. How about you?"

"What about me?"

"Why isn't there anyone here with you tonight?"

"I didn't see any point in bringing a date when I would only neglect him to perform my maid-of-honor duties."

Which answered his question without actually telling him whether or not she was involved with anyone right now. He decided to trust the reports of the local grapevine and assume that she was currently unattached.

But there was something else he was curious about. "You've known Erika for a while?"

"Since I moved here in the summer."

"So why were you uncomfortable in the limo when she thanked you for standing up with her?"

She lifted a shoulder. "Because I didn't really do anything that required thanks."

"You were—are—her friend."

"And she's mine."

He nodded. "But why—"

Someone nudged his shoulder.

He scowled and turned, an irritated retort on the tip of
his lips until he saw that it was his cousin Dax.

"Come on, Cor. We've got bottles of champagne ready
to toast the bride and groom."

"And I've got a beautiful woman in my arms," Corey
pointed out to his cousin.

"I'm not suggesting you let go of her," Dax said and
winked at Erin. "Bring her along."

And that was how she ended up with Corey at a table
where his friends and family were gathered.

During the time she'd been in Thunder Canyon, she'd already met most of the others at the table. The Traubs—Dax
and Shandie, DJ and Allaire, and the Cates—Marshall and
Mia—now back from their vacation, Mitchell and Lizabeth,
Marlon and Haley and Marlon's twin brother, Matt. Erin
realized that Matt Cates was the only one not married or
engaged, though he had brought Christine Mayhew as his
date. Her boss, Grant Clifton, was also there with his wife,
Stephanie, and Grant's best friend, Russ Chilton, was in
attendance with his spouse, Melanie. Erin had met the rest
of the groom's family at the rehearsal, but other than the
parents—Claudia and Peter—she didn't remember any of
their names, and she was grateful when Corey repeated the
introduction of his brothers, Ethan, Jason and Jackson, and
his sister, Rose.

Erin hovered on the periphery as glasses of champagne
were passed around, thinking that she might be able to

sneak away. But Corey kept an arm around her shoulders, making it clear that he had no intention of letting her go. So she stayed beside him as toasts were made and glasses refilled, and she found herself following the various conversations with avid curiosity.

When conversation shifted to the Thanksgiving holiday, only a few weeks away, Grant remarked that he expected his mother and his sister would both return to Thunder Canyon for the occasion.

"It's been a long time since Elise has been in town for her birthday," Grant said. "So I'm planning a surprise party for her while she's here."

"How old is she going to be?" Erin asked.

"Twenty-six," her boss replied. "On the twentieth."

Erin paused with her glass of champagne halfway to her lips.

Her twenty-sixth birthday was on the twentieth, too.

It was probably nothing more than a coincidence, but a sudden startling thought occurred to her. All this time she'd been looking for a man who might have had an affair with her mother, but maybe aunt Erma had been referring to something completely different.

Erin lowered her hand and focused her attention more intently on her boss, noticing—for the first time—that his eyes were the same blue color as her own. And that his hair was dark blond, also similar to her own. She shook her head, as if to rid it of the fanciful imaginings. But the questions that had rooted in her mind wouldn't be easily dismissed.

"I haven't seen Elise since high school," Matt remarked. "I'm not even sure if I would recognize her."

"I'm sure you would." Grant reached into his back pocket for his wallet. "She hasn't changed much."

Erin, who had been wondering how to ask Grant if he

had any pictures of his sister, leaned closer as her boss tugged a photo out from its holder and slid it across the table toward Matt.

"This was taken last summer," Grant told the other man.

Matt leaned closer to look at the photo, and Erin did, too.

"You're right," Matt said. "In fact, she hasn't changed at all."

Erin's first thought was that Grant's sister was an attractive woman—her blond hair was worn in a pageboy style that brushed her shoulders and she had pretty blue eyes and an innocence about her that made her appear younger than her years. Her second thought was that Elise didn't look much like her brother. In fact, the shape of her eyes and her chin was more like that of her own brothers, Jake and Josh.

She pulled back, her stomach suddenly churning, her heart pounding. The conversation continued around her, but she didn't hear a word of it. She couldn't think of anything but that picture of Elise.

"More champagne?"

"What?"

Corey held the bottle of champagne over her glass. Erin shook her head and set her glass on the table. "I, um, I need to get some air," she said, and slipped away from him and toward the exit.

She hadn't expected that he would follow her, but she'd only just pushed through the doors and barely registered the cold November wind on her bare shoulders before they were covered.

"You shouldn't be out here without a coat," Corey said, draping his tuxedo jacket around her.

"Now you are," she told him.

"I'm not wearing a sleeveless dress."

Her lips curved, just a little, at the thought of the all-too-masculine Texan in any kind of dress, and she slipped her arms into the sleeves of his jacket.

She could feel the heat from his body, smell the scent of his skin, and the quivering that reverberated low in her belly was almost enough to take her mind off of the kaleidoscopic thoughts swirling in her mind.

Twenty-six years earlier, on November twentieth, she'd been born in Thunder Canyon. Elise Clifton had been born on the same day in the same town. And Elise looked a lot like Erin's brothers—certainly more than she resembled Grant. Which made Erin wonder—was it possible that the hospital had somehow mixed up the two babies? Was it possible that the man she knew as her boss could be her biological brother?

"Erin?" Corey frowned and touched a hand to her cheek. "Are you okay? You look a little pale."

"Actually, I'm not feeling all that good," she told him. "I think I'd better call a cab and head home."

"I'll give you a ride, if you're sure you're ready to go."

"I am," she told him. "But you don't have to—"

"I'll take you home," he insisted.

Because he'd had a couple of beers earlier in the evening and knew he would be driving, Corey had barely touched his own glass of champagne. He didn't think Erin's had been refilled more than once, but she was obviously feeling the effects of the bubbly, and because he'd been the one who refilled her glass, he felt responsible and was determined to ensure she got home safely.

As they waited for the valet to bring his truck around, he noticed that some of the color had returned to her cheeks. Or maybe they were just pink from the cold. In either case, she didn't really look intoxicated. Her words weren't slurred and her steps weren't unsteady, but her eyes were a little glassy and, even with his jacket on, she was shivering uncontrollably.

He settled her in the passenger seat and immediately cranked up the heat. After a few minutes, her teeth stopped chattering but she kept her arms folded across her chest and continued to stare straight ahead out the window.

She was quiet during the short drive to her condo on the outside boundary of the resort property, only speaking when it was necessary to tell him to turn left or right. He kept stealing cautious glances at her, hoping for some clue as to how she was feeling, but neither her posture nor her expression gave anything away.

He'd been talking to DJ and Allaire and hadn't really paid attention to any of the other conversations. She'd been chatting with Grant and Matt, and he wondered now if either of those men had inadvertently said something that might have upset her. If so, no one else in the group seemed to have picked up on anything that might have caused her distress. Because the more Corey thought about it, the more convinced he was that Erin wasn't drunk—she was upset.

But whatever was on her mind, her silence clearly indicated that she had no intention of talking about it. Not with him, anyway.

"Right here," she said.

He pulled into a narrow driveway, behind a dark-green Kia, and turned off the engine.

"Thanks for the ride," she said, reaching for the handle before Corey could come around to help her out.

"I'll see you to your door," he told her.

"That's really not necessary."

"Necessary or not," he said, falling into step beside her,

"my mama would never forgive me if I left without making sure that you were safely inside."

"Okay, you walked me to my door," she said, stopping under the porch light. "Now your mother can hold her head up, confident she raised her boys right, and you can go."

"Not just yet," he said. "How are you feeling?"

"Fine."

She did look better, as if the effects of the champagne had already dissipated. *If* the champagne had truly been the reason for her abrupt departure.

"No nausea? No dizziness?"

She shook her head. "I'm fine," she said again. "Really. It was probably just too warm in the ballroom and once I got out into the fresh air, my head cleared."

"You're sure?"

"Yes, I'm sure." She smiled up at him, and though the smile didn't quite erase the shadows in her eyes, it made him forget his concerns and remember how much he wanted to kiss her.

"Good," he said and lowered his head to taste the sweet curve of her lips.

It was a testament to how preoccupied Erin's thoughts were that she didn't anticipate his kiss.

She'd been kissed plenty of times before, and she knew how to read the signs and signals that usually led to the first touch of lips on lips—and how to dodge that touch if she wanted to.

Not that she wanted to dodge Corey's kiss. In fact, she'd spent an inordinate amount of time wondering what it would feel like to be kissed by him. She'd wondered if the same spark and sizzle she felt when he looked at her would translate through actual physical contact…or if the anticipation of his kiss would be more exciting than the actual event.

No worries there, she thought, as his lips brushed against hers again, sending tremors of longing through her body.

He kissed the way he talked—softly and smoothly, as if he had all the time in the world. And as if he intended to spend all of that time just kissing her.

His hands skimmed up her back and, even through the fabric of the jacket she still wore, she could feel the heat of his fingertips tracing the ridges of her spine. Then his hands moved across her shoulders and down her arms.

The keys that she held slipped from her fingers and crashed to the ground.

Erin didn't even notice.

She was far too busy enjoying the slow, sensual assault on her mouth.

His tongue slid between her lips, licked lazily.

There was nothing leisurely or casual about her body's response.

Each flick and flutter of his tongue shot flame-tipped arrows of heat and hunger spearing toward her center. Every careful and unhurried pass of his hands made her blood pulse and pound.

She moved against him, and both the tempo and intensity of the kiss changed.

He drew her closer, his arms wrapped around her tighter, he kissed her deeper.

Erin felt her own arms glide up his chest, her hands sliding over impressive pecs and broad, hard shoulders to link behind his neck. He was so big, so strong, so wholly and undeniably male.

And her response was completely and helplessly female.

She shuddered and melted against him.

Corey groaned into her mouth and delved deeper.

Yeah, she'd been kissed before. But never like this. In

her experience, most men approached kissing as nothing more than a brief prelude to the main event, but not Corey Traub. His kisses were worthy of top billing. He kissed her as if she was the object of all desire and the source of all pleasure, and as if he never wanted to stop.

And Erin never wanted him to stop.

But just when Erin was about to throw all common sense and caution to the wind and drag Corey inside with her, he eased away.

"I think I should say good-night now, before I forget that my mama raised me to be a gentleman," he said.

She should have been grateful he'd backed off. She didn't know him nearly well enough to even kiss him the way she'd kissed him, never mind indulge in any of the other erotic fantasies her mind had conjured up while he'd been seducing her with his skillfully creative mouth and his dangerously talented hands.

He bent to scoop up the keys she'd dropped and put them in her hand, curling her fingers around them.

His other hand lifted to her face, his fingertips skimming lightly over the swollen curve of her bottom lip.

The gentle touch set off bursts of erotic tingles that warned her to put some distance between them before she urged him to forget his mother's teachings.

"Good night," she said softly.

He stepped back, and Erin fumbled with the keys in her hand for a moment before she found the right one for the door. She fumbled some more fitting it into the lock, but then the bolt released with a click.

Corey didn't say anything else, but he waited on the step until she'd slipped inside and locked the door again, then he turned away.

Erin watched from the window as he walked back to his car and reminded herself that she'd done the right thing, the smart thing, in letting him go. There was too much uncertainty in her life to consider any kind of personal involvement right now.

But that knowledge didn't stop her from wishing otherwise.

Chapter Three

It was a kiss, Corey reminded himself—for the umpteenth time—as he got dressed the next morning.

Yeah, it had been pretty spectacular as far as kisses go, but it was still just a kiss. Certainly there wasn't any reason for him to have lain awake into the wee hours of the morning thinking about that kiss—and the woman he'd shared it with.

But the truth was, even before they'd shared that one scorching kiss, he'd been haunted by thoughts of Erin Castro.

Thoughts of wanting to kiss Erin Castro.

He shook his head as he tugged on his jeans.

He didn't know what it was about the woman that had gotten under his skin. Sure, she was attractive in a classic blue-eyed, blond-haired, porcelain-skinned, soft curves sort of way.

Okay, more than attractive. He hadn't been giving her a

line when they were dancing and he'd told her she was the most beautiful woman at the wedding because from the first moment he'd set eyes on her, he hadn't seen anyone else.

And now that he had kissed her, now that he'd tasted the sweet seductive flavor that was hers alone, he worried that he'd made a mistake. Because now he wanted more.

Cursing himself for his weakness, he picked up his phone and dialed the number he'd obtained from directory assistance. She answered on the third ring.

"Hey, Erin, it's Corey."

"Corey?" She sounded distracted, as if he'd caught her in the middle of something. Or maybe as if she didn't recognize the name.

He was frowning over that possibility when she spoke again.

"Oh, Dillon's brother. Hi."

Dillon's brother?

That was how she thought of him? How about the man who'd taken her home the night before? The man who'd kissed her breathless and continued to kiss her until they'd both wanted a lot more?

But of course he didn't ask any of those questions. He didn't want her to confirm that he'd thought about her a lot more than she'd thought about him.

"I'm sorry I didn't make the connection right away," she said. "I just—you caught me when my mind was wandering."

"Is this a bad time?"

"No. I don't think so."

"You don't think so?" he prompted.

"Well, I guess that depends on why you're calling," she said.

"Partly just to find out how you're doing."

"I'm fine."

"You said you had too much champagne last night, so I wanted to make sure you weren't suffering any lingering effects today."

"Champagne. Right. Well, that certainly explains the… uh…"

She faltered, and he suspected that she was thinking about that kiss again. Or maybe he just wanted to believe she was thinking about it because he was.

"…the headache I had this morning," she continued. "But I took a couple of aspirin with breakfast and I'm fine now."

"Good," he said, even while silently wishing he could rid himself of the residual effects of the night so easily. But he suspected that the only thing that could cure his craving for Erin was Erin herself.

"And since you've already had breakfast—which was the other reason I was calling—why don't you let me take you to lunch?"

"Lunch?"

"You know—the meal usually served in the middle of the day," he teased.

"Yes, I do know what lunch is," she assured him. "I'm just not sure I understand why you're inviting me to have lunch with you."

"Because I don't like to eat alone. And because I really enjoyed spending time with you last night and I'd like to get to know you better."

Erin was tempted—too tempted—to jump at his invitation. And not just because she knew he would be able to distract her from the questions that had been pounding inside of her head since she'd seen that picture of Grant Clifton's sister the night before. Unfortunately, all of the reasons that Corey would be such a great distraction were the same reasons that she had to refuse. Because she was far too attracted to the man, because she couldn't think of anything else when he was near and because she could very well end up with her heart broken when he went back to Texas.

So instead of accepting, she said, "I'm afraid I may have given you the wrong impression last night."

There was a pause, as if he was surprised by her response. And he probably was because she'd no doubt given him the impression of a wild, willing woman who wanted to gobble him up in big, greedy bites.

And the impression wasn't really wrong, but it was misleading because nothing like that was going to happen between them. She couldn't let things move in that direction with him while her life was veering off course in so many other ways.

"The only impression I got," he finally said, "was that of a smart, beautiful woman who was the last thought on my mind before I fell asleep last night and the first when I woke up this morning."

"Oh. Wow." Erin didn't know what else to say. Was it the words, she wondered, that made her heart pound so fast? Or the sensual tone that turned the words into a verbal seduction?

She used her free hand to fan her flushed cheeks, grateful that he couldn't see what she was doing, couldn't know the effect that he had on her, even over a phone line.

"Then you definitely got the wrong impression because I'm really not looking to get involved with anyone right now."

"I invited you to lunch, darlin', not to shop for an engagement ring," he said.

The heat in her cheeks intensified. He was right—she was overreacting. But even an invitation to lunch was dangerous when she wasn't sure she could control her instinctive response to the man issuing the invitation.

"I know," she said. "But I still don't think lunch is a good idea."

"Because you're philosophically opposed to eating in the middle of the day?"

She had to smile. "Because you're far too charming for your own good."

"You think I'm charming?"

"I'm going to say goodbye now," she told him.

"Wait, Erin."

But she couldn't wait, because she knew that if she let him say anything else, she might very well give in—not only to his invitation but to the desire stirring again in her blood. "Goodbye, Corey."

Corey continued to hold the receiver to his ear, as if he didn't quite believe that he was hearing a dial tone instead of Erin's voice. He didn't think any woman had ever hung up on him before but, for some inexplicable reason, the realization made him smile.

As a management consultant, his professional reputation had been made on the basis of identifying a problem and determining the best solutions. He would simply analyze Erin's resistance in the same way. And if she thought he was the type of man to be dissuaded by one terminated phone call, well then, she was very soon going to learn differently.

But thinking of his business objectives made him remember that he had other reasons for being in Thunder Canyon than his brother's wedding and more reasons for staying than a pretty blue-eyed bridesmaid.

Pushing all thoughts of Erin Castro from his mind, at least for the time being, he pulled out his laptop and got to work reviewing the reports he needed for his meetings on Wednesday. The information he'd seen so far had been incomplete and often contradictory, warning him that the evaluation he'd expected to finish within a couple of weeks might take a lot longer than that.

At first, he'd been frustrated by this realization, but now—thinking of Erin—the idea of extending his stay in Thunder Canyon didn't bother him at all.

Erin called home on Sunday and spoke to both of her parents. Betty and Jack still didn't know her real reasons for going to Thunder Canyon, but they tried to be supportive of her decision. They asked about her new job and her friends and, as usual, when she would be coming home for a visit.

She had originally planned to go back to San Diego for Thanksgiving, certain she would have all of the answers she sought by then, but she warned her parents now that a trip at that time might not be possible. The holiday was the start of one of the busiest seasons at the resort and she wasn't sure that she would be able to get any time off. But she had another reason for changing her plans—she didn't want to leave Thunder Canyon just when Grant Clifton's sister would be arriving.

She continued to battle against the guilt she felt for not sharing her suspicions with them. She'd never really kept secrets from them before, and certainly never anything of this magnitude—if there could be anything else of such magnitude. Although she'd always felt a little disconnected from her parents and her brothers—as if they shared a deeper bond that somehow eluded her—she'd never been deceitful or dishonest, and the lie that she'd been living for the past several months was weighing heavily on her conscience.

When her mother said, "I love you, Erin," as she always

did at the end of a conversation, Erin's eyes filled with tears.

They *had* always loved her. She didn't doubt that. And she wondered now if the feeling that there was something missing in their relationship was actually indicative of something missing within herself. Maybe she was chasing after something that didn't exist except inside her own imagination.

The original seed had been planted by Erma, but her aunt was gone now and Erin was starting to wonder what purpose could possibly be served by continuing to nurture the old woman's suspicions. And if there was no purpose, then maybe it was time for her to forget everything Erma had said and just go home.

As she readied herself for bed, Erin realized the doubting and confusion had become as much a part of her Sunday night ritual as her call to her parents. Because talking to them inevitably made her realize how much she missed them, and missing them made her question why she was willing to upset the status quo.

Her family wasn't perfect, but they were hers.

Weren't they?

With a sigh, she pulled back the covers and crawled into bed.

As she settled back against her pillows, she acknowledged that it was entirely possible that her birthday being on the same day as Elise Clifton's was nothing more than a coincidence. And both of them being born in the same hospital was probably just another coincidence. But the physical resemblance she'd noticed in Elise's photo and her own brothers was a little harder to ignore.

Or maybe she'd just been looking for answers for so long that she was grasping at straws.

Determined to push these thoughts out of her mind, she

picked up the Stephanie Plum novel she'd just started reading. But she was too distracted to focus on the story and she set the book down again after reading only a few pages.

It took her a long time after that to fall asleep, and when she finally did, she had the strangest dream.

She was in the hospital, and the cry of a baby slowly penetrated the thick fog of pain that surrounded her.

No, not a baby. *Her* baby.

She struggled to sit up but felt as if she was strapped to the bed, unable to move.

"My baby." She tried to shout, but the words were barely a whisper.

"Your baby is fine. We're going to take her to the nursery so that you can rest."

She couldn't see the speaker, but the gentle tone both soothed and reassured her.

A short while later, after she'd rested, she wanted to see her baby. But the hall that led to the nursery seemed to stretch ahead of her forever. She walked faster but made no progress. So she started to run. She ran until her legs were weak and her lungs ached, and still she hadn't reached the end of the long, narrow corridor.

Then suddenly she was there, standing in the middle of the nursery, and her baby was crying again. But there were dozens of bassinets, dozens of crying babies, and she didn't know which one was hers. She ran from one to the next, desperately hoping for some sense of recognition, but they were all the same, all strangers to her.

But then another woman came into the room, and she went directly to one of the bassinets and picked up the crying baby and carried it away. Then another, and another, and another. Until it seemed as if a whole parade of women had come into the room and, one by one, taken away the crying babies until there was only one left.

She tried to rationalize that the one remaining had to be her own, but she wasn't certain. She didn't know how each of the other new mothers had been sure that the baby she was taking belonged to her. What if someone had taken her baby?

She lifted the last infant from its bed, yearning for some sense of connection. But there was nothing. Her eyes scanned the room frantically, searching for someone, anyone, to help her. But she was alone. And when she looked at the baby again, it was gone, too.

Erin awoke with a start. She struggled to sit up and pushed her hair away from her face. Her hands were shaking, her heart was pounding. It was easy to tell herself that it was only a dream. It wasn't so easy to shake the feelings of helplessness and fear that lingered.

There was no reason to believe that the scenario played out by her imagination had any foundation in reality, but she knew that the questions would continue to haunt her until she'd figured out the truth.

Maybe she should go home. Not forever, just for a while. If nothing else, the disturbing dream had proved that she definitely needed a distraction, something to stop her from thinking about hospitals and babies and questions that might never be answered. As if anything could distract her from these thoughts.

Unbidden, an image of Corey Traub came to mind.

Okay, there was a man who could make a woman forget her own name. Just one kiss had proved that. But she wouldn't—couldn't—let him get that close again. She snuggled under the covers, reminding herself that he would probably be heading back to Texas soon anyway, disappearing from her life as abruptly as he'd appeared.

She drifted back to sleep. But this time when she dreamed, she dreamed of Corey.

* * *

Corey wasn't used to chasing women. If anything, he'd become accustomed to being chased by them. Prior to his fifteenth birthday, he'd been short and scrawny and mostly overlooked by everyone. But in that magical year, things had started to change. He'd shot up in height, put on some muscle, started to shave. And when he'd gone out for football the next fall, he'd made the team.

By the time he'd started college, he was a first-string receiver and his family was known across the great state of Texas for the fortune they'd made in oil. Corey had been so caught up in the thrill of being popular that he hadn't questioned what he'd done to earn the attention. Truthfully, the reasons hadn't mattered. All that mattered was that the skinny kid who had been mostly ignored by the girls and laughed at by the older boys was no more.

Corey Traub was now in the spotlight. Guys wanted to hang with him, girls wanted to be seen with him, and he'd reveled in the attention. And then he'd met Heather, and everything had changed. He hadn't needed the adulation of fans so long as he had her attention; he hadn't wanted to be with anyone else so long as he was with her.

They'd dated for a year and a half. She was the first girl he ever loved, and she claimed to love him, too. And then he discovered that, during the entire time they'd been dating, she'd been lying to him, deliberately keeping certain parts of her life a secret from him. When he finally found out and confronted her, she cried and apologized, but learning the extent of her deception had destroyed his trust, and her tears didn't sway him.

It didn't take long for news of their split to make its way around campus, and the girls started coming around again. In the decade that had passed since his college graduation, little had changed. He was as successful in the business world as he'd been on the football field. And although there weren't any shy giggling girls hanging around outside of his locker room, there were plenty of bold, sexy women sneaking into his office after hours or slipping hotel room keys into his pocket.

He couldn't remember the last time he'd had to take the first step with a woman. And it had been a heck of a lot longer than that since any female had told him "no." But somewhere along the line, sometime within the last few years, he'd started to grow weary of empty relationships and meaningless hookups. He wanted what Dillon had found with Erika.

His brothers liked to tease that he fell in love too easily, but the truth was, Heather's deception had taught him to be careful with his heart. Not that he'd given up on falling in love. He was still hopeful that would happen, but the next time he opened up his heart completely, it would be to a woman who he could trust was capable of loving him the same way. Openly and honestly, without any secrets or lies between them.

There was something about Erin Castro that made him think she might be that woman.

Maybe he was putting the cart before the horse, considering that she hadn't even agreed to have lunch with him. But he refused to be dissuaded. If he'd believed that she was honestly not interested, he would have backed off. But he couldn't forget the way she'd looked at him when they danced, the way she'd trembled in his arms, the way she'd responded to his kiss. No way was the attraction one-sided.

When Monday morning came around and he still hadn't managed to put her out of his mind, he decided to track her down. Because he was staying in one of the resort's condo units, it would be easy enough to stop by the front desk of the main building and invite her to lunch and see where things went from there. Except that when he went down to the desk, he didn't see her anywhere.

"Erin isn't in today," Trina told him.

"Will she be in later?" he asked, wondering if she'd switched her shift for some reason.

"I doubt it. She called in sick."

Sick?

He knew she hadn't been feeling well Saturday night, but she'd sounded okay when he'd spoken with her Sunday morning. Did she have a touch of the flu or some other kind of bug and had suffered a relapse?

"Is there something I can help you with?" Trina's long lashes fluttered, the invitation in those green eyes obvious.

"No, thanks," he told her. "I'll catch up with Erin later."

"If you change your mind, you can catch up with me around four." Her glossy pink lips curved. "That's when I finish my shift."

"I'll remember that," he told her, determined to ensure that he was nowhere around when Trina got off work.

With any luck, he would be with Erin.

Erin prided herself on being a reliable employee, someone who could be depended on to get things done, whatever those things might be. But when she woke up Monday morning and still hadn't figured out what—if anything—to say to her boss about her suspicion that he might be her brother, she called in sick.

When her bell rang shortly after 10:00 a.m., she didn't think twice before responding to the summons. It wasn't until she'd peeked through the sidelight and saw Corey on her step, making her heart do a little hop and skip, that she hesitated. Unfortunately, he was looking through the same window from the other side, which meant there was no way she could now pretend she wasn't home.

Forcing a smile, she pulled open the door.

"Corey, hi."

He smiled back, and she felt that funny little quiver in her belly again.

"I stopped by the resort to see you, and Trina said you were home sick," he explained. His gaze skimmed over her, leisurely, appraisingly. "But you look pretty good to me."

"I wasn't feeling well when I got up this morning," she fibbed, conscious that her cheeks were burning. "I thought I should stay home…in case I was contagious."

"Well, I brought you some homemade chicken soup—my mother's favorite cure for whatever ails you."

"*You* made chicken soup?"

He chuckled at the obvious skepticism in her tone. "No, I bought chicken soup that was homemade by the wonderful chefs at the Gallatin Room."

She lifted a brow at his mention of the resort's fine dining restaurant and figured the little plastic bowl in his hand probably cost more than a whole meal at any other restaurant in town.

"Thank you," she said. "That was a really sweet gesture."

"But you've already had lunch," he guessed.

She nodded.

"So put it in the fridge for tomorrow."

It would be rude to refuse his offer, so she did as he suggested, though she wondered what kind of strings might be attached to the bowl in her hand.

"Thank you," she said again. "I'm sure I'll enjoy it."

"What are your plans for the afternoon? Because I know you're not working."

"I have no plans. I'm home sick," she reminded him.

His smile widened. "Don't worry. I won't turn you in for playing hooky…so long as you let me play hooky with you."

"You're blackmailing me?"

He shrugged. "Whatever works."

"What did you have in mind?" she asked warily.

"Just grab a jacket and put on a pair of boots."

Which, of course, told her absolutely nothing about what he had planned. "Look, Corey, I'm flattered that you'd go to such lengths to spend time with me, but I really don't understand why."

"There's nothing to understand. I just think some time outside in the crisp, fresh air will help you feel better," he assured her.

"I don't know," she hedged.

"Trust me."

It wasn't that she didn't trust Corey so much as she didn't trust herself to be alone with him. The attraction she felt whenever she was near him was both awesome and overwhelming.

As she went to get her jacket and boots, she couldn't help but think he looked as relaxed and unself-conscious in the jeans and flannel he was wearing today as he had in the designer tux he'd worn for his brother's wedding, making her curious to know which was the *real* Corey Traub. Not that it mattered. Her instinctive response to him was the same regardless of what he was wearing.

She didn't understand the attraction. She'd always dated guys who were…more subtle, she decided. There was nothing subtle about Corey. He was blatantly and undeniably male.

And the way he filled out a pair of jeans made her want to sigh. The cowboy boots didn't surprise her. He'd even worn a pair at the wedding, with his tux. But those boots had been polished, and these were battered and worn, like the hat on his head.

She'd never known a cowboy before she came to Montana. And even in the past few months, she'd never met anyone like Corey.

He wasn't just sexy. He was knock-the-breath-out-of-your-lungs sexy. And the way he smiled at her, he knew it.

She'd never liked arrogant men. Or maybe it was just that she'd always wondered why the men she'd known felt entitled to their arrogance. With Corey, there was no question of his entitlement. And it made her wonder, not for the first time, why he was interested in her.

She wasn't oblivious to her own appeal. Over the years, she'd received a fair share of compliments on her appearance, and she knew how to play up her attributes—how to apply makeup so her blue eyes looked bluer, how to dress so that her curves seemed curvier, how to walk into a room so that heads turned in her direction.

Since coming to Thunder Canyon, however, she'd deliberately downplayed her appearance. She'd toned down her makeup and dressed to blend in rather than stand out. No one looked at her twice, and no one asked any questions. At least, not until Erika's wedding.

When Erin agreed to be a bridesmaid, she'd been thinking that she could somehow hide beneath layers of pink organza ruffles. She should have remembered that her friend had exquisite taste and an eye for fashion. There had been no way to hide in the strapless satin gown that hugged her curves. And she could hardly refuse when the bride suggested that her maid of honor should have her hair and makeup professionally done.

The result was that, as she'd made her way up the aisle,

she'd been aware of the attention focused on her—and the speculation. She recognized some of her regular customers from the Hitching Post who had never looked twice when she'd waited on their tables and others who she'd met through her duties at the resort. None of them seemed to realize who she was. And although she'd been all too aware that the groom's brother wasn't the only man who had been watching her, he was the only one she'd watched back.

Corey snapped his phone shut when Erin came back with her jacket and boots.

"Everything's arranged," he told her.

"What is *everything?*"

"You'll find out soon enough."

"I don't like surprises," she warned, following him out the door.

"Everyone likes surprises," he insisted.

She shook her head as she turned her key in the lock, engaging the deadbolt.

He slid an arm across her shoulders and steered her toward his truck. "What happened, darlin'? Were you traumatized by a clown jumping out of your cake on your fifth birthday?"

"Nothing so dramatic. I just like to have a plan, and I don't like when things interfere with my plans."

He opened the passenger-side door for her. "Didn't John Lennon say something about life being what happens while you're making other plans?"

"Maybe that worked for him," she acknowledged, "but it's a strange philosophy for a management consultant."

"It's not my business philosophy," he told her. "But when I'm out of the office, I don't like being shackled by rules and schedules."

She stepped up into the truck, obviously thinking about

his response. He closed her door, then went around to the driver's side.

"My aunt died," she finally said.

He paused in the act of inserting the key into the ignition. "Today? Is that why you called into work?"

She shook her head. "No. A few months ago." She folded her hands, staring down at the fingers linked together in her lap. "You asked why I don't like surprises. Her death was a surprise. And she gave me some information just before she passed that was…unexpected. I had so many questions that I never got to ask her."

"I'm sorry," he said. "I know how hard it is to lose someone out of the blue, feeling as if you'd left something unresolved."

She looked at him, as if surprised by his response. "Who did you lose?"

"My father."

"I didn't realize—" She frowned. "I should have. When you introduced your mother and her husband, I just assumed your parents were divorced."

He shook his head. "My dad died in an explosion on an oil rig when I was eight. The last time I saw him, before he went to work that day, he swatted my butt for talking back to my mother. When he walked out the door, I was happy to see him go."

She touched a hand to his arm, and when she spoke, her voice was gentle. "You were eight," she reminded him.

"I know. I got over the guilt a long time ago but only after I'd carried it around for a lot of years first." He frowned.

Her hand dropped away. "What's wrong?"

"I was just thinking that it's mighty easy to talk to you."

"It is?"

"I haven't ever told anyone that story. Not anyone outside of the family, anyway."

"Sometimes it's easier to talk to someone who isn't close to a situation."

He turned into the long, winding drive that led to the Hopping H Ranch. "And sometimes a man just doesn't have the sense to hold his tongue around a beautiful woman."

Her cheeks flushed. "I might be a California girl, but I've heard plenty of stories about you smooth-talking cowboys to know that I'd be a fool to trust even half of the words that slide off of that glib tongue."

He pressed a hand to his heart as he pulled into a vacant parking spot. "Now you've wounded me."

The look of patent disbelief that she aimed in his direction changed to something more akin to wariness when she realized where he'd brought her.

Chapter Four

"This is Melanie and Russ's ranch."

Though it wasn't a question, Corey nodded anyway.

"What are we doing here?"

"I would have thought that was obvious." He got out of the truck and came around to her side.

This time Erin hadn't jumped out ahead of him. In fact, she didn't look like she had any intention of getting out at all. She hadn't even unfastened her seatbelt, so he reached across to release the clasp for her.

"This isn't a good idea," she said.

"Why not?"

"Because I already missed work today. I don't want to miss tomorrow, too, because I'm in a body cast in the hospital."

"You can't ride?" He deliberately infused his tone with both surprise and disbelief and a hint of challenge.

"Of course, I can ride," she said, then added, "waves."

"Waves?"

"I grew up on the coast, not in cowboy country," she reminded him.

The mention of surfing had distracted him with thoughts of Erin clad in a skimpy little bikini, her hair slicked back, her skin wet and glistening as she balanced on a longboard. He knew it was more likely that she wore a wetsuit and figured she'd probably look just as enticing in a full bodysuit of neoprene that hugged her feminine curves, but a man was entitled to his fantasies and Erin in a bikini was definitely one of his. Peeling the little scraps of fabric from her damp skin was another.

"Well, you're in cowboy country now," he said, forcing the all-too tempting images from his mind.

"I'm aware of that," she said, just as Russ came out of the barn.

The rancher came over to shake hands with Corey and Erin.

"Thanks for accommodating us," Corey said.

"Always a pleasure," Russ assured him.

Erin remained silent, wary.

"I've got Lucifer and Jax all saddled up and ready to go, but you just let me know if you need anything else."

"Will do," Corey promised.

And Russ disappeared into the barn again.

"Lucifer?"

Corey pointed out the spirited black stallion in a nearby enclosure. "And here—" he guided her to a closer paddock "—is Jax."

She hesitated a few feet from the fence.

"You've never ridden before?" He couldn't imagine going through life without experiencing the exhilarating freedom of racing over the open fields on the back of a horse.

"No, I have." Her gaze flickered cautiously toward the horse again. "Twice."

"When you were a kid?"

She shook her head. "A few weeks ago."

His lips twitched as he fought a smile. "What happened?"

"Haley convinced me that I couldn't live in Montana if I didn't know how to ride, so I decided to take some private lessons."

"And you had two?"

"I *suffered* through each one and decided the bruises on my butt were never going to go away if I kept them up."

Corey shook his head. "You don't strike me as the type of woman to give up so easily."

"You don't know me," she reminded him.

"I'm working on it."

"And accepting that something isn't working doesn't equal giving up."

"It sure sounds like giving up to me."

"If you came here to ride, go ahead," she said. "Don't worry about me."

"And what will you do?"

"I can watch."

He curved an arm around her shoulders and guided her closer to the docile bay gelding. He whistled softly, and the horse ambled over to the fence.

Erin looked at Jax.

It was an innocuous-sounding name, and the animal seemed well behaved, but he was just so big. Okay, not quite as big as Lucifer, and certainly not anywhere near as menacing as the powerful stallion that was pawing impatiently at the ground and tossing his head from side to side, but still pretty intimidating. But there was something about those big dark eyes that encouraged her to trust that, though he was big and strong enough to toss her around like a rag doll, he wouldn't.

She started to reach toward the horse, testing herself as much as the animal, then hesitated.

Corey caught her wrist before she could withdraw and guided her hand the rest of the way, until her palm was flat against the horse's neck. She felt the muscles quiver beneath her touch, and the gelding blew out a quiet breath that sounded distinctly like a sigh of pleasure.

Corey's hand dropped away, but he remained close while she continued to stroke the animal.

"I think he likes me," Erin told him.

He smiled. "Of course he likes you. He'd like you even more if you took him out for the run he's saddled up for."

Still, she hesitated.

"It's okay if you're afraid."

Her shoulders stiffened. "I'm not afraid."

His lips curved, just a little, and she knew that she'd fallen straight into his trap. He vaulted easily over the fence, then put one foot in the stirrup and swung himself into the saddle, then he held out his hand to her. "Come on."

Erin remained rooted where she was. "I thought you were going to ride Lucifer."

"I am," he said. "We're just going to take a walk around the paddock together, until you're comfortable with Jax."

Still she hesitated. "You expect me to get up on that horse with you?"

"You won't fall off," he promised.

"Won't we be too heavy for the horse?"

"We're just going to take a few turns around the paddock. He can handle it."

Erin remained skeptical.

"Trust me, darlin', I know what these animals are worth and I wouldn't do anything to risk harming any of them."

"Maybe I'm more worried about harm to me," she told him, but climbed up onto the fence—keeping a wary eye on the horse—and over.

"I won't let anything happen to you." He smiled. "Not anything that you don't want to happen, that is."

It was as much an enticement as a warning. She felt her cheeks flush but chose to ignore the innuendo.

She thought she was going to fall off before she ever managed to get on, but eventually she managed to climb up, straddling the horse's back behind the saddle.

"Put your arms around me and hold on," he told her.

She did so, all too aware of his solid warmth and masculine strength. His jacket was unzipped and she could feel the ripple of his muscles beneath the soft fabric of his shirt. Her mouth went dry—although whether it was from fear of the horse or awareness of Corey, she wasn't certain.

He nudged Jax into motion, and as Erin felt herself starting to slide, she fisted her hands in Corey's shirt and held on for dear life. He only chuckled. As the horse made its way around the paddock and she realized how easily he was controlling the powerful animal with the hard muscles of his thighs, her grip on the flannel gradually loosened.

Her own muscles felt watery; her limbs were weak. And her heart was pounding so hard inside her chest she was surprised he couldn't hear it. The rocking motion was somewhat familiar, and the familiarity made her tense. Her butt was definitely going to be sore tomorrow, and the knowledge made her wish that she'd never responded to Corey's knock on her door. She really did want to learn to ride, but maybe she just wasn't cut out to be a horsewoman.

"Relax."

She did and realized that when she stopped trying to anticipate the horse's movements, she didn't jolt up and down so much. In fact, she could almost enjoy the steady, easy rhythm. Lulled by this discovery, she closed her eyes and pressed her cheek against Corey's back, breathing in the heady scent of leather and horse and man.

She felt the familiar stir of desire low in her belly, and a tingling warmth between her thighs. Obviously as her worry lessened, her awareness heightened. With every step the horse took, her breasts brushed against Corey's back, and she was suddenly aware that her nipples had tightened into hard points that were straining against her bra, aching for much more intimate contact.

She wanted his hands on her, stroking over her bare skin, touching her everywhere.

He glanced over his shoulder. "Ready for more?"

She wondered, for a moment, if she'd said something out loud, but then she realized that he was referring to the horse's pace, and she nodded.

A nudge of his knees against the horse's flank and the animal moved from a jog to a canter—if she was remembering the terms correctly—and suddenly every nerve ending in her body was on high alert. She'd never found the experience of being on horseback anything but scary and awkward and painful, but with Corey it was exhilarating and incredible and sensuous.

It had been obvious to Corey that Erin had some apprehension about getting up on a horse again, so riding with her seemed like the perfect way to ease her worries. It had worked with his sister, Rose. When she was little, she'd fallen off the back of her pony and had been terrified to climb back up again. But she'd trusted her big brother, and riding with Corey had given her the courage to overcome her fears.

It didn't take a minute for Corey to realize that sharing a horse with a grown woman was a very different experience than doing so with his six-year-old sister. And when that woman was soft and sexy and snuggled up behind him, it was sheer torture.

Only for a few trips around the paddock, he promised himself, then she would be ready to handle Jax on her own—or Jax would be ready to handle her. The horse had a gentle nature and was well-trained, both essential qualities for the mount of a novice rider. He didn't know where Erin had gone for her lessons, but for her to have thrown in the towel after only two sessions, she'd either been given a difficult horse or had a horrible instructor. He was determined not to let that memory prevent her from enjoying the day.

He wanted to share this experience with her, to introduce her to pleasures that no one else ever had. And he wasn't just thinking about what they could do on horseback.

And while he tried to keep a tight rein on his thoughts, it was next to impossible. He was all too aware of her arms around him, of her soft breasts pressed to his back, rubbing against him. Though he was sure he couldn't actually feel the hard nubs of her nipples through the layers that separated them, he imagined that he could. He wanted to touch her, all of her. He wanted to strip away her clothes and—

He managed to lasso the runaway fantasy before it took him to the point of no return and, after another torturously slow turn around the paddock, he said, "Let's see what you can do on your own."

They headed out at a leisurely gait. Surprisingly, after half an hour in the paddock with Corey and Jax, Erin felt a lot more comfortable on the back of the horse than she had at any time during her two lessons. She had a moment of panic when they headed away from the barn, but Jax was so strong and steady beneath her that it was gone as quickly as it had come.

Lucifer wasn't nearly as complacent, and though Corey didn't have any trouble controlling the spirited stallion, it was obvious that the animal was eager to run. His feet danced impatiently and he tossed his head excitedly, but Corey held him in check and continued to keep pace with Erin and Jax.

When they broke through a stand of trees to yet another open field, Erin said, "Why don't you let him run?"

Corey looked over his shoulder. "I don't want to leave you."

"Well, I would appreciate it if you came back."

He grinned at her dry tone. "Are you sure you don't mind?"

"I'm sure," she said. "And I'm guessing that you crave the speed as much as he does."

He didn't deny it. "We'll be back."

She knew they would. And truthfully, she didn't mind letting them go. In fact, it was a pleasure to watch them streak across the fields. Horse and rider—two beautiful beings—so closely attuned to one another they moved as if they were one entity. As they raced off into the distance, Erin sighed.

What was she doing? She had no business being here with this man, no reason to think that getting involved with him could end up in anything but heartache. He was from Texas, she was from California, and it was only a coincidence that their paths happened to cross in Montana. She didn't even know how long he planned to stay in Thunder Canyon—or even how long she did.

But why couldn't she enjoy his company so long as he was here? For once in her life, why couldn't she be impulsive and irresponsible and just let things happen?

She heard them returning before she saw them. The thunderous pounding of the stallion's hooves in the distance made her turn just as they plunged through a copse of towering pines. The horse raced ahead, wild and reckless, and the man on its back looked every bit as dangerous. But it wasn't fear that made Erin's heart pound in her chest—it was excitement. Anticipation. Lust.

She wanted him. It was ridiculous to continue to deny it. It was also ridiculous to imagine that she could ever have him for anything more than a very hot, very short-term fling.

And what would be so wrong about that? her clamoring hormones demanded to know.

As he drew nearer, her heart pounded even harder.

What would be wrong, she reminded herself sternly, *was that she didn't even know the man.* Aside from the fact that he was Dillon's brother, she knew almost nothing about him. And she wasn't in the habit of falling into bed with men she didn't know.

Corey reined in the horse, reducing his pace to a canter, then a trot and finally slowing him to a walk as they approached Erin and Jax. She turned her mount around and began to head back, but she was less successful in redirecting her thoughts.

"You both look as if you enjoyed that," Erin said.

"I don't think there's anything I love more than exploring the great outdoors on horseback."

"This is beautiful country," she agreed.

"The prettiest in the whole world, apart from Texas, of course."

"Of course," she agreed drily.

He grinned. "Although I hear the West Coast has some good stuff, too. Like California girls."

"Are you going to break into song now?"

"I only ever sing in the shower," he told her, "so if you want to be serenaded—"

"Not necessary," she assured him.

Corey chuckled.

"So what did you think?" he asked a few minutes later. "Not just of the ranch, but the ride."

"I think I could learn to like this," she admitted.

"I knew you would," he said confidently.

There was that arrogance again—but it definitely suited him.

"You've probably been riding since you were little," she guessed.

"Since I was knee high to a grasshopper, to hear my mama tell the story."

She made a point of tilting her head way back to look up at him. "I can't imagine you were ever knee high to a grasshopper."

"I was," he surprised her by admitting. "In fact, I was short and scrawny almost all the way through high school. I couldn't even get a date to my junior prom."

"And your senior prom?"

He grinned. "Well, that was a different story."

"I'll bet."

"How about you? Did you go to your senior prom?"

She thought back, smiled. "Yes, I did. I went with Thomas Anderson. He was president of the chess club, editor of the yearbook, valedictorian of our graduating class."

"The first boy you ever slept with?" he prompted.

She shook her head. "No. But he was the first boy to break my heart."

"Where is he now? Want me to go beat him up?"

She laughed. "That's not necessary. I got over him a long time ago."

"Glad to hear that," he said. "How about more recently?"

"More recently what?"

"Have you been dating anyone in Thunder Canyon?"

"No. And I'm not looking to start, either."

"Why not?"

She shrugged. "I've been working a lot."

"You know what they say about all work and no play," he warned her.

"I don't play games."

"Some games are fun, darlin'."

She smiled at that, but her smile quickly faded. "I was dating someone in San Diego for a while."

"Did he break your heart, too?"

She shook her head. "But I think I might have bruised his."

"And you're still feeling guilty about it," he guessed.

"Maybe. I don't know. I didn't think our relationship was that serious. We hadn't been dating very long, but he was looking to make a commitment and I wasn't."

"Because you're not ready to settle down? Or because you didn't want to settle down with him?"

"I just didn't want to settle," she said and winced when she realized how the words sounded.

But Corey nodded, understanding. "There was something missing."

"A lot of somethings, actually," she admitted.

"How is that your fault?"

"Well, according to my mother, I didn't give him a chance, my expectations are too high, I need to understand that chemistry takes time—" she broke off, her cheeks burning. "Well, that's getting a lot more personal than I meant to."

"So, there was no chemistry with this guy, huh?"

She ignored his question because she knew the answer would lead her down a treacherous path.

They were at the barn now, and Corey dismounted before turning to help Erin down. She was grateful for his assistance, because as relaxed as she'd begun to feel in the saddle she wasn't at all confident in her ability to get out of it. She put her hands on his shoulders and slid down, the front of her body brushing against the front of his.

Like flint rubbing against rock, sparks flashed, heat flared. Her breath caught, her pulse pounded. His hands stayed on her hips, holding her close.

And suddenly she was smack in the middle of that treacherous path she'd been so determined to avoid.

"Did you guys have a good time?" Russ asked.

Erin jumped back, her cheeks burning.

"Oh, yes," she said. "It was wonderful. Thank you."

"Not a problem," Russ said. "Melanie's just about to put dinner on the table. There's plenty of food, if you wanted to join us."

"Oh." She wasn't sure how to respond to the invitation. She'd met Russ and Melanie a few times and didn't want to refuse his generous offer, but she wasn't sure she'd feel comfortable sitting down at a table with people she barely knew.

"Thanks for the invite," Corey said, coming to her rescue. "But Erin and I have other plans."

"You're sure?" Russ pressed.

"Positive. But please thank Melanie for us."

His friend nodded. "I will. And I hope you'll find your way out here again before you head back to Texas."

"You can count on it," Corey said, shaking his hand firmly.

The rancher tipped his hat to Erin, then led the horses into the barn.

* * *

"How are you holding up?" Corey asked when they were back in his truck and heading away from the ranch.

"Not too badly," she said.

"You should take a hot bath before you go to bed tonight," he suggested. "It will help ease any soreness in your muscles."

"That sounds like a wonderful idea." She tipped her head back and closed her eyes as if she was imagining herself sinking into a tub filled with bubbles.

Or maybe he just assumed that was what was on her mind because it was on his.

"And if it doesn't work, I'll call Stefan in the morning and see if he can squeeze me in for a quickie during my lunch."

"Stefan? A quickie?"

She laughed. "A quick massage," she clarified.

"Oh." But his frown deepened. "Don't they have women who give massages?"

"Of course. But Stefan has the most amazing hands."

"And you let him put them all over your body?"

"I pay him to put them all over my body." She didn't usually engage in this kind of flirtatious banter, but Corey's reaction to her statement was so typically and possessively male, she couldn't resist teasing him a little. "And he's worth every penny."

"I could do the same thing—for free."

She lifted a brow. "Show me your diploma, cowboy."

"Well, no one's ever called it a diploma, but—"

She laughed. "I was referring to a professional accreditation. Stefan trained in Sweden."

"I graduated from Texas A&M," he said, flicking on his indicator.

Instead of heading in the direction Erin lived, he turned the opposite way.

"Where are we going?" she asked, more curious than concerned.

"I told Russ we had plans for dinner," he reminded her. "You don't want to make a liar out of me, do you?"

"I just don't want you to feel obligated—"

"Erin."

She frowned at the interruption.

"You seem to be forgetting that I'm the one who tracked you down this morning and pretty much blackmailed you into spending the day with me."

"You did, didn't you?"

"Which should prove that if I didn't want to be with you, I wouldn't be."

"Okay," she finally said, but the furrow in her brow deepened when he pulled into the parking lot of the Super Saver Mart, still referred to by a lot of the locals as the Thunder Canyon Mercantile. "This is where we're going for dinner?"

He chuckled. "This is where we're going to get the ingredients for dinner."

She looked at him suspiciously.

"No, I don't expect you to cook dinner for me," he said before she could ask. "I'm going to cook for you."

"You are?"

"Why do you sound so surprised?"

"I guess because I am," she admitted, as they made their way toward the entrance. "No man has ever cooked me dinner before."

He eyed her warily. "Are you one of those—what do they call them—vegetarians or vegans or whatever?"

The tone of his voice left her in no doubt what this man

from cattle country thought of that possibility and made her lips curve. "No, I'm not a vegetarian or a vegan."

"Are you a picky eater?"

"There are some things I don't like," she admitted, "but I'm not picky."

"What don't you like?"

"Peas. Pickles. Pineapple."

He lifted his brows. "You have something against the letter 'p'?"

"I don't like squash, either."

"Like…pumpkin?"

She smiled again. "Any kind of squash."

"Well then, I think we're pretty safe," he told her. "Because there are no peas, pickles, pineapple or squash in my red sauce."

"I do like red sauce."

"How do you feel about pasta?"

"I love pasta."

He grinned. "Then let's go shopping."

Chapter Five

If she'd been surprised by his offer to cook for her, she was even more so by the ease with which he pushed the cart around the grocery store. He didn't just toss the vegetables into a bag, he checked the color of the tomatoes, tested the firmness of the garlic, gauged the texture of the peppers.

She made a face when he was sniffing the mushrooms. "Those aren't one of my favorite foods," she admitted to him.

"These are shiitake, not porcini," he teased.

"I'm just not a fan of any kind of fungus," she said.

"You won't even taste them."

She decided to give him the benefit of the doubt. After all, she was going to sit down for a home-cooked meal that she didn't have to prepare, and she was curious about his skill in the kitchen. Okay, she was curious about his skill in other areas, too, but she refused to let her mind go down that path. Again.

He added a head of romaine lettuce, a bag of carrots, a bunch of green onions and a cucumber.

Moving out of the produce department to the bakery, he grabbed a loaf of French bread, then a package of fresh fettucine, extra virgin olive oil, basil, oregano, a hunk of parmesan cheese and a bottle of red wine.

"You've thought of everything, haven't you?"

He took a mental inventory of the ingredients as they moved along the conveyor belt toward the cashier. "I hope so."

"Do you do this often?"

"Shop for groceries?"

"Cook."

"Do you mean cook for a woman or just cook in general?"

"Cook in general," she said, unwilling to admit that she was just as curious to know if he was in the habit of cooking for his female companions.

"I have to eat," he said logically.

"But—" She bit her lip, stifling the reply that had almost spilled out uncensored.

"But," he prompted.

She felt her cheeks burn. "I just thought you'd probably have women lining up to cook for you."

"Well, if you're offering …" He grinned.

"You said you were cooking for me," she reminded him.

"Tonight," he agreed. "But maybe next time you could show off your culinary skills."

"You're assuming there will be a next time."

"Not assuming," he denied. "Just hopeful."

She had enjoyed the time they'd spent together today and, so long as he wasn't looking for anything more than friendship from her—and so long as she remembered that she wasn't in a position to offer anything more—she wouldn't object to spending more time with him.

"I do make a mean enchilada," she told him.

"Spicy?"

"I guess I'll let you be the judge of that."

"I'll look forward to it." He smiled before he turned to the cashier to pay for his groceries.

Corey put Erin to work washing the lettuce and other vegetables while he got busy chopping and dicing. Her kitchen was laid out almost identical to the one in the condo he was renting, so he felt comfortable moving around in it and opening cupboards and drawers to find what he needed. He located a big pot to boil water for the pasta and a wok-style frying pan that he could use to make the sauce. He opened the bottle of wine to let it breathe while he heated a drizzle of olive oil in the pan and tossed in a couple of crushed garlic cloves.

"Where did you learn to cook?" Erin asked him.

He dumped the red and green peppers into the pan, stirred them around with a wooden spoon, then began peeling the tomatoes.

"Here and there," he said.

She lifted her brows at the vagueness of his response, but he didn't elaborate. He didn't think he'd score any points with Erin by admitting it was an ex-girlfriend who'd taught him the basics of the sauce he was currently making for her. Especially not if she knew that he'd appreciated Gina's marinara sauce more than he'd appreciated Gina and, once he'd realized that, he'd decided to learn to make it for himself so that he could enjoy his pasta without the complications of an unhappy relationship.

"Why don't you pour the wine?" he suggested.

She found two glasses in the cupboard and did as he suggested.

He finished dicing the tomatoes he'd peeled and tossed them into the pan, then added some spices and stirred everything around again.

"It smells good already," Erin told him.

He washed his hands and dried them on the towel that was hanging over the handle of the oven door before he turned to take the glass of wine she offered to him. "It will taste even better," he promised.

Her brows rose up again. "Cocky, aren't you?"

"Confident," he corrected.

When he stepped toward her, Erin felt an instinctual urge to retreat. But the counter was at her back, leaving her with nowhere to go.

His lips curved, slowly, seductively. Her heart hammered.

She had no doubt that he had reason to be confident. She knew enough about his background to know that he'd been born into a powerful and influential family, but he'd also achieved his own success. And men like Corey, men who wore success and self-assurance as comfortably as the designer labels on their backs, drew more than their fair share of female attention. Which made her wonder—what was he doing with her?

She wasn't oblivious to her own appeal, but she wasn't an heiress or a supermodel, and she didn't doubt that Corey had dated women from each of those categories—and a few more. She also guessed that he was a man accustomed to getting what he wanted, and the look in his eyes left her in no doubt that what he wanted, at least right now, was her. And though she had no intention of giving in to the desire that surged through her veins, she couldn't deny that she wanted him right back.

His gaze dropped to her mouth, and she knew that if he kissed her again, right here and right now, she would be lost. She put a hand out—a desperate, wordless attempt to hold him off, at least long enough for her to gather her wits about her—and realized she was holding her glass of wine in it.

"Well, then," she said, lifting her glass a little higher. "We should toast to dinner."

Amusement crinkled the corners of his eyes as he tapped the rim of his glass against hers.

"To dinner," he agreed, "with new friends."

She sipped her wine without tasting it, all too aware of his closeness and the intensity of his gaze on her.

"I should set the table."

"There's no rush," he assured her. "The sauce needs to simmer for about half an hour."

Half an hour?

It wasn't all that long, really, but somehow, it seemed like an eternity. Because the more time she spent with Corey, the more difficult it was to ignore the attraction she felt.

Her immediate response to him had been purely physical—the first time they met, she hadn't known him well enough for it to be anything more than a hormonal response to a good-looking man who practically oozed charm and sex appeal. But the more she got to know Corey, the more she found herself actually liking him.

Despite the attraction that zinged between them, she felt comfortable with him. Comfortable enough to laugh when he teased her, to respond in kind when he flirted with her and to enjoy the conversations they shared as much as the silences that sometimes fell in-between. Yeah, she was definitely starting to like him, and the combination of lust and like was a lot more difficult to ignore than a purely hormonal reaction.

But when they were alone together, as they were now, the pleasure she felt in his company grew into more, and she wasn't completely comfortable with that.

"Speaking of the sauce," she said, needing to break the spell that had woven around her like a spider's web, invisibly drawing her closer to him. And just like a fly caught in a web, she knew that it would be dangerous to let him get any closer.

"What about the sauce?" There was a hint of laughter in his voice, amusement sparkling in his eyes.

"Don't you need to stir it…or something?"

"Or something," he agreed and lifted a hand to trail a finger down her cheek.

Her pulse pounded, her breath caught.

Corey's eyes stayed locked with hers.

"You're a bundle of contradictions, Erin Castro."

She didn't dare ask what he meant, or maybe she was afraid that she knew. As clearly as she could read the desire in his eyes, she was sure he could see the same want echoed in hers. But she'd told him that she didn't want to get involved, and she'd meant it.

"I'm not trying to be," she told him.

He held her gaze for another minute before he stepped back. "I know. And that's why I'm going to focus on my sauce and let you set the table."

She exhaled slowly and turned to set her wineglass on the counter. As she reached into the cupboard for the plates, she assured herself that she was grateful he'd backed away.

Grateful and relieved.

And more than a little disappointed.

Half an hour later, they were seated at the table enjoying hot pasta, warm bread and crisp salad.

"You were right," she admitted. "It tastes even better than it smells—and it smells fabulous."

He twirled his fork in his own pasta. "I'm glad you're enjoying it."

"Are you kidding? This is one of the best meals I've had since…" Her words trailed off.

Since she'd come to Thunder Canyon, she suddenly realized and felt a pang of sadness thinking of the family she'd left in San Diego. But she'd had no choice. Not if she wanted to find the answers to the questions that Erma had planted in her mind. And she did want those answers. She *needed* the answers in order to understand who she really was.

"Since?" Corey prompted.

She forced a smile. "Since I can't remember when," she told him, keeping her voice deliberately light. "Really, this is amazing."

He took a slice of warm bread from the basket, tore it in half. "Do you want to talk about it?"

She swallowed another mouthful of pasta, then wiped her mouth with her napkin. "Talk about what?"

"Whatever's on your mind."

She reached for her wineglass. "There's nothing—"

He touched a finger to her lips, halting the automatic denial. She set her glass back down, nearly sloshing wine over the rim.

"If you don't want to talk about it, say so, darlin'," he told her. "But don't tell me there's nothing because it was obvious when I got here this morning that there was something bothering you and I can tell that your thoughts are wandering again."

She wondered if she'd been so obviously preoccupied or if he was more intuitive than she would have guessed. Either way, she couldn't imagine telling him what she'd been thinking. She couldn't imagine telling *anyone* about her suspicions, though she knew she should probably talk to someone before she took the next step.

Right now she had no idea what her next step was going to be, how to follow-up and find proof of her theory. Sure, she'd considered approaching Grant and saying, "I think I might be your sister." But as hard as she tried, she couldn't imagine how he might respond to such an announcement, except that she was confident he would *not* throw his arms around her and say, "Welcome to the family."

At the very least, he would be cautious; more likely, suspicious; possibly he would even question her sanity. All of which would be understandable reactions to such an unexpected claim, and all of which reaffirmed for Erin her decision to stay away from the resort today and avoid any chance of crossing paths with her boss.

But as much as her actions had been motivated by self-preservation, she couldn't deny that she was glad Corey had shown up and taken her mind off of the situation—at least for a while.

"I was just thinking that I was glad I played hooky today," she told him, because that was true.

His eyes narrowed, as if he knew she wasn't being completely truthful with him, but then he smiled. "I'm glad you played hooky today, too."

"Unfortunately, I can't keep playing hooky, which means that I have an early morning." She pushed her chair away from the table and stood up, taking her plate and cutlery to the dishwasher.

"Is that supposed to be my cue to take off?"

"Yes, it is," she said, but with more than a hint of reluctance.

She really had enjoyed her day with Corey—and she'd appreciated that he'd been able to take her mind off of her worries when nothing and no one else had done so.

"I'll head out as soon as the kitchen is cleared up," he told her.

"You cooked dinner, so I'll take care of the cleanup."

"That doesn't seem fair when I made the mess."

"It's more than fair, considering the delicious meal I just ate."

"Are you sure?"

"I'm sure." More importantly, she was worried that if she didn't get him out of her apartment as soon as possible, she might change her mind about wanting him to go.

"All right then," he relented. "But only because I have some early morning meetings myself that I need to prepare for."

"Meetings? I didn't realize…I thought you were just in town for your brother's wedding."

"I would have come just for the wedding," he agreed. "But as it turned out, I had a business opportunity come up in the area."

"Then you're going to be staying in Thunder Canyon for a while?"

He leaned closer. "Do you want me to?"

More than she should, and that was *not* an admission she was willing to make to a man who was all too aware of the effect he had on the female species. Instead, she only said, "I'm sure your plans have nothing to do with me."

His smile, slow and sexy, made her heart bump against her ribs.

"Don't be too sure, darlin'," he said in a tone that was as slow and sexy as his smile and shimmered over her skin like a caress. "While it's true that some new opportunities have come up, I'm not sure I would have been so willing to hang around if I wasn't also tempted by the possibility of spending some more time with you."

"I told you—" she had to look away to break the hypnotic

effect of those espresso-colored eyes "—I'm not looking to get involved with anyone right now."

"Yeah, you told me," he agreed. "But your kisses say somethin' totally different, darlin'."

"It was one kiss—and it never should have happened."

"My mama might have raised me to be a gentleman," he said, "but she also taught me to never back down from a challenge."

"That wasn't a challenge," she said.

"Wasn't it?"

"No," she insisted vehemently, desperately. "It was a statement of fact."

He smiled again. "We'll see about that, darlin'."

"And stop calling me *darlin'*."

"My apologies…Erin."

The way he spoke her name made it sound more intimate than any words of passion that had ever been whispered between lovers in the dark. She fought the urge to shiver. She refused to give any outward indication of the effect of his nearness on her.

"And the reason I said 'kisses' is because there will be more," he told her.

"That's quite an assumption to make," she said.

"I know."

His lips curved, just a little, before they covered hers.

It was a gentle kiss this time—teasing, testing. As if, despite the previous kiss they'd shared, he was unsure what her response would be this time.

Erin had no doubts. She was sure that she could— *would*—resist.

Her certainty lasted all of about two seconds. Because in the moment that his mouth first brushed against hers, every thought of protest, every ounce of resistance, simply melted away in response to the heat that churned through her body.

The sciences had never been her forte, but she did understand the basics of simple chemistry. And it didn't get much more basic than the rubbing of a man and a woman together resulting in physical attraction.

She knew there were exceptions to the rule. Trevor had been one of those exceptions. However, Corey was the poster boy for the rule. And in his arms, Erin was nothing more than a reactant.

She had no free will, no ability to control her own response where he was concerned, and no desire to be anywhere but in his arms.

Already the feel of his mouth on hers was familiar, his flavor addictive. She'd wanted this—wanted *him*—from the first, and the knowledge shook her. Or maybe it was the kiss that made her tremble.

Chapter Six

She'd said their first kiss never should have happened, and maybe she was right about that. But at this point, Corey thought that attempting to deny the attraction between them would be like closing the barn door after the horse had gotten out. And the desire that raced through his veins reminded him of Lucifer racing across the field, sampling his taste of freedom. Heady and reckless and desperate for more.

He desperately wanted more of Erin.

All of Erin.

He already knew how it would be between them, how she would feel, her naked body beneath his, moving against him, willing and eager. How she would wrap herself around him; how he would sink into her warmth and softness.

He could picture it clearly, and the details were so vivid and real, they made him ache.

But somewhere beneath the passion he tasted on her lips,

there was something else. Just a hint of uncertainty, a touch of wariness. He could make her forget all of her doubts. He could simply keep kissing her, touching her and enticing her to the point that her desire overwhelmed any lingering reluctance. But he knew that they would both have regrets if he did.

No, he wouldn't take her to bed until he was certain that she wanted him as much as he wanted her. So instead of letting his hands roam over her and touch her as he craved, he contented himself with holding her. Even when her arms lifted to link behind his head and her body softened against his, he held his own raging desire in check and continued to kiss her.

Just tasting.

Testing.

Tempting.

Except that he wasn't just tempting Erin, he was tempting himself, too. And because there was a definite limit to how much temptation he could endure, he gently eased away. Slowly. Reluctantly.

Her eyelids fluttered, opened, revealing beautiful blue eyes clouded with confusion.

He brushed his thumb over the curve of her bottom lip, moist and swollen from his kiss, and felt her tremble again. He dropped his hand, realizing he was venturing a little too close to the edge of his limits.

"I'll be seeing you again," he promised.

And then, before he could forget his resolution not to take more than she was ready to give, he turned and walked away.

As Erin closed and locked the door at Corey's back, she was more confused than ever. And considering how confused she was when she arrived in Montana, that was saying something.

She desperately wished she had someone to talk to about her feelings for Corey, but who?

Erika was probably the best friend she had in Thunder Canyon, but she was a newlywed who certainly didn't need to be troubled by her friend's romantic woes, not to mention that she was married to Corey's brother.

Haley was the first friend she'd made in town, but as a waitress, part-time student and volunteer counselor at ROOTS—an organization she'd founded to help troubled teens—Haley had more than enough on her plate. And on top of everything else, she was in the midst of her own romance with Marlon Cates.

Erin was pleased that her closest friends were blissfully in love. She wasn't so pleased that their happiness left her to figure out this situation with Corey on her own.

She really didn't want to get involved with him, but she had a feeling he was right—she was already involved. And now that she knew he was planning to stay in Thunder Canyon, at least for the short term, she would have to figure out how she was going to deal with him.

Sure, she could just continue to ignore the attraction she felt, but her attempts to deny the feelings he stirred inside of her had already proved futile. All he had to do was touch her and all of her resistance melted away. And when he kissed her…well, just the memory of his kisses, the masterful seduction of his mouth on hers, made her sigh.

She'd been attracted to other men before, and she'd had a few relationships in her twenty-five years. She'd also had her heart knocked around a few times, and that wasn't an experience she was eager to repeat. Of course, she'd been younger then and more naive, and she'd learned from her mistakes. She didn't lead with her heart anymore, she didn't believe everything a man told her (and she was especially skeptical of declarations of affection made while naked), and she wasn't ever again going to stay in a relationship with someone because she didn't want to hurt his feelings by telling him that there was no zing in the relationship—which is what had gone so wrong with Trevor.

Of course, lack of zing wasn't a problem with Corey. The problem was too much zing. So much zing, in fact, it was interfering with the normal, rational functioning of her brain.

What she needed to do, if she wanted to ensure that her hormones didn't overrule her head, was establish boundaries—and make sure that the man in question was aware of those boundaries. Because Corey Traub with his dark, bedroom eyes and slow, sexy smile and slower, sexier drawl was a cowboy who had undoubtedly left a trail of broken hearts all across Texas, and she had no intention of being his latest conquest. Even if the thought of being conquered by such a man held a certain undeniable appeal.

Which made her again consider that instead of ignoring the attraction, she should embrace it; instead of establishing boundaries, she should obliterate them. So long as they each knew what they wanted from the other, why shouldn't they enjoy being together?

Maybe it was foolish to think that she could indulge in a casual no-strings affair when she'd never done so before. Or maybe that was just another reason why she should go for it. When she'd made the trip to Thunder Canyon, she'd done so knowing that the journey would bring changes to her life. Meeting Corey had given her another opportunity to make another change.

She'd never known anyone like him—he was larger than life, a man strong enough for a woman to lean on, a man she wanted to be with. He didn't strike her as someone who did anything by half measures, and she knew that if she ever made love with him, it would be a spectacular experience.

What worried her was the possibility that he would seduce not just her body but her heart, and that when he was gone she would be left with only memories of the time they'd spent together and her heart in pieces.

Because he *would* go. She knew that. He had no more intention of staying in Thunder Canyon than she did—but she wasn't ready to pack up her bags just yet.

And although heading back to San Diego held a certain appeal, she knew she couldn't do it. She couldn't go back to her old life and pretend that everything was as it had always been. She'd come to Montana because she needed answers, and she wasn't going anywhere until she had them.

After another restless night, Erin got up Tuesday morning and readied herself for work as if it was any other day. Because her dreams had been mostly centered on Corey, she hadn't come up with any revelations about how to tell her boss about the possibility that he could be her brother. Instead, she decided to act as normal as possible, as if nothing had changed.

But she found herself making excuses to walk past his office, trying to catch a glimpse of him, trying to figure out if there was any familial resemblance between herself and her boss. She had two brothers, and she loved both Jake and Josh, but there was just something about Grant Clifton that had appealed to her from the start.

A man didn't rise to the position he was in without having a fair amount of drive and ambition, but he wasn't ruthless or hard. Her own experience had shown her that he was a fair and compassionate employer; according to his friends, he was loyal and steadfast; the love he obviously shared with his wife of three years proved he was faithful and devoted; and when he talked about his mother and his sister, he demonstrated that he had a strong sense of family.

Was it possible that she might be part of his family? If so, would he grow to care about her as he obviously cared about Elise? Of course, if it turned out that Erin was his sister, it would mean that Elise was not.

How would he deal with that revelation? Would he resent Erin for bringing it to light? Or would he accept that she was as much a victim of circumstances as everyone else?

"Is everything okay?"

Erin realized that she'd been standing in front of the reservation computer for several minutes without inputting any data. She looked up at Carrie and managed to smile. "Sorry. I don't know where my mind is today."

"I think I know," her coworker teased, nodding her head in the direction of the counter.

Glancing past her, Erin saw Corey standing there, and her heart gave that all-too familiar jolt.

"What's he doing here?"

"Looking for you," Carrie told her. "And honey, if you're not interested, feel free to give him my number."

Erin felt her cheeks flush as she moved past her coworker to the counter.

"Are you here to see if I was playing hooky today?" she asked him.

"Nope. Just to see you."

"Any particular reason?"

"You were on my mind. In fact, you've been on my mind since I left your house last night, a detail that did not go unnoticed by my associates at the meetings I had this morning."

She wasn't sure how to respond to that, so she remained silent.

"This is where you could say that you've been thinking about me, too," he prompted.

She didn't think his ego needed the boost of hearing the words, even if they were true. But she folded her arms on the counter and dropped her voice, as if making a confession. "What if I tell you that, as I drove to work this morning, I was thinking about playing hooky again because it's much too beautiful a day to be cooped up inside?"

He leaned closer, so their faces were only inches apart. "Did you think about playing hooky again with me?"

"A girl has to have a few secrets," she teased.

"Something tells me you have more than a few."

It was an effort to keep her smile in place as his words struck a chord. He was right. She had more secrets than anyone in Thunder Canyon knew, more than anyone would possibly guess. And the longer she stayed, continuing to perpetuate the myth that she was just a California transplant looking for a change of pace, the guiltier she felt. She'd made friends with the people in town, listened to their confessions and hopes and dreams.

But she hadn't told a single one of them her real reason for coming to Thunder Canyon. Not even Erika, who had chosen Erin to be the maid of honor at her wedding. And now Erika was married to Dillon, and Erin was fighting her attraction to Dillon's brother, who happened to be good friends with Grant Clifton, who might be Erin's brother. There were too many strings connecting all the players in the drama of her life, and they were getting all tangled up.

She'd been dishonest with so many people. Even if she wasn't guilty of telling lies, she certainly hadn't volunteered the complete truth. And she couldn't help but wonder what they would think of her when they found out. Would the people who had become her friends understand why she'd been silent about her true purpose for coming to Thunder Canyon? Or would the truth cost her those new but treasured friendships?

Her mother tried to instill in all of her kids the importance of being honest. If you tell the truth, she'd pointed out to them, you won't ever forget what you said. Erin understood the importance of the message and she'd tried to live her life accordingly. That had changed when she came to Thunder Canyon.

No, she admitted to herself, it had changed when she'd said that she was quitting her job in San Diego because she felt as if her life had stagnated since graduation and she wanted to explore some other opportunities. Her parents had been supportive—or tried to be. They'd also been hurt by her decision, but not as hurt as she knew they would be if she'd told him she was going to look for a family that Erma had told her was in Montana.

And that one little lie had led to more little lies. Since coming to Thunder Canyon, however, she'd been guilty of so many deceptions and half-truths she wasn't sure she could even remember them all. And she feared that those half-truths were going to come back to haunt her.

Maybe she'd believed they were necessary. Maybe she still did. She couldn't imagine how the tightly knit community would have responded if she'd slapped the newspaper clipping down on a table at The Hitching Post the first day she'd arrived in town and proclaimed that she was related to some or all of the persons in the photo.

Instead, she'd taken a more subtle approach. She'd gotten to know the residents of Thunder Canyon and asked some discreet questions about the families in that faded picture. Unfortunately, the responses she'd received to those inquiries had told her little. And although there was no shortage of skeletons in the closets of the residents of Thunder Canyon, she hadn't heard any murmurs about anyone losing a baby more than twenty-five years earlier.

And then, by sheer luck, she happened to be nearby when Grant Clifton pulled a picture of his sister out of his wallet. Coincidentally, that sister was born on the same day in the same hospital as Erin, and she had some similar features to each of Erin's brothers.

But Erin still didn't know what to do now, how to verify her suspicion that someone at the hospital had somehow mixed up those two babies.

A hand waving in front of her face jolted her out of her reverie. She looked apologetically at Corey. "Sorry."

"Are you sure you don't want to talk about it, darlin'?"

She could hardly deny that her mind had been wandering again, so she only shook her head. "No, I'm not sure. But it's not something I can talk about. Not right now."

"Will you keep me in mind, when you can?"

She wouldn't have blamed him for feeling dissed by her lack of attention, but he seemed more concerned than offended, and she was touched by his offer. "I will," she promised. "Thanks."

"So why don't we talk about your lunch plans?" he said. "Do you have a date with Stefan or can I steal you away for a little while?"

"Why are you so determined to take me to lunch?"

He shrugged. "It's lunchtime, I'm hungry and I enjoy your company."

"How could any woman refuse such a gracious invitation?"

"Stefan was booked, wasn't he?"

"Until four-thirty," she admitted.

"Then he won't be putting his hands on you today," Corey noted.

It was the hint of smugness in his tone that prompted her to tease, "Not until this afternoon."

Erin retrieved her purse from her desk and came around to the other side of the counter.

"How does DJ's Rib Shack sound?" Corey asked her.

"My mouth is watering already," she told him.

He reached for her hand and was pleased when she didn't pull hers away. It was a small thing, but it meant a lot to him because it proved that she was starting to feel comfortable with him.

"But we might have some trouble getting seated," Erin warned. "We have a conference group that booked several large tables for lunch there today."

"Are you forgetting that DJ is my cousin?"

"Does that family connection trump a group of fifty-five paying customers?"

He winced. "Well, I'm sure he can find a couple of chairs for us in the kitchen."

Erin laughed.

He liked to hear her laugh. She seemed so serious most of the time, as if there were heavy issues weighing on her mind. But when she laughed, it was like the sun breaking through on a cloudy day. The soft, sexy sound seemed to burst out of her, and her beautiful blue eyes danced and sparkled.

"For DJ's signature rib sandwich, I would happily sit in the kitchen," she told him.

As it turned out, DJ did manage to find them a small table on the opposite side of the room from the conference guests and with a fabulous view of the resort property. Because they both knew what they wanted to eat, he took their orders so that he could get it into the kitchen before the conference group started clamoring for its food. Corey ordered a beer and Erin, because it was the middle of a work day, requested a soft drink.

"So tell me," Erin said, "how you manage to have so much free time when you're supposed to be in town on business."

"I'm my own boss. When I first started out, I worked more than my share of eighty-hour weeks to ensure my business was successful. Now I have the luxury of being able to pick and choose my jobs and the hours that I'm going to work."

She eyed him over the rim of her glass. "Why did you start your own company instead of going to work at Traub Industries?"

"I did work at Traub Industries, as all of my brothers and my sister did. But, although the experience was memorable and I certainly won't complain about the opportunities the company has afforded me, making a career in the oil business wasn't what I wanted to do with my life."

"So who does run the company?"

"My mother took over at the helm when my dad died, and she's still the CEO. My brother Ethan is the CFO. My stepfather is on the board of directors."

"So it really is a family business."

"I guess it is," he agreed.

She tilted her head. "Are there issues between you and your stepfather?"

"No. Not really."

"Which is it—no? Or not really?"

"Peter's a good guy," Corey said. "And he makes my mom happy. It's pretty amazing to think about the fact that he was willing to marry a woman who was on her own with six kids."

"But—" she prompted.

He didn't say anything.

"But he's not your dad," Erin finished for him.

"No, he's not. I was so young when my dad died that my memories of him are pretty foggy, but it was still hard to accept anyone else trying to take his place. It's only recently that I've realized Peter made his own place—and I'm glad it's with my mom." He shook his head. "But it seems that we're always talking about my family—tell me something about yours."

"The Castros aren't nearly as interesting as the Traubs," she said.

"That's an opinion, not a fact," he chided.

She shrugged. "Okay, my parents are Jack and Betty. My dad's a harbor cop and my mom is a high school history teacher. I have two brothers, Jake and Josh, both of them older. Jake is a cop in New Orleans and Josh is a perpetual student. He's currently studying geosciences at Princeton."

"And what do your parents think of your decision to move to Montana?"

"They're trying to be supportive. They understand that I needed to make some changes in my life. They just wish I didn't have to make them so far away."

"It could be worse," Corey said philosophically. "You could have gone to New England."

She smiled. "Which is what I remind them whenever they start complaining about how far away Thunder Canyon is from San Diego."

"Do you get home to visit them very often?"

"Only once since I moved here," she admitted. "I'd hoped to go back again for Thanksgiving, but that doesn't look like it's going to work out now."

"It's hard being away from family, especially at the holidays."

She nodded. "I don't think I've ever missed a major holiday with them."

"So why don't you invite them to come here?"

She seemed startled by the suggestion. "I can't believe I didn't think of that."

"Sometimes it takes someone from the outside to see the possible solutions to a problem."

"That's exactly what you do, isn't it? Companies hire you to come in and determine what's not working, and you fix it."

"I offer suggestions," he clarified.

"And if a company doesn't take your suggestions?"

"People don't often ignore advice that they pay for, but it's always their choice."

The waiter brought their lunches.

Erin plucked a curly fry from her plate and bit off the end. "How long does it usually take—your review and analysis?"

"Are you trying to figure out how long I'm going to be in Thunder Canyon?" he teased.

"I'm trying to make conversation," she retorted, but the flush in her cheeks confirmed his guess.

"Well, the answer to that question is that it varies depending on the complexity of the problems. Is the company simply looking to improve its bottom line, or is it teetering on the edge of bankruptcy? Is it a mom-and-pop operation or an international conglomerate?" He picked up his spicy barbecue chicken sandwich and bit into it.

"So it could be weeks or months," she guessed.

He nodded, chewing.

"Do you enjoy it?"

"I enjoy the challenge."

"Is that why you're here with me now—because I turned you down the first time you asked me to dance?"

"*You're* here with *me*," he pointed out. "And if you'd accepted my original invitation, the only thing that would have been different is that we would have shared our first dance sooner."

"First dance?"

He grinned. "Yeah, I'm counting on there being more."

She smiled back, not protesting his assumption this time. Then her gaze slid away, caught by something across the room. Glancing over his shoulder, he saw that it wasn't a "something" but "someone"—her boss, Grant Clifton. But it wasn't the direction of her gaze that bothered him so much as the brief glimpse of yearning that he read in her eyes.

Then she focused on her plate again, and Corey was left to wonder if he'd just imagined the longing he thought he'd seen. He hoped so. He sure as heck didn't want to think that she was lusting after a man who was his friend, her boss and married to boot.

However, it would explain why she'd been resistant to his overtures. Not that he thought he was irresistible, but in his experience, most women were flattered by his attention and often sought him out, and he'd been trying to figure out why Erin seemed impervious to his legendary charms.

He'd considered the usual reasons—she was just getting over a failed relationship, she didn't like the color of his hair or his eyes, she thought he was too tall/too short or too young/too old, or she just wasn't attracted to him—although he'd discarded *that* possibility after their first kiss because he knew that a woman couldn't kiss a man the way she'd kissed him if she didn't feel at least some degree of attraction. It had never occurred to him that she might be infatuated with her boss.

"How's your sandwich?" Erin asked.

"Great," he said, and picked it up again.

They chatted casually as they finished their lunches. He noticed that Erin was both attentive and entertaining, her focus never again wavering. Maybe he had imagined the look she'd sent in Grant's direction. Maybe she'd actually been looking at someone else's lunch—or their dessert. He'd dated a lot of women who looked enviously at the cheesecake on someone else's plate but refused to order their own.

"Dessert?" he asked her.

There was still a handful of fries on Erin's plate when she pushed it aside, shaking her head. "I couldn't eat another bite."

"Not even a tiny slice of pecan turtle pie?"

She sighed wistfully. "As much as I love DJ's pecan turtle pie, I know they don't serve tiny slices."

He flagged down their server and ordered a slice anyway, asking for it to be boxed so Erin could take it home.

The cake was delivered along with his credit card slip, and Corey slid the dessert across the table to her.

"I really don't need the three thousand calories in this box," she told him. "But I'll say 'thank you' anyway, knowing that I will savor every last bite while I'm watching *American Idol* tonight."

"What do you watch on Fridays?" Corey asked, as they headed out of the restaurant.

"Nothing in particular."

"Then how about catching a movie with me?" he suggested.

"What movie?" she asked.

"I don't even know what's showing," he admitted.

"I would have expected you to find that out before you decided you wanted to go."

"I just thought it would be fun to go to a movie with you."

"I don't like horror flicks," she warned him.

"You could snuggle up to me during the scary parts." He wiggled his eyebrows suggestively.

She laughed but shook her head. "All the parts are scary parts, and I'd have nightmares for a week."

"Okay, no horror flicks," he promised.

"And I'm not big on sci-fi, either."

He nodded his understanding. "Aliens can be pretty scary."

Her gaze narrowed. "Are you mocking me?"

"Of course not," he said, but his lips twitched as he tried not to smile.

"Just for that, you have to buy the popcorn."

"It would be my pleasure," he told her, and he meant it.

She eyed him warily. "What are we doing, Corey?"

"Setting up a date."

"Is it that simple?"

"For now." They were back at the reception desk, and as much as he wanted to linger, he knew she needed to get back to work. "I'll give you a call to let you know what time on Friday."

"Okay," she agreed. "Thanks for lunch."

As she started around the counter, he caught her hand. She looked up at him, questioning, and he bent his head to touch his lips to hers. It was a quick and easy kiss that was over before she could think to protest about the inappropriateness of him kissing her at work.

"It was my pleasure," he said, and walked away with a smile on his face.

Chapter Seven

He called her on Wednesday, ostensibly to discuss the movie schedule for Friday night. They talked for more than an hour.

They went to the local theater on Friday to see a romantic comedy that Erin had expressed an interest in. Corey grumbled about "chick flicks" throughout the drive back to her condo, but she'd heard him laugh out loud at different parts of the film so she knew he was only teasing.

Because she'd missed work on Monday, she agreed to cover Carrie's shift Saturday morning. She planned to spend the afternoon catching up on the chores she'd neglected during the week—most notably her grocery shopping and housecleaning. But Corey's truck was in her driveway when she got home from the Super Saver Mart, and when he asked her to go horseback riding again, it sounded a lot more fun than scrubbing her shower.

Afterward, they picked up a pizza and a bottle of wine

and took them back to Erin's. As she sat beside him on the couch, watching the flames flicker in the fireplace, she found it hard to believe that she'd only met him a week earlier. So much time seemed to have passed since then.

Sunday morning she awoke to find the snow blowing outside of her windows and decided that the near-blizzard conditions were reason not to venture out of the house. But Corey had no similar qualms because he came over shortly after lunch with some movies he'd rented, and they spent the rest of the afternoon snuggled together on her couch, munching popcorn and watching the original *Star Wars* trilogy. Because, despite her admitted lack of appreciation for the sci-fi genre, he somehow managed to convince her that the George Lucas masterpieces couldn't be so simply classified, and she soon found herself deeply engrossed in the movies.

As the final credits of *The Empire Strikes Back* scrolled on the screen, Erin's stomach began to grumble. Glancing at the glowing numbers on the DVD player, she was surprised to realize how quickly the afternoon had gone and it seemed natural to invite Corey to stay for dinner. Though she hadn't consciously thought about it while she'd been grocery shopping the day before, she'd picked up all the necessary ingredients for her mom's famous enchiladas and Corey seemed pleased by her invitation and happy to eat with her.

After dinner, they tidied up the kitchen together, but when Corey suggested that he should head out, Erin was the one to protest. She wanted to know if Leia succeeded in rescuing Han, to which Corey reminded her that the movie was about a lot more than a romantic subplot. But, of course, he put the third movie on.

It was late by the time he finally said good-night, and several inches of snow had fallen. Erin cringed at the sight of the white stuff covering her car and her driveway, but she decided to ignore it until the morning. Corey wouldn't hear of it though and, after locating a shovel in the garage, insisted on clearing her steps and driveway. Although she appreciated not having to do it herself, she wasn't sure how she felt about his insistence on taking charge.

Not that she was really surprised—she'd instinctively known that he was the type of man who liked to be in control of any situation—but she didn't want him to think that she couldn't take care of herself. She prided herself on her self-sufficiency and independence. She didn't really want to battle with him over clearing snow, but she wanted him to know that she was capable. However, as she watched Corey clear her driveway, effortlessly tossing shovels full of snow aside, she had to admit that there were worse things than having a strong, handsome man around to perform such chores.

When he finished shoveling, she invited him to come back inside for a cup of hot chocolate to warm him up. He declined the drink but did come back inside to kiss her goodbye, and she couldn't deny that the heat they generated between them was—

She jolted as his ice cold hands slipped under her sweater and splayed against the bare skin of her back. Corey laughed and reached for her again, but she stepped away.

The wicked light in his eyes made her heart pound with anticipation; the sexy curve of his lips made her knees weak. She dodged around to the other side of the table, he feinted to the right and caught her when she turned in the opposite direction.

They were both laughing when her cell phone chimed. Corey frowned. "Who would be calling at this hour?"

"It's a text," she said, reaching for the phone to check the message. "From Grant."

His hands dropped away and he reached for the jacket he'd hung over the back of a chair.

"Carrie called in sick for tomorrow, so he just wanted to give Trina and me the heads-up that we'll be on our own," she explained.

"Didn't you cover for Carrie yesterday?"

She nodded. "She wanted the morning to get ready for a big date." Which made her suspect that her coworker wasn't sick at all but was simply having too much fun with her date to want it to end just yet.

"So she's probably not sick at all," Corey surmised.

Erin just shrugged because she knew she wasn't in any position to judge. Her own reasons for playing hooky the previous week might have been different, but she'd still called in sick when she really wasn't.

"Does that mean you'll have to work later tomorrow?"

"Only if someone on the afternoon shift calls in."

"Or if Grant needs you to fill in somewhere else around the resort," he guessed.

Was that an edge she heard in his voice, or was she imagining it?

"Since I started at the resort, I've never turned down any overtime that was offered because I never had any reason to. But if I have plans, I am allowed to say 'no' to extra shifts," she told him.

"Then you should know that we have plans for tomorrow night."

He was taking charge again, and she wondered if she should protest. But she wanted to see him, so there really wasn't any point. Instead, she asked, "Are you going to tell me what those plans are?"

"As soon as I figure them out," he said, and slid his arms around her waist again. She stiffened, remembering the shock of his icy hands against her skin, but he kept his hands on the outside of her clothes this time. "Right now, I only know that I want to be with you."

"That's good enough for me," she told him, and tugged his head down to hers.

She'd never initiated a kiss before, and she could tell that she'd surprised him by doing so now. He kissed her back, but he let her set the pace, and when she withdrew, he let her go.

As she watched him drive away, she was already anticipating seeing him again, and that worried her—more than a little.

They were spending a lot of time together and people were beginning to talk. Corey didn't seem to care and Erin knew that she shouldn't either, but it bothered her that being seen with him seemed a noteworthy event to the residents of Thunder Canyon. For months, she'd managed to avoid speculation and scrutiny by mostly keeping to herself. And in the space of a week, he'd managed to thrust her into the spotlight.

She could have stopped seeing him. She didn't have to answer his calls, she didn't need to accept his invitations and she certainly wasn't under any obligation to respond to his kisses. But she enjoyed talking to him, she had a good time when they were together, and the passion he stirred inside of her refused to be ignored.

The problem was that spending so much time with Corey meant she didn't have any time to search for the answers she'd come to Thunder Canyon to find. Yet she'd waited almost twenty-six years already, so there wasn't any pressing urgency right now. And because she didn't know how long Corey would be staying in town, she was going to enjoy spending every minute with him that she could.

The following Tuesday afternoon, Corey was feeling bored with his own company so he called Dillon and asked him to come out to the Hitching Post for a beer. He didn't really expect his newlywed brother to accept the invitation, but Dillon—abandoned by his wife and daughter for Holly Clifton's baby shower—said he'd be happy to meet him.

They opted to sit at the bar and within minutes were settled into their seats with frosty glasses of beer in front of them.

"I heard you've been spending a lot of time with Erin Castro," Dillon said.

Corey didn't bother to ask where his brother had heard. In a town the size of Thunder Canyon, rumors spread faster than a bushfire in July.

"I like her," he said simply.

But something in his tone must have given him away because Dillon's gaze narrowed. "You've only known her a week."

A week and a half, actually, but he didn't think the clarification would mean much to his brother. "Sometimes you just know."

Dillon shook his head as he munched on a pretzel.

"I think she might really be the one."

"You think every woman might be the one."

Corey couldn't deny that he'd made the same claim once or twice before. When he was younger, he'd trusted in the basic honesty and goodness of other people—and of women, in particular. As a result, he'd fallen in love readily and frequently. Then he'd met Heather, and he'd learned that people weren't always what they seemed. Although that experience had made him wary, there was something about Erin that urged him to open his heart and trust again, something about her innate sweetness that made him want to believe not just in her but in the way he felt when he was with her. "So I'm an optimist. But this time, it's different.

She's different—she's more real than any woman I've ever known."

"Just…be careful," Dillon cautioned.

He laughed. "You're warning me to be careful of Erin?"

"You don't know her very well," his brother reminded him, casting a pointed glance at the portrait of the town's original "Shady Lady" hanging over the bar. "In fact, no one in Thunder Canyon really knows Erin that well."

Corey didn't like the implication. "Why are you so suspicious? It's not as if entry past the town limits is by invitation only."

"I'm…uncertain…of her reasons for coming to Thunder Canyon," Dillon clarified.

"Maybe she just wanted a change of pace."

"Is that what she told you?"

"As a matter of fact, it is."

Dillon tipped his glass to his lips, drank. "A rather vague response, don't you think?"

He hadn't thought so at the time, but his brother's question had him frowning now. "I think that she'll tell me more when she's ready."

"Whenever that might be."

He picked up his beer. "What's that supposed to mean?"

"Just that she seems to ask a lot of questions without giving away any information about herself," his brother noted.

Corey had noticed the same thing, and he'd admired her ability to draw out other people. It was a valuable skill for someone working in the hospitality industry, and it irked him that his brother was turning it into something negative.

"What have you got against Erin?"

"Nothing," Dillon insisted. "I'm just suggesting that you take your own advice and look before you leap this time."

He took a long swallow from his glass and tried not to wince at the "this time." His brother was right—he had a habit of wanting to believe the best of people, and he'd ended up getting burned because of it. Maybe learning the details of Heather's job hadn't broken his heart, but the truth had dented the hell out of his pride and her lies had destroyed his trust.

But Erin was different. He was sure of it. "Maybe we should talk about something else," he suggested.

"Anything in particular on your mind?"

"The resort."

"What about it?" Dillon wondered.

"It's obvious that the recession has taken its toll on Thunder Canyon, and the resort is no exception."

"You're not telling me anything I don't know," Dillon said.

Corey reached for the bowl of pretzels. "I will," he promised, and proceeded to outline the basic plan he'd worked up to attract new investors and capital to the resort.

Corey had late meetings on Wednesday, so Erin didn't see him again until Thursday when he stopped by the reservation desk to ask her if she wanted to go out for dinner that night. She was conscious of Trina and Carrie watching and growing weary of the talk around town, so instead of accepting his invitation, she offered to cook for him at her place again.

Corey said that he would bring wine and dessert, and he showed up promptly at seven o'clock with a bottle of pinot noir and a bakery box containing two wide slices of DJ's turtle pecan pie.

She'd marinated strips of steak in teriyaki sauce and

stir-fried the meat with red and green peppers, snow peas and carrots, then served it on top of hot basmati rice. It was a favorite recipe of Erin's because it required little time to cook and even less to prep, but Corey obviously enjoyed it as much as she did, as evidenced by the second helping that he finished as readily as the first.

"So why Montana?" Corey asked, tipping the last of the wine into Erin's glass. "What brought you here?"

Their conversation during dinner had mostly touched on inconsequential topics, so his question now seemed to come at her out of the blue. But she'd been regretting all the secrecy and evasions that had been part of any conversations she'd had since coming to town, and she was almost grateful for this chance to tell someone the truth. Or at least part of it.

"I was born in Thunder Canyon," she told him now.

"No kidding?"

"I never actually lived here, but my parents were visiting my great aunt Erma when my mom went into labor ahead of schedule."

"Does your aunt still live here?"

She licked the last bit of caramel from her fork and then pushed aside her empty plate. "She's the one who recently passed away."

"Is that why you came here—to remember her?" he asked gently.

She gathered up their dessert plates and carried them to the counter. She heard the scrape of his chair legs against the tile floor as he pushed away from the table.

"I came here—" she hesitated, still not sure how much to reveal. She needed to confide in someone and she wanted that someone to be Corey, but she really didn't know him well enough to even guess how he might respond. "I came here because it was what she wanted."

"But why did you stay? I mean, a quick visit would have honored her wishes."

She washed and dried her hands before turning back to him. "I stayed partly because I don't yet have the answers I'm looking for and partly because I fell in love with the town the first minute I stepped into the Hitching Post."

"Love can happen like that," he agreed, settling his hands on her hips and pulling her closer. "Hitting you like a ton of bricks when you least expect it."

Corey could tell that Erin didn't know how to interpret his statement never mind respond to it, and he mentally cursed himself for not censoring his words. While he'd realized that the feelings he had for her were stronger and deeper than he'd expected, he shouldn't have assumed that she would feel the same way.

"I guess you're right," she said, looking at the button at his throat rather than at him. "Although I've never really experienced anything like that before."

Which wasn't an admission that she was experiencing anything like that now, but it also wasn't a rejection of his feelings.

"I know we haven't known each other very long—"

"Not even two weeks," she interjected hastily.

"You think I'm rushing things?"

"I think—" she sighed. "I don't know what I think. I have feelings for you—feelings I didn't expect to have. But—"

He could be satisfied with that, at least for now. And not wanting to hear whatever limitations or conditions she was probably going to put on her feelings, he silenced her words with his lips.

Her mouth softened beneath his, her lips parted.

He loved kissing her. She was so warm and passionate, so incredibly responsive. His tongue danced with hers, and his blood surged in his veins. She sighed and shifted closer.

His fingers made quick work of the buttons down the front of her shirt, then his hands slipped inside, cupping soft, round breasts encased in delicate lace. His thumbs stroked over her nipples, and they responded immediately to his touch. He circled the rigid points, felt her tremble.

His lips eased away from hers to trail kisses across her jaw. He touched his tongue to the rapidly beating pulse point at her throat, and she moaned. His mouth moved down her throat, toward the hollow between her breasts, and she shuddered.

He unhooked the clip at the front of her bra and filled his hands with her breasts. Her skin was so soft, so lush, so irresistible. He lowered his mouth to take one turgid peak between his lips. He swirled his tongue around the nipple, then suckled hard. She gasped. Her fingers sifted through his hair, holding him against her, silently urging him to continue.

He was more than happy to comply. He took his time, savoring the flavor of her flesh, learning what she liked by listening to her moans and sighs. As his mouth pleasured her breasts, his hands moved lower. He unfastened the button of her pants, slid down the zipper and dipped inside. Her panties were lace, like her bra, and he could feel her heat and wetness as he stroked her through the fabric. She moaned and arched into his palm, shuddering when he stroked her again.

Then, suddenly, her hands were on his chest, and she was pushing him away.

"No. We have to stop. I can't do this." Though her words were unequivocal, he heard the anguish in her voice and knew that she hadn't really wanted to push him away.

But Corey didn't have any trouble understanding "no" and, although he might regret that the war between desire and conscience had been won by her conscience, he couldn't deny that it had. He thrust his hands into the pockets of his jeans so that he wouldn't be tempted to touch her again, not until he had his own raging desires under control.

He caught a glimpse of tears in her eyes before she dropped her gaze, and he felt like a complete louse. "I'm sorry," he said, and winced at the inadequacy of the words.

Erin shook her head, her fingers trembling as she refastened the buttons on her shirt. "No, *I'm* sorry. I didn't mean to let things go so far. I'm not the type—"

He touched a finger to her lips, halting the flow of words. "You don't have anything to apologize for. I was rushing you," he admitted. "I can't seem to help myself. I want you, Erin. Every time I see you, I want you more."

"I want you, too, Corey, but I'm not ready for this."

He leaned his forehead against hers, frustrated beyond belief but unwilling to push her. He needed her to want him as much as he wanted her, and until then, he would try to be patient. "Then we'll wait until you are," he said simply.

"That might take some time," she warned him. "There's a lot going on in my life right now, personal issues that I'm trying to figure out, that I need to figure out, before I can even think about getting involved."

"We're already involved," he said again.

She sighed. "Only because you're stubborn and persuasive and far too charming for your own good."

He smiled at that. "And you admitted that you have feelings for me, so I'll be satisfied with that for now."

"I do have feelings for you," she acknowledged. "But I'm not sure what to do about them."

"Why do you have to do anything about them? Why can't we just enjoy being together?"

"Because I know you want more than I've given, and I'm not sure I'm ready to give any more."

"Because of Grant?" The question sprang out of his mouth without any forethought, and he immediately regretted the words. He hadn't realized how much he'd been thinking about her relationship with his friend until now, how much he'd worried about her apparent preoccupation with the man who was her boss.

He gauged her expression carefully, watching for a reaction. He hoped that she would be shocked by his question and immediately deny having any feelings for the other man. And he would believe her because he wanted to move forward with their relationship without the unease that prickled at the back of his neck whenever he saw her with Grant.

She sucked in a breath, obviously surprised by the question—or maybe just surprised that he'd voiced it aloud. When she spoke, her response was both weak and unconvincing and made frustration and anger churn in his gut.

"Wh-what does Grant have to do with any of this?"

"Why don't you tell me?"

"Grant is my boss."

"And my friend."

She only nodded.

"And he's married," Corey reminded her, in case she'd conveniently forgotten that fact.

"I've met his wife," she said. "On several occasions."

"They grew up together, here in Thunder Canyon. Their fathers were best friends."

She nodded again. "I've heard the story—about Grant and Stephanie finding their fathers' bodies after the two men were killed by rustlers."

He didn't detect anything but sorrow in her tone, and he wondered if he could be wrong about her feelings for Grant. He wanted to believe he was wrong, but her response to his mention of the other man's name wasn't something he could disregard. She'd been startled—almost acted guilty—and he couldn't shake the instinct that there was more going on than she was willing to admit.

But he knew Grant. He knew how devoted his friend was to Stephanie. And he didn't believe for a minute that the resort manager would ever cheat on his pregnant wife, so the idea that he was having an affair with Erin was patently ridiculous. Not to mention that she could hardly be tearing up the sheets with her boss when she'd spent most of her free time over the past two weeks with Corey.

But his brother's warnings continued to nag at the back of his mind. *You don't know her very well… she seems to ask a lot of questions without revealing any information about herself… look before you leap this time.*

Corey knew it was too late for that. He had already fallen for Erin. He only hoped that he hadn't fallen for a woman who was in love with another man.

After Corey had gone, Erin continued to think about the questions he'd asked. She didn't know why he'd brought Grant into the conversation; she could only assume that he'd picked up on her interest in her boss and misinterpreted it. She wanted to tell Corey the truth, and she wanted to stop tiptoeing around Grant, pretending that she wasn't carrying a huge secret.

Okay, at this point it was still more of a suspicion than a secret—nothing had been proven. And she didn't know what steps to take next, who to talk to, to confirm her suspicions.

Surprisingly, it was a conversation with her mother later that night that gave her an idea.

"The last time I saw Aunt Erma, she reminded me that she used to live in Thunder Canyon."

"That's how you happened to be born there," Betty reminded her.

"Well, I thought that since I'm here now, I might try to find some of her old friends."

"Erma only lived there a few years while she was married to Irwin, her third husband. When he passed away, she moved on."

"But she mentioned a friend who was a nurse, and I got the impression they may have kept in touch."

"Delores Beckett," Betty said.

"You know her?" Erin asked, surprised by her mother's immediate response.

"Of course. She was the nurse in delivery when you were born."

Chapter Eight

Erin's breath caught. "Aunt Erma didn't tell me that."

"She might not have remembered. It was almost twenty-six years ago," her mother reminded her.

But Erin knew that Erma had remembered, and she understood now why her aunt had mentioned the nurse's name.

If Delores Beckett—she scribbled the name down on the message pad beside the phone so she wouldn't forget it again—had been working when Betty Castro had given birth, then she would know what had happened in the maternity ward that day and if there was any chance that two babies had been mixed up.

"Speaking of which," Betty continued, oblivious to the thoughts swirling in her daughter's head, "your dad and I decided that, if you can't come home for Thanksgiving, we're going to have to come to you."

"Really?" Jack had sounded so doubtful when Erin issued the invitation that she hadn't let herself hope they might accept it. Because as much as she was trying to figure out the mystery Aunt Erma had dumped in her lap, she knew that Betty and Jack would always be her parents, and she missed them so much. "You're going to come here?"

"Do you think we'd pass on the opportunity to spend the holiday with our baby girl?"

Erin felt the sting of tears. "Thanks, Mom."

"You mentioned that it's a busy time at the resort," Betty reminded her. "Does that mean we should make a reservation somewhere else?"

"You don't have to make a reservation anywhere—I have plenty of room here at the condo."

She'd rented a basement apartment when she'd first moved out of the Big Sky Motel and she'd been happy in the unit and with the elderly woman who had rented it to her. But after only a few weeks, Erin had been informed by her landlady that her daughter was divorcing her husband and moving home with her two children, so she needed the space for them.

Thankfully, it was right around the same time that Erin had started temping at the resort, and when she'd mentioned to her boss that she was looking for a new apartment, Grant had suggested one of the condos on site. She'd hesitated, knowing that she didn't need as much space as a condo would provide and certain that she couldn't afford such luxurious accommodations. But the economic downturn had lowered the rents and as a resort employee, Erin was entitled to a further reduction.

The condo was completely furnished and the kitchen was fully equipped, which, for a woman who had arrived in town with two suitcases and a few boxes in her trunk, was essential. It had two fireplaces—one in the main floor living room and one in the master bedroom. And whenever she thought about returning to San Diego, she felt a strange tug in the vicinity of her heart.

But it was more than not wanting to move out of the condo—it was that she didn't want to leave Thunder Canyon. There was just something about the town that made her feel as if she'd finally found a place where she belonged.

"Are you sure?" her mother asked now. "We don't want to put you out."

"The condo has three bedrooms and I only sleep in one."

"In that case, we'll be happy to stay with you," Betty said.

"I'm so glad you're coming," Erin said, her throat tight. "I really miss you guys."

"We miss you, too."

She heard the emotion in her mother's response, and when she finally said goodbye and hung up the phone, she wondered—not for the first time—what she was doing in Thunder Canyon. So what if Betty Castro hadn't given birth to her? She and Jack had raised Erin as their daughter, they'd instilled in her the same values and morals as they'd given to their two sons and they'd loved her. Maybe she hadn't always felt as if she belonged, but she'd never had reason to doubt their affection for her.

And now she was digging into the past, and for what? Was uncovering the truth behind Erma's last words really worth tearing all of their lives apart?

Erin was afraid the answer to that question might turn out to be "no." But as she looked down at the name she'd scrawled on her message pad, she knew she couldn't let it go.

* * *

There were only two Becketts in the Thunder Canyon telephone directory. Neither one of them was a "D."

Erin called the number listed for "R & L Beckett" first. After the fifth ring, she waited, expecting her call to connect to an answering machine. But it rang a sixth time, then a seventh. Who, in this day and age, didn't have an answering machine or voice mail?

Aunt Erma, she remembered. Her parents had given her an answering machine one year for Christmas, but Erma had never even taken it out of the box. If she wasn't home, they could call back, she always said. It wasn't hard to believe that a friend of Erma's might have a similar attitude.

She was just about to hang up when the phone was finally picked up on the other end.

"Hello?" It was a man's voice, deep and strong and breathless, as if he'd had to run to answer the call.

"Mr. Beckett?"

"Yes, this is Reginald Beckett," he said cautiously.

"I'm sorry to bother you, but I'm trying to locate a Delores Beckett and I was wondering if she might be a relative of yours."

"No, there isn't anyone in my family by that name."

And that quickly, the hope that had only started to build was knocked down again. She apologized to Mr. Beckett again for bothering him and went to the next listing. This time, her call was picked up on the third ring.

"Yes, hello?" the woman who answered said impatiently.

"I'm looking for Delores Beckett," Erin said.

"Who is this? Why are you looking for Delores?"

"My aunt was a friend of hers, and she suggested that I look up Delores when I was in Thunder Canyon."

"What made you think she would be here?" the woman asked.

"It's not that I thought she would so much as I was hoping that you might be able to help me find her."

"I'm sorry. I can't do that."

She wasn't sure how to interpret that response. The woman who had been on the other end of the line—who never did identify herself—hadn't actually denied knowing Delores or where to find her.

As Erin listened to the dial tone buzzing in her ear, she noted the address beside the number and thought that maybe she would stop by to chat with Ms. T. Beckett in person.

Hollyhock Lane was located in a newer survey where all of the streets had picturesque-sounding names and postage stamp-sized lots. Number thirty-four was the center unit of a townhouse complex. Erin had driven past the stone-and-brick two-story on her way home from work the day before, but there had been no vehicle in the driveway and no indication that anyone was at home.

On Tuesday she ended up working late so the sun was already down by the time she left the resort. Considering that T. Beckett had been less than warm on the phone, she had no intention of approaching the woman's door in the dark.

But because she finished early on Wednesday if she was scheduled to work on Saturday morning, as she was this week, she was back on Hollyhock Lane by three o'clock that afternoon. She pulled up across the street, trying to get up the nerve to leave her vehicle and approach the door, when a little red Toyota pulled into the driveway.

Well, at least she knew someone was home.

But when the driver got out of her car, Erin realized there was no way she could be Delores Beckett. The woman was barely older than Erin herself. And then she opened the back door and a child—a little girl probably not more than three or four years old—climbed out. They went around to the trunk, and the mother lifted out several grocery bags, handing the lightest one to her daughter before juggling the rest of them along with her purse and keys as they made their way to the door.

With a resigned sigh, Erin pulled away from the curb and drove home.

Maybe Delores Beckett had left town just as Erma had done, moving away to make a new start somewhere else.

But if that was the case, where was Erin supposed to start looking for her?

As Erin was getting ready to leave work the next day, she overheard Grant mention to the afternoon desk manager that he would be at DJ's if there were any problems. She'd been distracted all day, trying to figure out a way to approach him. She had no intention of blurting out that she thought he might be her brother—she just wanted to have a conversation and possibly learn something more about his mother or his sister.

So when she'd finished assigning rooms for the last reservation that had come in through the website, she picked up her purse and headed to DJ's.

She watched the hostess lead Grant to the far side of the room. Her heart was pounding and her hands felt clammy, so she ducked into the restroom, needing a moment to shore up her courage. It was silly, she knew, to be so nervous when she talked to the man every day at work. But those were always work-related discussions and inevitably brief.

She washed her hands, ran a brush through her hair, dabbed on some lip gloss. Then she drew in another breath, pressed a hand to her still-pounding heart and prepared to go talk to the man who might be her brother.

Though she hadn't spoken the words aloud, they seemed to bounce off of the tiled walls and echo in her head.

…might be her brother…her brother…brother…

She nearly jolted when the door opened and another patron entered. Deciding that she'd stalled long enough, she exited into the foyer, hesitating in the entranceway that separated the restrooms from the main part of the restaurant to peek through the brass potted plants that flanked the arch.

She spotted Grant easily. He was sitting so that his profile was to her at a small booth with a curved leather seating area, a half-finished pint of beer on the glossy wooden table in front of him.

She smoothed her hands down the front of her skirt, drew in a deep breath and started toward his table. As she stepped out from behind the plants, she saw him rise to his feet.

She faltered. Had she dallied too long? Was he leaving already?

But he stayed standing where he was, his gaze focused across the room, smiling. And then Stephanie stepped into view. She crossed to her husband and leaned up to kiss him. His arm came around her, pulling her closer, prolonging the kiss.

And Erin knew that her moment had come and gone. It had been one thing to approach Grant when he was alone, and it was quite another to interrupt a private moment with his wife.

She turned away, tears of regret and frustration blurring her eyes and almost walked right into someone.

"Excuse me," she said softly. She stepped aside without looking up, then gasped when she felt a hand on her arm.

"What is going on with you?" Corey demanded.

She tugged her arm out of his grasp. "I don't know what you mean."

"I mean that I want to know why you're lurking in doorways, spying on another man...and his wife."

She didn't know how he knew she'd been watching Grant—unless he'd been watching her. But she didn't think challenging him on that point would do anything to erase the fury she read in his dark eyes. "It's not what you think," she said instead.

"Then what is it?"

She owed him an explanation, but she could hardly tell him what she hadn't been able to tell Grant, so she didn't say anything.

Corey shook his head. "I don't know which one of us is more screwed up—you, for lusting after your boss, or me, for wanting you anyway."

The accusation that she was lusting after Grant was so outrageous—and more than a little disturbing, considering what she suspected about her relationship to the man—that she chose to ignore rather than respond to it.

"I told you there was too much going on in my life to get involved in a personal relationship right now," she reminded him.

"You didn't tell me that what was going on was an infatuation with a married man."

She bit her tongue as another customer approached. When the door to the men's room had closed behind him, she finally said, "I'm not infatuated with Grant."

"Then why are you stalking him?"

His voice had risen, and she looked around, all too aware of their public surroundings. So far, no one seemed to be paying any attention to them, but the last thing she wanted was to draw attention to herself—at least not anymore than she already had.

"I'm not stalking him," she kept her voice quiet but firm. "And I'm not going to continue this ridiculous argument with you here."

She turned and walked away, choosing not the most direct route to the exit but the one that would ensure she didn't have to walk past Grant and Stephanie's table.

Corey followed her, and when they were outside of the restaurant, he stepped in front of her, blocking her path.

"Okay," he said. "If you don't want to continue this argument here, where do you want to continue it?"

"I don't want to continue it at all," she said, and brushed past him.

Corey's fingers closed around her wrist. "We're going to continue it because I want some damn answers about what's going on with you."

She tried to yank her hand out of his grasp, but his hold only tightened. "I don't know if this is how you treat women in Texas, but I don't appreciate being manhandled."

"You didn't object to my hands being on you the other day," he reminded her. "Or were you pretending that it was Grant who was touching you?"

"No," she denied, shocked that he would even suggest such a thing.

"So what is it, Erin?"

She swallowed, suddenly aware of the dangerous glint in his eye, the banked heat in their depths. "If you want to continue this conversation, we can go to my place."

"Fine. We'll take my truck."

"I have my own—"

"We'll take mine," he insisted.

Erin knew she should be annoyed with him, both with his high-handed attitude and his demands for answers. But as he led the way to his truck, she felt her annoyance fading. Looking at the situation from his perspective—seeing what he'd seen, thinking of her continued evasions—she could understand why he'd have questions.

She had to hurry to keep pace with him because his fingers were still firmly clamped around her wrist, but he wasn't hurting her. She also knew he *wouldn't* hurt her. Not physically, anyway.

He was a man who was used to taking charge and accustomed to getting what he wanted. But the other night, when he'd had her so aroused she'd almost begged him to make love with her, it had only taken a single word to have him backing off.

He helped her into the truck, then went around to the driver's side. Neither of them said anything during the short drive to her condo, leaving Erin with no escape from her own thoughts. And those thoughts kept taking her back to the intimate encounter in her kitchen.

He must have known that he could have changed her mind. Another kiss, a single touch, and she would have been putty in his hands. But he'd respected her need to put a halt to things; he'd accepted that she wasn't ready.

She was ready now.

She was shocked to realize it was true, but she was unable to deny it. She wanted him. Maybe it was the realization that she would be in control, that this incredibly strong and sexy man would accede to her wishes, pleasure her as she wanted—

Corey killed the engine. As they approached her front door, Erin drew a deep breath and reached for the door handle. Her fingers fumbled with her keys, but she finally managed to locate the right one and insert it in the lock. She was all too aware of Corey standing right behind her, so close that she could feel the heat from his body, and her knees trembled.

She set her purse and keys on the table, then stripped off her coat and hung it carefully on a hanger in the closet. Corey shrugged out of his leather jacket and tossed it over the arm of the sofa. When she turned to face him, he was standing with his arms folded across his chest, watching her. He was still angry, she could see it in his eyes. But there was something else there, a glint that hinted at the same heat that was churning through her own veins.

Her heart was pounding, her throat was dry. She had to lick her lips to moisten them before she could talk, and she noticed that his gaze zeroed in on the movement, and his already dark eyes grew darker.

"You said you wanted answers," she reminded him.

"Answers are the least of what I want, darlin', but that's probably a good place to start."

"Are you going to come in? Or did you want to finish this standing in the hall?" She started toward the kitchen. "I could put on a pot of coffee."

"Don't."

She halted in mid-step. "You don't want coffee."

"I don't want to have this conversation in the kitchen."

And suddenly she knew why—because he was thinking of the last time they'd been in her kitchen together, when she'd been half-naked and whimpering in his arms.

"Okay." She swallowed and pivoted toward the living room. "No coffee."

She needed to tell him about Grant, she wanted him to understand the true nature of her interest in her boss, but first she felt compelled to respond to the accusations he'd made outside of the restaurant.

"Before I explain about Grant, you need to understand that you were way off base when you accused me of having any kind of romantic interest in him. I was shocked and offended by the suggestion that I could be thinking of him while I was with you, but then I realized you don't really know me any more than I know you, and it's important to me that you believe I could never be with one man if I wanted another."

He took a step toward her. "So you were thinking of me, when I was kissing you and touching you and—"

"Yes," she admitted. "I was thinking of you."

"And you were wanting me?" he prompted.

She swallowed. "Corey—"

He touched his fingers to her lips, halting her protest. He traced the shape of her mouth. His touch was gentle now, infinitely seductive. And that quickly the mood changed.

The anger that had snapped and crackled in the air between them was something different now. But somehow the desire she saw was even more dangerous than the anger because she knew that her own desire was just as powerful, and that neither would be denied this time.

His fingertips skimmed over her cheek, traced the outline of her ear, making her shiver. "Corey, please, I need to explain—"

"I don't want to argue about this anymore," he told her.

His fingertips slid down her throat, over the curve of her breast. Her breath caught, her legs went weak.

"Corey."

He dipped his head to brush his lips against hers. "Tell me what you want, Erin. If you tell me to go, I'll go. But if that's truly what you want, you better say it loud and fast because what I'm seeing in your eyes is something very different."

"I don't want you to go," she said.

"Then what do you want?"

"You," she said, and lifted her arms to link them around his neck, drawing his head down so that she could kiss him. Long and slow and deep. "I want you."

He pulled her tight against him, proving that he wanted her, too. "Should we go upstairs?"

She shook her head. "I want you here. Now."

"Sounds good to me," he agreed.

But he took a moment to set the scene. He found the remote and started the fire, then he removed the blanket from the back of the sofa and spread it on the floor by the hearth.

"Should I get a bottle of wine?"

"Later," he said, and reached for her again.

He kissed her, gently at first, as if wanting to ensure that this was really what she wanted. She could hardly blame him for his doubts. Only a few days earlier, she'd told him she wasn't ready—but that wasn't entirely true. Even then she'd wanted him, more than she'd ever wanted any other man, but the intensity of those feelings had scared her.

She was still scared. She wasn't the type of woman who gave herself easily to a man. In fact, she'd only ever had two lovers, and both had been men that she'd believed herself in love with, men that—at the time—she'd believed she was building a future with. She had no such illusions about Corey, but she could no longer deny the inevitable. The attraction between them had been escalating to this point since their first meeting.

He nibbled on her bottom lip, tugging with his teeth, teasing with his tongue. His kiss was hot and demanding now, and when his tongue stroked the ultra-sensitive skin on the roof of her mouth, sparks shot through her body and her knees nearly buckled.

She yanked his shirt out of his pants, her fingers fumbling just a little as they made quick work of the buttons that ran down the front. Then her hands were on his skin—hot and smooth—tracing the hard ridges of muscle. The man had the kind of body she'd only ever fantasized about.

She could have spent hours admiring those rippling muscles, exploring all that taut golden skin. But he was still half-dressed and she was suddenly desperate to see all of him. To touch and taste every inch of him.

He was so strong and hard—so undeniably male—and everything that was female inside of her responded to his nearness. When he walked into a room, she could barely tear her eyes away. Now she had him in *her* living room, and she wasn't even going to attempt to keep her hands off of him.

She wasn't usually impulsive or reckless, and she knew that getting naked with a man she hardly knew—a man who obviously had questions and doubts about her—was both impulsive and reckless, but she couldn't continue to deny what they both wanted. What they needed.

Though she hadn't even been aware of him unfastening her skirt, she felt it drop away, pooling at her feet. Her blouse was dispensed with as quickly, leaving her clad in only her bra and panties and stockings. His hands curved over her buttocks, his fingertips skimming down the backs of her thighs before they encountered the lace band at the top of her stockings.

He pulled back, holding her at arms' length to look at her. His eyes glittered in the light of the fire, but it was the heat in their fathomless depths that stoked the flames burning inside of her.

"Do you have any idea how much I want you?" he asked, his voice hoarse with desire.

"Hopefully as much as I want you," she told him and reached for the button at the front of his jeans. She struggled a little with the zipper that was straining over his erection, but when she managed to slide it down and slip her hand inside, she almost moaned with pleasure. Even through the cotton barrier of his briefs, she could tell that he was rock hard and huge, and the discovery made her knees weak.

She slid her hand down the length of him, felt him respond to her caress. A low growl reverberated in his throat and he scooped her off of her feet.

Her heart fluttered inside her breast, though she knew his action wasn't a romantic one so much as a purposeful one. He was the type of man who was used to taking what he wanted, and right now he wanted her.

He lowered her onto the blanket, then straddled her hips with his knees. The gaze that raked over her was hot and hungry and as intimate as a caress. Her whole body ached for him, but now that he had her mostly naked and horizontal, he didn't seem to be in any hurry.

When he did touch her, it was only to push the thin, pink straps of her bra off of her shoulders. Then he lowered his head and nibbled gently along the ridge of her collarbone.

She enjoyed foreplay. Although her experience with sex was admittedly limited, she'd usually found the "before" parts more pleasurable than the "during." But now, with Corey, she wanted nothing so much as she wanted him inside of her.

"Corey."

He lifted his head, and the glint of amusement in his eyes told her that he'd heard the plea in her voice, that he knew exactly what she wanted. And the slow, sexy curve of his lips warned that he was going to enjoy torturing her a little bit more.

"I thought about what you said, darlin'," he told her. "About rushing things. And I've decided that I don't want to rush anything now."

"At this point, I wouldn't object to rushing things a little."

He chuckled softly, then brushed his lips against hers. "Relax."

Relax? How the heck was she supposed to relax when every nerve ending in her body was aching with wanting?

But she let her head fall back and her eyes drift shut.

His fingertips skimmed the curve of her breasts, then dipped into the hollow between them. He unhooked the clasp, then stripped the bra away. Her nipples immediately pebbled, begging for his attention. He didn't disappoint. He bent his head to one breast, taking the rigid peak in his mouth and suckling deeply. The other he palmed, rolling the nipple between his thumb and finger. Sparks of white, hot pleasure shot through her, seeming to bombard her from every direction, arrowing toward her core.

His mouth moved from one breast to the other, laving and suckling and teasing her right to the edge of ecstasy… only to leave her dangling.

With a wicked smile, he abandoned her breasts and took his exploration lower. His mouth left a trail of hot, wet kisses as he made his way down her belly. He hooked his thumbs in the sides of her panties, slowly drew them down her legs, tossed them aside.

"These are nice," he said, his tone almost casual as he stroked his fingertips lightly up the length of her stockings, from her ankles to the inside of her knees to the bands at the top. He traced the lacy edging, slowly, his gentle touch making her shiver.

"Very nice," he amended. "But I think your bare skin will feel even nicer."

She couldn't speak. He had her so completely and desperately aroused she was speechless…and very close to whimpering.

He took his time removing the stockings. He bent one leg at the knee, then traced the lace border again, all the way around this time. Then he slowly rolled down the band, just to her knee, then his fingertips drifted upward again, a feather-light touch against her bare skin. She bit down on her lip to keep from moaning aloud. He lowered his head and kissed the inside of her thigh, then kissed his way down to the sensitive spot at the back of her knee. He rolled the stocking down to her ankle, following the path of the silk with more hot kisses. Then he repeated the same routine with the other stocking, treating her other leg to the same close, personal attention until she was quivering and aching and ready to beg.

His hands stroked over her, from her shoulders to her breasts to her hips, and she trembled everywhere that he touched.

"Corey—please."

He drew away from her only long enough to strip away the last of his clothes and put on protection, and when he lowered himself over her again, she sighed and thought, *Now—finally now.*

Corey had pictured her like this, wanted her like this. Her eyes were glazed, her skin was hot, and she was breathless and trembling, as desperate for him as he was for her.

He could take her now—he could plunge into the slick, wet heat between her thighs and give them both the release they craved. He wanted to take her now, to finally ease the ache that had been building inside of him for weeks, an ache that only she could lessen. But he was determined to give her more. To give her more pleasure than anyone else had ever given her, to be more than anyone had ever been to her.

He knelt between her legs, and she sighed. His hands stroked the soft skin of her inner thighs, and her knees fell open a little farther, silently encouraging his exploration. His thumb stroked over her nub, and she shuddered. He slipped one finger, then two, inside of her, the slick wetness confirming that she was ready for him—more than ready. His erection throbbed painfully, urging him to take what she was offering.

Instead, he curled his hands around her bottom, lifting her hips off the blanket, and lowered his head to take her with his mouth.

She gasped and arched, as if to pull away, but he held her fast and feasted. She tasted as he'd imagined—sweet and seductive—and he savored her feminine flavor. Her shallow, breathless pants assured him that she'd stopped fighting and had surrendered to the pleasure. With his lips and his tongue, he teased her back to the edge where he'd left her teetering so precariously before, but this time, he pushed her not just to the limit but beyond.

He'd known she was a passionate woman. The kisses they'd shared had proved that. What he hadn't known was how incredibly arousing it would be to watch her finally succumb to the passion that burned so hot and bright between them.

He saw her eyes glaze, heard her breath quicken then catch and finally release on a sob. She bucked…shuddered… shattered. Then sank bonelessly back onto the blanket, her eyes closed, her cheeks flushed.

He made his way slowly back up her body, stroking and kissing her until she was trembling again. He kissed her belly, her breasts, her throat. She pulled him up, seeking his mouth with her own, kissing him with the same frenetic passion that was raging inside of him, using her lips and tongue and teeth to drive him as wild as he was driving her.

His body pressed down on hers, his erection nudging at her slick, wet center. She arched her hips, rocking against him. The rhythmic friction was nearly enough to send him over the edge. He scrambled to hold on to the last fraying threads of his self-control with a slippery fist.

"Tell me you want me," he demanded.

"I want you."

"Say my name." He needed to hear his name on her lips, to know that she had no illusions about who she was with.

Her hands slid up his arms, over his shoulders, her fingernails biting into his muscles. "I want you, Corey." She tugged on his bottom lip with her teeth, and he felt the ache spread through him. "Only you."

He'd fantasized about this moment, about the texture of her skin beneath his hands, the taste of her damp, quivering flesh, the sounds she would make as he pleasured her. Even his most explicit fantasies paled in comparison to the reality.

Unable to hold back even a single moment longer, he yanked her hips high and thrust into her. She gasped and arched, pulling him deeper, her muscles clamping around him as she climaxed again. Perspiration beaded his brow as he battled against the pulsing waves that washed over her and threatened to drag him along in their wake. He clenched his teeth as he fought the tide, his fists clutching handfuls of blanket as he rode out her release.

She was gasping and shuddering as he plunged into her, again and again, deeper, harder, faster, and she matched him stroke for stroke. Her nails scored his back, but he didn't feel the pain. He wasn't aware of anything but the desperate urge to take, to claim, to possess.

He fought the haze that blurred his vision, needing to see her, to watch her surrender to the sweet pleasure of their mating. And he swallowed the cries of pleasure that spilled from her lips as another climax pulsed through her and finally dragged him over the edge and into oblivion with her.

Chapter Nine

Erin had always believed that sex was a generally enjoyable if highly overrated experience. Of course, that had been her opinion *before* she had sex with Corey Traub.

After she was seeing things differently.

Or maybe she was still seeing stars.

Later she might worry that there were still secrets between them, but she wouldn't—couldn't—regret making love with him.

Corey had slipped away to deal with the protection, but he'd returned almost immediately and snuggled up with her again.

The flickering flames of the fire cast golden shadows on his face, emphasizing the strong planes and sharp angles. Just looking at him nearly made her sigh again. All those hard, taut muscles, all that smooth, bronzed skin. How was it possible to look at him and not want him?

He was probably too rugged to be considered beautiful,

but in that moment, she thought he was truly the most beautiful man she'd ever known. Certainly he was the most considerate and thorough lover. And though her body had been completely and unquestionably sated, when he stroked a hand down her arm, she felt her blood start to heat again.

"What are you thinking?" he asked.

Her lips curved. "That I was wrong."

He propped himself up on an elbow. "About?"

"Sex."

"How were you wrong?"

His hand had slid from her hip to her breast, his thumb tracing lazy circles around her nipple. An already tight and aching nipple.

"I always thought that the anticipation was so much more exciting than the main event," she admitted.

"And now?" he prompted, nuzzling her throat.

"Now—" she sighed contentedly "—I don't."

His mouth came down on hers, as gentle as a whisper. Not possessing but coaxing, not demanding but giving. And the more he gave, the more she wanted.

She lifted her arms, drew him down to her.

He pressed her back down onto the blanket, then abruptly drew away.

"You know what? I'm starving."

She blinked, stunned by his sudden withdrawal. "I could maybe throw something together," she offered. "But I was supposed to stop and get groceries on my way home, so the fridge is pretty bare."

"Why don't we order something and I'll go pick it up?" He was already reaching for his pants, starting to dress.

"That sounds better than cooking, but why don't we order something and have it delivered?"

"I don't mind going out."

She tugged the blanket up to cover her nakedness. He'd

been so wonderful and attentive earlier that she hadn't felt the least bit self-conscious. But now it seemed that he couldn't get away from her fast enough, and that made her wonder what she'd done wrong.

"So what do you want—Chinese? Pizza? Pasta?"

"I want to know why you're so anxious to get out of here."

He paused with one arm in his shirt. "What?"

She tucked her knees up beneath her chin and stared at the fire. "If you're done with me, just say it. Don't make up excuses to race out the door."

He was immediately beside her, squatting down so that they were at eye level. He touched his hand gently to her cheek. "I'm sorry, darlin'. It never occurred to me that you would think I was running out on you."

"Isn't that exactly what you're doing?"

"No," he denied and brushed his lips against hers. "I only wanted to make a trip to the pharmacy without admitting where I was going."

She drew back. "The pharmacy?"

His smile was wry. "Well, I didn't actually plan for this to happen tonight and we've already used my emergency condom."

"Oh." She felt her cheeks flush. "Well, I didn't plan for this to happen tonight, either, but I thought I should be prepared for...eventually."

"You have protection?"

"A whole box. Upstairs."

He tugged the dangling shirt off his arm, tossed it aside, then scooped her into his arms, blanket and all. "Then I guess we should be upstairs."

"I thought you wanted food."

He was already halfway to her bedroom. "We'll have something delivered."

* * *

Later, they ordered Chinese and opened a bottle of wine. They ate fried rice, Cantonese chow mein and lemon chicken and washed it all down with a light, crisp Chardonnay. Then they made love again.

Corey didn't know what it was about Erin that had gotten so completely under his skin, but no matter how many times he had her, he couldn't seem to get enough. But his feelings for her went much deeper than physical attraction, and there was still so much that he didn't know about her.

He needed to know what was going on, why she seemed so preoccupied with the man who was his friend and her boss. He no longer believed that she was infatuated with Grant. He knew she wouldn't have made love with him as willingly and passionately as she had if she had feelings for another man, but there was definitely something that she wasn't telling him.

He wanted answers, but as connected as he felt to her right now, he wasn't ready to let anything come between them.

They were in her bed, snuggled together beneath the covers. The only light in the room was from the flames of the fire, but he didn't need to see. He'd memorized every detail of her face, every curve of her body.

He lifted a hand to brush a strand of hair off of her cheek. Her lips curved, though her eyes remained closed. "Tired?"

"Exhausted," she admitted.

"Do you have to work tomorrow?"

She shook her head. "No. Although I will have to go pick up my car."

"I'll take you in the morning."

Her eyes flickered open. "You're going to stay?"

"If that's okay."

"That's definitely okay."

"Are you going to make me breakfast?"

"If you consider coffee and toast 'breakfast.'"

"You have to get groceries," he remembered.

She nodded, her eyes drifting shut again.

"Erin—"

He wanted to apologize for the way he'd confronted her at the resort, for what his brothers would undoubtedly refer to as typical high-handed behavior. But he was afraid that mentioning what had happened earlier would lead into a discussion about Grant and after everything they'd shared tonight, he wasn't sure he was ready to have that conversation.

"Mmm," she said.

He brushed his lips to hers. "Sweet dreams."

After the intense physical workout of the night before, Erin suspected that Corey would have preferred a hearty breakfast of eggs and bacon and fried potatoes, but he didn't complain when he got only the toast and coffee she'd promised. In fact, he even helped prepare the simple morning meal.

While Erin set coffee brewing and put the bread in the toaster, Corey embarked on a search through her cupboards for peanut butter and jam. While she buttered the toast, he filled two mugs with coffee and carried them to the table. When they finally sat down together, she noticed that he went for the peanut butter but she preferred jam, that he drank his coffee black while she added lots of milk and sugar to hers.

It was funny, she thought, the things you could learn about a man when you woke up with him in the morning. She'd rarely had that experience before. Though she was almost twenty-six years old, she'd still lived with her parents, and Betty and Jack Castro were not the type to casually accept their daughter spending the night at a man's house.

She'd had a boyfriend from out of town visit her in San Diego for a weekend once. They'd started dating while he'd attended USD and had stayed together after he'd graduated, but it had been difficult to sustain a relationship over the long distance and when he had visited, her parents had put him in her brother Jake's room and made sure they kept their own door—located directly across the hall from their twenty-two-year-old daughter's—open throughout the night.

Of course, Corey had probably slept with a lot of women, and, although she didn't intend to dwell on that thought, the realization did make her feel more than a little awkward. Especially in the morning, when she woke up with her hair in tangles and her face bare of makeup. She didn't know if he sensed her self-consciousness, but he eliminated all traces of it by making love with her again.

It was certainly an effective way to get her blood flowing in the morning, but even as she'd snuggled again in the warm comfort of his arms, she'd been all too aware that things could change in a minute—the minute she told Corey the truth about her reasons for coming to Thunder Canyon.

He hadn't pressed her for an explanation, but she knew he hadn't forgotten their aborted conversation of the day before. More likely, he was giving her an opportunity to explain, as she wanted to do. But she was hesitant to say anything that might jeopardize the comfortable rapport they'd established.

So she was silent about it while they tidied up the kitchen, after which Corey took her to the supermarket to do her grocery shopping. Erin assured him that she could shop on her own—if he would just take her to get her vehicle—but he insisted that he wanted to spend the time with her, and because Erin wanted to be with him, too, she didn't protest too much.

After they'd finished shopping, he took her home again and helped her put away the groceries. It was a routine chore, and one that she'd performed dozens of times by herself. But somehow, with Corey, it was cozy and domestic and it was all too easy to imagine that it could become *their* Saturday morning routine.

Dangerous territory.

She knew that physical intimacy didn't necessarily imply a committed relationship, and she wasn't looking for any long-term promises. She hadn't been looking to get involved at all. But being with Corey had decimated all of her reservations. Being with Corey allowed her to forget that the unanswered questions about her past made it difficult for her to plan a future. Being with Corey made her forget everything except how very much she wanted to be with him.

She tried to play it cool. She didn't want him to know that she'd already given him a very big piece of her heart. Despite the reference he'd made to his feelings for her, she knew that those feelings might change when he learned the truth about her reasons for being in Thunder Canyon. As she'd gotten to know him better, one of the things she'd learned about him was that he was loyal to his family and friends, and she suspected that his uneasiness in believing she had a crush on her boss originated more from his friendship with Grant and Stephanie than any personal jealousy.

It was the issue they'd been ignoring, pretending it didn't exist. But they couldn't continue pretending.

"Looks like it would be a nice day to go riding," Corey said.

Erin looked out the window, at the big, fat flakes of snow that had started to fall. "It's snowing."

"The horses love the snow—it makes them frisky."

"I *don't* love the snow," she told him.

"California girl," he teased.

"Yep."

He chuckled. "Okay, so what do you want to do?"

"Stay indoors where it's warm."

"By the fire?" he prompted huskily.

Her blood heated with the memory of what they'd done by the fire the night before…and in her bedroom…and in the shower.

Yeah, she could think of a lot of ways to pass the time inside with Corey. But first, they had to talk.

"I need to tell you about Grant," she said.

The teasing light faded from his eyes; the muscle in his jaw flexed.

"I'm listening," he said, but the coolness in his tone warned her that he'd started to withdraw already.

"I think—" she drew in a deep breath, blew it out "—I think that Grant Clifton might be my brother."

She knew he'd be surprised, probably even skeptical, but she hadn't expected that he would laugh in response to her statement.

But after a minute of stunned silence, he did just that. "You've got to be kidding. That's why you're so interested in your boss—because you think you're related?"

"I know it sounds unbelievable—"

"Sounds? Darlin', my family has known Grant's family forever, and I can assure you that he only has one sister. What on earth would ever have given you such an outrageous idea?"

She couldn't help but feel irritated by his immediate dismissal of her suggestion. "For starters, Elise Clifton and I share the same birthday."

"Lots of people share their birthdays with other people," he pointed out.

"I was born in Thunder Canyon."

"Again, nothing more than a coincidence," he insisted.

"And Elise looks a lot like each of my brothers," she continued, determined to make her case.

His brows rose. "What are you saying—that you and Elise were switched at birth?"

"It could have happened."

"Maybe—if this was a Sunday afternoon movie."

"Life is often stranger than fiction," she pointed out.

"And what possible motive would someone have for mixing up babies?"

"I'm not suggesting that it was a deliberate switch but an accident."

"Yeah, because that's much more likely," he said drily.

She reminded herself that his skepticism was expected, but it was his obvious disbelief that hurt. She tried to understand—she knew her explanation had surprised him—but she couldn't comprehend how a man who claimed to care about her could so completely disregard something that was so important to her.

"The last time I visited my great aunt Erma, she told me that my real family was in Thunder Canyon."

"And you told me that she was dying when you saw her." His tone was gentle now, sympathetic. "She was probably pumped up on medication and didn't have any idea what she was saying. You can't take someone's delusional ramblings and run with them."

"She was dying but she wasn't delusional," Erin insisted.

"She just wanted to be sure that I knew the truth about my family."

"Did she actually tell you that you and Elise Clifton were switched at birth?"

"No," she admitted, some of her conviction fading, "but—"

"And what does your family think of these claims?" he challenged.

She dropped her gaze, sighed. "I haven't told them."

"Why not?"

"Because I didn't want to upset them until I had proof," she admitted. And maybe because she knew they would be just as skeptical as Corey.

"But you're willing to upset Grant and his sister and their mother?"

"I don't want to upset anyone. I only wanted to talk to Grant, to find out more about his family."

"Is that why you've been asking questions around town? Do you think there was some kind of conspiracy? That the whole town was somehow involved in covering up a baby switch?"

"Of course not," she denied, wondering how he'd managed to twist her words around so completely, and wondering why his obvious lack of faith in her hurt so much.

"Well, if you think you can make that kind of claim and not upset a whole lot of people, you're sorely mistaken, darlin'."

"I just want to know the truth," Erin insisted. "All my life, I've never really belonged—it's like I'm an outsider in my own family."

"Lots of people feel disconnected, but they don't go looking for a new family to replace the one they've got."

"I'm not looking to replace my family. I love my parents and my brothers—"

"If you truly love your parents and your brothers, you'll let this go," he said.

"I can't. I need to find the truth."

"What if the truth is that you are their biological child?"

"What if I'm not?" she countered. "What if Elise Clifton is?"

"What will that change? Even if you're right, what do you hope to accomplish? Do you think anyone will thank you for digging this up?"

Probably not, she admitted to herself. And while the absolute last thing she wanted was to hurt anyone, she knew that continuing to live a lie would hurt, too. Why couldn't he see that she needed to know the truth—that she couldn't begin to move forward until she'd answered the questions about her past?

"Obviously we have a difference of opinion on this."

"I won't help you cause heartache for people I care about. You need to decide what really matters to you—our relationship or this wild goose chase you've set yourself on."

There was something in his tone that was so determined, so final. Was it possible that this was the same man she'd spent the night with? The man she'd not only made love with but realized she was falling in love with? "What are you saying?"

"I'm asking you to forget about this…to just let it go."

She didn't understand why he was so adamant, but maybe he was right. Maybe it was unfair of her to turn other people's lives upside down for something that was, at this point, only speculation.

Still, she couldn't help but feel disappointed. She'd finally found the courage to confide in Corey about her reasons for coming to Thunder Canyon, foolishly hoping that he would support her quest for the truth. Instead, he was asking her to abandon it.

"Okay," she finally said. "I won't say anything to Grant—"

Corey pressed a brief kiss to her lips before she could finish. "Thank you. The Cliftons have had enough crises to deal without having their lives turned upside by something like this."

She felt uneasy. He'd obviously assumed she was willing to forget about her potential connection to Grant when all she'd intended to say was that she wouldn't mention anything to her boss *until* she had concrete proof of their relationship. Because there was no way she could abandon the quest she'd already started.

They spent the rest of the weekend together, and while Corey had apparently managed to put their conversation aside, it continued to weigh on Erin's mind.

For a minute, when they'd faced off in her kitchen and he'd told her she had to choose, he'd reminded her of Brandon. He'd been her first serious boyfriend, her first lover, and she'd been so infatuated with him she hadn't realized that he was slowly trying to take control of her life. She wasn't allowed to have thoughts and opinions unless they supported his thoughts and opinions. He made suggestions on what she should wear, how she should cut her hair, and he didn't hesitate to express his displeasure when she exhibited her own style choices. He told her he wanted to marry her, but she realized he didn't want a partner but an accessory.

Since then, she'd been careful to steer clear of men with domineering tendencies—until Corey. He was a cowboy through and through, confident and self-assured, the type of man who could walk into any situation and take charge with little effort. He was also attentive, considerate and charm-ing. He listened to her when she talked and he seemed to respect her ideas and opinions. So why had he reacted so strongly—and so negatively—to the possibility that she might be related to Grant?

More importantly—why hadn't she stood up to him? Why hadn't she told him that he had no right to make de-mands or issue ultimatums? Why hadn't she told him to go to hell?

Because she wanted to believe that he had a valid rea-son for responding the way he had. Because she wanted to believe that, when she had proof of her claim, he would support her.

Although it carried the same name, Erin knew that the Thunder Canyon General Hospital on White Water Drive wasn't actually the same hospital where she'd been born. The two-story building was less than a dozen years old, having been built during the economic boom to better serve the town's growing population.

But Erin also knew that the records from the old hospital would have been transferred over along with most of the staff. As she stepped beneath the covered portico toward the entrance, she mentally crossed her fingers that if Delores Beckett wasn't still working there, she might at least find someone who could help her track the woman down.

She checked in at the information desk and got direc-tions to the maternity ward on the second floor. As she made her way through the halls, she was surprised by the bright and modern décor. If not for the antiseptic smell and tiled floors, she might have believed she was in an office building rather than a hospital.

The corridor in the maternity wing had a lovely floral border in shades of pink and green and lilac. She stopped at the nurse's station, where a dark-haired nurse wearing blue scrubs decorated with teddy bears was inputting data into a computer.

She looked up and smiled. "Can I help you?"

Erin wiped her suddenly damp palms down the front of her skirt. Now that she was here, she was a bundle of nerves. And she had a sudden urge to turn around and walk away, to "let it go" as Corey had urged her to do.

But she couldn't because she knew that the questions that swirled through her mind would continue to haunt her until she had the answers. Besides, the woman dressed in teddy bears—Beth Ann, according to her name tag—was watching her, waiting.

"I'm, uh, looking for Delores."

Beth Ann glanced at a chart on the wall, but she was already shaking her head. "We only have three new moms here now and no one named Delores. Maybe she went to Billings to have her baby," she suggested helpfully.

"She's not a patient," Erin explained. "She works here."

"Delores?" Beth Ann frowned. "And she works in maternity?"

"Who are you looking for?"

The question came from behind her, and Erin jolted at the sharpness of the tone. Turning, she found herself face-to-face with a tall, steely-eyed doctor.

"Delores—" Her hand went to the scrap of paper in her jacket pocket, the one on which she'd scrawled the nurse's name. Delores Beckett. She didn't need to pull out the paper to verify the name, and she was reluctant to do so. There was something about this doctor's confrontational posture and suspicious glare that made her wary, though she didn't understand why.

Do you think there was some kind of conspiracy? That

the whole town was somehow involved in covering up a baby switch?

Corey's words echoed in the back of her mind, but instead of challenging, this time they sounded like a warning. And while she didn't believe the whole town was involved, it occurred to her that someone other than the nurse might have been aware of the situation. Possibly even the doctor who had delivered the babies.

Erin swallowed. "I knew her before she was married, and I've blanked on her new last name," she fibbed.

"Well, it doesn't matter because we don't have anyone named Delores who works here." The doctor went behind the counter to retrieve a stack of patient charts, effectively dismissing her.

Erin was surprised they had anyone on staff who would be willing to work with such an obnoxiously rude doctor, and even more surprised that anyone would want to give birth in this hospital if it was under his watch.

"Beth Ann—"

The nurse sent Erin an apologetic glance before she turned her attention to the doctor.

"—I need the Warner file."

She closed the cover on the folder beside her computer and held it toward him. He snatched it from her hand and strode away without a backward glance.

"That was Doctor Gifford," Beth Ann said to Erin.

"Friendly guy," she muttered.

The nurse smiled. "This woman you're looking for—" she hesitated "—is it possible that you mean Doris Becker?"

Erin was sure both Erma and her mother had said "Delores," but "Delores" and "Doris" weren't so very different. Maybe Erma had known her as Delores and had introduced her by that name to Betty, but the nurse shortened her name at work. And maybe Erin was grasping at straws again.

But there was something in the tone of Beth Ann's question—it was almost as if the nurse was suggesting that Erin should talk to Doris, as if there was something she wanted her to know but was afraid to say with the disapproving doctor within earshot.

She shook her head, worried that she was starting to see conspiracies where none existed. However, she had nothing to lose by talking to Doris and she certainly didn't have any other leads to follow.

"I've always called her Delores," she finally said. "I forgot that she sometimes goes by Doris."

Beth Ann checked the schedule that was posted on the wall beside her computer. "She's actually off today, but she's working the afternoon shift the rest of the week. That means she starts at three and usually has her first break around four-thirty."

Erin mentally reviewed her own schedule. She usually worked until five, but if she worked through her lunch the next day, she could probably get away a little early and be at the hospital by four-fifteen. "That's great," she said to the nurse. "Thanks."

She left the hospital disappointed but not entirely dejected. Her visit hadn't been as successful as she would have liked, but something about Beth Ann's demeanor had given her new hope.

Was she on the right track now? Or would Doris end up being another dead end?

Hopefully, within twenty-eight hours, she would have the answers to those questions.

Chapter Ten

Corey was invited to Grant and Stephanie's for dinner Monday night. Grant, apparently having heard through the infallible Thunder Canyon grapevine that his friend was seeing a lot of Erin Castro, extended the invitation to include her as well. Corey knew that Erin would be thrilled to join them, and he hesitated only a second before declining on her behalf.

He couldn't forget what she'd said—her ridiculous belief that Grant was her brother. And he felt it was best not to give her any opportunities to poke into his friend's life more than she already had. Not that he believed she'd slip away from the dinner table to rifle through Grant's home looking for nonexistent proof to support her claim. Especially since she'd decided not to follow up on her suspicions.

He felt a twinge of guilt when he remembered that she *had* agreed to back off and a sharper twinge when he recalled that he'd practically demanded it of her.

He'd reacted strongly, impulsively. But he'd known Grant for a long time; he remembered how his friend's world had fallen apart when John Clifton had been killed. Grant's mother, Helen, had lost any interest in ranching when she lost her husband, and she'd eventually taken her daughter with her to Billings, for a new start away from the horrific memories. Grant had stayed. Eventually he and Stephanie—whose father had been killed along with Grant's—had fallen in love. They'd overcome tragedy and heartache and would soon be expanding their family. They deserved to be happy, to feel secure in the life they were building together.

What Erin had suggested was impossible, he truly believed that. But he also believed that telling Grant there was a chance—however minute—that she might be his sister and that Elise might not be another blow to a man who had already dealt with so much. He didn't even want to imagine the effect that such a claim would have on Elise.

Or maybe he was projecting. Maybe the scars from his own life weren't as long buried as he wanted to believe. He knew what it was like to have his whole world change in a heartbeat. It had happened for him and his brothers and sister when their father was killed by an oil rig explosion. He might have only been eight years old at the time, but he remembered, all too clearly, the sense of complete helplessness. And he remembered thinking that he would have done absolutely anything to put things back the way they were—to leave his life unchanged.

He'd experienced that same powerlessness when his four-and-a-half year old nephew, Dillon's son from his first marriage, died. He would have done anything, would have given anything, to save Toby, but of course, nothing could.

Since then, he'd worked hard to control every aspect of his life. He liked to call the shots. He liked to know not just what was happening but to feel as if he had some command over the outcome of a situation. And when Erin had suggested that she might be Grant's sister, all he could think was that she was going to send his friend's world spiraling out of control, and he wasn't willing to sit back and let that happen.

But he wondered now if he'd been unfair to Erin. He knew that she hadn't come to Thunder Canyon to stir up trouble, that her intentions weren't cruel. More, he could tell that she believed what she'd told him. As outrageous as her claims seemed to him, she honestly thought it was possible that someone at the hospital had mixed up babies. And he'd dismissed her suggestion practically out of hand.

He pushed those recriminations aside. He'd done what he thought was best. And in any event, why would Erin want to be preoccupied with the past when they had so much to look forward to in the future—together?

Erin was more than a little distracted at work the next morning. She lost track of what she was supposed to be doing, and when Corey showed up just before noon, she couldn't think of why he might be there.

"Did we have plans for lunch?" She was sure they didn't—she wouldn't have forgotten something like that. But she'd forgotten a lot of things today that she didn't think she would.

"Not yet," Corey said, giving her one of those smiles that never failed to jumpstart her heart. "But I was hoping we could make some."

"I'm sorry," she said, and she was. Even if he didn't have time to go for lunch or coffee, it always perked up her day when he stopped by. And she felt guilty that she was not only brushing him off, but that she couldn't tell him the reason.

"I switched breaks with Carrie and I'm working through lunch so that I can leave early to meet…a friend."

She cringed inwardly at the lie. It was one thing to stretch the truth when she was trying to get information from Beth Ann, and something else entirely when she was talking to the man she was very personally involved with.

But she couldn't tell him the truth because she knew he would try to talk her out of meeting with Doris. And she'd come too far to back out now. She needed to find out what—if anything—Doris could tell her.

She touched his hand. "I won't be late, though. So if you wanted to come by later for dinner…"

He smiled and leaned forward to brush his lips against hers. "I definitely want to come by later for…dinner."

She felt her cheeks flush in response to the deliberate innuendo. It amazed her, after all the time they'd been together and all the things they'd done together, that he could still make her blush.

"What time?" he asked.

"Seven?"

He kissed her again. "I'll be there."

"I know we're encouraged to provide personal service," Trina said, walking past, "but I'd say that goes above and beyond."

Erin managed a smile, but she didn't miss the edge in her coworker's voice. Obviously Trina was still annoyed because Corey had rejected her advances at Erika and Dillon's wedding.

After he'd gone, she forced herself to focus on her work so that Trina wouldn't have anything else to complain about. The afternoon seemed to stretch out interminably, but at last it was three thirty and she started counting down the last half hour of her shift.

Unfortunately, she got caught up on a long-distance call

that seemed as if it would never end. An executive assistant for a wealthy German businessman was trying to make arrangements for a corporate retreat for twenty-two employees. Erin wanted to transfer the call to group bookings, but there was something of a language barrier in their communications and, in the end, she decided it was probably just easier to make the arrangements herself.

By the time she finalized the details and managed to get away from the desk, it was after four o'clock. Thankfully, she didn't run into any more snags between the resort and the hospital.

As a result of his conversation with Grant the night before, Corey had come up with a business proposition that he wanted to discuss with his brother. But when he caught up with Dillon, who was still helping out at the resort, he found that the doctor had a waiting room full of patients—compliments of a nasty seasonal flu that was making the rounds—and a stack of files and insurance forms on his desk—courtesy of his admitted abhorrence for paperwork.

But the nurse snuck him into Dillon's office, promising that the doctor would check in with him as soon as he had a minute. Half an hour later, his brother finally breezed through the door with a cardboard box under one arm and another handful of patient folders under the other.

"Busy place today," Corey said to his brother.

"Please tell me you don't have a fever, nausea or diarrhea."

"I don't have a fever, nausea or diarrhea," Corey repeated obediently. "What I do have is a proposition."

Dillon dropped the box and the files on his desk and glanced at his watch. "Can you outline it in thirty seconds or less?"

"I think we should invest in the resort."

"And twenty-seven seconds to spare," his brother noted.

"I don't expect you to answer right now. I just thought I'd put the idea out there, give you something to think about."

"I will," Dillon promised.

"Then I'll let you get back to your patients."

"Hey—where are you going now?" Dillon asked.

Corey paused at the door. "Why?"

"Any chance you're headed by the hospital? Because I have some samples from the pharmaceutical rep who was in today that I promised to drop off for Dr. Tabry."

"That *you* promised to drop off," Corey echoed.

Dillon picked up the box again, held it out to his brother. "But if you're headed in that direction…"

He was, but only because it had occurred to him that he and Erin had missed a few of the usual steps in the development of their relationship, and he'd decided to remedy that with old-fashioned courting. Because she was making him dinner tonight, he thought it would be appropriate to take her some flowers. Coincidentally, the flower shop was across the street from the General Hospital.

"Do I look like an errand boy?" Corey asked, not willing to accede too easily to his brother's request.

Dillon gave him a once-over. "Now that you mention it."

Corey snatched the box out of his hand. "Fine. But you owe me."

"Add it to my tab."

"I will."

"How about dinner on Saturday?"

"Are you asking me for a date?"

"Smart ass," Dillon muttered.

Corey just grinned.

"I'm inviting you—and Erin—to come over for dinner Saturday night."

"I thought you didn't like Erin."

"I didn't say I didn't like her," Dillon told him. "I said I didn't know her. Maybe if we all spend some time together, that will change."

"I'll check with her and let you know."

This time, it was a younger, blonde woman who was at the nurse's station.

"I was in yesterday trying to track down an old friend," Erin explained, "and the nurse on duty suggested that I come back this afternoon."

"Oh, yes, Beth Ann told me that someone had stopped by looking for Doris Becker."

She nodded.

"That would be me," the nurse told her.

In that moment, Erin realized two things—Doris Becker knew her cover story was a lie, and there was no way she'd been in attendance when Erin was born. In fact, it was likely Erin had been born before Doris.

"I'm sorry—obviously I made a mistake."

"Not necessarily," Doris said and smiled when Erin frowned. "It's quiet in here today. Why don't we go grab a cup of coffee?"

"I don't want to take up any more of your time."

"I've got time," Doris insisted.

So Erin found herself following the nurse down to the cafeteria. Like the rest of the hospital, it was modern and efficient, if somewhat stark. The floor was white, the tables and chairs were blue, but there were lots of tall windows looking into the lobby on one side and outdoors on the other.

Doris led the way to a self-serve beverage station where she poured herself a large cup of dark roast. Erin opted for the same, generously doctoring her cup with milk and sugar. She insisted on paying for their beverages, in appreciation for Doris's time, and they took their cups to a table over-looking the courtyard.

"It's a much better view in the summer," Doris told her. "When everything is lush and green instead of dull and brown."

"It's a nice hospital," Erin said.

"I've only worked here a few months, but I like it. I'm guessing this…friend you were looking for worked here some time ago."

"She was actually a friend of my aunt's. I never even met her—" she paused there but decided that the nurse having been present at her birth didn't require her to alter that statement "—but I thought, since I was in town, I would look her up."

"She was a labor and delivery nurse?"

"Apparently she delivered me."

Doris sipped her coffee. "I think you might be looking for Delores Beckett."

Erin bobbled her cup, sloshing hot coffee over the rim. She grabbed a napkin from the dispenser on the table to mop up the spill.

"I thought I was looking for Delores Beckett, too," she agreed. "But when I mentioned the name Delores, no one seemed to know who I was talking about."

"That's odd." Doris frowned. "Or maybe not so odd."

"What do you mean?"

"There were whispers of a scandal a while back. No one seemed to know exactly what it was about, but the implica-tion was that it could be huge. Then, just as suddenly as the rumors started, they stopped. And Delores Beckett was gone."

"Gone?" Erin asked, startled.

"Early retirement," Doris clarified. "As I understand, everyone thought she would work another ten or more years before she retired, but I guess she had some health issues that prompted her to give up the job early.

"I wasn't even working here then," the nurse continued. "So everything I'm telling you is complete hearsay, but I do remember hearing some rumblings that the administration was worried Delores had said or done something that might result in a lawsuit against the hospital."

Something like mixing up a couple of babies? Erin wondered but only asked, "Do you have any idea how I might get in touch with Delores?"

Doris shook her head. "I don't. I'm sorry. I'm sure personnel would have current contact information, but I don't know that they'd give it out."

"That's okay," Erin said. "I appreciate everything you've told me."

"I gave you a bad impression of a family friend, and I didn't mean to. For what it's worth, everyone who knew Delores only had good things to say about her."

Erin finished her coffee. "Even Dr. Gifford?"

"Dr. Gifford doesn't have good things to say about anyone," Doris told her. Then she asked curiously, "How do you know Dr. Gifford?"

"I don't, but I crossed paths with him when I was here yesterday."

"Well, apparently he worked with Delores a lot. In fact, there was speculation that if the scandal came to light, it might tarnish his stellar reputation, and that's why he turned on her." She shrugged. "Like I said, I've only been here a few months, so I have no idea what he was like before, but I'll admit that I wouldn't be at all disappointed if he followed in Delores's footsteps and took early retirement, too."

Corey considered the usual flower choices as he made his way toward the reception desk in the main lobby of the Thunder Canyon General Hospital.

Carnations? Too casual.

Roses? Too formal.

A mixed bouquet? He shook his head. Too lazy. That was the type of thing that a forgetful husband picked up for his wife at the grocery store when he stopped to grab a quart of milk on his way home and suddenly remembered that it was her birthday/their anniversary/some other occasion.

Orchids? A more thoughtful choice, he decided, but also a little pretentious.

Corey continued to mull over the possibilities after he'd left the pharmaceutical samples for Dr. Tabry.

Tulips? Probably difficult to get in November.

Lilies? A definite possibility, he thought, then did a double take when he saw someone who looked just like Erin walk out of the cafeteria.

No—it wasn't someone who looked just like her, it was Erin.

But what was she doing at the hospital?

Whatever she was doing there, she obviously didn't expect him to be there because she walked right past without even seeing him.

"Erin."

She spun around. "What are you doing here?"

He gestured back toward the reception area. "I promised to drop off a package for Dillon. What are you doing here?"

"Oh. Um."

She wasn't usually at a loss for words and the fact that she was now concerned him.

"You said you were meeting a friend," he reminded her and realized now that she hadn't been telling him the truth. But why would she have lied? And then he had another, even more disturbing thought. "Did you have an appointment? Are you sick?"

"No," she said quickly. "I'm fine."

His heartbeat slowed to something closer to normal. "Then why are you here?"

"I came to see someone in maternity."

Now that the initial wave of panic had subsided, his brain started to clear. She wasn't at the hospital because she was sick, she was visiting someone.

"Your friend had a baby?"

Erin shook her head. She was muddling everything up. No matter how many half-truths she told, they were never going to add up to the whole until she stopped keeping secrets from everyone. Starting with Corey.

"No. I came to see…" She trailed off as she spotted Doris exiting the cafeteria a minute behind her.

"I'm so sorry about that," the nurse said, apologizing for the cell phone call she'd received just as Erin had been saying goodbye.

"No worries," Erin said. "I knew it was time for you to be getting back to work anyway."

"Unfortunately, yes," the nurse agreed, but her eyes shifted from Erin to Corey, her brows winging upward to meet the fringe of her bangs.

Erin had to smile. The first time she'd seen the sexy cowboy, her own reaction had been very similar.

"This is Corey Traub," she told the nurse. Then, to Corey, "And Doris Becker."

Doris shook his proffered hand, smiling. "Any relation to DJ Traub of DJ's Rib Shack?"

"He's my cousin."

"I absolutely love his sauce," Doris said.

"I'm not sure that's one he's heard before," Corey teased, "but I'll be sure to pass it along."

She laughed. "You do that."

"So, are you and Erin old friends?" he asked the nurse.

Doris winked at her. "Oh yeah, we go way back."

Erin knew the nurse was joking, but Corey took her words at face value. Of course he would because Doris's response confirmed the fib Erin had told him earlier.

And somehow the hole she'd started digging so many months before kept getting deeper and deeper, and Erin was beginning to worry that she would end up over her head.

Chapter Eleven

She had to tell him the truth. Tonight.

Erin spooned the sauce over the grilled chicken, then slid the pan into the oven and checked on the rice.

She would never have made it as a spy—she wasn't cut out for a life of deception. Every single untruth she'd told since she'd arrived in Thunder Canyon weighed heavily on her, but none more so than those that she'd told to Corey.

They were lovers, but she knew that true intimacy between two people was about more than a joining of their bodies. It required openness and honesty and a willingness to share their thoughts and dreams. And if she wanted that with Corey, she had to tell him the truth, not only about her meeting with Doris Becker, but also her plans to find Delores Beckett and uncover the truth about what happened at Thunder Canyon General Hospital on the day that she was born.

At six fifty-eight the doorbell rang, making her smile.

Corey was nothing if not punctual.

But as she wiped her hands on a dish towel and made her way down the hall, her heart started to race and the nerves in her belly twisted into knots.

When she opened the door, she saw that he had a bottle of wine in one hand and flowers in the other. Before she could offer to take either, he had his arms wrapped around her and was kissing her breathless.

"Mmm, you smell delicious."

She laughed. "I think what you smell is the chicken."

"The chicken smells good, too," he said, nuzzling her neck, "but you smell even better."

She stepped away from him. "Does that wine need to go in the fridge?"

"Sure." He handed her the bottle, then the flowers. "And those need to go in a vase."

"I think there's one in the kitchen."

She peeked in the oven at the chicken, stirred the rice, then dug a tall, narrow vase out of the back of the cupboard.

It had been a long time since anyone had brought her flowers, and she was touched by the gesture. She untied the bow, then unwrapped the paper and sighed when she saw the snowy white calla lilies inside.

"Oh, they're gorgeous."

"The florist said they were 'timelessly beautiful.' I thought that described you as much as the flowers."

She traced a finger around the outside of one snowy white trumpet, her eyes misting with tears.

"What's wrong?"

She shook her head. "I guess I'm just feeling a little sentimental," she explained. "My aunt Erma was a big fan of lilies."

"Then she'd probably suggest you put them in water."

She smiled. "I'll do that."

She turned on the faucet and filled the vase, then cut the long, thick stems and carefully arranged the flowers in the water. "So what did I do to deserve these?"

He wrapped his arms around her from behind. "Maybe it's not what you did but what I'm hoping you'll do."

"You think you're going to get lucky tonight?"

"I'm hoping."

She turned to brush her lips against his. "Your chances were pretty good, even without the flowers."

His hands skimmed up her back, down again. "Any chance of getting lucky before dinner?"

She was tempted to say "yes," to take him by the hand and lead him up to her bedroom. When they were together, when their bodies were linked and their hearts were pounding in unison, it was as if the rest of the world didn't exist. Nothing else mattered, certainly not some regrettable half-truths and misunderstood evasions.

But after her conversation with Doris, she'd been more determined than ever to find Delores Beckett and learn the truth about what happened at the hospital on the day she was born. And because that truth might very well affect other people in Thunder Canyon—people who were friends of Corey's—she had to tell him about her intentions. Even if she knew that he would disapprove.

"Not if you want dinner to be edible," she warned, and ducked out of his embrace.

"I'm really not that hungry," he assured her.

But she was already taking the pan of chicken out of the oven and Corey inhaled deeply, then sighed. "Mmm, that does smell good."

He reached into the cupboard to get the plates for her.

"I thought you weren't that hungry," she teased.

"Well, since you've gone to so much trouble, we should eat."

She dished up the chicken and rice while he opened the wine. Conversation during dinner was easy, casual. Erin wanted to tell him what she'd learned from Doris, but there didn't seem to be any natural segue into that topic of conversation. Or maybe she was more chicken than what was on her plate.

Corey was up to his elbows in soapy water when the bell rang. Though Erin had insisted that the dishes could wait, he figured a little washing up was the least he could do to repay her for another fabulous meal. Plus he wanted to make sure that once he got her upstairs, she wouldn't be distracted by thoughts of dirty plates and glasses in the sink downstairs.

Not that he had any doubts about being able to keep her mind as thoroughly occupied as her body—or any shortage of ideas on how to do so.

"I'll get it," Erin said.

He watched her walk down the hall toward the door, enjoying the subtle sway of her hips beneath the slim skirt she was wearing. She really had a great butt. And fabulous legs. And when she was dressed in one of those neat little suits she usually wore to work, he couldn't help but think about how much fun he would have getting her out of it. Because beneath all that buttoned-up style was a warm and passionate woman.

Of course, she dressed more casually on her days off and was equally appealing in faded denim and fuzzy sweaters. Even more appealing in nothing at all. He pushed those thought aside and dried his hands just as Erin opened the door.

"Are you Erin Castro?" the visitor, a sixtyish woman, asked.

He had come around through the living room, and he could see the wariness in Erin's expression.

"Yes, I am. Who are you?"

"I'm Delores. Delores Beckett."

The name meant nothing to him, but obviously it meant something to Erin because her eyes went wide and her breath caught.

"Oh. I didn't—I mean—how—why—*what* are you doing here?"

"I heard you were looking for me," Delores said.

"I was. I am." Erin was obviously flustered, and her gaze went from the older woman to him and back again, her eyes narrowing. "It *was* you. I spoke to you on the phone."

"Yes," Delores admitted. "But I wasn't sure who you were or what you wanted then. It wasn't until after I'd hung up that I made the connection between the aunt you mentioned and Erma and finally realized why you were looking for me."

Of course, Corey still didn't know why Erin had been looking for Delores, but he had an uneasy feeling—bolstered by her refusal to meet his gaze—that he wasn't going to like the answer to that question.

"Will you come in, please?" Erin invited.

The older woman stepped into the foyer.

"Do you want me to make coffee?" Corey asked.

Erin seemed surprised by the offer—or maybe she'd forgotten he was there, which meant that his plans for the rest of the evening had taken a sudden detour.

"This is Corey Traub—a friend of mine," Erin told Delores. Then, to him, "Delores was a friend of my aunt Erma's."

"Coffee would be great," Delores said to him.

"I'll put it on," he told her.

"Thanks," Erin said.

When the coffee had finished brewing and they sat down together in the kitchen, it occurred to Corey that whatever Erin wanted to discuss with her visitor had nothing to do with him. But he was afraid that if he offered to leave, she would let him and he would never find out what was going on. Because he knew that there was something going on, something she hadn't told him.

Like Heather.

No, he wasn't going to go there. He wasn't going to assume that Erin had deliberately kept anything from him. She wouldn't do that.

"How did you find me?" Erin asked Delores now.

"Reverse lookup."

"Obviously you're not as opposed to technology as my aunt was," Erin said, smiling just a little.

Delores chuckled. "I'm an old woman who lives alone with a cat and a computer—I'm a registered member of twenty-nine chatrooms."

"You live alone? But I saw a young woman and a little girl…" Her words trailed off, her cheeks turned pink.

"My daughter and granddaughter." Delores smiled. "And I thought that was probably you parked across the street last Wednesday."

Corey didn't say anything, but he also didn't fail to make the connection between the date and the memory of Erin brushing off his invitation to go riding that same afternoon. Of course, he hadn't realized she was brushing him off or that her purpose had been to stake out this grandmother.

"Well, thank you for finding me," Erin said. "Because I was beginning to give up hope that I would ever locate you."

"I'm sure you have questions," Delores said. "And I've got some explaining to do."

Explaining? *That* definitely caught his attention.

Erin's gaze shifted to his again. "Delores isn't just a friend of my aunt's," she told him. "She was also the nurse who was working in labor and delivery at Thunder Canyon General Hospital the night I was born."

Erin could practically see all of the pieces click together in Corey's mind, but she wasn't going to worry about his reaction right now. She would explain everything to him later—after she got the answers to her questions from Delores.

"How did you know Erma?" she asked.

It wasn't the foremost question on her mind, but she wasn't quite ready to dive headfirst into the murky waters of her birth. She was still feeling a little unsettled by the knowledge that the woman who could answer her questions was sitting in her kitchen. The truth was finally within her grasp, and she wasn't entirely sure that she was ready for it.

"I grew up in the house next door to where she and Irwin lived," Delores explained. "I was just a kid, but she always took the time to talk to me. She knew more about my life and my friends and my ambitions than my own mother, and I was devastated when she left Thunder Canyon. I only saw her a few times after she moved away, but we kept in touch faithfully if not regularly.

"Then I had a stroke last February," she continued. "It was mild, as far as those things go, but it made me realize that I wasn't going to live forever. If I wanted to confess my sins, so to speak, I needed to do so before it was too late. So I went to visit Erma.

"She told me that she was going to tell you what happened

at the hospital the night you were born. But then, when she passed away and I didn't hear from you, I wasn't sure she had."

"What did happen?" Erin asked. "Did you mix up the babies?"

Delores's eyes filled with tears. "I don't know, but I'm not sure that I didn't."

She glanced at Corey. His cool, narrow-eyed stare proved he was angry that she'd continued to pursue investigating exactly this possibility when he'd asked her not to, but she had to trust that he would understand once he realized she was only trying to find the truth.

"Can you tell me exactly what happened?" she asked Delores.

"There were two women in labor that day, and they gave birth literally within minutes of each other. Not an unusual occurrence in a bigger hospital, but hardly commonplace in Thunder Canyon. Plus, we were short-staffed that night, so I was assisting both deliveries.

"Everything seemed fine, but then one of the mothers starting hemorrhaging, and suddenly there was chaos. Dr. Gifford took her into surgery and I took the baby to the nursery."

Dr. Gifford? Erin only had a moment to register that the rumors were true—that the scandal everyone at the hospital had been whispering about could tarnish the doctor's good reputation—before Delores forged ahead with her story.

"Now we have computer-printed labels and the ID bracelets are snapped around the babies' ankles before they're ever taken out of the delivery room," she explained. "But back then, the attending nurse printed the information by hand. That's what I was doing when I was called out to assess another mother who had been admitted in the early stages of labor.

"I was only gone a few minutes, but when I came back, both of the babies were gone. A young nurse, new on staff and trying to be helpful, had taken them down to the nursery, not realizing that I had yet to put the ID bracelets on either one."

Erin was frustrated that such a mistake had been made, but there was no doubt in her mind that it was a mistake. Neither Delores nor the other young nurse had any malicious intent, and she didn't think it was fair that Delores had essentially been forced into retirement because of the mistake.

And as much as she hadn't been impressed with Dr. Gifford during their brief meeting, she didn't want his career to be ruined over something that had happened twenty-six years before. She just wanted to make things right—except that wasn't possible now.

There was no way to go back in time and ensure that Betty Castro and Helen Clifton had gone home with the right babies—if, in fact, they had not done so. Right now, Erin was so confused, she wasn't sure what she believed.

You need to find your family. They're in Thunder Canyon.

She didn't doubt that Erma believed it was true.

And in her heart, she believed it, too. The first day that she'd driven into Thunder Canyon, she'd felt as if she was finally home; the first time she'd been introduced to Grant Clifton, she'd felt a connection, as if she knew him even though they'd never met before.

She'd also felt worry and guilt, wondering what her search for the truth would mean for the family she'd grown up with, for the parents and brothers who had always loved her even if they didn't always understand her.

She loved them, too, and the very last thing she ever wanted to do was hurt them. But she also knew that she couldn't ignore the truth. She couldn't pretend the mistake hadn't been made. She didn't want to. She wanted to know Grant as her brother; she wanted to meet his mother—the woman who had given birth to her.

And what about what they wanted?

Although he hadn't said anything in a while, it was Corey's voice that she heard, asking the question that echoed in the back of her mind.

What if they only wanted to enjoy the status quo and not have their entire lives turned upside down?

And she couldn't help but wonder, "How could someone leave the hospital with the wrong baby?"

"Neither mother thought she had the wrong baby—no one had any reason to suspect that a mix-up may have occurred."

"I guess I just thought that, after carrying a baby for nine months, there would be a natural bond between mother and child."

"The maternal bond is an amazing thing," Delores said. "But it's not always instantaneous. It can happen within minutes or it can take days or weeks, especially if the mother and child are separated for some reason immediately following the birth."

"As happened when my mother was taken into surgery," Erin guessed.

Delores nodded. "She was in rough shape for a few days after that, and by then, Helen Clifton had already left the hospital with her daughter."

"Still, you could have said something then," Erin said. "You could have admitted there might have been a mix-up and fixed it then."

"I could have," Delores agreed sadly. "And I should have. But I was scared, terrified. It had been my mistake—I would have lost my job. And it didn't seem like any real harm had been done. After all, both mothers went home with beautiful baby girls."

"That's how you justified it?"

Delores looked down at the hands she'd wrapped around her mug. "I'm not proud of what I did. And not a day has gone by in the past twenty-six years that I haven't thought I should have done things differently. But the longer I waited, the harder it was to admit my mistake. If it even was a mistake."

"Did you tell anyone what had happened?"

"Dr. Gifford. We didn't only work together, we were… involved. He urged me to keep quiet, insisting that no one would ever find out what I'd done. I was sure he was wrong, that someone would start asking questions.

"I didn't sleep for days. But then, as the weeks turned into months, I started to think maybe he was right. As the months turned into years, it seemed more and more believable that no one would ever know.

"But I knew. And the longer I held on to the secret, the more it ate away at me, haunted me.

"I knew where both of the babies were. Elise Clifton had grown up in Thunder Canyon, so I knew that—despite her father's tragic death—she had a family who loved her. And through my correspondence with Erma, I knew that the same was true about you. But then Erma began to make comments that caused me to worry that everything wasn't as great as I wanted to think."

"What kind of comments?" Erin asked, curious.

"She said that your parents didn't understand you, that if she hadn't been there when you were born, she'd have thought you were left on their doorstep."

"Do you think she knew?"

"I don't know how she could have." She paused, as if considering the possibility, then smiled. "And yet, Erma seemed to have a knack for seeing things others didn't—that's why people called her crazy.

"And then, when I went to see her in the spring, when I told her that I might have mixed up the babies, she said, 'Well, that explains everything.' To her, it wasn't a possibility but a fact."

"I know she was adamant that my family was in Thunder Canyon," Erin said.

Delores nodded. "She told me that she was going to tell you what happened all those years ago. I've been waiting on pins and needles for months, expecting that any day you would show up."

"I didn't get the whole story from Erma, only a few pieces that I struggled—unsuccessfully—to put together. That's why I came to Thunder Canyon, to try to get more information. I didn't even remember your name until my mother mentioned it. And when I couldn't track you down through the telephone listings, I decided to go to the hospital, looking for someone who might be able to help me find you. As it turns out, I ran into Dr. Gifford when I was there."

"And he pretended he'd never even heard my name," the nurse guessed.

"He certainly didn't give any indication that he'd worked with you."

"David excels at nothing more so than covering his own behind," Delores said. "Not that I can blame him, in this case. He only knew about the possibility of a mix-up because I told him. He wasn't there—he'd gone into surgery with Betty. And he wasn't responsible for ID'ing the babies—that was my job."

"But he encouraged you to keep quiet about your concerns." Erin didn't quite manage to keep the bitterness out of her tone.

Delores didn't make any more excuses for her former lover. "And now that you know, what do you plan to do about it?"

"I guess we need to prove that the mistake was made."

"You're sure that's what you want to do?"

"Of course."

"And are you prepared for the consequences whatever the truth may be? Because if it's true that I put the wrong bracelet on the wrong baby, that Helen Clifton gave birth to you and Betty Castro gave birth to Elise, then the truth is going to turn a lot of lives upside down."

Erin was quiet for a long time after Delores had gone.

Corey left her alone, figuring she needed some time to fully assimilate everything she had learned. He finished tidying up the kitchen while he tried to do the same.

He may not have grown up in Thunder Canyon, but he had family and friends in this town. They were a close-knit community, and this kind of news—if it was true—could devastate them. It would certainly devastate Grant and Elise.

"You haven't said anything," Erin noted softly.

"I don't know what to say," he admitted. "All I can think is that you lied to me."

She winced but didn't deny it.

"You told me you were going to forget your theory about babies being switched," he said.

"No, I didn't—at least, not intentionally. I only meant to promise that I wouldn't say anything to Grant until I had proof."

"You didn't say anything about continuing to look for proof."

"Because you didn't give me a chance."

"So it's *my* fault you lied to me?"

She sighed. "No. I should have made my intentions clear. But you were being so unreasonable and—" She cut herself off, as if realizing that being critical of his attitude wasn't an effective defense of her own actions. "It doesn't matter. I should have been honest."

"Yes, you should have," he said. "And now you're still determined to drag all of this out into the open, aren't you?"

"'All of this' happens to be my life. I need to know who I am," she insisted.

"Delores admitted that she *may* have put the wrong ID bracelet on the wrong baby. Even she can't say for sure that she did. I'm willing to admit that it's possible that she got the babies mixed up. Why can't you admit the possibility that she didn't?"

"Because there are too many coincidences to ignore, and because Elise looks more like my brothers than I do."

"But what purpose can be served by bringing a twenty-six-year-old mistake to light now?"

"How about the truth?"

"But at what cost?"

She frowned at that.

"Erin, if you go to anyone with your suspicions—whether it's your parents or Grant—there are a lot of people who will be hurt."

"Do you really think it would be better if I didn't say anything? Do you really believe the truth can be buried forever?"

"I'm wondering if a woman who could deceive so many people so easily can even recognize the truth," he told her.

She recoiled as if she'd been slapped. He hadn't intended to hurt her, but he couldn't just stand back and watch as she hurt other people—people he cared about.

"Because the truth may be that Delores Beckett was distracted from her duties the day you were born but still managed to put the right ID bracelet on the right baby," he continued.

"No one else has any clue what's going on—not your parents or Grant or Elise or their mother. You've had *months* to think about this, to put all the pieces together. Do you really think they're going to be happy when you start throwing around these allegations?"

"You can't understand how I feel," she told him. "Because you know exactly where you fit into your family, but I can't make plans for my future when I have so many unanswered questions about my past."

"I can't—I *won't*—be a part of this. If you insist on following through with this, you're on your own."

Her eyes—those beautiful blue eyes that could never hide her feelings—were filled with anguish. "Don't do this, Corey. Please."

"I'm not doing anything."

"You're forcing me to make an impossible choice," she told him.

"Is it impossible? Or has your choice already been made?"

She looked away but not before he saw the shimmer of her tears. "I guess it has."

He left without saying anything else.

From his perspective, there was nothing left to say.

Chapter Twelve

Erin didn't know what to think when she was called into Grant's office the next day.

At first, she'd worried that Corey might have gone to her boss after he'd left her condo the night before, but she dismissed that idea almost as quickly as it had come to her. Corey had been adamant that he wouldn't have any part in bringing to light the information she'd obtained from Delores Beckett.

"Is everything okay?" her boss asked.

"That's what I was going to ask you," Erin said.

Grant smiled, but he still looked concerned. "You seem a little…preoccupied today."

"I'm sorry—"

"I don't want an apology. I want to know if there's anything I can do to help."

She could only shake her head, not meeting his gaze.

"You're a good employee, Erin. An asset to the resort.

And if you're dissatisfied with any part of your job, I want to know."

She looked up now. "I love working here," she assured him.

"Then it's personal," he guessed.

She nodded.

"And none of my business?"

She wanted to open up to him, but she didn't know what to say. It was hardly the time or the place to tell him that she believed his mother had also given birth to her.

Now that she'd spoken with Delores Beckett, she was closer than ever to the answers she'd come to Thunder Canyon to find. But in her search for the truth, she'd found something she'd never expected to find—and lost it. And when Corey had walked out on her the night before, he'd taken her heart with him.

"Just not anything you can help me with," she told him.

"Okay," he said. "But I want you to know that I have an open-door policy here, and I hope that you'll come to me if there's ever anything you think I can help you with."

"Thank you. I will."

"On another topic," he said. "It's my sister's twenty-sixth birthday on the twentieth."

She nodded. "You mentioned that at Erika and Dillon's wedding."

He seemed surprised that she would have remembered. She probably wouldn't have if not for the fact that it was her birthday on the same day, but of course he didn't know that.

"Anyway, I thought if you weren't doing anything, you might want to come. I've already invited Corey—"

"Corey and I—we aren't dating any more," she told him.

"Oh," Grant said, in a sympathetic tone that suggested he suddenly understood why she'd been distracted. "Well, there will be other people there, too, and Stephanie and I would like you to come."

"That's very kind of both of you," Erin said. "But I don't even know your sister."

"Elise and my mom have been living in Billings for so long now that there are a lot of people in town that she doesn't know, but I'm hoping this party will give her the opportunity to get to know them and maybe entice her to move back to Thunder Canyon," he admitted.

"You must miss her a lot."

"I do. It's hard to play the annoying big brother when she's so far away."

Erin managed a smile. "I have two big brothers—they seem to manage even from a distance."

Grant chuckled. "Elise would probably say the same thing about me."

"I'd like to meet her."

"Then you'll come to the party? We're taking over DJ's at seven o'clock for the event, so you know the food will be good."

"I'll think about it." Erin stood up. "But right now I should get back to work before my boss catches me slacking off."

"I'll put in a good word for you." Grant walked with her to the door, pausing with his hand on the knob. "Corey and I have been friends for a long time, but if he doesn't come to his senses soon, there are plenty of other single guys in this town that I could introduce you to. And a lot of them will be at the party."

"I appreciate the offer but—"

"None of my business," he filled in for her.

She smiled to show that she wasn't offended, then ducked out of his office before she burst into tears and completely humiliated herself.

Corey decided to head to The Hitching Post on Monday night to grab a beer and maybe find someone to shoot some pool with. He needed a distraction—something to help him forget about Erin and all of her lies. His mind kept replaying the scene between Delores and Erin, but he was still having trouble accepting that the nurse's story had confirmed Erin's suspicions. Maybe he'd been hasty in dismissing the suggestion that she could be Grant's sister, and maybe it had been unfair to expect her to leave the past in the past. But in the end, what he couldn't forget—what he couldn't forgive—were her lies.

Every day that passed and she didn't tell him the truth, she'd lied. He felt angry and betrayed. And maybe he was hurting, too, because when it came right down to it and she'd had to make a choice, she hadn't chosen him.

He pushed open the door and was greeted by a familiar country song about a woman who'd done a cowboy wrong. Yeah, he'd come to the right place. Or so he thought until a cursory glance around the room showed his brother having dinner with his new family.

He moved toward the bar.

The last thing he needed tonight was an invitation to join Dillon and his bride and their two-year-old daughter. Technically Emilia was Dillon's stepdaughter, of course, but Corey knew his brother didn't think of the little girl that way. When he'd married Erika, she'd become his wife and her daughter had become his daughter, too. Dillon didn't seem to care about Erika's past relationship or the man who had fathered her child.

It was probably one of the reasons Corey found it difficult to understand why Erin was so obsessed with knowing who gave birth to her when, by her own admission, she had a family who loved her. Why wasn't it enough that he loved her, too?

Of course, he hadn't actually spoken those words to her. He'd never had a chance to tell her what was in his heart. Would the words have changed anything between them? He didn't know.

He was on his second beer when Dillon slid onto the vacant stool beside him. Corey looked around but didn't see any sign of his brother's wife or child.

"Erika took Emilia home," Dillon answered the unspoken question. "It's long past her bedtime."

"So why are you still here?"

"Because you don't look like you should be drinking alone." He signaled to Carl, who was tending the bar tonight, for a draft beer.

"I'm fine," Corey said.

The statement was so blatantly untrue that his brother didn't even bother to dispute it. "How are the evaluations at Rycon coming along?"

"Fine."

With a nod of thanks to the bartender, Dillon picked up the mug that had been set in front of him. "How about your discussion with Grant about the Resort?"

"Fine," Corey said again.

"How's Erin?"

"Look, Dillon, as much as I appreciate the brotherly concern, I really wish you'd just go home to your new family and leave me the hell alone."

Dillon nodded. "So she *is* the reason you look like you want to knock some heads together."

"And if you insist on hanging around here, yours might be the first."

"I'm not worried," his brother said. "Because as often as we've gone head-to-head, I've always had your back, and I know you've always had mine."

Corey sighed, silently damning his brother because he spoke the truth. And because it was true, because Dillon had always been there for him, he wouldn't get any satisfaction from turning on him now.

"So are you going to tell me what happened to make you so miserable?"

"Let's just say that I learned something I didn't want to know."

"Everyone has secrets," Dillon said.

"Weren't you the one who warned me about Erin's?"

His brother shrugged. "Only because I know you have a tendency to leap before you look."

He didn't say 'Like with Heather,' but they were both thinking it.

He'd met Heather while he was in college. She was the first woman he'd ever fallen in love with and he'd actually thought they would get married someday. One of the things he liked about her was that she didn't expect him to pay her way just because he was rich. Unlike several other women he'd dated, she prided herself on supporting herself through her job as a waitress. At least, that's what she'd told him she did. He later found out that she wasn't waiting tables but dancing on them, and it wasn't an exclusive upscale restaurant but a private men's club.

He didn't care that she'd taken off her clothes for money. Not that he was thrilled to think of all the men who had stared at and undoubtedly lusted for her naked body, but he didn't blame her for taking a job that paid her bills. He couldn't forgive her for lying, though.

After his experience with Heather, he had no tolerance for half-truths. Maybe Erin hadn't actually lied to him, but her failure to tell him the whole truth was just as much a breach of trust. He'd been played for a fool…again. And he was as furious as he was hurt by her deception.

"But in retrospect, I may have been too quick to pass judgment," Dillon was saying now.

"You weren't," Corey told him.

"And maybe you are, too."

He frowned.

"The thing is, Erika and Erin are really close, and Erika isn't easily taken in."

"As you learned when she kept saying 'no' to you," Corey couldn't resist teasing, although the effort was half-hearted.

His brother shrugged. "As a single mother with a young child, she had reason to be wary. But she never had any misgivings about Erin."

Maybe she should have, he thought, but he didn't say the words aloud because he didn't want to cause his brother undue concern. After all, Erin's reasons for being in Thunder Canyon really wouldn't affect the life Dillon was building here with Erika and Emilia.

"Do you ever think about Emilia's biological father?" he asked.

"Of course," Dillon answered without hesitation.

"Okay—fast forward twenty years and think about how you would react if the daughter you'd raised since she was two years old suddenly told you she wanted to know her father."

Dillon sipped his beer, considering. "I'd hope I could be supportive," he finally said.

"Wouldn't you think she was…ungrateful?"

His brother shook his head. "Six months ago, I might

have given you a different answer." He smiled. "Of course, six months ago, I didn't know Erika or Emilia. But Peter's recent heart attack has made me see a lot of things differently. Now I can appreciate everything he did over the years. Not just as a husband to Mom, but as a father to six kids he had no biological tie to. I can also see how tough it has been for some of the others—Rose, in particular—to have no memory of the man who contributed half of her DNA, and I can understand that the not knowing can leave a void no one else can see."

Corey finished his beer and shook his head when Carl looked over to see if he wanted another refill.

...the not knowing can leave a void...

Maybe that was what Erin had meant when she said that she needed to know her past before she could plan her future.

But her lies had undermined the foundation of what was between them, and Corey couldn't forgive her for that.

Erin couldn't go to a birthday party empty-handed, but never having met the guest of honor made it difficult to know what kind of gift might be appropriate. She wandered through the resort shops on her lunch hour, hoping something would catch her eye. What finally did was a collage-style picture frame with the word "Family" etched in the bottom corner of the glass.

She wondered at the irony that would have her give such a gift to a woman whose family she might tear apart with the information she had. But that wasn't her intention. Yes, things would change—for both Erin and Elise—but she refused to look at it as a negative. She had no intention of walking away from Betty and Jack and her brothers if it turned out that Betty Castro hadn't given birth to her, and she certainly wouldn't expect Elise to turn her back on Helen or Grant.

As the salesclerk wrapped the gift, Erin continued to wander through the store. She paused at a display of decorative perfume bottles and caught a glimpse of someone through the store window. For one brief, heart-stopping moment, she thought it was Corey. But then the man turned to speak to the woman at his side, and she saw that it was actually his brother, Dillon, with his new wife. Erika smiled at something her husband said, then he bent his head and kissed her gently.

Erin felt a pang in her heart, and she had to look away from the obvious love between them. She'd started to think that she'd found something similar with Corey. She'd let herself believe that if Erika could find love, maybe she could, too.

Obviously she'd been wrong.

Corey hadn't expected that Erin would show up at the birthday party Grant was hosting for his sister. He wouldn't have thought she'd have the nerve. But not only did she come, she came with Erika and Dillon.

And when she walked through the door, his heart knocked hard against his ribs, forcing him to admit how much he'd missed her. It had only been a few days since he'd last seen her, since he'd learned of her deception, but those few days had seemed like a lifetime.

He noticed that she'd brought a gift—a good way to get an introduction to the birthday girl, he figured, then remembered that Erin should be celebrating her birthday today, too.

She set the wrapped package on a table that had been set aside for that purpose and unbuttoned her coat. As she shrugged it off of her shoulders and turned to hang it on a hook, he nearly choked on the beer he'd been about to swallow.

She was wearing a dress. He wasn't sure he'd ever seen her in a dress before—other than the day of Dillon and Erika's wedding, of course. She often wore skirts to work, but he'd never seen her in something so flirty and feminine. There were no sleeves, so her long, slender arms were bare, and the short, fluttery skirt showed off miles of shapely leg.

She looked…stunning.

As if sensing his perusal, she turned. They were separated by the width of the room, but even over that distance their eyes met, held. And then she looked away.

Corey lifted his glass to his lips again, then realized it was empty. He went back to the bar, but this time he ordered a Coke. He obviously didn't need alcohol fogging his brain when just being in the same room with Erin had the same effect.

If he'd expected that she would be so devastated by their breakup that she'd be hiding out in her condo, he was obviously mistaken. Of course, why would she be devastated? She was the one who'd decided their relationship was over.

He watched her hips sway as she walked, appreciating the way her soft, flowing skirt swirled around her thighs as she moved. Unfortunately, just admiring those legs from a distance reminded him of how they'd felt wrapped around him—

He turned away, mortified to realize that he was getting aroused just thinking about her.

Of course, the physical parts of their relationship had been phenomenal. Everything between them had clicked.

He'd thought they were clicking in other areas, too.

They'd had so much fun, talking and laughing and just being together.

And then he'd found out about her lies, and he'd realized they had nothing if they didn't have trust.

But the heart didn't always defer to the logic of the mind, and, although he told himself that she was just like Heather, his heart wouldn't accept that it was true.

Because he loved her.

Regardless of what she'd said and done—or not said and failed to do—his heart urged him to give her another chance, to give *them* another chance.

The first time he'd set eyes on her, he'd felt something stir inside of him. He hadn't even known her name, but he'd somehow known that she was the woman he was meant to be with. And so he'd pursued her, relentlessly and single-mindedly.

And then he'd found out that she wasn't quite the woman he'd wanted her to be, that she had secrets he couldn't have guessed and didn't want to believe. And still, he couldn't shake the feelings he had for her. He couldn't stop wanting her, needing her, loving her.

But he'd abandoned her when she needed him. All she'd asked for was some compassion and understanding, and he'd turned on her because he didn't want to rock the boat. It wasn't even *his* boat, but the peacemaking instinct of the middle child was so deeply ingrained in him it had a tendency to carry over to all areas of his life. How ironic that his desire to maintain the status quo for his friend's family had led to his conflict with Erin.

Maybe it wasn't about giving her a second chance but asking if she would give him one.

...I can't make plans for my future when I have so many unanswered questions about my past.

He didn't think she'd actually come here tonight to answer those questions, but maybe he should stick close to her—just to be sure.

Erin didn't feel as awkward as she thought she would at Elise Clifton's party. Although she'd never met Grant's sister, she was surprised by how many of the guests she did know. Obviously she'd met more people and made more friends than she'd realized during the few months that she'd been in Thunder Canyon.

In fact, she didn't feel uncomfortable at all except for that brief moment when she'd glanced around the room and found Corey watching her. She'd known he would be there, but she hadn't expected that she would feel so rattled by his presence.

But she should have. After all, they'd been more than casual acquaintances—they'd been lovers. And although their time together had been brief, it had also been more intimate and intense than any other relationship Erin had ever had.

Of course, that was over now, she reminded herself. And although she might regret the way their relationship had ended, there was no point in wishing things had turned out differently. She couldn't deny herself the answers she'd sought for so long just because he wanted her to. And the fact that he could even ask it of her, knowing how important it was to her to find the truth, proved that he didn't care about her half as much as he'd claimed.

Anyway, it was inevitable that, in a town the size of Thunder Canyon, she would cross paths with Corey every now and again. And she was relieved that the first meeting had happened. They hadn't actually exchanged words, but she was okay with that. She was still too raw to be able to hide the hurt she was feeling.

She wandered around the buffet table, more out of curiosity than hunger, examining the assortment of finger foods. Her stomach was too knotted to contemplate putting anything into it right now, but she might eat later, when Corey was gone—or at least when he stopped watching her.

Was she being paranoid—or was he shadowing her every move? Probably he was sticking close so he could intervene if she got too close to one of his friends.

But he didn't make a move when Grant and Stephanie sought her out, or even when Grant pulled his mother and his sister over to meet her.

Truthfully, Erin wouldn't have minded if he'd interrupted just then because coming face-to-face with Elise Clifton for the first time, she was absolutely speechless. It wasn't just that the resemblance to her own brothers was more evident in person—it was the tiny brown birthmark on the side of Elise's nose, exactly where Jake and Josh each had identical birthmarks.

Erin hadn't noticed the birthmark in the photo, or maybe the angle from which the picture was taken had hidden it from view. But she knew that the presence of that birthmark couldn't possibly be a coincidence—it had to mean that Elise was Betty and Jack Castro's child.

After Grant had made the introductions, while Erin was still reeling from the shock of this revelation, Helen Clifton looked at her thoughtfully.

"Would your mother be Betty Castro by any chance?" she asked.

Erin's heart was pounding hard and fast as she faced the woman who had not raised her but who, she was now certain, had given birth to her. But she could hardly say, 'Actually, you're my mother,' and because Betty had been her mother in every other way, she answered, "Yes, she is."

"Erin's mother and I gave birth on the same day, practically at the same time, right here in Thunder Canyon," Helen informed them.

"No birthing horror stories, please," Stephanie said quickly.

"I don't have any to tell," the older woman assured her expectant daughter-in-law.

"Good." Stephanie breathed a sigh of relief as she rubbed her baby bump. "But just in case, I'll excuse myself to get this rapidly growing baby some food."

"I'll make sure she skips the seafood and sits while she eats," Grant said, following his wife.

"If your mom gave birth the same day as mine, then it's your birthday today, too," Elise said to Erin after her brother and sister-in-law had gone.

She nodded, feeling more than a little self-conscious that the attention had shifted in her direction.

"Are your parents here to celebrate with you?" Helen asked. "It would be a hoot to see your mother again."

"No," Erin said. Despite this most recent and shocking revelation—or maybe because of it—she realized she missed her family more than ever. "They live in San Diego, but they are coming for Thanksgiving."

"Well, maybe we'll have a chance to get together while they're here."

"In the meantime," Elise said, "I should see if someone in the kitchen can add your name to the cake."

"No." The protest was as immediate as it was instinctive.

"Why not?" Elise asked.

"Because this is *your* party."

"But it's *our* birthday."

She was so gracious and generous and her easy acceptance made Erin feel all the more guilty about the secrets she carried deep inside.

"That's really kind," Erin said, "but—"

"But we need to be going," Corey interjected, touching a hand to her back. "We have another birthday celebration to attend."

While she was grateful to have been rescued, she wasn't entirely sure how she felt about Corey being her rescuer. But she was desperate enough to escape that she played along.

"Oh. Of course," Elise said, though she sounded more than a little disappointed.

"Enjoy the rest of your night," Erin said and impulsively hugged her.

Grant's sister hugged her back; then Helen did, too.

"It was a pleasure to meet you—again," she said and laughed.

Erin forced a smile, but her throat was tight and her eyes were stinging.

Corey said his goodbyes, then ushered her toward the exit.

"I'll grab your coat," he said.

She only nodded.

He slipped the garment over her shoulders and guided her out of the restaurant.

"Why did you do that?" she finally asked him.

He shrugged. "You looked like you needed to get out of there."

"I did," she admitted. "Thanks."

"What are you thinking now? Do you still believe Delores made a mistake at the hospital?"

"I know she did," Erin told him.

He frowned. "Why are you suddenly so certain?"

"Because Elise has a little birthmark on her face in exactly the same spot that both of my brothers do."

He didn't say anything.

Erin pulled her wallet out of her purse. Her fingers trembled as she pulled out photos of each of her brothers. "Look."

Corey did, his frown deepening.

"Are you thinking that this is yet another coincidence?" she asked.

"No, I'm wondering why you didn't say anything in there," he admitted.

She stared at him. "Did you really think I would just blurt something like that out? Is that why you're here? To make sure I didn't cause a scene?"

"I'm here because I was invited."

"So why were you hovering around me rather than visiting with your friends?"

"Because the minute I saw you walk through the door, darlin', I realized how much I've missed you."

Her traitorous heart bumped against her ribs. She couldn't do this—she couldn't let him get to her. She didn't have any emotional reserves left to deal with him right now.

"You were the one who walked out," she reminded him.

"I made a mistake."

Oh, she wanted to believe him. She needed to feel as if she had someone on her side when all of her family allegiances suddenly seemed so uncertain. But he'd hurt her already, and her heart was still feeling too bruised to endure another beating.

"Look, I appreciate the rescue in there, but if you don't mind, I'd really just like to go home now."

"But it's your birthday," he reminded her. "And I'd really like to take you out to celebrate it."

She didn't feel like celebrating, but the thought of spending the few hours that were left of her birthday alone was too depressing to contemplate. And while the thought of spending those hours with Corey was tempting, she knew it would be dangerous to do so.

"Come on, Erin," he cajoled. "You didn't eat anything at the party. Let me at least buy you a burger."

"A burger?"

"Or steak and lobster—whatever you want."

She was too raw and vulnerable right now to resist him—and too pathetically needy to refuse. And she was kind of hungry. "I think I'd like a burger."

He took her hand, linking their fingers together. "Just a burger—or are you going to go crazy and order a side of fries?"

"Maybe onion rings."

"A woman after my own heart," he teased, squeezing her hand.

Erin forced a smile as she let him lead her to his truck.

Maybe she did want his heart—but she no longer believed that he would ever give it to her.

Chapter Thirteen

They went to the Hitching Post. Being a Saturday night, they expected to have to wait for a table, but they lucked out by walking in just as another couple was getting up to leave.

Corey helped Erin with her coat, hanging it on the hook beside their booth.

"Is that a new dress?"

She glanced down, as if she wasn't sure what she was wearing, then shook her head. "The only thing I've bought new since I came to Montana are jeans, flannel shirts and boots."

He slid onto the bench across from her. "I guess a California girl's wardrobe is pretty short on those."

"If by 'short' you mean 'nonexistent,' then yes."

"Well, you sure know how to wear them," he told her. "Although I must admit, I really like the way this fluttery little skirt shows off your legs."

She glanced at him over the top of her menu. "Are you flirting with me?"

"Why do you sound so surprised?"

"The last time I saw you, you made it pretty clear that we were done."

Corey started to respond, then noticed the waitress approaching. They ordered their drinks and burgers with a side of onion rings. When their server had gone, he said, "I was caught off guard by Delores's visit and my response was probably both impulsive and unfair."

"Is that an apology?"

"I am sorry," he told her. "And I don't want to lose what we had."

"What did we have, Corey?"

"If you're trying to make me squirm by asking me to talk about our relationship, you're going to be disappointed, darlin'."

The waitress returned with their drinks. Erin picked up her glass of wine and took a sip.

"I came here for a burger, not a relationship analysis," she told him.

"I'm not sure how much longer my business is going to keep me in Thunder Canyon," he said.

"I never expected you would stay here forever." Her tone was casual, but she looked away, giving him hope that she wasn't as unaffected by his announcement as she wanted to seem.

"How about you?" he asked. "How long do you think you'll be in Montana?"

She shrugged. "Right now, I don't have any plans to be anywhere else."

"Ever thought of spending some time in Texas?" he asked.

"No," she said bluntly.

"You're determined to make this difficult, aren't you?"

"That's not my intention," she denied.

"Just a lucky coincidence?"

"*You* would think it was a coincidence."

He winced. "Okay—I deserved that."

She sighed. "No, you didn't. I'm just not very good company tonight."

"Turning twenty-six is getting you down?"

Her lips curved, just a little. "That must be it."

He reached across the table, touched her hand. "Are you missing your family?"

"I guess I am. Which is silly because they're coming for Thanksgiving, but I've never been away on my birthday before."

"Tell me some of your favorite birthday memories," he suggested.

"Why?"

"Because it might help you feel less homesick."

"I'm not homesick," she denied automatically. Then, when his brows rose, she relented, "Not really."

"Would you have gone out for dinner if you were celebrating your birthday in San Diego?"

She shook her head. "My mother would have cooked—anything I wanted. And she would have made her famous triple-layer dark-chocolate coconut cake."

"Instead you're getting a hamburger."

Erin smiled as the waitress set her plate in front of her. "Yeah, but it's a really good burger. And onion rings," she said, plucking one from her plate and biting into it.

They didn't talk much while they ate, but the silence wasn't at all uncomfortable. Corey wasn't entirely sure that Erin had forgiven him for his dismissal of her baby-switch theory, but she seemed to be warming up to him, at least a little.

He excused himself when he'd finished his burger but detoured on his way to the men's room to track down their server and arrange for dessert. When their plates had been cleared away and Erin was finishing her second glass of wine, the waitress brought a chocolate fudge brownie with coconut sprinkled on top and a single candle stuck in the middle.

Erin's eyes widened.

"I'm sure this can't compare to anything your mother would have made, but it was the best I could do on short notice."

"You didn't have to do anything," she told him.

He nodded toward the dessert. "Make a wish and blow out your candle."

She focused on the candle, closed her eyes and blew softly. The flame flickered, then disappeared in a wisp of smoke.

She cut the brownie in half and insisted on sharing it with him. He didn't really like coconut, but since it was the first overture she'd made in his direction, he accepted happily.

When the plate was empty and the bill had been paid, he helped her into her coat again.

"Thank you," Erin said as she walked beside him toward the exit.

"For what?"

"For the rescue, for dinner and for hanging with me so that I didn't have to spend my birthday alone."

"Anytime," he told her.

She puzzled over his response.

A few days earlier, Corey had refused to consider the possibility that there had been a mix-up at the hospital. Of course, a few days earlier, Erin hadn't known about Elise's birthmark and proving that Jake and Josh had the same mark might have helped Corey see things from her point of view. But she hadn't shown him the photos of her brothers until after they'd left the party, after he'd unexpectedly come to her rescue.

So what had caused his change of heart? Did he really want to pick up their relationship where they'd let off? Why was he suddenly willing to forgive her deception?

She had no idea how to answer those questions and too many other things to worry about right now. Top of the list of her worries was how to tell her parents—Jack and Betty—what had happened at the hospital on the day that she was born. Thankfully, she had a few days to come up with the right words.

She was quiet on the drive back to her condo, thinking about their upcoming visit. And maybe it was because they were on her mind that she didn't find it strange when she saw their car in her driveway.

"You have company," Corey said.

His words made her realize that what she was seeing was real and not an illusion.

"My parents," she said.

"Did you know they were coming?"

She shook her head. "Not today."

Her hand was on the door handle even before he'd come to a complete stop, and then she was flying down the driveway and into her dad's arms.

"Dad." Tears filled her eyes as she moved from Jack's embrace to Betty's. "Mom. I thought you weren't coming until Wednesday."

"Well, that was the original plan," Jack admitted.

"But your birthday is today," Betty pointed out. "And there was no way I was missing my little girl's birthday if I didn't have to."

"What time did you get here? Why didn't you call me and let me know you were coming?"

"We wanted it to be a surprise."

"Well, it is," Erin said and hugged her again. "A wonderful surprise."

"Then you don't mind that we didn't get you a present?" Jack teased.

"Just having you here is the best present ever," she assured them.

"You're sure it's okay that we came a few days early?" Betty asked, glancing pointedly at Corey.

"Of course it is," Erin said, but she felt her cheeks flush as she imagined what they were thinking and how to introduce the man who had been her lover and now…was not. "This is Corey."

He shook hands with each of her parents, who didn't even try to be subtle as they sized him up. Her father's narrow-eyed gaze warned her that he was reserving judgment; her mother's warm smile suggested a willingness to be accepting. Of course, her mother had been willing to accept Trevor, too, and now that Erin was twenty-six years old (officially "over-the-hill" to a woman who had married when she was barely twenty), her matchmaking efforts would undoubtedly kick into overdrive.

"Are you going to make your parents stand in the driveway all night?" Corey asked her.

"Of course not," Erin denied. "Although as I stand here, I am wondering if I left my breakfast dishes on the counter this morning."

"I won't be surprised if you did," Betty said.

"And I don't care if you did," Jack said. "I'm just hoping you've got a cold beer in your fridge."

"I'm sure we can find one," Erin said, digging in her purse for her keys.

"I'll say goodbye then," Corey said to her, "so that you can have some time alone with your parents to catch up."

Erin was relieved by his offer. She didn't want her mother making more of her relationship with Corey than it was—especially when she had no idea what exactly it was right now.

"Thanks again for dinner," she said.

"You don't have to run off on our account," Jack said, obviously wanting more time to make up his mind about the man who'd been out with his daughter.

"And you can't go until you've had cake," Erin's mom insisted, reaching into the backseat for a covered plate.

"Triple-layer dark-chocolate coconut?" Corey asked.

Betty positively beamed. "Erin told you?"

"She said it didn't feel like her birthday without it."

"Then you really have to try a piece," she insisted.

So Corey came in and had a piece of cake and a cup of coffee.

Erin had thought it would be awkward to have him there, but her thoughts were so preoccupied that she was grateful for his efforts to keep the conversation flowing. While he was chatting with her father, she went upstairs to put sheets on the bed in the spare room. She was just pulling up the comforter when her mom came in.

"Your young man is helping Jack with the bags," Betty told her.

And so it begins, Erin thought, but with more indulgence than annoyance. "He's not my young man," she warned.

Not unexpectedly, her mother sighed. "Only because you're not trying hard enough, I'm sure."

She had to smile. It was either that or take her mother by the shoulders and shake her. But she couldn't deny that Betty had her best interests at heart—they just didn't always agree on what was "best" for Erin.

Thankfully, the arrival of Corey and her dad with the suitcases saved her from having to answer. While her parents got ready for bed, she saw Corey to the door.

"Should I apologize?" she asked him.

"For what?"

"Whatever my father may have said to you outside."

He grinned. "No need. In fact, I think we came to something of an understanding."

"What kind of understanding?"

"I understand that if I make a move on his daughter while he's sleeping under her roof, he's going to kick my ass."

"He's always been a little overprotective."

"You're his little girl," Corey said simply.

But was she? The automatic question brought tears to her eyes.

Corey tipped her chin up. "You are," he said, somehow reading the doubts that were in her mind. "And I suspect that you always will be, no matter how many birthdays you celebrate and no matter what a DNA test might prove."

She nodded.

"I'm glad I got to meet them," he told her.

"If I don't have to apologize for my dad, I should at least warn you about my mom."

"Why?"

"Because you made a very favorable impression on her and, if you're not careful, she'll have me out shopping for china patterns before the end of the week."

"Maybe I don't want to be careful," he said.

"Corey—"

"I know. I've done a complete one-eighty and you're trying to figure out why."

She eyed him warily.

"I'm not sure there's a simple explanation. As a result of my own history, I can handle almost anything but dishonesty. And when I thought you'd lied to me, well, I may have overreacted," he admitted. "But after I'd had some time to think about it, I realized that even if you had promised not to pursue the truth about the circumstances of your birth, I had no right to ask you to make such a promise."

"I needed to know," she said, needing *him* to understand how important that knowledge was to her.

He nodded. "And maybe you had a point when you said that I couldn't know how you felt because I'd never had reason to question where I fit in my family."

"Are you saying that you understand now?"

"I'm trying," he promised her. "But mostly, I'm saying that our relationship is worth the effort and if we have differences of opinion, we should work through them."

"You were the one who gave me the ultimatum," she reminded him.

"I was wrong."

"And if I told you I was taking out a billboard to announce that I'm Helen Clifton's daughter?"

"I'd try to talk you out of it," he said. "But only because I think the situation should be handled a little more discreetly."

She must have frowned, because he rubbed his thumb over her brow. "You're tired and you've had a long day. Don't stress about it now, darlin'."

"How can I not?"

"Try to think of something else," he said, and touched his lips to hers.

It was a fleeting kiss—filled with more promise than passion. She only wished she knew what he was promising.

Erin woke up the next morning to the mouthwatering scents of frying bacon and perking coffee. She slipped out of bed and into her robe and followed her nose downstairs to the kitchen.

"I didn't think I had any bacon," she said, pouring herself a cup of coffee from the pot.

"You didn't," Betty agreed. "You never have much more than the bare essentials, so I brought a few things in a cooler."

Erin opened the refrigerator to get the milk to add to her coffee and immediately realized that her mother had brought more than a few things—her fridge had never been so thoroughly stocked.

"Even out here in the wilds of Montana, there are grocery stores," she told her mom.

Betty stacked a couple of slices of French toast on a plate, added a few slices of bacon, then passed the plate to her daughter. "Sit and eat."

Erin sat and ate.

Usually breakfast was a bowl of cereal or some fruit and yogurt. She couldn't remember the last time she'd had French toast. And as much as she loved bacon—she took another bite of the deliciously salty meat—she never took the time to cook it for herself.

She picked up the bottle of maple syrup, poured some more onto her plate and swirled a piece of toast in it. "There are probably a gazillion calories in this breakfast."

"Calories don't count when food is prepared with love," Betty said.

"You always say that," Erin noted, dropping her gaze to her plate again so her mom wouldn't see the tears in her eyes.

"And you look like you could use a good meal—honestly, Erin, you're little more than skin and bones now."

She smiled at that because she knew it was far from the truth. She weighed exactly the same as always, but if Betty wasn't personally feeding her daughter, she had a tendency to assume that Erin wasn't eating.

"Where's Dad?" she asked, as much to shift the conversation as because she wanted to know.

"He had his breakfast already and went out for a walk—he was curious to check out the resort property." Betty carried her own mug of coffee to the table. "If you had to leave San Diego for a while, you couldn't have picked a prettier spot."

The front door opened and heavy footsteps pounded on the mat. "Brr, I think I've got ice on my glasses," Jack called out.

Erin smiled. "It is a little colder here than in California, though."

"A little?" Betty wrapped her cardigan more closely around herself.

"There's my girls," Jack said, coming into the kitchen. He pressed his cold cheek to his daughter's, then to his wife's.

Betty yelped. "Goodness, Jack. You're freezing."

"The air is brisk out there," he said. "But it sure does get the blood flowing."

Erin pushed her now-empty plate aside, smiling as she watched her dad make his way around her kitchen, finding the mug he'd obviously used earlier and refilling it with fresh coffee.

She'd missed these casual morning conversations with her parents, but she had different routines now—daily rituals that were her own. And maybe that was all part of growing up. Before she'd come to Thunder Canyon, she'd only occasionally thought about moving out of their home. Sure, she'd realized that she would have to make her own way eventually, but she'd had no real complaints about living under their roof, and the advantages had certainly outweighed the disadvantages.

But now that she had been living on her own for several months, she understood that it was what she'd needed—to be completely independent, to be responsible for herself, to make her own decisions. There was one decision in particular that she'd wrestled with late into the night—when to tell them what she'd learned about the events surrounding her birth at Thunder Canyon General Hospital. And she knew that she couldn't delay any longer.

"Mom. Dad." She took a deep breath, looked at each of them in turn and sent up a silent but fervent prayer that she was doing the right thing. "There's something I have to tell you."

Chapter Fourteen

"Do you remember last June, when I went to visit Aunt Erma?" Erin asked them.

"She had asked to see you," Jack recalled.

"It was just before she passed away," Betty added.

Erin nodded. "Well, she wanted to talk to me because she had some information that led her to believe that I had family in Thunder Canyon."

Betty looked to Jack, as if he might know something she didn't.

He shook his head. "If Erma had any relatives here, I didn't know about it."

"She didn't mean that she had family here, but that *I* did," Erin clarified.

"I don't understand," her mother said.

"I didn't understand either," Erin admitted. "She gave me some bits and pieces of information, but I never got a chance to ask her to explain."

She was making a mess of this, trying to break the news gently rather than blurting out 'I'm not your daughter.' But even if she could have spoken those words, she realized they weren't true. Corey was right—even if Betty Castro had not given birth to her, she would always be her mother.

"Is that why you came to Thunder Canyon?"

"Partly," Erin said, then realized her response was yet another half-truth and that she needed to be completely honest. "No, I left San Diego partly for the reasons I told you—because I was feeling stifled at the hotel and with Trevor. But I chose Thunder Canyon because of the questions I had."

"Because of Erma," Betty said, annoyance in her tone.

Jack laid his hand over his wife's. "What kind of questions?" he asked.

So Erin summarized, as best she could, her final conversation with her father's aunt and the information she'd uncovered since coming to Thunder Canyon, including the sense of recognition she'd felt when she saw the photo of Grant's sister at Erika and Dillon's wedding and the revelations from her recent conversation with Delores Beckett.

Her parents listened, silently absorbing what she was telling them, but she could tell that they were both confused and distressed by the implications.

"It seems…unbelievable," Jack said.

"Because it is," Betty insisted. "And I refuse to give any credence to Erma's crazy rants or to…"

Her words trailed off when Erin slid her digital camera across the table.

On the display was a picture of Elise that she'd snapped just before leaving her party the night before. She was with Grant, laughing at something he'd said, and the angle of the shot clearly showed the birthmark on the side of her nose.

Obviously Betty noticed it, too, because her breath caught. "Who is this?"

"Her name is Elise Clifton. She was born in Thunder Canyon General Hospital on November twentieth, twenty-six years ago."

Jack touched his wife's hand again.

"Helen Clifton's little girl." Her mother's words confirmed that she also remembered the woman she'd met in the maternity ward that day so many years earlier. "I didn't think it was possible—I didn't want to believe it was possible. But, oh, my Lord, the birthmark, and the shape of her eyes is exactly like Jake's, and the chin is so much like Josh's…"

She trailed off again and looked at Erin, who smiled wryly. "I know. She looks a lot more like my brothers than I do."

"But that might just be a coincidence," Betty said now, though not very convincingly.

"And I might believe it was," Erin said, "if not for all of the other coincidences."

Betty sighed, her eyes filled with tears. "Oh, honey. I don't know what to say."

While his wife and daughter fumbled, it was Jack who found the words. "I think the most important thing to remember at this point," he said to Erin, "is that we love you. We always have and we always will, and even if it turns out that a mistake was made and you aren't ours by blood, that will never change. You are our daughter in our hearts and that's more important than anything else."

It was probably the longest speech Erin had ever heard her father make, and though his tone was gruff, she knew that he meant every word. And because she finally understood that it was true, she fell into his arms and sobbed.

* * *

A while later, after all the tears had been dried, Betty asked, "What do you want to do now?"

"I want to tell Helen and Elise and Grant, Helen's son. But Corey told me that John's death hit them all hard, and I'm worried about how they'll react to finding out that their ties to one another aren't quite what they believed."

"You've talked to Corey about this?" Jack asked.

"I had to talk to someone," Erin told him.

"Then we'll talk about Corey later," her father promised.

"Why?"

"Because I know what it means when a man looks at a woman the way he was looking at my little girl, and I want to know what's going on with you two."

"Jack," Betty chided gently, as if she hadn't tried to pry the same information from Erin the night before. "She's a grown woman now."

"I said we'll talk about it later," he repeated.

And Erin smiled because she realized that although her entire life had been turned upside down, some things never changed.

"Getting back to the topic at hand," Betty said, looking pointedly at her husband before turning her attention back to her daughter. "I think you should talk to Helen first—a mom usually has a good idea about how her kids will deal with tough news."

"And my mom always has the best ideas," Erin said, making Betty smile. "If I could set up a meeting, would you go with me?"

"Absolutely," her mother said, proving once again that her support was unconditional and unwavering.

Corey was pulling into the Super Saver Mart parking lot, thinking about Erin instead of the groceries he needed, when he saw her walk out of the store. He recognized her Kia and pulled into a vacant spot beside it.

She looked up when he opened the door.

"Did Mother Hubbard find the cupboard was bare?" he asked lightly.

Her face was pale and her eyes looked tired, but she smiled, just a little. "I'd swear my mother brought half of the Whole Foods Market from San Diego in coolers," she told him. "But she somehow managed to forget butter."

"You don't have butter?" he asked curiously.

"No, I have margarine, and when my mother bakes, she does not substitute margarine for butter."

He stroked a finger gently over the shadow beneath her eye. "Rough night?"

"I didn't sleep well," she admitted.

"Probably because you were sleeping alone," he said teasingly, earning another half-smile from her.

"I told my parents this morning."

"How did they react?"

"They were shocked. Skeptical. But when they saw Elise's picture, they couldn't deny the possibility. We're going to talk to Helen before any other steps are taken."

"Sounds reasonable," he said.

She nodded.

"Speaking of next steps," he said. "How about catching a movie with me tonight?"

"My parents are visiting," she reminded him.

"They can come, too. Or are you worried that they won't approve of you dating me?"

"You know that's not the issue. And I'm not dating you."

"Don't shut me out, Erin."

"I'm not shutting you out," she denied. "I just need time to figure some things out."

"You don't have to figure everything out on your own," he told her. "Or are you saying 'no' to punish me for not supporting you?"

"I'm not punishing you."

He wasn't sure he believed her, but he also couldn't blame her. He'd treated her carelessly and she had every right to be wary. But he wasn't going to give up. He would do whatever he needed to do to prove his feelings for her, to prove that they were meant to be together because he really believed that they were.

"Okay," he finally said. "I'll give you some time to figure things out. But while you're doing that, there's one other piece of information you might want to consider."

"Which is?"

"That I'm in love with you."

Erin stared at him, stunned, breathless, terrified.

"Yeah, that's kind of how I felt when the realization hit me," Corey told her. "And I probably shouldn't have said those words for the first time in the middle of a parking lot, but I wanted you to know."

It wasn't the location but the words that left her speechless. They'd broken up; he'd walked out on her. "You don't—you can't mean it."

His brows rose. "Why can't I?"

She didn't know why, she only knew that he couldn't. It didn't make any sense. She looked away from him, trying to order her scrambled thoughts, and bought some time for herself by unlocking the doors and putting the butter inside her car.

He took her hands and linked their fingers together. "I know you're confused and probably more than a little scared because of your family situation. But although Helen may have given birth to you and genetics might make Grant your brother, Betty and Jack Castro are still your parents—they raised you and loved you and helped you become the woman you are now. The woman *I* love."

He sounded sincere and she wanted to believe that he meant what he said, but it wasn't that long ago that he'd dumped her. He'd walked away from her when she'd needed him and, in the process, he'd trampled all over her heart with his size thirteen boots. And now he thought he could toss those three little words out and she would welcome him back with open arms? Not likely.

But you love him, too.

The voice didn't echo in her head this time but in her heart, but she refused to listen.

"I can't do this right now," she told him.

"I'm not asking you to do or say anything," he told her. "I just wanted you to know because I'm going back to Texas—"

"You're leaving?" She didn't know why the thought sent her into such a panic. After all, she was the one who'd told him to go, but she'd only wanted him to give her a little space—not fifteen-hundred miles.

And now that she knew he was leaving Thunder Canyon, she suddenly wanted to cling to him and ask him to stay. Because she was afraid of being alone? Or because she was afraid that if he walked out the door he might never come back?

"Only for a while," he promised. "And I will be coming back."

When?

The question sprang to her lips, but this time she managed to bite back the instinctive response. She had no right to ask questions, no right to expect anything from him. And she should know better than to expect anything from a man who could say he loved her in one breath and tell her that he was leaving in the next.

It was for the best, she decided. Because she needed to figure out her own life before she could decide where he might fit into it—or even if she wanted him to.

"When are you leaving?" she asked instead.

"Tomorrow."

She nodded and tried to ignore the tightness that had taken hold of her chest.

"I'm giving you some time." He tipped her chin up and pressed a brief, hard kiss to her lips. "But I'm not going to wait forever for you to decide what you want."

He started across the parking lot.

"Corey."

He paused, turned.

She wasn't sure what she'd intended to say, what she could say, that would erase the aching emptiness that filled her heart as she watched him walk away from her. In the end, she only said, "Have a safe trip."

He nodded.

She watched until the automatic doors of the store had closed behind him, then she got into her car and drove home.

The Clifton and the Castro families spent Thanksgiving together. Bo and Holly Clifton were in attendance, and even Erin's brothers, Jake and Josh, made the trip to Thunder Canyon for the holiday. Erin knew their decision was partly motivated by a desire to reassure her that they would always be around to nag her, as big brothers are required to do, and partly motivated by curiosity about their new sister. Although they were still waiting for the DNA results to officially confirm that the babies had been incorrectly ID'd at the hospital, no one doubted that it was true. Betty shared the information that she had with Helen and was, in turn, given one final piece of the puzzle.

When Helen first held her baby girl in her arms, she hadn't had a birthmark on the side of her nose. A few hours later, after the baby had been bathed and swaddled and returned to her, she'd questioned the nurse about the tiny brown mark that she saw on her daughter's face and that she was certain hadn't been there before. The nurse had brushed off her question, assuring her that birthmarks weren't always present at birth and often did appear hours—or even days and weeks—later.

Because of the hemorrhaging, Betty hadn't seen her baby until after her surgery, so she couldn't say for sure that her daughter had been born with a birthmark, but she remembered that the marks had been evident on each of her sons right away.

Learning that she had a second mother and a father again, after losing John so many years earlier, seemed to have completely overwhelmed Elise.

Erin could understand—she'd felt the same way when she'd come to Thunder Canyon on the impetus of only her great-aunt Erma's cryptic words. And though her suspicions about her background had continued to grow over the past few months, hearing Delores Beckett give credence to those suspicions had made her question everything she knew about her roots and her family. Elise, having never had any reason to doubt who she was or where she came from, was still reeling from the revelations. Erin hoped that in time Elise would agree that they weren't losing the families they'd known but gaining new ones, with the added bonus that sharing brothers made them honorary sisters. But she understood that the other woman needed some time to absorb the revelations that had been thrown at her. As Corey had once pointed out to her, Erin had been thinking about the possibility of a baby mix-up for several weeks, and Elise had known the truth for only a few days.

As always, just thinking of Corey made her heart ache. She hadn't heard from him since he'd left Thunder Canyon, and through everything else that had happened, she'd remained conscious of his absence, of how empty her life seemed without him. True, she'd told him she needed time, but she thought he could at least have called.

Or you could've called him.

Damn, but there were times when she hated that rational side of her.

She knew it was her turn to make the next move. No way was she going to let her last memory of Corey Traub be of him walking across the parking lot of the Super Saver Mart.

Erin had to work the Friday and Saturday immediately following Thanksgiving, but her parents stayed through to Sunday morning and spent a lot of time with Elise and Helen. As she went about her usual routine, it surprised Erin how normal everything seemed. On the outside everything was exactly the same, but on the inside so much had changed—and definitely for the better.

Since the summer, she'd been living in limbo—trying to answer questions about her past and not at all certain about her future. Recent events had somehow solidified her relationship with her parents and her brothers, and she was building new ones with Helen and Elise and Grant and Stephanie. It was her new sister-in-law who pointed out to Erin that she was going to be an aunt very soon, and she knew that both she and Elise would spoil the baby terribly when he or she finally arrived.

She had so much to be grateful for—her life was full

and rich. And still, there was an emptiness inside of her, a space that she knew only Corey could fill.

I'm not going to wait forever for you to decide what you want.

His words echoed in the back of her mind.

Okay, seven days wasn't exactly forever, but it certainly felt like it.

When she went into work the next day, she was going to ask Grant for some time off, and if she had to play the sister card, well, she wasn't above doing so. She wasn't going to wait another seven days to book a plane ticket to Texas.

Just making the decision made her heart feel lighter, and she resolved to check the flight schedule to Texas so that she could discuss specific options when she talked to Grant. She was booting up her computer when the doorbell rang.

Erin peeked through the side window, but she didn't see anyone on her porch. All she could see was a huge evergreen tree, but she was pretty sure it hadn't pressed the bell.

She pulled open the door for a closer look. The tree topped six feet and was at least that wide at the bottom. And behind it—laden down with shopping bags—was Corey.

Her heart started pounding; her knees trembled. She wanted to throw her arms around him, but there was no way she could get near him with that forest between them, so instead she only asked, "When did you get back?"

"Can I come in and put this stuff down?" he asked.

She automatically stepped back. Somehow he maneuvered around the massive tree and through the doorway.

"Late last night," he answered her original question.

"What the heck is all of that?" she asked, indicating the bags in his arms.

"Decorations."

"Why?"

He nodded in the direction of the evergreen propped up on her porch. "Because the tree will look much more festive when it's dressed up."

"Okay, maybe the question I should have asked is, why did you bring me a Christmas tree?"

"Because Erika said you didn't have one yet."

She watched as he wrestled the tree through the doorway. It occurred to her that maybe she should offer to assist him, but she would probably be more of a hindrance than a help, so she just stayed out of his way.

When the tree was inside, he stepped into the family room and turned in a slow circle, surveying the location. "Between the window and the fireplace?"

She pushed the wing chair aside to make room.

He came over to help her—then pulled her into his arms. He felt so good—so solid and strong—that she melted against him. And for a moment, she just held on, breathing in the warm, masculine scent of him and marveling at the fact that he was there. He was really there.

"I guess I won't have to make that trip to Texas after all," she said.

"You were planning to go to Texas?"

"Well, I wasn't going to wait for you forever."

"Forever?" His brows rose. "I've been gone a week."

She slid her arms around his neck and pulled his head down to hers, kissing him softly. "It was a really long week."

"Tell me about it, darlin'," he said.

She shook her head. "I don't want to talk."

He caught her hands as they began to tug at his clothes. "I promised myself that I wasn't going to pressure you. I wanted to give you the time you said you needed, and it hasn't been that much time, but—"

"It was enough," she interrupted.

Ever since he'd walked away from her in the parking lot of the grocery store a week earlier, Corey had lived with an uncomfortable pressure in his chest. With Erin's words, her kiss, and her touch, the painful tightness finally eased.

She touched her mouth to his again. He let her set the pace, content to just hold her, so happy to have her in his arms again. But when she deepened the kiss, when her soft breasts flattened against his chest and her hips pressed against his, he felt the pressure building again, but it was much lower this time.

As passions escalated, clothes fell away, until they were both naked and panting and wanting.

"I should take you upstairs," he said.

But she shook her head. "I want you here—like our first time."

So he tugged the blanket off the back of the sofa and spread it out on the floor.

Her skin was pale, creamy silk that trembled when his hands stroked over her. He wrapped her hair around his hand, and tugged her head back, feasted on the long, slim column of her throat, savored the frantic pounding of her pulse. His lips moved lower until he found her breast, and he laved and suckled until she was whimpering and shuddering beneath him.

She reached down between their bodies, seeking and finding the hard length of him. And when her fingers wrapped around him, he knew that he was as close to the edge as she was.

"I want you inside me," she told him.

"I want to be inside you," he admitted.

Later he might regret that he hadn't taken more time with

her, that there had been no quiet words or soft caresses. But in the moment, the need was too great. They would have a lifetime to take things slow—at least if he had anything to say about it—but for now, her hands were as rough and frantic as his, her kisses equally greedy and demanding.

"Now," she said breathlessly.

Now, his body echoed her plea, and he sank into the sweet, wet haven between her thighs.

Her muscles clamped down on him, and he groaned at the pleasure of being so tightly and intimately embraced. Then he began to move, and her head fell back as she closed her eyes and surrendered to the delicious friction of their mating.

She'd missed him.

Not just the intimacy of their lovemaking, but simply being with Corey. And as Erin lay cradled in the warm strength of his arms, her body still joined with his, she knew that she had finally found where she wanted to be.

"I've figured out what I want," she said.

"What's that?" he asked, skimming his fingers down her back.

"I want you in my life. It doesn't matter whether I'm in San Diego or Thunder Canyon or Texas, so long as I'm with you."

"Well, lucky for me, that fits right into my plans."

"Which part?"

"The part where we're together."

"I love you," she said softly.

He brushed her hair away from her face, kissed her gently. "It seems as if I've waited forever to hear you say those words."

"Forever? You were only gone a week," she said, echoing his earlier statement.

"It was a really long week," he told her.

She pressed closer to him. "Tell me about it."

He rolled away from her, laughing. "We can't spend all day on this floor."

"Why not?"

"Because we've got a tree to decorate, darlin'."

It took them a while, but they finally did get the tree set up. Erin tried to help Corey with the lights, but the needles were sharp and after she'd hissed several times in response to being poked, he sent her into the kitchen to make hot chocolate.

By the time she returned with two steaming cups, the tree was illuminated from top to bottom with hundreds of tiny colored lights.

"What do you think?"

She thought it was perfect, but she wasn't going to tell him that. Instead, she looked it over carefully, critically. "There are more lights at the top than the bottom."

"I was running out." He came over to stand beside her, eyeing the tree up and down, then shrugged. "Well, next year you're doing the lights, no matter how much you whine."

Next year.

She liked the sound of that but felt compelled to protest, "I did not whine."

"You did so whine." He looked at her out of the corner of his eye, grinned. "And now you're pouting."

"I don't pout," she denied.

Corey took one of the mugs from her hand and sipped. "I dated a woman once—well, I've dated a few women," he said, as if telling her something she didn't know, "but this was one I was dating around the holidays—and she had this stunning Christmas tree. Every branch was full and precisely shaped, the decorations were beautiful and color coordinated. It was the most perfect tree I'd ever seen."

She wasn't sure where he was going with the story, but she couldn't resist cocking her head slightly to the side, so that the slightly off-balance tree would appear straight. "You mean like this one?"

He shrugged. "It may not be perfect, but it's real. Which is what I realized was wrong with my relationship with Rebecca—she was always so precisely put together, so perfect and unreal. And the longer I stood there, looking at the tree that was so much like Rebecca, the more I realized that I didn't want perfection."

"I'm not perfect," she warned him.

"Neither am I," he admitted, "but I think we're perfect for one another."

She smiled. "I can live with that."

"Can you live with me?" he asked.

Her heart skipped. "Are you asking me to?"

"Actually, I don't want to live with you—I want to marry you."

She'd barely had a chance to get her head around the idea of living with him and he'd moved straight into talk about marriage. "For a man who talks slow, you sure move fast."

"The usual response is a 'yes' or a 'no,'" he told her. "Preferably 'yes.'"

"If those are my only options, I'll go with 'yes.'"

"Really?"

"Do you want me to change my answer?"

"No way." He pulled her close and brushed his lips against hers. "I've got you now, darlin', and I'm never letting you go."

She settled into his embrace, not wanting him to ever

let go, not wanting to be anywhere but precisely where she was.

So much had changed in her life since that last meeting with her great aunt Erma, and though there were times when she'd questioned her decision to come to Thunder Canyon, she wouldn't wish any of it away because it had brought her here—to this time and place and this man.

She wondered what Erma would have thought of Corey, if she'd had a chance to meet him. No doubt her aunt would have loved him.

"What are you smiling about?" Corey asked her.

"Just thinking about how very lucky I am."

He kissed her again. "I'm glad you came home to Thunder Canyon."

"Me, too." She'd come to town in search of a family, but she'd found so much more.

She snuggled deeper into his arms, secure in the knowledge that she was where she truly belonged.

* * * * *

A THUNDER CANYON CHRISTMAS

BY
RAEANNE THAYNE

All the characters in this book have no existence outside the imagination of
the author, and have no relation whatsoever to anyone bearing the same name
or names. They are not even distantly inspired by any individual known or
unknown to the author, and all the incidents are pure invention.

First published in Great Britain 2011
by Mills & Boon, an imprint of Harlequin (UK) Limited,
Eton House, 18-24 Paradise Road, Richmond, Surrey TW9 1SR

© Harlequin books S.A. 2010

Special thanks and acknowledgement to RaeAnne Thayne for her
contribution to MONTANA MAVERICKS: THUNDER CANYON
COWBOYS.

ISBN: 978 0 263 88925 3

23-1111

Harlequin (UK) policy is to use papers that are natural, renewable and
recyclable products and made from wood grown in sustainable forests. The
logging and manufacturing processes conform to the legal environmental
regulations of the country of origin.

Printed and bound in Spain
by Blackprint CPI, Barcelona

Dear Readers,

I love stories about secret crushes that unexpectedly turn into something more, especially if that shift happens when a woman is least expecting it…and when she most needs something solid to hold on to.

Elise Clifton has always had a bit of a thing for (mostly) reformed troublemaker Matt Cates—but right now she's not looking for love. The foundation of her world has been shaken after the discovery that her entire identity had been based on a mistake. Hurting and alone during the holidays, she desperately needs a strong shoulder and turns to her old friend Matt. Much to her shock, Matt wants much more from Elise.

I had a truly magical time writing their story, giving Elise and Matt the happy ending they deserve and coming to know all the Thunder Canyon Cowboys!

All the best of the season to you and your loved ones.

RaeAnne Thayne

RaeAnne Thayne finds inspiration in the beautiful northern Utah mountains, where she lives with her husband and three children. Her books have won numerous honors, including three RITA® Award nominations from Romance Writers of America and a Career Achievement Award from *RT Book Reviews* magazine. RaeAnne loves to hear from readers and can be reached through her website at www.raeannethayne. com.

To my sister Carrie Stevenson, military wife
extraordinaire, for courage and strength in the face
of tough times. You (and your hero of a husband)
inspire me!

Chapter One

Rock bottom was one thing. This had to be a new low, even for her.

Elise Clifton hunched onto the bar stool at The Hitching Post, painfully aware of her solitary status. She wasn't sure which made her more pathetic—showing up alone at Thunder Canyon's favorite watering hole or the fact that she would rather be anywhere else on earth, including here by herself, than home with her family right now.

She sipped at her drink, trying to avoid meeting anyone's gaze.

So much for the girls' night out she had been eagerly anticipating all week. She was supposed to have met her best friend Haley Anderson here for a night of margaritas and girl talk, accompanied by a popular local band.

Two out of three was still a winning average, she supposed.

The band was here, a trio of cute, edgy long-haired cowboys belting out crowd-pleasing rockabilly music. Margaritas, check. She was almost done with her second and heading fast toward number three.

But the girl talk was notably lacking…maybe because Haley had called her twenty minutes ago, her voice hoarse and full of apologies.

"I'm so sorry I didn't phone you earlier," Haley had rasped out. "I completely zonked and slept through my alarm. All day I've been hoping the cold medicine would finally kick in and I would be ready to rock and roll with you at The Hitching Post. No luck, though. It's only making me so sleepy I'm not consciously aware of how miserable I feel."

"Don't worry about it," Elise had answered, trying to keep any trace of her plummeting mood out of her voice. She couldn't really blame Haley for her bad luck in coming down with a lousy cold on a night when Elise was particularly desperate for any available diversion. She would be a poor friend to make a big deal about it, especially when Haley probably felt even worse than she sounded, which was pretty bad.

"We can reschedule as soon as you're feeling better," Elise had said. "The Hitching Post will still be here in a week or two."

"Deal," Haley croaked out. "If I ever get feeling better, anyway. Right now that doesn't seem likely."

"You will. Hang in there."

That was about the time Elise had gestured for her second margarita as her plans for the evening went up in smoke.

"Thanks for understanding, honey. First round is on me next time."

Elise sighed now as the band switched songs to one she hadn't heard before. She watched the blinking of Christmas lights that some enterprising soul had draped around the racy picture of Lily Divine adorned in strategically placed gauze that hung above the bar.

Even Lily Divine was in a holiday mood. Too bad Elise couldn't say the same.

Usually she enjoyed coming to The Hitching Post. Once rumored to be Thunder Canyon's house of ill repute, the place was now a warm, welcoming bar and grill. Locals loved it for its enduring nature. Unlike the rest of Thunder Canyon, The Hitching Post had remained unchanged through the ebbs and flows of the local economy.

With hardwood floors, the same weathered old bar and framed photos from the 1880s on the walls, the restaurant and bar likely hadn't changed much since the days when Lily Divine herself used to preside over the saloon she'd inherited from the original madam.

Elise had never been here by herself, though, and was quickly discovering how that created an entirely different dynamic. She felt more alone than ever as she sipped her drink and tried to avoid making eye contact. With a lone woman in a bar like The Hitching Post, it probably looked as if she was on the prowl, in search of some big, strong cowboy to help her while away a cold winter's night.

One such cowboy—a little heavy on the outdoorsy aftershave—sat three stools away. He'd been eyeing her for the past ten minutes and she was trying her best to pretend she didn't notice.

Maybe if she had stayed at Clifton's Pride, she might have been snuggled up right now in a fleece blanket watching some movie on the big-screen television at her family's ranch house instead of perched here at the bar like some kind of sad, pathetic loser.

She took a healthy swallow of her margarita and gestured to Carl, the longtime bartender, for another one as she swung her foot in time to the music.

Who was she kidding? If she had stayed at the ranch, she wouldn't be snuggled up with a movie and a bowl of popcorn. Not when her mother and brother had company—hence her escape to The Hitching Post, so she wouldn't have to smile and nod and make nice with Erin Castro. Right this moment Erin was having dinner with her miraculous, newfound family—Elise's own mother, Helen, her brother Grant and his pregnant wife, Stephanie Julen Clifton.

Escaping the family gathering had probably been cowardly. Rude, even. Helen and John Clifton had raised her to be much more polite than that. But the truth was, she wasn't sure she was capable of spending a couple of hours making polite conversation just now, even though she liked Erin.

She couldn't blame this twisted tangle on the other woman. It wasn't Erin's fault that a nurse's error twenty-six years ago during an unusually hectic night at Thunder Canyon General Hospital and a string of mistakes had resulted in two baby girls—born on the same night to mothers sharing a room—being inadvertently switched.

Erin might have set into motion the chain of events that had led to the discovery of the hospital mistake—and the shocking truth that Elise's birth parents were a couple she had never even met until a few weeks ago—but she had only been trying to look into a mysterious claim by a relative that the truth of her birth rested somewhere in Thunder Canyon. She had come here several months ago to investigate why she looked nothing like her siblings and had finally discovered that she was in reality the child of Helen and the late John Clifton, while Elise—who had spent her lifetime thinking she knew exactly who she was and her place in the world—had been stunned to learn she was the biological child of Betty and Jack Castro.

Elise understood the other woman hadn't set out to drop an atomic bomb in her life, only to find answers. But every time Elise saw how happy her mother and Grant were now that they had found out the truth about the events of twenty-six years ago—and in effect gained another daughter and sister—Elise felt more and more like she didn't belong.

She took another healthy swallow of her drink, welcoming the warm, easy well-being that helped push away that sense of always being on the outside, looking in.

The funny thing was, she couldn't really blame Erin

for that, either. She always felt like an outsider whenever she came to town because she *was* an outsider. Oh, she had lived in Thunder Canyon through elementary and middle school. She had loved it here, had thought she would stay forever—until the horrible events of that day more than a decade ago when her father and a neighboring rancher were murdered by cattle rustlers.

She couldn't say she was exactly a stranger in town. She and her mother came back occasionally to visit family and friends. Scattered throughout the bar and grill were various people she recognized. Her family's ties here ran deep and true, especially since Grant and Stephanie had revitalized Clifton's Pride, in addition to her brother's work as general manager of the Thunder Canyon Resort.

Grant certainly belonged here. Her mother, too, even though Helen had escaped the bad memories after her husband's violent death by moving with Elise to Billings when Elise was thirteen.

Elise didn't feel the same sense of connection. She had come back temporarily with her mother for the holidays while their family absorbed the shocking developments of the last month. But she was beginning to think she might have been better off booking a month-long cruise somewhere warm and exotic and an ocean away from this Montana town and all the pain and memories it held.

The desire was reinforced when The Hitching Post door opened with a blast of wintry air. Like everybody else in the place, she instinctively looked up to see who it might be, but quickly turned back toward Lily Divine, her stomach suddenly as tangled as those wisps of material covering Lily's abundant charms.

Matt Cates.

She averted her face away from the door, mortified at the idea of him noticing her sitting here alone like some pathetic barfly.

He didn't seem to be on a date, which was odd. From the rumors she heard even after she moved away, Matt and his twin brother, Marlon, both enjoyed living up to their wild reputation.

Marlon was apparently reformed now that he was engaged to Haley. She didn't know about Matt, though.

Out of the corner of her gaze, she spotted him heading over to a booth in the corner where several other guys she vaguely recognized from school years ago had ordered pizza and a pitcher of beer.

Some of her tension eased. From his vantage point, he wouldn't have a direct line of sight to her. Maybe he wouldn't even notice her. Why would he? She had always been pretty invisible to him, other than as an annoying kid he always seemed to have to rescue.

She crossed the fingers of her left hand under the bar and reached for her third—or was it fourth?—margarita with her right.

"How'd I get so lucky to be sitting next to the prettiest girl in the place?"

Elise turned at the drawl, so close she could practically feel the hot breath puffing in her ear. She had been so busy hiding from Matt, she hadn't realized the cowboy had maneuvered his way to the bar stool next to her.

She definitely should slow down on the margaritas, since the ten gallons of Stetson cologne he must have used hadn't tipped her off to him.

"Oh. Hi." Her cheeks heated and she cursed her fair skin.

"I'm Jake. Jake Halloran."

She should just ignore him. She wasn't the sort to talk to strange men in a bar. But then, everything she knew about herself had been turned upside down in the last two weeks, so why not? It had to be marginally better than sitting here by herself.

"Hi, Jake. You from around here?"

"I'm working out at the Lazy D." His heavy-eyed gaze sharpened on her. "You sure you're old enough to be in here? You must have used a fake ID, right? Come on, you can tell me the truth."

"I—"

"Don't worry, darlin'. I won't say a word."

He smiled and mimicked turning a key at his lips. He was good-looking in a rough-edged sort of way, with tawny blond hair beneath his black Resistol and a thin, craggy, Viggo Mortenson kind of face.

She supposed she was just tipsy enough to be a little flattered at his obvious interest. Not that she had the greatest track record where men were concerned. She sighed a little. Her one and only serious relationship had been a total disaster. Kind of tough to see it any other way after the man she'd considered her first real boyfriend—and had surrendered her virginity to—introduced her to his lovely fiancée.

She'd dated on and off over the three years since

then, but most guys tended to see her as a buddy. Jake Halloran obviously didn't. Though she thought it was more than a little creepy that he would be willing to flirt with somebody he thought might be underage, she figured there was no harm in flirting back just a little.

"I appreciate that, Jake," she answered. "But I've known Carl, the bartender over there, since I took my first steps. He knows exactly how old I am and would be the first one to tan my hide if I were caught trying to pass a fake ID in The Hitching Post."

"Is that right? So how old are you?"

"Old enough," she answered pertly.

"Well, however old you are, you are about the prettiest thing I've seen in this whole town."

"Um, thanks." She forced a smile.

"How come I haven't seen you around before now?"

"I'm from out of town, here visiting family for the holidays." Or at least visiting the people she had always considered her family.

"What's your name?"

It was a simple question, really. Just about the most basic question a person could be asked. She still hesitated before answering, for a whole host of reasons.

"Elise. Elise Clifton."

The words came out almost defiantly. She *was* Elise Clifton. That's who she had been for twenty-six years, even if it turned out to be a lie.

She gestured to Carl for another margarita, even though she was usually a one-drink kind of gal.

"Well, Elise Clifton," Jake said. "This is goin' to

sound like a cheap line but what's a sweet-looking girl like you doing in a place like this all by herself?"

Now that was a very good question. She took a swallow of the new drink Carl delivered as the music shifted to a cover of a rocking Dwight Yoakam song. "Listening to the guys," she finally answered. "They're one of my favorite bands."

At just that moment, she spied Matt over Jake's shoulder. He stood at the other end of the bar, talking to a middle-aged man she didn't know.

He was so gosh-darned gorgeous, with that streaky brown hair and warm brown eyes and broad shoulders. She sighed. She'd always had more than a bit of a crush on Matt, ever since the day in first grade when he had taken down a big third-grade boy who had pushed her into a mud puddle.

Matt didn't see her as any sort of romantic interest. She knew that perfectly well. To him, she was small-for-her-age Elise Clifton, bookish and shy and clumsy, always in need of some silly rescue.

He turned in her direction and she quickly angled her body so she was hidden by the cowboy's big hat and his broad shoulders.

Jake's eyes widened with surprise at her maneuver, which also happened to put her closer to him, then she saw a gleam of appreciation spark there and he tilted his head even more closely.

"They are a mighty fine band," he agreed. "Makes you want to get up there and dance, doesn't it?"

"The bass player went to school with me," she said, trying her level best to act as if practically sitting in a stranger's lap was an everyday event. "He used to play tuba in the school band."

"Is that right? What did you play?"

"Clarinet," she answered. "I'm really good at blowing things."

He choked on his drink. It took her several beats of listening to him cough and splutter to figure out what she'd said and then she gasped. Her face flared—she wanted to sink through the floor. She was apparently a really cheap drunk. After three and a half margaritas, she excelled at unintentional double entendres.

"That's not what I meant," she exclaimed. "I really did play the clarinet. Oh!"

He laughed roughly, wiping his mouth with a napkin he'd grabbed off the bar. "I'd love to see you…play the clarinet."

Okay, she should really leave. Right now, before Jake Halloran got any ideas about checking out her embouchure.

Despite her discomfort, she laughed at her own joke but when she looked up, Lily Divine seemed to be undulating up there on the wall like a snake dancer. Elise blinked. Maybe she needed to switch to water for a while. Apparently the fourth margarita hadn't been her greatest idea.

"Hey, you wanna dance?" Jake suddenly asked. Either he was slurring his words or her ears weren't firing on all cylinders.

She considered his invitation, taking in the small dance floor that had been set up in front of the small stage where the band had now switched to a bluegrass version of Jingle Bells. Only a handful of couples were out there: an older man and woman doing a complicated Western swing like they were trying out for some television dancing show, another pair who weren't really even dancing, just bear-hugging like they were joined at the navel, and a couple about her age, dancing with a painful awkwardness she instantly pegged as a first date, even through her bleary brain.

Ordinarily she loved to dance. But since she had probably spent enough time in the Thunder Canyon spotlight the last few weeks, she decided she didn't need to be the center of attention by dancing out there in front of everyone. Everyone being primarily Matt Cates.

"I'm not much of a dancer," she lied. "Why don't we just talk? Get to know each other a little better?"

"Talking's nice." Jake grinned and put his hand on her knee. Through the material of her favorite skinny jeans, his hand felt uncomfortably hot. "Gettin' to know each other better is even nicer."

Drat Haley and her stupid rhinovirus.

She tried to subtly ease her knee away, wondering if she ought to ask Carl for a cup of coffee.

"Where are you from, Jake?" she asked a little desperately. "Originally, I mean."

"Over Butte way. My daddy had to sell off our little ranch a few years ago so I've been on my own since then. What about you?"

"Um, I live in Billings most of the time. I'm only in town for the holidays. I think I said that already."

"You did. And doesn't that work out just fine for me?"

She barely heard him. Out of the corner of her gaze,

she saw a woman in tight Wranglers and a chest-popping holiday sweater approach Matt's table and a moment later, he headed out to the dance floor with her. Elise refused to watch and shifted a little more so her would-be Romeo was blocking her from view.

He didn't seem to mind. "Hey, what do you say we get out of here? Take a little drive and see the Christmas lights?"

She might be tipsy, but she wasn't completely stupid. She wouldn't go with him, even if his breath *wasn't* strong enough to tarnish the frame on Lily's picture.

"I'd better not. I don't want to miss the music. That's the reason I'm here, after all."

Just her luck, at just that moment, the lead singer stepped up to the mike. "We're going to take fifteen, folks. Meantime you can keep dancing to the jukebox."

"What do you say? Want to at least walk outside and get some air?"

Air might be nice. Even cold air. The faster she worked the margaritas out of her system, the faster she could leave. Where she would go until the dinner party with Erin was over was a question she didn't want to consider yet.

Though she was leery about going anywhere with a man she had just met and didn't trust, how much trouble could she get into walking out into the snowy parking lot on a frigid Montana night? Anything had to be better than sitting here trying to avoid being seen.

"Sure. Let me grab my coat."

The coat and hat racks at The Hitching Post lined

the hallway on the way to the restrooms. She decided
to make a quick stop at the ladies' room first to check
her lipstick and maybe splash a little water on her face
to clear her head.

It helped a little, but not much. When she emerged
a few moments later, she found Jake lurking in the
hallway.

"I thought you might be having trouble finding your
coat," he murmured. For some reason, she thought that
was hilarious. As if she was so stupid she couldn't recognize her own coat, for heaven's sake.

"Nope. I just stopped to fix my lipstick."

"It looks real pretty."

"Um, thanks." Maybe going outside with him wasn't
such a great idea. Actually, she was beginning to think
walking through The Hitching Post doors tonight ranked
right up there with her worst decisions ever. Second only
to her ridiculous lapse in judgment in ever agreeing to
date that cheating louse Jeremy Kaiser in college.

Jake cornered her just to the edge of the row of coats.
"Bet that lipstick tastes as good as it looks," he said in
what he probably thought was a sexy growl. Instead, he
sounded vaguely like a cat whose tail just had a close
encounter with a sliding door.

He leaned in closer and she edged backward until
her hands scraped the dingy wood paneling.

He dipped his head but she managed to shift her face
away at the last minute. "Um, I think I changed my mind
about going outside. Too cold. Let's go dance."

"I reckon we can do a pretty good tango right here,"
he murmured.

He tried again and she planted her palms on the chambray of his Western-cut dress shirt. "No, I really want to go dance," she said and realized her voice sounded overloud in the still-empty hallway.

Where was everybody? Didn't anybody in the whole place need to use the bathroom, for Pete's sake?

They struggled a little there in the hallway and she started to feel the first little pinch of fear when she realized she wasn't making a lick of headway against those cowboy-tough muscles.

"Come on, darlin'. A little kiss won't hurt nobody."

"I don't think so. I don't know you."

His face hardened and she wondered why she ever thought he looked a little like Viggo. More like Ichabod Crane. "You sure knew me well enough to be all snuggly over at the bar," he snarled.

"Hey," she exclaimed when his hand slid behind her to hold her in place. She pushed at the pearl buttons on his shirt. "Let go."

"Come on. Just a kiss. That's all."

"No!" She wriggled and squirmed but was faced with the grim realization that her 110-pound, five-foot-four frame was no match for somebody who wrangled tons of Angus cattle for a living. "Let me go!"

"Looks to me like the lady's not interested, Halloran."

The familiar steely voice managed to pierce both her sudden attack of nerves and her muzzy head.

She swallowed a curse. Matt. Her miserable night just needed this. Her face blazed and she knew she must be more red than a shiny glass Christmas ornament. Of every single person out in the crowded bar, why did he have to be the next one who happened into the hallway to come to her rescue?

Chapter Two

Matt stood a few feet away from them in the otherwise empty hallway, an almost bored look on his rugged features.

Jake Halloran had muscles, but he was no match for Matt, who helped run his family's construction business. He loomed over the other man, big and dark and dangerous.

"This ain't none of your concern, Cates," the wrangler currently trying to wrangle *her* snarled. "You don't know what you're talkin' about, so just walk on by."

"I don't think so." Matt stepped forward, looking tough and dangerous and heartstoppingly gorgeous. Elise slammed her eyes shut.

"Hey, Elise."

She opened them to find him watching her, a slight

smile playing around his mouth. She certainly wouldn't be wriggling and squirming like a lassoed calf if *that* mouth had been the one coming at her.

"Hi," she whispered. She was never drinking again. Never drinking and certainly never talking to strange men in bars again.

"Let's let the lady decide, why don't we?" Matt said calmly. "Elise, you want me to walk on by and leave the both of you to whatever was going on here that you didn't particularly appear to be enjoying a minute ago?"

What kind of choice was that? She didn't want him here, but she certainly didn't want to be the star attraction in octopus cage fighting anymore.

"No," she whispered, then cleared her throat when she heard that pitiful rasp. "No," she repeated more firmly. "Don't go."

"That sounded pretty clear-cut to me, Halloran. The lady isn't interested. Better luck next time."

Matt reached around the cowboy to grab her arm and extricate her from yet another humiliating situation. With a tangled mixture of relief and trepidation, she reached to take his hand.

She wasn't sure exactly what happened next. One moment she was stuck to the cowboy's side, the next Matt had her elbow firmly in his grip and was leading her away.

"Come on, Elise. Let's get you something to eat."

They took maybe three steps away from the situation when the wrangler grabbed her other arm and yanked her back. Pain seared from her shoulder to her fingers and Elise gave an instinctive cry.

Why in *Hades* hadn't she just put on her big-girl panties and stayed at the ranch to deal with Erin? Anything would be better than this. She did not want to be here right now, caught in a tug-of-war between two tough, dangerous men.

Something dark and hot flared in Matt's expression as he eyed the other man. "You're going to want to let go of her arm now," he said in a low voice, all the more ominous for its calmness.

"I saw her first," Jake muttered, just as if she were the last slice of apple pie in the bakery display case.

Elise managed to wrench her wrist out of his grasp and after a moment, Matt continued leading her back toward the bar, but apparently Jake didn't get the message.

"I saw her *first,*" he said more insistently and shoved his way in front of them to block their path.

A muscle flexed in Matt's firm jaw. He certainly didn't look like the kind of guy *she* would want to tangle with. "Come on, Halloran. Take it easy. The lady wasn't interested, but I'm sure there are plenty more back at the bar who will be."

"Want this one," he said, reaching for her arm again. This time Matt stopped him with a sharp block from his own arm. In the tussle for her appendage, Matt shoved the wrangler away. Halloran stumbled back, but came up swinging with a powerful right hook that connected hard with Matt's eye.

Elise gasped and jerked away from both men in time to evade Matt's defensive punch in return.

And that was it. Halloran leaped on him, yelling and swinging.

"Fight!" somebody yelled inside the bar, resulting in a mad rush of people into the narrow hallway. The only thing patrons of The Hitching Post liked better than a good band was a rousing brawl.

Matt's buddies at his booth joined in to pull the wrangler off. As soon as he was clear, he grabbed Elise and pushed out toward the nearest booth and out of harm's way, but apparently the cowboy had friends at The Hitching Post, too, and soon it was a free-for-all that spilled from the restroom hallway into the main room of the bar.

Everybody seemed to be having a grand old time until Carl took matters into his own hands.

"Knock it off, you idiots," the bartender yelled out, working the pump action of an old Remington shotgun, just like he was out of some cheesy old Western like the kind her dad used to love to watch.

Another voice joined in. "What the hell is going on here? Who started this?"

About a dozen hands pointed toward Matt and Jake, roughly equally divided between the two, as Elise recognized Joe Morales, a Thunder Canyon sheriff's deputy, who didn't look happy to have his dinner interrupted when he was obviously off duty.

"Cates. Should have known you'd be involved," he grumbled, his brushy salt-and-pepper mustache quivering. "What the hell happened?"

Since he seemed to be focusing on the two of them, the rest of the crowd seemed happy to slip away from any scrutiny and return to their drinks and their food. Elise really wanted to join them all and started easing away, but Matt pinned her into place beside him with a glare, as if this was all *her* fault.

"Sumbitch stole my girl." A thin trail of blood spilled out of the corner of Jake Halloran's mouth and he wiped at it with a napkin.

The deputy frowned at Elise. "You his girl?"

She shook her head, grateful she was still sitting down in the booth when the room spun a little. "I just met him tonight."

"You're Elise Clifton, aren't you? Grant's sister?"

Wouldn't her brother just love to hear about this little escapade? She couldn't wait to try explaining to Grant why she had let herself get cornered in an empty hallway by a drunk cowboy. "Yes."

"Well, Ms. Clifton, the guy seems to think there was more to it than a little chatting at the bar."

"He's wrong," she said, then was appalled at the note of belligerence in her voice. Must be the margaritas. She normally was not a belligerent person. Just another reason she needed to swear off drinking for a long time.

"We were only talking, Deputy Morales," she went on in what she hoped was a much more cooperative tone of voice. "I met him maybe half an hour ago. We talked about walking outside for some fresh air while the band was taking a break. I came back here to get my coat and he just…kissed me."

She drew in a shaky breath, more mortified than she

ever remembered feeling in her life. Even more embarrassed than the time she had been bucked off by
her horse in the junior rodeo for Thunder Canyon Days
when she was eleven and Matt had been the first one to
her side.

"I tried to tell him I wasn't interested but he didn't
listen," she said. "Then Matt came into the hallway and
saw I was having a tough time convincing him to stop,
so he stepped in to help me and Jake hit him."

"How much have you had to drink, Ms. Clifton?"

She looked down at the speckled Formica tabletop
then back up, drawing a breath and hoping she sounded
more coherent than she felt. "Not so much that I don't
know how to be perfectly clear when I'm saying no to
a man, sir."

"That what happened?" he asked Halloran. "Did she
say no?"

"I heard her say no, Joe," Matt said. "Loud and
clear."

"I don't believe I asked you," the deputy growled.
Elise suddenly remembered he had a younger sister who
had once carried a very public torch for Matt back in
Matt's younger, wilder days when bar fights probably
weren't an uncommon occurrence.

"Did the girl say no?" he asked Jake again.

"Well, yeah. But you know how women can be."

The deputy gave him a long, disgusted look, then
turned back to Elise. "Do you want to press charges for
assault?"

She gave him a horrified look. "No. Heavens no! It
was just a misunderstanding." Yes, the man had been

wrong to paw her, especially when she'd made it clear she didn't want him to. But she had been wrong to flirt with him back at the bar, to use him only so she could hide from Matt.

"What about you, Cates? You want to press charges?"

Matt shook his dark head. "I know how things can get out of hand in the heat of the moment."

"Fine. All of you get out of here, then, so I can go back to my wife and my steak. Can you make sure she makes it back to Clifton's Pride okay?" he asked Matt.

Matt gave her a look she couldn't decipher, then nodded.

The moment the deputy ushered Jake over to the other Lazy D cowboys who had come to his rescue, Elise rushed back to the hallway, grabbed her red peacoat off the rack and twisted her scarf around her neck. She had to escape. What a nightmare. As if she needed more gossip about her flying through town.

She heard someone call her name but she didn't stop, only pushed through the front door out into the cold night.

The streets of Thunder Canyon glittered with brightly colored Christmas lights. They blinked at her from storefronts and the few houses she could see from here. A light snow drifted down, the flakes plump and soft. Away from the front door, she lifted her face for a moment to feel their light, wet kisses on her face.

She found a strange sort of comfort at the realization that she'd been seeing the same holiday decorations in Thunder Canyon since she was a girl. Her entire life may have changed in the last few weeks, but some things remained constant.

"You're not thinking about driving in your condition, are you?"

She opened her eyes, somehow not very surprised to find Matt standing a few feet away, looking big and dark and dangerous in a shearling-lined ranch coat. His eye was beginning to swell and color up and he had a thin cut on his cheek she very much feared would leave a scar.

"Thinking about it," she admitted.

"Sorry, El, but I can't let you do that. You heard what the deputy said. I need to take you home."

"And how are you going to stop me?" she asked, with more of that unexpected belligerence.

He smiled suddenly and she blinked at the brilliance of it in the dark night. That must be why she was taken completely off guard when he reached for her purse. After a moment of fishing through the contents, he pulled her keys out, dangled them out for a moment, and then pocketed them neatly in his coat.

"I can give you a ride back to the ranch and find somebody later to take your car home. Face it, Elise, you're in no shape to drive."

She couldn't go back to Clifton's Pride yet. Just the thought of walking inside the ranch house in her condition made her queasy.

She didn't need to see that same wary look in everyone's eyes she'd been dealing with since before Thanksgiving, as if she were somebody who had been given some kind of terminal diagnosis or something. Her mother hugged her at the oddest moments and Grant and his wife, Stephanie, went out of their way to include her in conversations.

She especially didn't want to show up tipsy when Erin was there in all her perfection, the daughter they *should* have had.

"I don't want to go home yet," she whispered, grimly aware the words sounded even more pathetic spoken aloud.

"No?"

"Not yet. I'll only be in the way. My...my mother and Grant have...well...guests for dinner."

He gave her another of those long, considering looks and she could feel herself flush, certain he could guess what—or rather whom—she meant.

"Want to go back inside?"

She shook her head. "I don't think I need to see the inside of The Hitching Post for a while."

Or ever again.

"Fair enough. Do you want to go grab a bite to eat somewhere? I'm sure we can find somewhere still open."

"Not really."

He gave a half laugh. "Well, I'm running out of options. You'll freeze to death if you sit out here in the parking lot for another hour or two until your head clears."

"I know."

After another pause, he sighed. "My place is just a block or two away. If you want to, I can get cleaned up and fix you something to eat and we can hang there until you think the coast is clear back at Clifton's Pride."

She hated that he had to come to her rescue, just like when they were kids. She had been a clumsy kid and it seemed like every time she fell, he had been right there to help her back up, brush off the dirt, gather her books, whatever she needed.

From the time he had fought two schoolyard bullies bigger than he was—and won—he had been stepping in to protect her from the world.

She was twenty-six years old. Surely it was high time she found the gumption to fight her own battles. Still, the idea of somebody else taking care of her for a few minutes sounded heavenly.

"Don't you ever get tired of rescuing me?" she asked.

Instead of answering, he laughed and tucked a strand of hair behind her ear. His hand was warm in the cold December air and she wanted to lean into him, close her eyes and stay there forever.

"Come on. Let's get you out of the snow."

Chapter Three

Though Matt only lived a few blocks from The Hitching Post, Elise dozed off beside him in his pickup truck before he reached his house—a small, run-down cottage on Cedar Street he had purchased a few months back to rehab in his spare time away from his work at Cates Construction.

Before the first snow a few months earlier, he'd rushed to put new shingles on and managed a new coat of white paint and green shutters. From the outside, the place looked fresh and tidy.

Inside was an entirely different story.

He thought about driving around for a while to let her sleep off the alcohol in her system, but he had a feeling she probably needed food more than sleep. Back in the day when he used to enjoy the wild weekend here or there, that's what always helped him most.

He pulled into his driveway and put his truck in gear, though he left his engine running to keep the heater blowing. He shifted his gaze to her and shook his head.

Elise Clifton.

She was still as sweet and pretty as she had always been, blonde and petite, with delicate features, a slim little nose and her cupid's bow of a mouth.

She always looked a year or two younger than the rest of their grade. Now she probably considered that a good thing, but when they were kids, he knew she had hated being mistaken for a younger kid.

Maybe that was why she always stirred up all his protective instincts. She was right, it seemed like he was always coming to her rescue. He hadn't minded. Not one damn bit. He only had brothers—a twin and two older ones—and didn't know much about dealing with girls back when he was a kid. But his father had taught them all that a guy was supposed to watch out for those who were smaller than him.

Elise certainly fit the bill—then, and now. She looked small and fragile with her blond hair fanned out on the pickup's upholstery and her bottom lip snagged between her teeth.

Elise had always seemed a little more in need of rescuing than others. Even before the terrible events when she was thirteen, something about her seemed to stir up all his protective impulses.

Her long lashes fluttered now as she blinked her eyes

open. For a brief instant, she smiled at him, her eyes the soft, breathtaking blue of the Montana sky on an early summer morning. As he gazed at her, he felt as if he'd just taken a hit to the gut from a three-hundred-pound linebacker.

He drew in a breath, trying to shake off the unexpected sensation. This was Elise, he reminded himself. Little Elise Clifton, whose junior-rodeo, barrel-racing belt buckle had nearly been bigger than she was.

Except she wasn't little. She hadn't been in a long, long time. Though still petite, he couldn't help but notice she was soft and curvy in all the right places.

"Feeling better?" he spoke mostly to distract himself.

Her brow furrowed a little, as if she were trying to figure that out herself. After a moment, she nodded a little shyly, a trace of color on her cheeks. "Actually, I think I am. At least there's only one of you."

"Until Marlon shows up," he joked about his identical twin, and was rewarded with her sweet-sounding laugh.

"I hope he's with Haley right now, tucking her in and bringing her tissues and chicken soup. She and I were supposed to have a girls' night out to see the band at The Hitching Post together tonight but she bailed on me at the last minute."

She sat up and stretched a little and he tried not to notice how her sweater beneath her unbuttoned coat hugged those soft curves. "Since I was already there and…well, didn't really want to go home yet, I decided to stay and listen to the band."

Ah. That explained why she'd been sitting by herself at the bar. He had spied her the moment he walked in and had been keeping an eye on the cowboy she'd been sitting beside. At first, he thought maybe they'd been on a date. The little spark of inappropriate jealousy had come out of nowhere, taking him completely by surprise.

When she walked down the hall toward the ladies' room, he had watched the cowboy follow her. When neither of them emerged after a moment, he'd gone looking for her. And just in time.

"Poor Haley," he said now. "Being sick bites anytime, but especially at Christmas. Still, I'm sure Marlon loves the chance to baby her. He's crazy about her."

"He'd better be," she said darkly. He hid a smile at the belligerent tone he'd noticed her adopting earlier. He didn't know how much she'd had to drink. With her small frame, it probably wasn't much, but he definitely recognized the signs of somebody on the tipsy side.

"Let's get you inside and find you something to eat."

"I'm really not hungry."

"Humor me, okay?"

After a moment, she shrugged and reached for the passenger-side door handle. He climbed out of the truck and hurried around the front of the pickup. His work truck was high off the ground so he reached inside and grabbed her hand to help her to the ground.

Her fingers felt small and cool inside his and when her high-heeled boots hit the ground, she wobbled a little. He reached out to steady her and found he was strangely reluctant to release her.

He held her, gazing into those blue eyes far longer than he should have while the fat snowflakes drifted down to settle in her hair and cling to her cheeks.

He hadn't seen her much over the years since she and her mother moved away from Thunder Canyon. Last time was probably over the summer when she'd come for a visit and he had ended up pulling over to help her change a flat tire.

Every time he saw her, he was struck again how lovely she was.

He had missed her, he suddenly realized. More than he ever could have imagined.

She shivered suddenly and the delicate motion jolted him back to his senses. "Let's get you inside."

"Thanks," she murmured.

He gripped her arm so she didn't slip on the skiff of snow covering his sidewalk as he led the way up the porch. He twisted the key in the lock and was greeted by one well-mannered bark that made him smile.

As soon as he opened the door, a brown shape snuffled excitedly and headed toward them. Elise took a quick, instinctive step backward on the porch, wobbling a little again on her dressy boots.

He reached for her arm again, feeling the heat of her beneath the red wool coat she wore. "Sorry about that. I should have warned you. Tootsie, sit."

His chocolate Labrador immediately planted her haunches on the polished wood floor of the entry, her tail wagging like crazy.

Elise reached down to pet her head. "Tootsie?"

He winced. "When she was a puppy, she looked like a big, fat Tootsie Roll. My mom named her."

Tootsie waited patiently until he gave her the signal to come ahead, then she hurried to his side and nudged his leg for a little love.

"She's beautiful, Matt."

"The sweetest dog I've ever had, aren't you, baby?"

She snuffled in response and he obediently scratched her favorite spot, right behind her left ear.

He loved having a dog to keep him company. When the weather wasn't so cold, she rode with him to construction sites. After the cold weather set in, his favorite evenings were spent at home watching a basketball game with her curled up at his feet.

Used to be Marlon would join them but these days his twin had better ways to spend his time.

Matt supposed it was only natural that lately Tootsie's company didn't seem quite enough anymore, especially since it seemed like everybody he knew was pairing up.

"How long have you lived here?" Elise asked.

He shifted his attention from the dog to his house and winced again at its sorry shape. The place was a work in progress. He had stripped years worth of ugly wallpaper layers, down to the lath and plaster. He'd finished mudding the walls a few weeks earlier but had been so busy rushing his crew to finish Connor McFarlane's grand lodge in time for Christmas, he hadn't had time to paint.

At least the kitchen and bathroom were relatively

presentable. He had started with the kitchen, actually, installing hand-peeled cabinets, custom tile floors and gleaming new appliances.

He had also taken out the wall of a tiny bedroom to expand the bathroom into one big space and he was particularly satisfied with the triple heads in the tile shower and the deep soaking tub.

But he couldn't exactly entertain his unexpected guest in his bathroom. Maybe he should have spent a little more time working on the more public areas of the house.

"I've got lots of plans but I have to fit the work around the jobs I'm doing with my dad," he said.

She nodded. "That's right. I heard you were working for Cates Construction these days. Do you like it?"

He was never sure how to answer that question. Most of the time, he was only too aware of the subtext behind the question. *You really dropped out of law school to work construction? Couldn't hack it, huh?*

That hadn't been the truth at all. His grades had been fine after his first year of law school. Better than fine. Great, actually. He'd been in the top ten percent of his class and had fully intended going back for his second year—until he realized after he came home to Montana for the summer that he was much happier out at a work site with his dad, covered in the satisfying sweat of putting in a hard day's labor, than he'd ever been in a classroom.

"I do like it. There's always a new challenge and it's great to watch something go from blueprints to completion, like the McFarlane Lodge."

"Haley told me about that. It sounds huge."

"It is. More than 10,000 square feet. It's been a fun project but a little time consuming. That's why I only have bits and pieces of time to work on this place. This is the third house in town I've rehabbed on my own."

She cast her gaze around the room. "Um, it looks good."

He smiled at her obvious lie. "No, it doesn't. Everything's a mess out here. As soon as we wrap up the McFarlane Lodge, I'll have more time for the finish work here. But come on back to the kitchen and see what I've done there. I'd love a woman's perspective."

Surprise flashed in her eyes. "Mine?"

"You see any other women around?"

"Not right this very moment," she muttered. "I'm sure that's not typical for you."

He shouldn't be irritated by her words but he was. Yeah, he'd been wild in his younger days. Not as wild as Marlon, maybe, but he'd had his moments. How long and hard did a man have to work to shake off a wild reputation?

"Come on back," he said again and led the way through the compact cottage to the kitchen.

When she saw the room, the shocked admiration on her features more than made up for the dig about his reputation.

She did a full three-sixty, taking in the slim jeweled pendant lights over the work island, the stainless-steel, professional stove, the long row of paned windows over the dining area.

"Wow! You really did all this by yourself?"

"You sound surprised. Should I be insulted by that?"

She made a face. "I guess I just never realized you were such a…what's the word? I can't think. Artisan, I guess."

"Nothing so grand as that," he protested. "I'm just a construction worker."

She slicked a hand over the marble countertop and he was suddenly entranced by the sight of her long, slim fingers sliding along his work.

He cleared his throat. "How does pasta sound? I've got some lemon tarragon sauce in the fridge I can heat up while I throw a pot of water on to boil."

"You cook, too? I guess with a kitchen like this, you must."

"Not much," he was forced to admit. "The kitchen's for whoever eventually buys the place. I've got a few specialties and know enough so I don't starve. That's about it. My mom sent over the pasta sauce. She thinks I live on fast food and TV dinners."

"I don't want you to go to any work."

"How much effort does it take to boil a pot of water on the stove and push a few buttons on the microwave? Have a seat. If you'd rather go in and watch something on TV, the family room isn't in too bad of shape, as long as you don't mind a few exposed wires."

"I'll stay here. Could I have a drink of water?"

"I can make coffee. That would clear your head faster."

"Water is okay for now."

He pulled a tumbler out of the cabinet by the sink

and dispensed ice and cold, filtered water from the refrigerator. When he handed it to her, she took a seat at one of the stools around the work island. Tootsie, always happy for someone new to love, settled beside her and Elise smiled a little and reached down to pet her before the dog curled up on the kitchen floor.

"Maybe you ought to put something on that black eye, don't you think?"

How had he managed to block out the throbbing from both his eye and his cheek where Halloran had gotten off a cheap shot? She was a powerful distraction, apparently. "Right. Let me get the fight washed off me first and then I'll fix you something to eat."

"Do you need help?"

He thought of those fingers, cool and light on his skin, and felt his body stir with interest. This was Elise, he reminded himself. Not some bar babe looking for a good time.

"I think I can handle it," he finally answered. He wasn't sure he trusted himself around her right now. "Hang tight. I'll be back in a minute."

It took him about ten to wash away the blood, most of it belonging to the idiot who had mauled her, and to change his shirt. When he returned to the kitchen, some of the tension had eased from her features. She was leafing through a design book he'd left on the kitchen desk and she looked sweet and relaxed and comfortable.

As if she belonged there.

She looked up and he watched her gaze slide to the bandage he'd applied just under his colorful eye.

"Does it hurt?"

"I've had worse, believe me."

That didn't seem to ease her concern. "You could have been really hurt. He might have damaged your vision."

"He didn't. I'm fine."

She closed the book, her fine-boned features tight and unhappy. "I'm really sorry about…everything. I feel so stupid."

"Why? You didn't do anything wrong except maybe pass the time of day with a cowboy who'd had a few too many."

"I can't really blame him for getting the wrong idea," she admitted. "I might have…acted more interested in him than I really was. If you want the truth, I was using him to hide from you."

He raised his eyebrows. "Why would you need to hide from me?"

She suddenly looked as if she wished she'd never said anything. "I was embarrassed about being there by myself. It's not something I usually do."

"I'm glad you were there," he said as he headed to the refrigerator for the sauce. "Except for your little episode with the jerk, it's great to see you. So are you back in Thunder Canyon to stay?"

She sighed and sounded so forlorn that Tootsie must have sensed it. She nuzzled her leg. "I don't know. Everything's in…limbo. My mother wanted to come home for the holidays and begged me to come with her so I took a temporary leave from my job until the new year. After that, I don't know what I'll do."

He really hoped she would decide to stay. He liked

having her around. He started to say so but she spoke before he could get the words out.

"I guess you heard about my…about what happened twenty-six years ago."

"Who in town hasn't?"

Her sigh this time sounded even more forlorn and he cursed himself for his tactless response.

"Sorry. Was that the wrong thing to say?"

"I really hate having everyone gossiping about me. I hated it after my dad's murder and I hate it more now. Everything is such a mess."

He couldn't begin to imagine what she must be going through. "How are you holding up?"

"Not too great," she confessed softly.

He set down the box of pasta he'd just pulled from the cupboard and crossed to give her a reassuring squeeze on the shoulder.

Instead of comforting her, as he'd intended, his gesture made her big blue eyes brim with tears.

"My mom wants the family together for Christmas. Everyone, including Erin."

"And that's a problem?"

She sighed. "I feel like I don't even belong at Clifton's Pride anymore."

He stared. "You most certainly *do* belong at Clifton's Pride! It's your home and the Cliftons are your family. Why would you feel otherwise, even for a moment?"

"I'm not a Clifton. Not really. If not for a quirk of fate and a moment's mistake by a nurse, I never would have known any one of them. I'm not a Clifton. But I'm not really a Castro, either. I barely know those people. I don't know who I am."

A tear brimming in her eyes dripped over and slid down the side of her nose and his heart broke.

He grabbed a tissue box and couldn't resist the compulsion to pull her into his arms. She felt small and feminine and he wanted to hold tight and take on all her demons for her.

"You're the same person you've always been. You're Elise Clifton, daughter of John and Helen and sister to Grant. Blood or not, that's who you are."

"I wish it were that easy."

"Why isn't it? They're your family."

She frowned. "They're not my parents! I don't belong in Thunder Canyon at all!"

A dozen arguments swarmed through his head—he hadn't been in law school without reason. But then, she wasn't a hostile witness on the stand, either.

"So blood and genetics is everything? According to your reasoning, anybody who's been adopted into a family should always feel like an outsider."

"I wasn't adopted!" she exclaimed. "I was switched for their real daughter. For the child Helen and John should have had. They didn't choose to be stuck with me. My whole life is a mistake! *I'm* a mistake."

"Do you really think that's what your mother and Grant think?"

"I don't know. They're so happy about Erin," she whispered.

Her tears started flowing in earnest now and she added a few sobs in there to really twist the knife.

Nice, Cates, he thought. *Take a vulnerable woman who has already had a rough night and reduce her to tears.* He had definitely lost his touch.

"Hey. Easy now. Come on." He pulled her back into his arms.

"I'm sorry. I'm so sorry." She sniffled.

"For what? Being human? Anybody would be upset."

"Oh, I'm making a big mess of your shirt and you just changed it for a clean one," she wailed.

He tightened his arms. "No worries. I've got a good washing machine."

His words only seemed to set her off again and Matt held her, hating this helpless feeling. With no sisters and a mother who rarely lost her cool in front of her boys, his experience with crying women was extremely limited. This was a novel experience, trying to offer comfort instead of instinctively seeking any handy escape route.

She clutched his waist as if he was the only thing keeping her from floating away on her wild emotions, her cheek pressed against his chest. Her hair smelled like fresh raspberries just plucked from his mama's garden behind their house and he inhaled, doing his best to ignore how soft and curvy she felt in his arms and feeling powerless to do anything but hold her.

He moved into his half-finished family room where he could sit down on the sofa, pulling her with him.

After a few moments, her intense sobs quieted. She took a few slow, hitching breaths and he could feel the shudders against him subside.

With vast relief, he felt her regain control until some

time later when she eased slightly away from him, though she didn't seem any more eager to leave the shelter of his arms than he was to let her go.

"This is the single most embarrassing night of my life," she finally said, her cheeks flaring with color. "Apparently, I'm a maudlin drunk. Who knew?"

He laughed a little roughly, still unnerved by the intensity of his attraction to her, which somehow far outweighed all those protective impulses.

Elise always had the ability to make him laugh, he remembered. She had a funny, quirky sense of humor and he remembered back in school feeling privileged to be among the few she revealed it to.

"I haven't cried once since…well, since Erin told us all what she suspected."

"Then you are probably long overdue, aren't you?"

She said nothing for a long moment and then she smiled at him and he felt like he was seeing his first taste of springtime after weeks of fog and gloom.

Even with her reddened eyes and tear-stained cheeks, she was beautiful. He gazed at her upturned face a long moment, then with a strange sense of destiny or fate or inevitability—he wasn't sure—he leaned down and pressed his mouth to that smile.

Chapter Four

Elise froze at the first warm touch of his mouth. He tasted delicious, like fresh-baked cinnamon cookies, and his arms around her seemed the safest place in the universe.

She couldn't quite believe this was happening and wondered for a moment if she was hallucinating. No, she hadn't had quite *that* much to drink. She wasn't sure about a lot of things but she knew that, at least.

Matt Cates, who had never looked twice at her all these years, really was kissing her, holding her, like he couldn't get enough.

Elise would have laughed at the sheer, unexpected wonder of it if she wasn't so preoccupied with the sexy things his mouth was doing to hers.

This all seemed so surreal. She wasn't exactly a

femme fatale. Most guys tended to think of her like the girl next door, somebody sweet and fairly innocent. Blame it on her blond hair or the blue eyes or her small stature. She didn't know exactly what, she only knew that she wasn't the kind of girl men considered for a quick fling.

Now, twice in one night in the space of only an hour or so, she found herself in a man's arms. Not that the two things were in any way comparable. Kissing Matt Cates was a whole different experience than trying to fight off Jake Halloran in the hallway outside the ladies' room at The Hitching Post.

Then, she had been doing everything she could to avoid the man and wriggle away from him. With Matt, she had absolutely no desire to escape. She wanted to stay right here forever, where she was warm and safe.

She should be curling up behind the sofa with a blanket over her head. Even as he kissed her, she couldn't shake her lingering embarrassment when she remembered her emotional breakdown.

Definitely must have been the margaritas. Why else would she spill everything to Matt when she hadn't talked to another soul about her emotional turmoil over learning of the hospital mistake? She hadn't told her mother or Grant or even Stephanie, Grant's wife, who along with Haley Anderson had been her closest friend when they were kids.

Matt only had to show her a little sympathy in those brown eyes and she started blubbering all over him.

Her stomach muscles quivered as he shifted his mouth over hers. What was the matter with her? After all these years of wondering what it might be like to kiss him, she finally had her chance and she was wasting the moment being embarrassed about the events leading up to this. Was she completely insane?

She leaned into that hard, solid chest and opened her mouth for his kiss. He made a sexy little sound in his throat that rippled down her spine as if he'd run his thumb from the base of her neck to her tailbone.

He wrapped his arms more tightly around her and slid his tongue inside her mouth and she forgot everything else but Matt.

She slid her hands in his hair. Funny, she might have expected his thick dark hair to be short, coarse, but it felt silky and decadent against her skin.

Time seemed to shift and slide and she had no idea how long they stayed there on his sofa, wrapped together. She only knew she didn't want him to stop. Matt suddenly felt like the only solid, secure thing she had to hang on to since Erin Castro shook the foundations of her world.

His hand burned through the cotton of her sweater and she ached for closer contact. As if in answer to some unspoken request, his hand slid beneath her sweater and glided to the small of her back. She shivered at the heat of him and murmured his name.

Well, that was a mistake, she thought as he froze. Next time she would keep her lovesick murmurings to herself.

He wrenched his mouth away and she felt even more like an idiot. His breathing was ragged and he looked like he'd just been kicked off a prize bull.

He stared at her for a long moment, then raked a hand through his hair. He didn't move, though, and she was still sprawled against him.

"I'm sorry, Elise. That was the last thing you needed, another stupid cowboy pawing you."

"Was it?" she murmured.

"Yes! You're upset and vulnerable and I completely took advantage of that."

"No, you didn't." She was exhausted suddenly, her muscles loose and fluid, as if his kiss had been the only thing keeping her upright. "I'm glad you kissed me. You're a great kisser. All the girls used to say so. I'm glad I finally had the chance to find out. You really were. Great, I mean."

He gave her a skeptical look but she thought she saw a hint of color over his cheekbones. She was too tired to know for sure, though. She just wanted to close her eyes and ease into sleep like she was sliding into sun-warmed water.

"I never did rustle up something for you to eat."

She opened one eye. "I'm not hungry. Do you mind if we stay here like this for a minute?"

He looked startled for only a moment, then shook his head. "What man with a brain in his head would mind having a chance to hold a pretty girl for a while longer?"

She smiled, though the last remaining rational part of her brain was sending out a whole host of warning signals. Matthew Cates was exactly the sort of man who could make a woman completely lose her head.

She was definitely going to have to take care around him.

The thought slid through her mind but she pushed it away. She wouldn't worry about a little detail like that. Not right now. For now, she only wanted to stay right here, savoring the warmth of his arms around her and the steady rhythm of his breathing, and indulging in this rare, precious moment of peace.

It was her last thought for some time.

This should have been the perfect way to spend a December Friday night. The lights on his Christmas tree glistened brightly and through the window, he could see those plump snowflakes still drifting down.

When Elise had first fallen asleep, he had taken a chance and reached with his free hand for the remote. Somehow he had managed to turn the TV on low without waking her and had turned to one of the digital music stations offered by his satellite provider, this one playing soft, jazzy holiday music.

Matt shifted on the sofa. His legs tingled and he was pretty sure he'd lost all feeling in one arm.

He didn't mind any of that. What worried him was this unaccustomed tenderness coiling through him as he held the slight woman in his arms.

He had always cared about Elise and considered her a friend. Maybe he'd been more protective of her than most of his friends over the years, in part because she'd been small for her age and had appeared delicate, even if she really wasn't, and in part, of course, because of the terrible event in her family when she was still a girl—her father's brutal murder.

A desire to watch out for her was one thing. This desire for *her*—to taste her and touch her and explore every inch of that delectable skin—stunned him to the core.

He had never been so aroused by a simple kiss. If he hadn't suddenly remembered that she'd had a little too much to drink, he wasn't sure just how far he might have let their kiss progress.

Just remembering her sweet response—those breathy sighs, the trembling of her hands in his hair—sent a shaft of heat through him now.

He tightened his arms around her. What a hell of a mess. He didn't want to hurt a sweet girl like Elise, but his track record at relationships wasn't the greatest. He usually leaned toward women who preferred to keep things casual and that was exactly what he told himself he wanted. Fun, easy, no strings.

He thought briefly of Christine. She was the perfect example. The last thing she wanted from him was a serious commitment. The only reason they started seeing each other in the first place was because neither of them was romantically interested in the other. She wanted to avoid a persistent ex-boyfriend and he wanted to escape his mother's transparent matchmaking attempts.

He had enjoyed taking Christine around town for the last couple of months and they had a good time together, but the few experimental kisses they'd shared just to see if things might progress in some sort of natural order had left both of them shaking their heads and wondering why they just didn't spark the magic in each other.

Christine was far more his usual type than Elise. His few long-term girlfriends had each been dark-haired and tall like her, funny and social.

Elise couldn't be more different from what he had always considered his usual taste, yet he'd never known a kiss as explosive and stirring as theirs, or this soft, easy tenderness flowing through him, just from holding a woman in his arms.

He shifted on the sofa and finally drew his legs up along the length of it, sliding as far as he could to the side to make room for both of them. She murmured something in her sleep then nestled against him, her arm around his waist.

Her straight blond hair reflected the Christmas lights and he watched them for a moment, then closed his eyes. He would let her sleep for a little while until the effects of the alcohol she'd consumed were out of her system and then he would take her back to Clifton's Pride.

He was only thinking of her, he told himself. Not about how terrifyingly perfect she felt in his arms.

So much for good intentions.

When Matt awoke, Elise was still asleep snugged up against him, her arm across his chest, her hair brushing his chin and one of her legs entwined with his.

As he slid back to consciousness, he became aware of her first, small and soft against him. Not a bad way to wake up, he thought, with the sweet scent of raspberries surrounding him and a beautiful woman in his arms—and then he heard a little well-mannered whine and noticed Tootsie stretched out in front of the door, waiting to go out, something she usually only did first thing in the morning.

He shifted his gaze to the window. That couldn't be right, could it? It looked as if the first pink rays of dawn were sneaking through the slats of his window blind. Had they really slept here all night?

He was going to have a crick in his neck all day from sleeping like this and he could only hope he would regain feeling in his arm one day. Working construction might be difficult if he didn't have the use of his right arm.

Tootsie whined again and Elise made a soft little sound in her sleep and he decided all his discomforts didn't matter—a small price to pay for the pleasure of holding her.

As he watched, her eyelashes fluttered against her skin and a moment later her eyes opened. She gazed at him for a long moment and her brow furrowed.

"Matt? What are you…"

The words were barely out before she groaned. "Ow," she muttered and squeezed her temples.

He suddenly remembered her excess the night before and winced in sympathy.

"Headache?"

She sat up and opened one eye to glare balefully at him. Her hair stuck up a bit on one side and her cheek was creased with a funny little pattern from the material of his sweater but he still thought she was just about the prettiest thing he'd ever seen.

"Headache," she groaned. "That's one word for it. If you like understatements. I don't suppose you've got coffee?"

"Sorry. I've been a little preoccupied all night."

She looked at him and then at the couch and color rose up her cheeks in a rosy tide. "I fell asleep."

"We both did. I hadn't planned a sleepover. Sorry about that."

She looked at the pale light outside the window with something akin to panic. "What time is it?"

He glanced at the clock above the gas fireplace. "Early. Looks like it's not quite six. I need to put the dog out."

"Oh. Of course."

He winced a little as he stood on numb legs but still managed to make it to the door without falling over. A few more inches had fallen in the night, but not enough to be more than an annoyance. Tootsie bounded out when he opened the door and he turned back to find Elise looking distressed.

"I've gone all night. Mom must be frantic. And Grant is going to kill me."

He had a feeling if Grant had *anyone* on his hit list, Matt's name would be right there at the top after last night.

"You're twenty-six years old, Elise. Surely you've been out all night before."

"Of course I have." She spoke the words with more than a trace of defiance. "But not when I'm staying with my mother and my brother. Or at least not without letting them know I'll be late. Maybe they'll just think I stayed over at Haley's."

He sighed. "When I let Tootsie back in, I'll run a comb through my hair and then I'll take you back to Clifton's Pride. We'll just explain what happened. I took you home to feed you after we left The Hitching Post and we both fell asleep."

"I'm sure that will go over just great."

"It's the truth. Or most of it, anyway."

She pressed her fingers at her temples again. "It's the 'or most of it' I think we might have a problem explaining."

"I wouldn't worry about it, El. Your brother knows me well enough to know I'm not the kind of guy to take advantage of a vulnerable woman."

No matter how much he might have wanted to. Okay, as much as he *still* wanted to.

Much to her relief, Matt was right. Grant hadn't kicked up any kind of fuss about her rolling in just after sunrise from a night on the town.

Her brother had just been leaving the house when they pulled up. He didn't say so but Elise suspected he'd been on his way to look for her since he generally didn't go to work at the resort this early in the morning.

She had feared some sort of scene. Grant could have a temper and was the only male she knew more overprotective than Matt. But Grant—the closest thing she had to a father figure since John Clifton's murder a dozen years ago—had given Matt one long, searching look, then apparently accepted the story.

"I really appreciate you keeping her safe," Grant said, clapping Matt on the shoulder. "Somebody without your scruples might have taken advantage of the situation."

Elise remembered that searing kiss and her intense reaction to it. She could feel a blasted blush creep up her cheeks and had to hope Grant didn't notice.

"Glad I could be there. We left her car at The Hitching Post. Need me to shuttle it home for you?"

"No. I can have somebody from the resort drive it out here later this morning."

Elise felt supremely stupid and about ten years old again. She was grateful when Matt said goodbye quickly and left, saying he needed to get to the McFarlane job site early that morning.

After the door closed behind him, she was faced with her headache and Grant, who watched her with a concerned frown.

"I don't get it. After Haley pulled out of your plans, why didn't you just come home and have dinner with us?" he asked. "Erin was sorry she missed you."

She didn't want to sound whiny or self-pitying, especially not when Grant and Helen were so happy about finding Erin. "I was already at The Hitching Post and you all weren't expecting me home so I just decided to stay and enjoy the band. In retrospect, maybe not the smartest decision I ever made, but it worked out okay in the end."

"You were lucky," Grant growled.

She sighed. "I know."

"I don't even want to think about what might have

happened to you if Cates hadn't been there," Grant growled.

"If Cates hadn't been where?"

Her mother walked into the kitchen wearing her favorite green bathrobe and Elise mentally groaned. So much for her furtive hope that she might sneak away from Grant's lecture and climb back to bed to nurse her blasted headache before her mother came downstairs. She was in for it now.

"Elise had a little run-in with a drunk cowboy last night down at The Hitching Post. Matt Cates came to her rescue. That's why she's just rolling in at 6:00 a.m."

"What a nice boy. Those Cates brothers are always so thoughtful." Helen smiled. "They must take after their father. He's always been the nicest man."

Her mother tended only to see the good in people. Either that or she hadn't paid any attention to the Cates twins' antics over the years. Matt and his brother had been wild hell-raisers until recently.

They hadn't completely worked all the wildness out of their systems. She remembered the fierce way Matt had taken on Jake Halloran to protect her and then the stormy, wondrous heat of his kiss.

"Tell me again how you ended up spending the night at Cates's place instead of coming back here after you left The Hitching Post?" Grant asked pointedly, which she found the height of hypocrisy coming from a man who'd enjoyed a healthy reputation as a ladies' man before his surprise marriage to Stephanie three years earlier.

To her surprise and relief, her mother stepped. "I

think that's really Elise's business, don't you?" Helen said with a reassuring pat to Grant's arm.

"I fell asleep on his couch. Relax, Grant. You can put your mind at ease. Matt was a perfect gentleman," she answered. Mostly.

"I would think a perfect gentleman would have made sure you spent the night safe and sound in your own bed."

"I'm here now. Look, don't blame Matt for any of this." Her head hurt and she was embarrassed and wanted nothing more than to crawl into bed and sleep the rest of the morning away but she had to set the record straight first.

"It's all completely my fault. The truth is, I'm embarrassed to admit I wasn't paying attention to my drink quota and I had a little too much on an empty stomach. You know I don't have much tolerance for alcohol."

Last night had truly been full of anomalies and she would be wise to remember that. She rarely drank more than a glass of wine with dinner and the kisses she'd shared with Matt had been a fluke, something that wouldn't happen again.

"Where does the drunk cowboy come in?" her mother asked.

Elise sighed. Maybe they ought to go wake up Steph so she didn't have to go through the story again. "I struck up a conversation at the bar with a Lazy D ranch hand. He mistook our conversation for more of a flirtation than I intended and he…didn't take my attempt at brushing him off with very good grace. He tried to…to kiss me and didn't seem to believe my no really meant no."

"You could have been in serious trouble."

"I know. Believe me, I know." She shivered, remembering again that moment of fear when she had felt overpowered and helpless. "But Matt saw I was having trouble and he stepped in before anything could happen. The two of them got into it a little bit, mostly shoving, pushing, that sort of thing. When it was over, Matt took me back to his place so I could help him clean up and to grab a bite to eat. I'm afraid we both fell asleep. And here we are."

She was leaving out a few details, like how she had cried all over him and then kissed him until she couldn't think straight.

Some things were no one else's business but hers and Matt's.

"I guess I owe the man for looking out for you," Grant said.

"You don't owe him anything. I do."

"Well, you're home now and that's the important thing." Helen pulled her into a hug and Elise held on, closing her eyes and inhaling the clean, wholesome scent of lilacs and Tide detergent that clung to her mother.

Tears stung her eyes and not just from the headache pulsing through her veins. This was the scent of her childhood, when she had felt warm and safe and beloved.

Before she knew anything about wicked people who could kill men because of greed, or innocent hospital mistakes that would come back years later to destroy everything she thought she knew.

"I wish you had stayed," Helen said. "We had a

perfectly lovely evening with Erin. Corey Traub came with her. They make such a wonderful couple."

Elise forced a smile and eased away from her mother. "They seem great together."

"She was sorry to miss you, too. I think she's looking forward to having a sister after growing up only with brothers."

But they weren't sisters. They weren't related at all except for the weird, sadistic twist of fate that had brought them all together.

Elise decided she must be a terrible person. Erin obviously wanted to be friends and Elise couldn't seem to put any effort forward in that direction.

She should have stayed home and tried last night, she thought again. A few hours of being polite seemed a small enough price compared to her humiliation at causing a scene at The Hitching Post and, worse, spilling her angst all over Matt Cates and then sharing a kiss with him.

Her mind replayed those stunning moments at his house—his mouth warm and sexy against hers, the strength of his arms around her, the safety and security she felt near him. The man could definitely kiss. She'd always suspected it and now she knew without a doubt all the whisperings she'd heard around town were based on fact.

For a few moments there, she hadn't been able to think about anything but his touch. Not hospital mistakes or drunk cowboys or even her own name—Elise Clifton or Elise Castro or whoever the heck she was this week.

Chapter Five

"Nice bit of color you've got there, son. Thought I taught you how to duck a little better than that."

Matt made at face at his father, who leaned on the doorjamb of the bedroom at the McFarlane Lodge where they were putting up the last bit of finish trim around the windows and doors.

A guy got in one lousy fight and the whole town wanted to talk about it. He supposed it didn't help when he sported the worst shiner he'd had since he was fourteen, when he and Marlon had gotten a little too physical over a cute cheerleader from Bozeman.

He'd realized he had a long and painful history of fighting over women.

"Heard you got into it with a drunk cowboy over a girl down at The Hitching Post," piped in Bud Larsen, one of their workers, as he carried in another load of trim from the truck.

Matt used the fine-planed black walnut he was measuring as an excuse to avoid the gaze of either Bud or his father.

"Something like that," he answered evasively.

"Was Christine involved?" Frank asked.

He supposed he couldn't blame his father for jumping to that conclusion. His parents thought he and Christine Mayhew were serious since they had been "dating" steadily for the last few months.

"She wasn't even there, Dad. She had a baby shower last night so I went to hang out with some of the guys."

Frank set the level on the trim to double and triple check, as he always did. "She know you got into a fight over another girl?"

His parents liked Christine. Now that both of his older brothers were married and Marlon was engaged to Haley Anderson, Matt often found himself the object of much teasing and speculation from his family about when he planned to take his turn on that particular merry-go-round.

He had tried to be evasive to his family about his and Christine's relationship but it was becoming more difficult without blatant prevarication, something he tried not to do to his parents very often since they always seemed to catch him at it anyway.

"I don't know if Christine has heard or not. I haven't had a chance to talk to her, but you know how the grapevine works around here."

"Women like to hear those sorts of things straight from the horse, if you get me," Bud offered with a wink.

"I'll keep that in mind," Matt said. He decided he didn't need to mention that he wasn't about to take relationship advice from a man who had been married four times, two of them to sisters.

"Anyway, it was just a misunderstanding."

"So if the girl you tussled over down at the bar wasn't Christine, who the heck was it?" Frank asked.

For some reason, Matt found himself strangely reluctant to tell his father the truth. He knew this was just what Elise had feared, that she would find herself the subject of gossip and speculation.

But he also knew that look in his father's eyes. Frank wouldn't stop until he'd extracted every ounce of available information out of Matt. Sometimes he wondered if his father had undergone interrogation training somewhere in his distant past or if he was just particularly gifted at squeezing information out of his reticent sons.

He should probably just blurt it out, rather than hem and haw and obfuscate, when Frank would just find out sooner or later.

He sighed. "Grant Clifton's sister."

"Elise?" His father registered a moment of surprise then he shook his head. "That poor little thing. She's had a rough time of it this last month, hasn't she?"

"She has."

"If some no-account cowboy was messing with her, you did the right thing, son. She all right?"

He thought of her sobbing out her confusion and pain in his arms and then the stunning, unforgettable kiss that never should have happened. "I think so."

"She's tough, our little Elise."

"Not so little anymore, Dad. We're the same age."

His father again looked surprised. "I guess you are at that. I always forget you went to school with her. Well, I'm glad you were there to watch out for her. Christine will probably understand."

"If she don't and throws you out on your butt, you mind if I have a go?" Bud asked eagerly. "That is one fine-looking woman."

The man was twenty years older than Christine. Hell, he had kids who were older than she was. Matt was trying to come up with a diplomatic response but his father didn't bother.

"Shut up, Bud, and get back to work now before I throw *you* out on your butt," Frank growled.

Bud grumbled but headed back out for another load.

When the other man left, Frank turned to him, his brown eyes uncharacteristically serious. "As much as I hate to say it, I think Bud's probably right about this, anyway. You might want to get out in front of the story. Call Christine and explain your side of the story before she hears a rumor and gets the wrong idea. Be careful there, son. She's a nice girl. You don't want to hurt her."

An image of Elise in his arms flashed through his mind again, a picture he hadn't been able to shake all morning. He didn't worry about hurting Christine. They were only friends. Elise was an entirely different story. "Yeah. I know."

His phone rang just a few moments after his father left to direct the other workers, leaving Matt alone with the work and his thoughts.

Matt pulled it from the holder on his belt and glanced at the caller ID.

"Hey, Christine," he said. "I was just talking about you."

"You're a busy guy, Matt. Rumor has it you pulled the white-knight act last night at The Hitching Post."

How the heck did rumors manage to fly so fast and furiously in a small town? "A guy might think nothing exciting ever happens in Thunder Canyon," he complained. "Doesn't anybody in town have something more interesting to talk about?"

She gave that rich, husky laugh he had always enjoyed. "I guess tongues all over town are going to wag when one of the supposedly reformed hell-raising Cates boys comes out of retirement."

"Yeah, yeah."

She laughed again. "That's why I'm calling, actually. I'm just wondering if you want to cancel our plans for tonight."

"Why would I do that?"

"I just figured, now that you've apparently taken on the cause of some other damsel in distress, you might be too busy."

Elise might have returned his kiss the night before with a sweet passion, but for all he knew, that might have only been the margaritas talking. "I'm never too busy for you, Chris. As far as I'm concerned, we're still on."

"And the bar fight I'm hearing about? From what I understand, you whomped on a Lazy D cowboy."

"All a misunderstanding," he repeated what he'd told his father.

"And the girl?"

"Elise is just an old friend," he lied. "I'm definitely looking forward to dinner."

"So am I. I owe you. Taking you to The Gallatin Room is the least I can do to repay you for helping me out these last few months."

"How many times will I have to remind you I was happy to be able to help, before you start to believe me?"

"A few more, maybe."

He smiled. "It's been fun, Christine. And I think your devious plot worked. You haven't been bothered by Clay for a while, have you?"

"Not much. The stray email here and there and message on voice mail but I can always delete those."

"So does seven tomorrow still work?" he asked.

"Perfectly. Try not to get into any more barfights between now and then. I might have a tough time explaining why my supposed boyfriend is ripping it up down at The Hitching Post over another woman."

"Maybe because you won't give it up," he teased.

She laughed hard. "Ewww. Don't even go there, Matt. Don't get me wrong, you're gorgeous and all, but it's like kissing a brother."

He couldn't fault her for that since he'd had a very similar reaction.

"Sorry, I've got to run," she said a few moments later. "This place is crazy with Christmas shoppers today. I'll see you tonight, okay?"

After he hung up, he paused for a moment, gazing out the window at the spectacular view of the mountains from the McFarlane Lodge. Some part of him really wished he could stir up something more than friendship with Christine. She was perfect for him in many ways. Fun and exuberant and undeniably beautiful.

A few months ago, he never would have believed it, but he was beginning to feel ready to start thinking about the next phase of his life. Maybe it was Marlon's relationship with Haley that had set him on the road, but his life had begun to seem empty.

He loved the job. He loved the challenge of rehabbing houses on the side. He enjoyed hanging with the guys and going fly-fishing and watching basketball games. But something had been missing for a while.

His thoughts filled with Elise again—the softness of her mouth, the startling hunger racing through him, that incredible wash of tenderness as he held her while she slept.

He had a fierce desire to see where things might take them but it was tempered by the awareness that this was abysmal timing for her. She was dealing with a lot right now, stresses he couldn't begin to imagine. Maybe what she needed most from him was a little patience, something that had never been one of his strengths.

He sighed. He wasn't going to get this project finished

in time for Connor McFarlane's grand lodge opening if he didn't focus.

He had to stop thinking about Elise. A pleasant evening with Christine would be the perfect diversion.

He hoped.

"We'll have your table ready in just a moment, Mr. Clifton."

"No problem, Sara. We don't mind waiting."

Elise felt a pang of sympathy for the hostess at The Gallatin Room at the Thunder Canyon Resort, who looked on the verge of a full-fledged panic attack that her boss and his family had to wait even thirty seconds.

Grant had been running the ski resort—now a four-season destination—for several years. He seemed to be highly respected by his employees, with perhaps a healthy amount of fear added to the mix.

She had a hard time reconciling his professional persona with her teasing, sometimes annoying older brother.

After her disaster of an outing the night before at The Hitching Post and the gossip she knew likely had galloped through town, her first instinct was to stay at the ranch where she was safe, to avoid showing her face around town. But her usually sweet mother could be stubborn about certain things.

"We've hardly had a moment with Grant and Stephanie since…well, since everything happened with Erin and since you and I came back to Thunder Canyon," Helen had said that afternoon. "With Grant's busy schedule from now until New Year's, who knows when we'll have time for a family dinner again."

Elise hadn't known how to wiggle out of it. As the hostess finally led them through the always-crowded restaurant toward the best table overlooking the snow-covered mountains, she wished she'd tried a little harder.

Many of the guests were tourists in town for holiday skiing but she recognized several locals, who all seemed to follow the Cliftons' progress through the restaurant with avid, hungry gazes.

"I hate this," she muttered under her breath.

She really hadn't meant to say the words aloud but she must have. Stephanie, Grant's wife, tucked her arm through Elise's. "Hate what, honey?"

"Everybody's staring and whispering at us," she finally said. "I feel like some kind of circus freak."

Stephanie's blue eyes warmed with compassion and she smiled, squeezing Elise's arm. "And here I thought they were staring at me, in all my voluptuous glory."

Elise had to laugh. Steph was seven months pregnant, due in February, but carried the baby well on her slim, athletic frame.

"You're right." Elise smiled back, grateful at Steph for yanking her out of her pity party. "What else would they be looking at but how utterly, gorgeously pregnant you are? How narcissistic of me to automatically assume I'm always the center of attention."

"Wait until you're either a bride or pregnant for that," Steph said.

By then they had reached their table and Grant pulled

out the chairs for all three of the women. "Aren't I the luckiest guy here, to have the three most beautiful women in town at my table?"

"Suck-up," Elise muttered, earning a grin from her older brother. She couldn't resist returning his smile. Elise reached for her water glass when the hostess filled it, then nearly dumped the whole thing over when she spotted the couple sitting only three tables away from them.

Matt Cates seemed to be enjoying a very cozy dinner for two with a slender, lovely brunette. The woman was laughing at something he said and leaning into him, her body language clearly telegraphing an easy, comfortable familiarity. While they spoke, the woman kept one hand on his arm as if she didn't want to let him go—the same arm that the night before had pulled Elise to him and held her close while she slept.

She told herself to look away. His choice in dinner companions was absolutely none of her business, and she would do well to remember that. She was not about to spend the evening gawking at him.

She had just started to heed her own advice and shift her attention back to her family when he suddenly happened to look straight at her. Rats. Caught. Just like in junior high when she used to moon over him in Mrs. McLarty's algebra class.

Something flashed in his eyes as he smiled at her. She jerked her gaze away, fumbling with her flatware and knocking her salad fork into her lap.

"Everything okay?" Stephanie asked in an undertone.

"Sure. Fine. Just great. Why wouldn't it be?"

She let out a breath. Naturally, she had a clear view of the two of them from her vantage point. If she didn't suspect it would spark a host of questions she wasn't in the mood to answer, Elise would have asked her mother to switch places so she didn't have to sit and watch him. Instead, she would just have to force herself not to stare.

There were plenty of other restaurants in town. Why did they both have to choose tonight to come to this particular one? she wondered. His presence—complete with that spectacular black eye—was certain to generate plenty more conversation among anyone who might have heard even a whisper of a rumor about the altercation the night before.

Grant spied him at the same moment and lifted a hand. Matt returned the greeting before turning back to his companion.

"His shiner's looking even prettier," Grant said just as their waiter approached with an obsequious smile.

Grant cut him off at the pass before he could even go into his spiel welcoming them to The Gallatin Room.

"Listen, Marcos. I need you to do me a favor."

"Of course, Mr. Clifton. Anything."

"Send a bottle of our best Cabernet Sauvignon to table seventeen, with my compliments," he answered.

Curiosity flashed briefly in the man's eyes but he quickly concealed it and nodded. "Of course, sir. Right away, sir."

He hurried away and Elise rolled her eyes at her

brother with an exasperated sigh. "Was that really necessary?"

Grant smiled. "He protected my baby sister from a sticky situation and has the battle scars to prove it. I'd say it is."

Would Grant be so amused by the whole thing if he knew about the heated kiss she and Matt had shared?

Elise snapped her napkin out onto her lap, trying not to remember the heat of his mouth and the strength of his arms and the liquid pool of desire seeping through her.

A moment later, the sommelier delivered a bottle to Matt's table. He acknowledged Grant's gift with a wry smile to her brother, which Elise pretended not to notice.

The next hour was a definite challenge. Through each course, she had to work hard not to gawk at Matt and his companion. She made a pointed effort to enjoy the delicious dinner, though each bite seemed a chore.

Halfway through the main course, she excused herself to use the restroom, located just outside the restaurant in the main lobby area. When she emerged, she was somehow not surprised to find Matt waiting for her.

He looked far more delicious than the roasted chicken and new potatoes she had ordered, in a cream-colored sweater that made him look dark and gorgeous in contrast.

"How's the head?" he asked.

She made a face. "Better. Just be glad you didn't ask me that a few hours ago or you would have a headache of your own after I bit yours off."

He smiled. "I'm glad you're feeling better."

Why did he make her feel so safe and warm just inhabiting the same air space? It was completely ridiculous, this yearning of hers to stand here and bask in his smile.

She suddenly remembered his companion. "Your date is lovely," she said, working hard to ignore the sinking sensation in the pit of her stomach, that pinch of jealousy she had no right to feel.

For an instant, he looked slightly taken aback, as if he'd forgotten all about the poor woman, then he nodded. "Do you know Christine Mayhew?"

"I'm not sure we've met."

They lapsed into awkward silence. She was just about to excuse herself when he gestured toward the dining room. "You look as if you're enjoying your dinner. How are things with your family? Better?"

She fidgeted, embarrassed at the reminder of her emotional breakdown at his house. "Yes. Fine."

"I've been worried about you today."

Her cheeks felt hot and she cursed her fair skin that revealed every hint of embarrassment. "Don't. I'm fine, mostly just embarrassed that I fell apart like that. I learned a hard lesson, that too much alcohol turns me into a bawl-baby. You'll notice I'm not having anything stronger than ginger ale tonight. I really am sorry, Matt, for putting you through that and dumping all my troubles on you."

"I'm glad I could be there. If you, you know, need to talk or anything, you know where to find me."

He looked completely sincere and Elise felt a tiny

little tug on her heart. "Thank you. I appreciate that. I think I'm done feeling sorry for myself for a while. I've even got a job. Well, sort of. Haley called and asked me to help her with the ROOTS Christmas party next week. Staying busy will help."

"Good. That's great. I'll be there, too. Marlon has demanded—I mean, asked me in no uncertain terms—that I help out at the party."

Apparently she wouldn't be able to completely avoid him during the rest of her stay. She didn't know whether to rejoice or be depressed by that.

Elise glanced inside the dining room where the rest of her family members looked to be finishing up their meal. Stephanie was already gesturing for Marcos to take away her plate. "I should go. And you probably need to return to your date."

"Right."

He followed her gaze to the other diners, then shifted his attention back to her. He seemed strangely reluctant to leave her company, but she must be misinterpreting things. He was here with a date. A beautiful, vivacious date. Why would he want to hang around in a hallway with her when he could be sitting out there with a pretty brunette? She knew the thought shouldn't depress her so much.

"I guess I'll see you around ROOTS, then," he said.

"Enjoy your evening," she answered, then hurried back inside the restaurant to rejoin her family, trying hard not to wish *she* were the one sharing that bottle of wine with him.

* * *

"So that's Elise."

Matt returned his napkin to his lap, careful not to meet Christine's gaze. She was entirely too perceptive. For some reason, he was hesitant to let her see the depth of his attraction for Elise. Even though he and Christine were strictly friends, showing such blatant interest in another woman seemed rude.

"Yes. Grant's little sister."

"But she's not really, right? Grant's sister, I mean. She's the one who was switched at birth with Erin Castro."

"That doesn't make her any less Grant's sister," he answered, more curtly than he intended. He couldn't shake the memory of her anguish the night before as she had sobbed out her confusion in his arms.

Christine raised an eyebrow but said nothing and he squirmed. Yeah. Entirely too perceptive. So much for concealing his growing feelings for Elise.

"She's very pretty," Christine said after a moment. "Has she moved back to Thunder Canyon for good?"

He was wondering that same thing. "Not sure yet."

She was quiet for a moment then she touched his forearm. "Whenever you want to stage a breakup, you only have to say the word. You've been wonderful these last few months but this arrangement of ours was never supposed to be open-ended."

"Why do we need to change anything?"

She smiled. "I don't know. Maybe because you haven't stopped sneaking glances over at the Clifton table all night."

He took a sip of the delicious wine Grant had sent over to thank him for doing what any decent man would do. "I'm sorry," he murmured.

"Why are you sorry? This isn't a real date, Matt. You're not breaking any unwritten rules here. I'm just saying, I'll step out of the picture whenever you want me to."

He mulled her offer, not sure exactly how to respond. How was it possible that one crazy evening with Elise seemed to have changed everything?

"What about Clay?"

Christine shrugged. "I'll deal. If he hasn't gotten the message by now that I've moved on, the man needs serious help. I don't know what more I can do."

He had thought more than once that Christine was too softhearted. From the moment she broke up with Clay Robbins, she should have been clear that she was breaking up with him because he was clingy and obsessive. Instead, she had tried to let him down gently. When that didn't work, she had enlisted Matt's help to convince the other man she had moved on.

In Matt's opinion, the man needed somebody to knock him ass over teakettle until he clued in that Christine wasn't interested. Sort of like Jake Halloran the night before at The Hitching Post.

They finished their dinner not long after that. A surreptitious peek at the Cliftons' table while he was waiting for their server to return the check revealed they were lingering over dessert. He supposed it would be better to leave before they finished to avoid any awkwardness with Elise or the embarrassment of having to endure more unwanted gratitude from her family over the events of the night before.

He and Christine walked out into the lobby of the resort, with its leather sofas and life-size elk sculpture. He grabbed her coat and was helping her into it when her shoulders suddenly tensed beneath his hands and she inhaled sharply.

"Sorry. Did I pull your hair?" he asked, feeling big and fumbling.

"No," she whispered with a panicked look at a group that had just entered the lobby carrying holiday presents, obviously out for a night of festive celebrating.

"That's Kelly Robbins, Clay's cousin."

"Which one?"

"The one in the plaid sweater."

He saw exactly when the thin-as-a-rail other woman recognized Christine. Her eyes widened and jumped between the two of them, resting on his hands still at Christine's shoulders as he finished helping her with her coat.

"She's the biggest gossip in the whole blasted county."

"Is that right?" Some spark of recklessness must still be lingering in him from the tussle the night before at The Hitching Post. Heedless of the consequences, he threw an arm over Christine's shoulders.

"She's coming this way," he muttered. "Smile. It's about damn time Clay got the message once and for all."

"What are you going to do?"

"Just play along," he said. "Let's go say hello."

"Matt…" Christine said in a warning tone, but before she could finish, Matt dragged her over to the group of chattering women, who happened conveniently to be located near the entrance to the valet parking, anyway.

Christine gave a polished sort of smile. "Hi, Kelly. I thought that was you."

The other woman gave a high-pitched squeal, just as if she hadn't already seen them five minutes earlier. He could already tell she was exactly the sort of woman who always grated on his nerves, plastic and gushy.

"Christine! Hi! You look *gorgeous!* I haven't seen you in *ages!* Not since you and Clay…well, not in *forever.* How are you?"

Christine sent him a help-me sort of sidelong look as if she were waiting for his grand master plan.

"Good. Great. Um, Kelly Robbins, this is Matt Cates. Matt, Kelly lives over in Bozeman. I used to…um, date her cousin."

"You're Clay Robbins's cousin?" he asked, forcing a note of intrigue in his voice.

"Yes," she said slowly with a wary sort of look.

"How is Clay these days?" Matt asked. "I guess I should feel sorry for the poor guy but I just can't."

He squeezed Christine's shoulders, laying the cheese on as thick as he dared.

"Why is that?" the other woman asked, her overbright friendliness beginning to show a few hairline fractures.

"He really did me a favor, breaking up with Christine. If things had worked out with the two of them, I wouldn't be about to become the luckiest guy in the world."

He kissed her temple, lingering there with his mouth in her hair as if he couldn't bear to lose contact with her, in exactly the sort of public display of affection that always gave him the creeps.

He was probably going overboard here. Christine obviously thought so, at least judging by the heel of her boot that was currently digging into his instep.

"You're getting married?" Kelly squealed. She yanked Christine out of his arms and pulled her into a hug and even from here he could smell the spicy holiday-scented perfume she must have spritzed heavily before walking out the door. "When is the big day?"

Christine slanted him a sour look over the other woman's shoulder and Matt grinned back at her.

He tried to dissemble as much as he could manage to get away with. "You know how it is. Nothing's official yet. We're, uh, still working out the details. Keep it to yourself though, okay?"

Kelly gushed for a moment or two more. "I'm happy for you. Really I am." She frowned as if she'd suddenly thought of something, when Matt knew damn well she'd only been trying to figure out a way to work it into the conversation. "It's just, well, Clay's gonna be pretty upset, you know."

Christine sighed and then sent Matt a swift look. "I'm sorry for that but I guess it's time he moved on and found someone else, like I have."

"I s'pose," she said.

She looked as if she might say more but the hostess

at that moment came out from The Gallatin Room to let her party know their tables were ready.

"Congratulations again," Kelly said. "Let me know when the big day is, won't you?"

"Nothing's official," Christine protested, with another sideways glare at him.

"That ought to do it," he said, dropping his arm as soon as Kelly was out of view inside the restaurant. "If Robbins doesn't get the message after that, he's more of an idiot than I thought."

Christine somehow managed to look relieved and upset at the same time. "You're crazy, do you know that?" she said, shaking her head. "What are you going to do when the rumor starts flying around Thunder Canyon that we're engaged?"

"Who's going to talk? I didn't recognize a single one of those ladies and I know everybody in town. They must be from Bozeman. Who are they going to tell?"

"Don't you think Clay will figure out something's hinky when this engagement of ours never materializes?"

"Who knows?" Matt shrugged. "By then, he'll hopefully have found some other poor woman to cling to."

She was quiet for a moment as they walked out of the lodge and into the December night, starry and cold and lit by little twinkling gold lights adorning the lodge.

"What about Elise Clifton?" she asked as they waited for the valet to bring his pickup. "What if she hears rumors we're engaged?"

"There's nothing going on between Elise and me," he said, even though the words weren't precisely true.

What would it matter if she did find out? She probably wouldn't care, even if it were true. Elise was a friend—that was all.

Yet he was suddenly shocked to find himself wanting much more.

Chapter Six

"You need to march straight home and climb back to bed, missy. I'm not going to listen to any more arguments."

Elise stared down at Haley. Her best friend, who was currently huddled at her desk at ROOTS with a blanket over her shoulders, a nearly empty box of tissues at her elbow and complete misery on her features.

"I can't be sick another minute. I have way too much to do!" Haley wailed, then gave a wretched-sounding cough. "The Christmas party is only four days away and I still have to finish the decorations and make sure the caterers are ready and organize the swag bags from all the donations we've received."

"And if you don't get some rest and take care of yourself, you're going to be in a hospital bed while the rest of us throw a party. Go home, Hale."

"I can't just dump it all on you."

"I don't mind. Knowing you, I imagine your notes are extensive enough that I can figure out everything."

"It still doesn't seem right."

Elise wasn't always the most firm person on the planet, but she wasn't going to budge about this. "Go home," she repeated. "If not for your own sake, think about all these kids you love so much. What if you pass on all your pesky little germs and make them sick for the holidays?"

Haley opened her mouth to answer, then closed it again and slumped a little further down in her chair. "You're right. Darn it, you're right."

"Of course I am. Come on, I'll help you to your car."

Haley sighed heavily as if the very idea of moving just then was far beyond her capabilities. She lifted her hands to the arms of her desk chair but before she could rise, the door to ROOTS opened with a blast of cold air.

For a moment, Elise felt her heartbeat skitter at the tall, muscled figure who walked through, then she shook herself. Not Matt. Despite the fact that he shared the same brown hair and eyes and those sturdy, cry-on-me shoulders, this was Marlon, Matt's twin brother. She could tell in an instant, though she wasn't exactly certain how she knew.

He stood inside the renovated storefront that now housed Haley's volunteer organization aimed at helping

Thunder Canyon's troubled youth. Marlon looked between the two of them. "What's going on?"

"I'm trying to convince your stubborn girlfriend that she needs to be home in bed."

He raised his eyebrows. "Funny, that's exactly what I told her when she managed to crawl out this morning."

"It's just a cold," Haley insisted, though her brown eyes were bloodshot, her nose red, her skin pale. "I'll be fine."

"Sure you will." Elise said briskly. "You'll be good as new in a day or two. In the meantime, I can handle things here. I don't want you to worry for a single moment. I think I can manage to answer phones and make some Christmas decorations without ROOTS falling completely apart."

"It's such a lousy time to be sick. I have so much to *do*."

Elise shared a sympathetic look with Marlon and was struck again by the similarities yet differences between him and Matt.

"Nothing that's so important it's worth jeopardizing your health to accomplish," Marlon said sternly. "Come on, I'll drop you back at home and tuck you in with a cup of tea and a good book."

Was she a terrible person that she actually envied her friend? Oh, not for the lousy cold. She would happily leave that to Haley since Elise hated being sick worse than just about anything. But Marlon's tender concern for the woman he loved touched a chord somewhere deep inside, left her with a nameless ache in her chest.

Though she dated here and there, she had avoided any serious entanglements the last few years after a nasty experience with her ex-boyfriend. As she watched Haley and Marlon together, Elise had to wonder if she'd been wrong. A broken heart—or more accurately, probably, bruised ego—from one cheating louse didn't mean she had to give up all hope of finding what Haley and Marlon shared.

"Go home and go back to bed," Elise said again. "When you wake up later today, you can email me your to-do list. Meantime, I can start with the Christmas decorations for the party."

"Are you sure?"

"Positive. Go home. If you don't go on your own, I have a feeling Marlon over there will toss you over his shoulder and haul you out of here."

"Really?" Haley shifted her gaze to the man. For the first time since Elise had walked into ROOTS a half hour ago, she saw a tiny smile on her friend's face.

Marlon grinned. "In a heartbeat, sweetheart. Want to try me? Come on, let's get you home."

Though Haley still looked far from convinced, Elise and Marlon finally managed to usher her out the door and into Marlon's vehicle.

After they left, Elise turned around to survey this place her friend loved so much. The place wasn't fancy but Haley had managed to turn it into a comfortable hangout for troubled local teens. The wall facing the street was covered in a mural that Haley painted—kids with books, computers, sports images. A couch covered with a slipcover took up one wall and in a corner was a TV with video games.

Haley loved it here and was passionate about helping her teens. Elise knew Haley came up with the idea after her own brother Austin ran into trouble and was helped through it by some local ranching folk. Haley had more than paid it forward by providing a foundation for kids who might be feeling similarly rootless.

Elise envied Haley her dedication and determination. She wasn't sure she had ever cared as passionately for anything.

Oh, she had worked hard to earn her bachelor's degree in business and had enjoyed her job managing a bookstore in Billings. She wanted to think she had been good at her job—good enough that her district manager had assured her he would only accept a temporary leave of absence rather than a full-on resignation when she made the decision to come to Thunder Canyon for the holidays after Erin's stunning revelation.

While she had enjoyed the challenges of running a small bookstore, she couldn't say she really missed it. What she *had* missed was the chance to do something constructive. The last two weeks, she had tried to stay busy by helping out at the ranch but Stephanie had everything running so smoothly there, Elise had mostly been in the way.

She actually relished the chance to help Haley out at ROOTS for a few days, if only to provide a distraction from everything that had happened in the last month.

If the work also helped divert her mind from Marlon's gorgeous twin brother, she considered that a definite bonus.

* * *

Several hours later, Elsie was questioning her sanity. Her fingers had a dozen pinpricks from stringing popcorn and cranberries for the tree garlands, her neck had cramped about an hour ago and her eyes were blurry and achy from concentrating.

Added to that, all afternoon, ROOTS had been a madhouse with people coming in and out to make deliveries of donations for the party and the phone had been ringing off the hook with people asking questions she couldn't answer.

Since the high school let out, a couple dozen teens had descended to do homework or play video games or just to hang out.

Now, near 6:00 p.m., they had all dispersed, leaving her alone again to finish up the Christmas decorations.

Night came early at this latitude as Montana was headed for the shortest day of the year in a week, and outside the Christmas lights up and down the streets of Old Town Thunder Canyon had slowly flickered on.

There. One more cranberry and she was calling this one good. She tied the knot on the string then carried the garland to the back room to go with the rest of the decorations, twisting her neck from side to side as she walked, to stretch her achy muscles. She laid it carefully across the folding table she had unearthed from a corner and had set up to hold the decorations. She flipped off the light to return to the front when she suddenly heard the jingling bells on the door.

So much for locking up. Who would be coming this

late? Probably somebody with another donation. The generosity of the townspeople had been a definite eye-opener.

Elise gave a weary sigh and headed out to greet the newcomer.

As soon as she spied the tall, dark-haired man near the door, her heart gave a ridiculous little leap and this time she didn't even wonder for an instant which Cates brother it was.

"Matt. Hi!"

He entered the room with that long-legged, loose-hipped walk of his and her stomach sizzled.

Surprise and something else—something that left her hot and edgy—flashed in his eyes. "Oh! You're not Haley."

"No. She's a few inches taller and her hair is brown and quite a bit longer. And you're not Marlon."

He sent her a sidelong look and she saw the teasing sparkle in his eyes. The Cates boys had been notorious in school for playing tricks on people, pretending to be each other at the most inconvenient moments.

"You sure about that?" he asked.

She stacked stray papers on Haley's desk so her workspace would be neat in the morning. "Completely. Marlon's the good-looking one."

Surprise flickered in those brown eyes again and then he laughed. "Wow. A little harsh, don't you think?"

All the stresses of the day seemed to shimmer away like silvery tinsel on the wind. How did he have that effect on her? she wondered. She had no idea—but she was very much afraid she might become addicted to it.

"You know I'm joking. You're identical twins, both of you too gorgeous for your own good."

As soon as the words were out, she couldn't believe she had actually spoken them aloud. She wasn't exactly the flirty, lighthearted type. Actually, she had always been a little on the shy side when it came to men, especially big, sexy men like Matt Cates.

He didn't seem to find her remark out of character but it did seem to make him uncomfortable. He rolled his eyes and she thought she detected a slight hint of color on his features. Really? Could he honestly not be aware of his effect on the opposite sex? He had been breaking girls' hearts since grade school.

"Seriously, how can you tell?" he asked her with a quizzical look. "Sometimes our own parents aren't sure."

"Besides the black eye, you mean? I'm not quite sure. I just know." She studied him, trying to figure out the signs she took for granted. "Your chins are shaped a little differently, I guess. Your hair's just a little more streaky than his. Oh, and your lashes are just a bit longer."

He still looked baffled and Elise could feel herself blush. How could she tell him she had spent a long time staring at him when he wasn't paying her any attention, from the time she was old enough to even notice him?

"However you do it, it's amazing. Not many people can tell us apart." He looked around. "So is Haley here?"

"No. Your brother—"

"You mean the good-looking one?" he interrupted. She smiled. "Right. Marlon took her home earlier.

She's got a bad cold and is feeling lousy. She tried to tough it out here at ROOTS for a while but seemed to be getting worse, not better. I offered to step in to help her with the Christmas party Friday so she could recover and keep her bad juju to herself."

"Oh, right. I forgot about the party."

She pointed to the boxes of donations. "If you'd like, I've got about a hundred gift bags to fill that might jog your memory."

"Tonight?"

He sounded as if he was completely willing to sit right down and start throwing bags together, which she found rather wonderful.

"No. I'll probably work on them a little later in the week once all the donations come in. But thanks for the offer. Haley might take you up on it if she comes back in time to crack the whip over all the volunteers." She paused. "Sorry, you must have had a reason for coming in to see Haley. Is there something I can help you with?"

He didn't say anything for several beats, only looked at her with that glittery look in his eyes again, until her skin felt achy and tight.

After a moment, he cleared his throat. "Actually, I had a good excuse to come visit Haley but that's all it was. An excuse. In reality, I was trying to be sneaky."

"You? Sneaky? Imagine that!"

He ignored her dry tone. "You know, finding you here instead of Haley works out even better for me. You're the perfect person to help me out."

"Am I?"

He sat on the edge of the desk and she tried not to feel overwhelmed by all that rugged strength so close to her. "You've been friends with Haley for a long time, right? So you know her pretty well."

"She and Steph have been my closest friends forever."

"Great!" He grinned and she had to remind herself to breathe. "This is perfect. You can come to Bozeman with me tonight."

She blinked. "Excuse me?"

"I'm trying to find a Christmas present for her. Not just any Christmas present, the perfect Christmas present. She's the only one left on my list."

That he had a list in the first place struck her as odd. That he was enlisting her help to cross Haley's name off that list was even more surreal. "She's really the only one whose present you haven't bought yet? You still have another week and a half before Christmas. I thought most guys tended to wait until the last minute."

He manufactured an affronted look. "That is a blatant stereotype, Ms. Clifton, and I am personally offended by it."

She couldn't help herself—she smiled. She couldn't remember the last time she had felt this, well, happy. "Oh, sorry to be a reverse chauvinist. But every man *I* know waits until the last minute. Grant and my cousin Bo are the worst."

He shrugged. "I happen to love Christmas and the whole giving-presents thing. I've had almost everything done and even wrapped for a while now, except for Haley's gift. She's still fairly new to our family circle and since this is her first Christmas with us, I wanted to find something special. I'm heading into Bozeman right now before all the stores close and dropped by ROOTS hoping I could finesse a few hints out of her about what she would like before I leave."

"I'm sorry she's not here."

"Not at all. Now you can come with me, which is even better. I'll even spring for dinner. What time are you closing up shop here?"

"I was just about to. But I can't just…"

"Sure you can," he said over her objections. "Come on, it will be fun."

She could think of a dozen reasons why she shouldn't go with him. She was tired. She had a headache. She wasn't thrilled about her silly, futile crush on him and had been warning herself since Saturday morning when he dropped her off back at Clifton's Pride that she needed to keep her distance so she didn't make an even bigger fool of herself over him.

But her words to Grant that morning after he drove away still echoed in her mind. She owed him for coming to her rescue the other night at The Hitching Post—and he still had the vividly colored eye to show for it.

Without him, she might have found herself in serious trouble with Jake Halloran. He had stepped in to rescue her from a jam at considerable risk to himself. All he wanted now was the simple favor of helping him select a gift. If she went with him to Bozeman, perhaps she wouldn't feel quite so indebted to him.

The trick would be making it through the evening alone with him without completely humiliating herself while the memory of that stunning kiss simmered under her skin.

"Fine." She spoke quickly before she could change her mind. "But since you apparently love Christmas so much, I'm still going to expect you to help me fill those gift bags."

"It's a deal." He grinned and helped her find her coat.

"Are you sure about this?"

Two hours later, they stood inside an art gallery just before closing time looking at an elaborate—and elaborately priced—needlework sampler that depicted an old, gnarled oak tree. In the thin, topmost branches perched a stately, magnificent eagle with its wings outstretched, gleaming gold as if reflecting sunlight.

"Positive. Oh, Matt. It's perfect. Haley will love it."

He studied the piece. It was lovely, in an artsy sort of way. He could see where Haley would probably enjoy it. Elise seemed convinced, anyway. The moment they had walked into the gallery after searching fruitlessly through three or four other crowded stores, she saw it hanging on the wall and gasped with delight.

"You're the expert, I guess," he said now.

"Trust me, she's going to love it. It's perfect," she said again. "So perfect it might have been custom made for her. You know that's the reason she named her teen organization ROOTS, right? Because of a sampler her mother had hanging on the wall. It said something about how there are but two lasting bequests we can give children—roots and wings. This covers both of those things.

I mean it. With this present you're going to win the best future brother-in-law race, hands down."

"Well that's something, at least," he said dryly. "I wouldn't want her favoring Marshall or Mitch over me."

"Haley's going to love it," she assured him. "In fact, she just might wonder if she's marrying the wrong twin."

He made a face as they headed to the salesperson seated behind a discreet counter. "I doubt that. The two of them seem to forget that anybody else on earth even exists when they're together."

He paid for the needlework, gulping a little at the price tag but grateful again that Cates Construction had managed to avoid the worst of the economic downturn so he could splurge a little for his twin's future wife.

"Would you like this gift wrapped?" the saleswoman asked.

"Please. Gift wrapping isn't one of my particular skills."

While the salesclerk carried the piece over to a nearby table where wrapping supplies were neatly organized, Elise picked up their conversation.

"Do you mind? About Marlon and Haley, I mean? The two of you have always been so close. Do you worry she'll interfere with that bond?"

He thought about Haley and the changes she had wrought in his brother. She was sweet and loving, as different as he could imagine from his formerly wild twin. Somehow the two of them managed to still perfectly complement each other.

"Haley's been great for Marlon," he answered honestly. "She centers him, you know? Before she came along, the only thing Marlon really cared about was having a good time and making the next deal. Now he's as passionate about ROOTS as Haley is. They're crazy about each other."

"I noticed." She smiled a little and gave him a considering look. "I guess that leaves you the last Cates standing, which is probably exactly where you want to be, right?"

He gazed at Elise, bright and lovely in the recessed lighting of the gallery. Whenever he looked at her, something soft and tender lodged just under his chest.

Maybe he ought to be a little uneasy about how quickly everything he always thought he wanted had shifted in the last few days, but all he could manage to drum up was gratitude that she had come back to Thunder Canyon.

"I don't expect that particular situation will last long," he said, purposely vague. A guy had to hope, right?

She gave him an uncertain look but he decided not to explain yet. He could be patient, give her time to figure out her feelings.

"Well, whoever manages to capture the last Cates will be a very lucky woman, I'm sure. Especially if you're always so generous with your gifts."

Now would probably be a really good time to change the subject, he decided, before she started to probe too deeply into areas he wasn't quite ready to discuss.

"What about you?" he asked her. "What's on your Christmas list this year?"

She shrugged. "My gifts are already all wrapped this year. When you work in a bookstore, it's easy to find something perfect for everyone on your list."

"I meant for yourself. What are you asking Santa to bring you?"

She looked reluctant to answer and he saw relief in her blue eyes when the saleswoman brought back his wrapped gift for Haley before he could probe a little more.

"Will there be anything else?" the woman asked in the brisk, tired tone of someone who had spent hours on her feet dealing with holiday shoppers.

"Not tonight. But thank you. This is perfect," he said.

He held the door open for Elise and they walked out into the frosty night. A light snow was falling and a few flakes landed on her crimson knit hat and then on her eyelashes.

"You were saying about your Christmas list…" he prompted.

She made a face. "You're about the most persistent man I know."

"I haven't even gotten started yet."

She sighed. "I'm not a big Christmas fan, if you want to know the truth. I haven't been in a long time. Probably since my dad's murder. It's always a difficult time but I'm afraid this year I feel even less like celebrating."

He studied her there in the fluttery snow and that soft tenderness swelled up inside him again. She had certainly been faced with a rough road to walk. He thought of his own family, the parties and traditions and craziness of a Cates family Christmas.

So much had been taken from Elise. He wanted to give her something back but he didn't have the first idea how to help her enjoy Christmas again.

"Come on," he said suddenly. "Let's lock Haley's present in my truck and then take a walk through town before we grab a bite to eat."

She stared at him in the light reflected from the gallery's front window. "Take a walk? It's got to be fifteen degrees out! Are you crazy?"

"Maybe. Probably." He grinned at her. "Come on, let's enjoy some of the Christmas decorations and then I'll buy you dinner at my favorite steak house."

She laughed, though he saw a little lingering sadness in her eyes. "You're in a very strange mood tonight."

"What's strange about being happy? It's Christmas and I'm with the prettiest woman in Bozeman. What guy wouldn't be happy about that?"

Rosy color climbed her cheeks and he knew it wasn't from the cold. Her blushes fascinated and charmed him. On impulse, he pulled her toward him with his free arm for just a moment, leaning in to kiss her forehead. Up close, her eyes were wide and startled and impossibly blue.

He wanted to stay there holding her for a long time while the snow eddied around them and the Christmas lights twinkled in the storefronts, but he sensed she needed a cautious approach.

He eased away and took her hand. "Come on. Let's see if we can find you a little holiday spirit."

They took their time dropping off the package for Haley in his truck then wandering through the streets of Bozeman, listening to the carols playing from speakers out front of the businesses and peering into the all the storefronts like they were children dreaming about the biggest, best bicycle in town.

He found every moment magical, especially watching her eyes lose a little of that lost, haunted look. She laughed and joked with him like the girl he remembered and through the knit of her gloves, her fingers curled inside his as if she didn't want to let go.

By the time they reached his favorite restaurant, his toes were numb from the cold but he wouldn't have changed an instant.

Though the popular steak house could be crowded, business was slow this late on a weeknight and they didn't have to wait long for a table.

She looked lighter somehow, he thought as the hostess seated them and rattled through the evening's specials. Maybe that's what she needed most. Someone to make her smile and help her forget her troubles for a moment.

He wanted to give her the gift of a happy, lighthearted evening where she could forget her worries—and this was definitely one present he didn't need anyone else's help to deliver.

Chapter Seven

How did he do it?

Elise studied the man across the low-lit table from her, strong and dark and gorgeous. Though both Cates twins had been wild, Marlon had always been the charmer while Matt had always seemed more the studious type—one reason he had gravitated toward law school, she supposed.

But tonight, he was making every effort to charm her…and it was definitely working. If she wasn't careful, she would fall hard and fast for him.

She would just have to be careful, she warned herself as her insides trembled from another of his smiles.

"So you never really answered me the other night. How long do you think you're staying in Thunder Canyon?" he asked, in a tone of voice that made her think he had genuine interest in her answer.

She refused to let him fluster her. Matt might be the studious one but he had a reputation as being every bit the player that Marlon used to be.

"I'm not sure," she answered. "I promised my mother I would spend the holidays in town. For now that's what I'm focusing on, just spending time at the ranch and helping Haley at ROOTS while I'm here. Once the holidays are over, I don't know. I'm considering my options."

"What are they? Maybe I can help."

"My job is still waiting for me in Billings if I want it. That's a definite possibility. My life is there. My friends are there. For now, I still have a house until my mother decides whether to sell it or rent it out."

She paused, then added reluctantly, "Jack and Betty Castro haven't exactly made it a secret that they would like me to go down to San Diego for a while so they and…their sons can get to know me beyond phone calls and emails."

He studied her out of those surprisingly perceptive brown eyes. "You're not so sure about that one, are you?"

She sighed, moving her undeniably delicious pasta around on her plate. At the reminder of the Castros, the happy bubble around them she suspected he had carefully nurtured seemed to fizzle and pop.

"It's all so difficult. They're strangers to me, you know?"

"Sure they are." He paused and reached across the

table to entwine his fingers around hers. "You know, they're going to stay strangers to you until you make an effort to get to know them better."

"You sound like my mo—like Helen."

"Your mother," he said, squeezing her fingers lightly. "Helen is your mother, no matter what the DNA says."

His words brought a lump to her throat and she had to reach for her water glass. "My mother is urging me to spend more time with them."

"Don't you like them?"

"Sure I like them. They're very nice people."

How could she explain that spending time with them, coming to know them, would make this strange, twisted journey seem more real, somehow? She didn't understand her tangle of emotions, she only knew she wanted everything to go back to the way it was a few weeks ago, before she'd ever even heard of Erin Castro.

She couldn't continue in this limbo, she knew. Something had to change. She just wasn't sure she was ready yet.

"Jack and Betty are coming back to Thunder Canyon as soon as school lets out in San Diego to spend the holidays in Montana with Erin. Betty is a teacher there. History. Jack's a police officer. They have two sons in addition to Erin, one who's a police officer like his father and one who is a student."

"Are the brothers coming, too?"

"As far as I know, only Jack and Betty. They want to get to know me better while they're here."

"That's a start."

"We'll see."

She didn't want to talk about the Castros. She wanted that bright, happy bubble back. "What about you? What are your plans? Do you think you'll ever consider going back to law school?"

"Right now, I doubt it. I like working with my dad. I've discovered I really love the whole building process, seeing a place take shape under my direction. I'm not sure I'd get that same high from practicing law.

"So you think you'll be sticking around Thunder Canyon, then?"

He gave her another one of those intense, unreadable looks that made her blush, for reasons she didn't fully understand. "I guess you could say I'm pretty content with my life right now. For the most part, anyway."

She wondered if he was serious about the woman she'd seen him with the other night at dinner. Probably not. Matt probably had a dozen beautiful women like that, all eager to hang on his every word.

That probably shouldn't depress her so much, she thought. She wasn't doing a very effective job of protecting herself around him.

They finished eating a short time later and somewhat to Elise's surprise, she found she was grateful he'd parked some distance away so she could stretch out the enjoyable evening. He took her hand to help her over a patch of ice, then didn't release her. They walked hand in hand through the quiet streets.

She was fiercely aware of his heat seeping through her gloves, of his solid strength beside her.

She sighed, knowing perfectly well she shouldn't find such comfort just from his presence. Matt made her feel…safe. He had a tendency to watch out for anything smaller than he was but for some reason he had singled her out for extra protection.

She didn't know why but it seemed as if every time she found herself in trouble, Matt was there to help her out. Whether she was falling off a swing at the playground, tripping in the halls, schoolyard bullies, even suffering that flat tire last summer. Whenever she needed him, he seemed to be there.

What a comfort that was, she realized. A girl could definitely find herself getting used to that.

She had missed him after she moved away. Oh, she had made several good friends at her new high school in Billings, friends she kept to this day, but none who would step up to look out for her like Matt.

This time, they walked back to his truck by a more residential route, passing the small, close-set houses of downtown Bozeman. All seemed to be adorned with holiday decorations, from elaborately lit facades to a simple Christmas tree in the window and a wreath on the door. They were still a block from his pickup when Elise suddenly grabbed Matt's arm, peering around him to the shadows near a white clapboard house.

"What was that?"

He looked around. "What's the matter?"

"I saw something out of the corner of my eye. Something huge." She squinted in the direction of the blur, vaguely aware even as she did that Matt had moved his body protectively in front of her, even though he didn't know what she was talking about or even if anything posed a threat.

Maybe it was just a shadow. No. There it was again.

Her gaze sharpened and she gasped. "Do you see it?" she asked him. "Over there by the corner of that house across the street. Near that big pine tree."

He scanned the area and then laughed. "A moose! Right in the middle of town. Think he's Christmas shopping?"

"How cool is that?" she exclaimed. "I've seen plenty of mule deer in town, even in Billings, but never a moose."

She stood with her hand in Matt's, heedless of the cold seeping into her bones as they watched the massive creature leisurely nibble on a bush as if he were standing at the buffet at a Christmas party.

They watched for a long time, until Matt suddenly snickered. "He'd better watch out for the colored lights on the next bush or he's going to find himself a not-very-merry crisp moose."

She groaned and laughed at the same time. "Oh. You had to go and ruin a lovely moment with a lame joke."

"Sorry." He smiled at her and reached to push a loose strand of hair away from her face, his suede gloves caressing her skin.

"You need to do that more often," he murmured.

"What? Complain about your corny jokes? Sure. Anytime."

"I meant laugh. I've always thought you had the sweetest laugh of anyone I know."

She stared at him for a long moment, her heart pulsing. What would he do if she kissed him? Just reached up on tiptoe and pulled his head down to hers? The moment stretched out between them, as bright and hopeful as those fairy lights dripping from the eaves of the nearby house. She drew up on her toes inside her boots…then chickened out and slid back down to the ground.

"The people inside have no idea he's even out here," she said, her voice hushed.

He was quiet for a moment, then he spoke in an equally hushed voice. "It's amazing what you can miss when you're not paying attention."

Her gaze flashed again to his and her stomach trembled at the intensity in his eyes and a moment later, his mouth brushed hers.

His lips were warm and firm and he tasted of chocolate and mint from the piece of gourmet candy their server had delivered with their check at the restaurant.

She closed her eyes and leaned into his strength. The night seemed magical. The lights, the moose, the easy flutters of snow. She felt so safe here, warm and content, a slow peace soaking through her.

She finally followed her impulse of earlier and rose up on her toes so she could wrap her arms around his neck, savoring the heat of him.

She was in deep trouble. Since Friday night she had wondered what it would be like to kiss him again. To really kiss him this time, not when she was slightly tipsy from too many margaritas but when she was completely clearheaded and rational.

Now she knew exactly how his mouth tasted and his arms felt around her, exactly how silky his hair was sliding through her fingertips and the strength of his muscles against her body.

What she didn't know was how, in heaven's name, she would manage to endure the rest of her life without more of this—without more of *him*.

She shivered suddenly, cold despite his heat engulfing her, and Matt immediately slid his mouth away.

"You're freezing," he murmured. "I'm a brute to keep you out here in the cold."

She couldn't tell him her reaction wasn't from the temperature but from reality slapping her around. Better to let him think she was in danger of freezing to death than to admit she was afraid of having her heart broken.

"That's probably a good idea."

They left the moose to his browsing and Matt grabbed her hand to lead her the rest of the way to his truck.

A single kiss shouldn't leave him feeling as if his world had been rocked off its whole foundation.

A half hour later as Matt drove back to Thunder Canyon, his heartbeat still hadn't managed to settle. Every time he looked at Elise in the seat beside him, blond and delicate and lovely, he felt that little tingle of awareness, the urgent throb of hunger.

He felt as if everything in his world had changed. A week ago, he thought he had everything figured out. He was happy with his life in Thunder Canyon, content working for his dad.

And then Elise Clifton blew back into town and

everything he thought was important seemed to have shifted.

For a few moments after they had returned to his pickup, they had made small talk. But even before they left the Bozeman town limits, she started to yawn. Now she appeared to be fast asleep.

He risked another quick glance across the cab of the truck. She seemed comfortable enough with her cheek pressed against the upholstery but he still had to fight the urge to ease her onto his shoulder and tuck her under his arm, which wasn't the most safe position when the roads were slick and icy from the light snow.

He sighed. What was he supposed to do with her now?

He hadn't missed that when she was talking about her options for the future, not once had she mentioned staying and settling down in Thunder Canyon for good. She had talked about returning to Billings and about spending time with her newly discovered birth parents, but never anything about staying in town.

What would he have to do or say to convince her to add that to her plate of possibilities? he wondered.

He had a feeling he would have to take things slow and steady with her. Anticipation curled through him. He didn't mind. He could be patient when the payoff promised to be everything he had never realized he wanted.

He was still mulling his options when he finally drove up to the Clifton's Pride ranch house.

"Elise? Sweetheart, we're back."

Her eyes blinked open. For a few seconds, she stared

at him with a disoriented look in her eyes and then she gave him a slow smile that made him wish he was seeing it from the comfort of his own bed, with her on the pillow next to him, instead of in the cramped cab of his pickup truck.

"Hey," she murmured. "Sorry I fell asleep. It was a crazy day at ROOTS today. I never realized just how exhausting a bunch of teenagers could be. I guess I was more tired than I thought."

"No problem. It was warm and cozy in here. I don't blame you a bit. I would have liked to sleep, too."

"I'm really glad one of us decided to stay awake."

She reached to open her door, but he quickly held out a hand to stop her. "Thank you again for your help picking out Haley's gift. I don't know what I would have done without you. I think she's going to be very happy with it."

She smiled. "You're welcome. I… It was really a lovely evening."

He couldn't help himself. Despite all his plans to give her time, he had to kiss her again, especially when she looked so soft and sleepy and adorable.

He leaned across the width of the pickup and cupped her chin, then lowered his mouth to hers. She seemed to sigh against him, just about the sexiest sound he'd ever heard and after a long moment, he felt her arms around his neck.

The kiss was slow and gentle, like an easy ride into the mountains on a summer evening. He intended to keep it that way, but then her mouth parted slightly and he couldn't resist deepening the kiss.

She froze for just a moment and then she was kissing him back, her mouth eagerly dancing with his, her curves pressed against him.

After several long, delicious moments, she finally jerked away, her breathing ragged. Her knit cap had fallen off and her hair was tousled. She shoved it away from her face with fingers that trembled slightly.

Her mouth was swollen from his kiss and he drew his fingers into fists to keep from reaching for her again.

She stared at him for a long moment, then she shook her head, that curtain of hair swinging with the movement. "This really isn't a good idea."

He pretended to misunderstand, even as he felt a hard knot of unease lodge under his breastbone. "I know. Been a long time since I made out in the cab of a pickup truck. Seems a lot harder than it used to be."

"You know that's not what I meant."

"Elise—"

She shook her head. "Don't. Let me finish. I'm obviously attracted to you. I have been for, well, a long time. But I…I'm not in a very good place right now for a casual fling. I need to tell you that."

He opened his mouth to argue that he wanted much more than that but she again cut him off.

"I'm still trying to sort out everything that's happened the last few weeks and I'm afraid I really can't afford this sort of…of distraction right now."

"I can wait."

She looked stunned by his words but quickly shook her head. "I'm not asking you to wait. That's not fair to either of us. Matt, you've always been a great friend to me. I don't want to risk losing that by complicating everything."

Now there was a tidy little bit of irony. He eased back into his seat. How many times had he used similar phrases while trying to let a woman down gently? He didn't know quite how to react. Mostly he was confused. How could she kiss him with such sweet passion and then try to brush him off in the next moment?

"I think you're just trying to come up with any excuse to run away," he finally said.

She narrowed her gaze. "Oh?"

"I think you sense we could have something really fantastic together and that scares you right now so you're taking the safe road."

She looked out the window. "We might have been friends in grade school, Matt, but it's been years. I'm not the same person I was then. Don't make the mistake of thinking you know anything about me or about what I feel right now."

"I know enough to recognize when someone's running away. Believe me, I've been doing it long enough myself that I recognize all the signs. You're scared."

"And you're unbelievable." She reached for her door.

"Elise, don't. I'm sorry." He was blowing this. Hadn't he just vowed to give her whatever time and space she needed? Now here he was jumping on her for being cautious. He needed to back off. He could be patient, especially with something this important.

"Forget I said anything. You're right. The timing is

lousy. You want to be friends, we'll be friends. I'm fine with that. Come on, I'll walk you to the door."

"That's really not necessary."

He gave her a pointed look that seemed to shut her up in a hurry. They trudged through the thin skiff of snow to the porch of the ranch house. It was past midnight and most of the windows were dark, though someone had thoughtfully left a light burning on the porch for her and a colorful Christmas tree blazed from the front window.

"Please don't be mad at me, Matt," she said in a low voice when they approached the front door. "I really did have a great time with you tonight. More fun than I've had in…a while now."

"I'm not mad," he protested, though it wasn't quite true. He was mad at circumstances—at Erin Castro for stirring up the past, at her family for not seeing how upset and lost Elise was, at himself for the lunacy at falling for her right now when she had other things to cope with.

He would deal, he told himself. What other choice did he have?

"Good night." He forced himself to give her only a kiss on the cheek, even though he wanted much, much more, then he turned around and walked back through the cold.

While she removed her coat and scarf and slid off her boots, Elise kept her gaze fixed out the window, watching Matt turn his truck around in the driveway then head back in the direction of Thunder Canyon.

She watched until his taillights faded pink in the lightly falling snow and then disappeared.

She wanted suddenly to be the sort of woman he was probably used to, someone who could flirt and laugh and kiss without thinking anything of it. But kisses meant something to her. Especially *his* kisses. She couldn't pretend otherwise.

A month or two ago, she might have been happy just for the chance to indulge her foolish daydreams about him, even at the risk of a little inevitable heartbreak. He was Matt Cates, for heaven's sake.

But she didn't have room in her life for that sort of mess and chaos right now.

She made the right choice, she told herself as she walked into the kitchen for a glass of water before heading to her room. Friendship with him was a much more safe option than these tantalizing kisses and terrifying emotions.

She saw a light glowing from the kitchen and just assumed her mother or Stephanie had left it on for her. She walked in to turn it off and discovered her sister-in-law sitting at the kitchen table with a mug bearing a silly blue snowman in front of her.

"Hey, you!" Elise exclaimed softly. "What are you still doing up?"

Stephanie gave her a quick smile and Elise thought how happy she was that her brother and one of her dearest friends had found love together. They had been married for three years now and seemed happier than ever.

"I couldn't sleep," Steph said.

"Everything okay?"

Stephanie made a face. "The baby's restless tonight. He's rolling around like he's calf roping in there."

Elise forced a laugh. "Maybe the kiddo is practicing the pre-Christmas hijinks to get the parents psyched and ready for all the sleepless nights a few years from now when he's a little kid waiting for Santa."

"Oh, don't remind me of that." Steph gestured to her mug. "I'm already having nightmares about putting together toys on Christmas Eve. I had a craving for cinnamon hot cocoa and thought it might help me and the baby relax a little. Want to join me?"

"Think I'll pass on the cocoa but I'll keep you company for a minute."

She sank into a chair across from Stephanie, thinking again how very much she had always loved the kitchen at Clifton's Pride. After she and her mother moved to Billings, Elise had missed many things about the ranch. Moonlit rides into the mountains, the excitement of roundup, the thrill of watching a newborn foal come into the world.

One of the things she had missed most of all was this kitchen, warm and comfortable and homey.

Steph and Helen had decorated the kitchen for Christmas, with greenery and lights and pinecones covering every unused space. As she sat with her sister-in-law in the hush of a December evening, she could fully understand why Steph and Grant loved it here so much.

She reached down and rubbed her feet, sore from her long day at ROOTS and then their snowy walk through Bozeman. Better not to think about that, she told herself, especially if she wanted to stick to her resolve to be only friends with Matt.

"How was your evening?" her sister-in-law asked.

Her mind flashed to the two kisses she and Matt had shared, both very different but equally intense.

"Nice," she paused, then added in what she hoped was a casual tone, "I went to Bozeman with Matt Cates."

"Helen mentioned you left her a message on her cell phone that you were going with him."

Elise heard the curiosity in her friend's voice and she purposely avoided her eyes. Steph and Haley both knew she'd had a major crush on Matt when they were girls. They had all giggled about him and Marlon and the other cute boys often enough at recess and sleepovers.

"Matt was trying to pick out a Christmas present for Haley and he asked for my input," she said.

"Did you find something?"

"Yes. I took him to that gallery near Grand Avenue, the one with all the embroidery. We found a gorgeous piece with an eagle alighting with outstretched wings in an oak tree. It will go beautifully in the ROOTS clubhouse."

Stephanie's eyes lit up. "That does sound perfect. Haley will be thrilled."

"I think so. It fits perfectly with her concept for ROOTS, a place where teens can stretch their wings while remaining rooted to values and traditions."

"I didn't realize art galleries stayed open this late," Stephanie said.

Elise shot her a quick look but her sister-in-law merely sipped at her hot cocoa with an innocent look. "We went to dinner afterward at that steak house you and Grant took me to a few years ago."

Stephanie was quiet for a moment, then she looked at her with concern in her eyes. "I guess Matt's fiancée must be an understanding sort."

Elise froze as her heart gave one hard, brutal kick in her chest. "Sorry. His…what?"

Stephanie looked apologetic. "Well, I'm not sure it's official yet, but someone in town asked me about it today."

"I'm sure it was a mistake." Oh, heavens. Let it be a mistake. Fate wouldn't play that particularly nasty trick on her twice.

"I don't know. My source sounded pretty credible. Remember we saw him at dinner last night with Christine Mayhew? Tall, leggy brunette?"

"Yes," Elise said, her voice low. She remembered the woman vividly and the way she and Matt had appeared so cozy together.

"The mother of one of my riding students works at the front desk of Thunder Canyon Resort. Joanie Martin. After the lesson today, we were chatting about the party next week at the McFarlane Lodge and about how hard Matt and his father had rushed to finish it. In the course of the conversation, she asked me if I'd heard about Christine and Matt yet. She said she overheard Matt telling someone after dinner last night that he and Christine were making plans for their future together. Speculation is they're going to announce it at Connor's big party on Christmas Eve."

The dinner she had barely touched at the Bozeman

restaurant seemed to congeal into a hard, nasty ball inside her stomach. She thought of his kisses and the tenderness in his arms.

We could have something really fantastic together.

Had that just been a line? She tried to remember their conversation and realized he had never once said anything that implied he wanted anything more from her than the fling she'd accused him of wanting except for that—which in the abstract was vague enough it could mean anything. He could have just been talking about great sex, since they seemed to strike such sparks off each other.

Engaged. How could he be engaged? She wanted to deny it, to chide Stephanie for listening to gossip. But Steph wouldn't lie and she wouldn't repeat something unless she considered the source credible. Elise had seen them too, talking and laughing, had seen Matt's arm around the other woman.

Hadn't she always known he was a player? Oh, he might kiss her with breathtaking intensity but it obviously meant little to him.

She felt nauseous, remembering another time, another place, when she had been forced to stand politely by while the man she thought she loved, the one she had given her virginity to just a few weeks earlier, had introduced her to his very lovely bride to be.

Was it really possible that she had completely misread the situation with Matt? Now she couldn't meet Stephanie's concerned gaze, afraid of what her sister-in-law might read in her foolish, foolish eyes.

"Matt and I are just friends," she mumbled, wondering why her lips suddenly felt numb and achy.

Friends. The word rang hollow. She certainly couldn't consider any man a friend who would put her in this position—and worse, when he would betray his fiancée with such callous disregard.

How foolish she was, still hanging on to childish dreams. That she would even consider for a moment that Matt might genuinely have feelings for her made her just about the most pitiful woman in the county.

For just a moment, she fought down a vicious stab of jealousy that some other woman would know the sweetness of those kisses, the strength of his arms, the tenderness of his lying, cheating smile.

"I'm sorry, El," Steph said.

She forced her own smile, hoping it looked more genuine than it felt.

"About what? Matt and I are friends," she repeated. Friends who neglect to mention an impending engagement. Who laugh and tease and kiss and betray.

"Whether he's engaged or not is no business of mine," she lied. "He needed a favor, I owed him one for rescuing me the other night at The Hitching Post. Now we're square. He's free to be engaged to a dozen women, as far as I'm concerned."

Steph didn't quite look convinced. Small wonder, since Elise couldn't even convince herself.

"You know, I'm beat. Think I'll leave you to your cocoa and the quiet. I wouldn't want to get the little one riled up again now that you've calmed him down."

Stephanie smiled a little but touched Elise's hand with concern still in her eyes.

"It's really been wonderful having you back here at the ranch. Just like old times. I don't think I've told you that enough since you came back."

Tears pricked the back of her eyelids as she hugged her sister-in-law and friend. She told herself it was just exhaustion from the busy day. "It's fun to watch you growing that baby in there. You're going to be a great mom, Steph."

Stephanie made a face. "We'll see about that. I have a lot to learn. But at least I can make a mean cup of hot cocoa."

Elise forced a smile and said good-night, then headed for her bedroom—the same one she had used when she was a girl, before her father's murder, when life at Clifton's Pride was warm and joyful.

By the time she closed the door behind her and sagged onto her bed with its blue-and-violet quilt, she was shaking with anger and something else, something dark and forlorn.

The anger was wholly justified. But she had no business entertaining even for a moment this yawning sense of betrayal, of loss.

Matt had never been hers. Not a half hour ago, she had bluntly told him she wasn't interested in a relationship. How pathetic must that had sounded to him, when he obviously wasn't interested in anything so formal, anyway?

She had a lucky escape, she reminded herself. Some wise part of her had warned her not to let herself be swept away by the moment, by the seductive magic of being in his arms.

Good thing she had listened to it and hadn't done something supremely foolish like allow her heart to get tangled up with his.

Right?

Chapter Eight

"**Y**ou're sure everything will be ready by the end of the week so we can bring in the decorators?" Connor McFarlane surveyed the kitchen where Matt was currently installing the knobs and handles on the custom cabinetry.

"That's the plan," Matt answered, carefully setting another hole. "Everything is on schedule. The carpet layers will be here tomorrow and we'll do the floor trim and hang the closet systems the day after that, and that should wrap it all up."

"Good. Excellent. I've got a team of designers coming in from McFarlane House hotels to finish up and they've informed me they need at least four days."

"We should be good," Matt said again. Better than

good. He loved a job well done. Finishing that job ahead of schedule was icing on the cake.

Connor ran a hand over the Italian marble countertops. "Cates Construction has gone above and beyond to bring the work in early. I want you to know I won't forget the work you've done here."

"It's been a pleasure." The words might seem polite but Matt sincerely meant them and he hoped Connor knew it.

He was proud to have his name associated with this particular construction project. McFarlane Lodge would be a showpiece in Thunder Canyon, tasteful and well-crafted. More than that, it would be warm and comfortable, a home for Connor, his son CJ and his wife to be, Tori Jones.

The only thing he loved more than setting the last tile and hammering the final nail was the other side of any building project: that first scoop of dirt in the backhoe, those heady days of pouring the foundation and framing the first few walls, when everything was still only possibilities.

He was particularly pleased about the chance to be part of building McFarlane Lodge, with its expansive views and the massive river-rock fireplace that served as the focal point in the open floor plan.

"I've got other irons in the fire around Thunder Canyon," Connor said with a significant look. "I'm going to need a dependable contractor. I'd love to keep Cates Construction at the top of that list."

Matt experienced a sharp burst of pride and a not inconsiderable degree of elation. He didn't doubt that the hotel magnate had various projects underway. Connor always seemed to be cooking up something and in this economy, anything that allowed Cates Construction to keep its workers swinging a hammer was a blessing.

"If we can fit in the job with our other commitments, we'll be happy to consider whatever work you send our way," he said, moving on to the next cabinet.

Connor smiled and patted the countertop. "I'm sure we can work something out. I'll be in touch."

"Sure thing."

After McFarlane left the kitchen a moment later, Matt glanced toward the adjacent laundry room. A grizzled gray buzz cut bobbed there and he could see his father lurking, pretending not to listen.

"You catch all that, Dad?" he asked with a grin.

Frank walked into the kitchen. "I heard. He's right. You've done a hell of a job with the place."

"This isn't a one-man show. The whole crew worked their tails off to get 'er done by Christmas."

"Don't be humble, son." Frank gave him a stern look. "It doesn't fit you. You're the one who made it happen on time and under budget and every single man on the crew knows it."

Matt flushed at the unexpected accolades. Frank was a good man and a wonderful father but he wasn't one for outright praise—his style was more like subtle encouragement. Matt didn't know quite how to respond.

"You've done so well the last few years, you're starting to put ideas in your mother's head."

Matt looked up and found his father looking remarkably ill at ease. "Oh? What sort of ideas?"

"Crazy ones." Frank sighed. "She's talking about taking a cruise. Maybe even a couple of them. She's even brought up maybe heading somewhere warm for the winter. Southern Utah, maybe, or Arizona. You know how the cold bothers her."

The idea of a Thunder Canyon without his parents was just too strange to contemplate. "What do you think about her ideas?"

His father was silent for a long moment. "I'm considering them. I've been in this business a long time. I've got old habits, old ways. Maybe it's time somebody else shook some new life into Cates Construction."

"Dad—"

"Your brothers aren't much interested in construction, son. Marshall's busy at the hospital and Mitch and Marlon both have their own companies. I don't suppose it's a surprise to you or any of them that I would like you to take over for me. Hell, you're doing most of the work, anyway. I'd just like to make it more official."

Excitement pulsed through him. This was what he wanted, he realized. Taking over the operations of Cates Construction fit him much better than law school ever could.

"I would have asked you before but I didn't want you to feel tied down to Thunder Canyon. You're still young. Your mother and I have always wanted you boys to feel free to experience the world on your own terms, not ours. But now that it looks like you're settling down, I figured this would be a good time to get things out in the open."

Matt stared. "Now that I'm what?"

His father looked uncomfortable. "Your mother's got some crazy idea you're getting married."

"Where did you hear that?" he asked.

"Apparently Edie heard a rumor last night at her bunco club about you," he answered. "A couple different people dropped a bug in her ear that you and Christine are talking about tying the knot."

The hammer suddenly slipped out of his fingers and he barely managed to snag it before it would have clattered onto the Italian tile floor.

He mentally hissed an expletive he wouldn't dare say aloud in front of his father. He should have known his impulsive gesture Sunday at The Gallatin Room would come back to bite him in the rear one day. He hadn't been thinking clearly or he never would have started the charade.

What the hell was he supposed to say to his father now?

"Um, don't believe everything you hear, Dad. Christine and I aren't getting married."

Frank narrowed his gaze. "What are you up to, son?"

"Nothing. This is all a big misunderstanding."

"I thought I taught you boys better than to mess around when it comes to this sort of thing."

"You did. I haven't been messing around."

Frank cleared his throat, looking ill at ease. "A woman's heart is a fragile thing, son. It's like that tile down there. If you'd dropped your hammer a minute ago, you might have chipped one of them fancy tiles. We might have repaired it, filled it in a bit. On the surface, it might look good as new, but there would always be a weakness there."

His father gave him a stern look. "Christine is a nice girl. If you're not serious about her, you need to cut her loose so she can find somebody who will be."

He did *not* want to be having this conversation with his father right now. "I hear you, Dad. Thanks for the advice."

"So you're going to do the right thing by Christine?"

"If by doing the right thing you mean marry her, then no. Trust me, Dad. Christine is not expecting an engagement ring from me. We're good friends, that's all."

His father continued to study him. "I hope you're right. I guess I need to tell your mother she won't be planning another wedding anytime soon."

For one insane moment, Matt pictured Elise in a white dress, something feminine and lovely, flowers in her blond hair and her face bright and joyful.

Whoa. Slow down. He drew in a sharp breath, astonished at the yearning trickling through him.

He wasn't at all ready to go there yet. Even if *he* was—which he clearly wasn't, right?—Elise certainly had made it apparent the night before that she didn't want to have anything with him beyond friendship.

That seductive image faded like an old photograph under a hard western sun. He had his work cut out for him to convince her he wanted more. But Matt had never been the sort to back down from a challenge.

* * *

Three hours later, Matt drove through town on his way to drop off a bid at a restaurant in Old Town Thunder Canyon that was planning a big remodeling project.

If the restaurant just happened to be on the same street as ROOTS, well, that was a happy coincidence. It would give him a chance to implement his new strategy for winning Elise over.

She claimed she didn't want to lose their friendship. Great. Fine. He had decided he would be the best damn friend she'd ever had. He would offer a sympathetic ear, a helping hand, a shoulder—whatever part of his anatomy she needed, until she discovered she didn't know how she could survive without him.

Though it was a weekday afternoon, Christmas shoppers were out in force in town. He happened to spy Bo Clifton and his very pregnant wife Holly heading into a clothing store, and Tori Jones and Allaire Traub coming out of the florists with their arms full of what looked like poinsettias and evergreen branches.

After he dropped off the bid to the restaurant owner, he dodged holiday shoppers and slushy snow piles down the street a few storefronts to the ROOTS clubhouse.

Connor McFarlane's son CJ sat with Ryan Chilton and a couple of other boys at one of the tables with textbooks open in front of them, though they didn't seem to be paying them much attention. A couple of teen girls he didn't know looked bored as they leafed through magazines on the couch.

As he had hoped, Elise was at Haley's desk, the

phone pressed to her ear. Her gaze lifted at the sound of the bells on the door chiming, a ready smile on her features.

The moment she spied him coming through the door, her smile slid away and her expression turned stony, much to his consternation.

He eased into the chair across from the desk. By the time she finished her phone call, her eyes were the wintry blue of the Montana sky on a clear January afternoon and her jaw looked set in concrete.

She hung up the phone, a muscle twitching in her cheek. "Can I help you?"

Not a good sign, when her voice was even colder than her eyes.

"Um, I was in the neighborhood dropping off a bid and figured I'd walk down and see if you need help filling the gift bags."

"They're done," she said curtly. "I finished them today."

This wasn't going at all as he'd hoped. "Okay, then. Any idea what my assignment might be for the Christmas party? Haley said something about needing some muscle for setting up tables, that sort of thing."

"I don't know. You'll have to ask her that."

"I'm assuming since you're here and she's not that she's still laid low with the flu," he hazarded a guess.

Elise jerked her head in a nod. "She sounded better this morning when she called. She should be back tomorrow. I'm sure you can talk to her then."

So much for his grand master plan. Elise was acting as if she didn't even want to share the same air space

with him. The night before, she had said she didn't want
to lose their friendship. Had he screwed that up now?

"What's wrong?" he finally asked warily. "You seem
upset."

She made the same sort of sound his mother did
when he tracked job-site mud on her mopped floors.
"Do I?"

He looked around the ROOTS clubhouse to make
sure none of the teens were paying attention to them,
then he leaned forward. "Is this about last night?"

Her jaw hardened even more and for a long moment,
he didn't think she would answer him. When she spoke,
the chill in her voice was nearing arctic proportions.

"I suppose you could say that. You put me in a terrible
position."

He glanced at the teens, who seemed to be arguing
about some super-hero movie and paying absolutely no
attention to them.

"Why? Because I kissed you?" he asked in a low
voice. "You weren't complaining at the time."

Whoops. Wrong thing to say. The ice queen disappeared in an instant. Elise shoved her chair back and
rose, her color high. He wouldn't have expected it, but
apparently his quiet, sweet Elise could pack a pretty
decent temper.

"You haven't changed a bit," she snapped. "You're
the same wild, irresponsible cowboy who thinks he can
use his charm to get away with anything!"

Where did that come from? "Hold it right there," he
said, pitching his voice low. "What the hell did I do?"

"You kissed me!" she hissed.

That drew the attention of the teens. A couple of them—the girls especially—cast sidelong looks in their direction. Maybe this conversation would be better in private, he thought, about five minutes too late.

He gestured with his head to the teens and then pointed to a back room. Mortification replaced some of the anger in her eyes but she gave a short nod and headed into the back room, closing the door behind them.

"I guess I haven't read the Thunder Canyon town ordinances closely enough," Matt said when they had some measure of privacy. "I didn't realize kissing a beautiful woman had been outlawed when I wasn't looking."

Two high spots of color flared on her cheeks. "It might not be a crime, but it's wrong on so many levels I don't even know where to start."

"Why?"

"You're engaged to marry someone else!"

He stared at her for about twenty seconds. He closed his eyes, cursing his big mouth and the white knight syndrome he couldn't seem to shake.

"This is about Christine?"

"Of *course* it's about Christine! I can't believe you even have to ask! I always knew you were a player, I just never imagined you would take things this far."

He had a feeling this was a disclaimer he was going to have to provide a few times before the rumors around Thunder Canyon started to fade. "I'm not engaged to Christine. I never was. We're only friends."

"Funny, that's not the rumor going around town. The minute I walked in the house last night, Stephanie was bending my ear about your engagement. And she's not the only one. I've now heard it from more than one person."

He loved living in Thunder Canyon but life in a small town where everybody cared about your business had some definite downfalls. A stray bit of gossip could run rampant like an August wildfire. With just a little fuel, it would spread to every corner, wreaking havoc in its path.

And he had stupidly been the one to set the match to this particular rumor. He should have expected this, damn it.

The hell of it was, he couldn't go around putting out this particular fire completely, not if Christine was going to convince her jackass of an ex that they were done.

He might not be able to tell everyone, but he could certainly confide the truth to Elise, he decided. "Look, if I tell you something, I need you to keep it to yourself, at least for a little while."

She crossed her arms over her chest, obviously not at all in the mood to listen to anything he had to say. Still, she didn't toss him out so he figured he would take what he could get at this point.

"The truth is, Christine had an overenthusiastic ex-boyfriend a few months back who couldn't seem to get the message they were really over. I wouldn't exactly put him in the stalker category, but maybe a step or two down from that. She confided in me one night what she'd been going through and somehow we decided to pretend to be dating in hopes the ex would finally figure out it was over."

"So out of the goodness of your heart, you agreed to pretend to date a beautiful woman with absolutely pure and altruistic motives."

He fought down annoyance at her sharp tone. "I never said that. I'll be honest, it was a mutually beneficial arrangement. My parents stopped bugging me for a while about settling down for the first time since Haley and Marlon got together. And I enjoy Christine's company. She's a very fun person. But we're not engaged and never will be. Neither of us feels that way about the other."

She didn't look convinced. "For the sake of argument, let's say I was stupid enough to believe you. Don't you think becoming engaged to the woman is taking your charade a little too far?"

He sighed. How to explain this part without sounding like a complete idiot? "We bumped into a cousin of the ex-boyfriend outside The Gallatin Room the other night. Completely on the spur of the moment, I figured this was the perfect opportunity to convince the guy things were over, once and for all. I never really stopped to consider the consequences, that word might trickle out and we would have to explain the truth someday."

He thought he detected a slight thaw in her expression but it was barely perceptible so he pressed harder.

"I'm telling the truth, Elise. Come on, think about it. Do you really believe I'm the kind of guy who would announce his engagement one night, then spend the next night kissing someone else?"

She gave him a long, considering look. "I can't answer that, Matt. I guess that's part of the problem. I've been away from Thunder Canyon for a long time. All

I know are the rumors I've heard about your wild past. Didn't you and Marlon get engaged a few years ago to twins you'd barely met?"

He winced. She *would* have to dredge up that little gem of a story, one of his less than stellar moments. "We were young and stupid. I think it was more of a joke than anything. Marlon and I have both changed over the years. Look at him, happily engaged to Haley. And he was always the reckless one, not me. I was mostly along for the ride."

He thought the ice thawed just a little more. At least she didn't look ready to feed him to the wolves yet.

"Trust your instincts, El," he said softly, reaching for her hand. "We're friends. I wouldn't treat any woman like that, not Christine and not you."

She stared at him for a long moment and he could feel the tremble of her slender fingers. She swallowed hard and opened her mouth to say something, but at that moment the door was shoved open.

CJ McFarlane burst in, all auburn hair and lanky skater boy. He didn't seem to notice any of the fine-edged tension in the room. "We're starving, Miz Clifton. Okay if we nuke a couple bags of popcorn? Haley keeps a supply back here."

"Um, sure." She stepped away from Matt and tucked a strand of hair behind her ear. "Anything else you need?"

"No. Popcorn ought to do it."

She gave Matt a long look, then returned to the other room. He followed, frustrated and more than a little annoyed that she was being so stubborn.

"I guess I'll give Haley a call about what she needs me to do for the party. Sorry I bothered you," he said tersely and headed for the door.

"Matt. Wait."

He turned. "Yeah?"

She twisted her fingers together and chewed her bottom lip. "What was I supposed to think?" she finally said with a quick look at the kids. "Stephanie's not the sort to make up stories."

"And I'm not the sort to string two women along. You ought to know me better than that."

She sighed. "I've been in that position before, in college. The other woman, I mean. My first real boyfriend was a…well, a jerk. I dated him for three months and never knew he had been engaged for a year to marry a girl in his hometown right after graduation. Then I bumped into them one day while they were picking out wedding flowers and had to stand there, stunned and heartbroken, while he introduced me as some girl he had a class with."

She paused, fidgeting with a stapler on Haley's desk. "It was an awful situation. I hated thinking you could do the same thing to me or to Christine."

He sighed. He felt like he was doing nothing but taking one step forward and two or three giant steps backward with her.

"I'm sorry you were hurt that way. But I'm not some idiot you knew in college, Elise. You've known me for a long time. You should have given me a chance to explain before you jumped to all kinds of crazy conclusions."

He was hurt, he realized. It was a feeling he wasn't

very accustomed to when it came to his dealings with women.

"I've got to go." He didn't want her to see it, didn't want to reveal the depth of his feelings for her just yet, not when she was fighting him every step of the way. "Tell Haley I dropped by and I'll do whatever she needs me to for the party."

"Matt—"

He didn't wait for whatever else she wanted to say, only pushed open the door and walked out of the ROOTS clubhouse and into the December afternoon that seemed to have lost all its good cheer.

Chapter Nine

"Everything looks absolutely perfect!"

Haley slung her arm over Elise's shoulders and pulled her close as they stood in the doorway admiring the winter wonderland they had spent all day creating in the ROOTS clubhouse.

"You did a fantastic job with the whole thing. You should be a party planner, El. You didn't need me after all," Haley said.

"Not true. I never could have thrown it all together without you the last two days. I still think you're overdoing it, though. Are you sure you're up to this?"

"I'm feeling almost back to normal, if I can only shed this stupid cough." As if to illustrate her point, she suddenly had to step away from Elise in order to cough into the corner of her sleeve.

"Sorry. I really am feeling better," she said after a moment. "Those garlands you made are fantastic and the swag bags are perfect."

"The kids are going to have a great time." She smiled at her friend, noting all the changes in Haley over the last few months. Her friend glowed with happiness, even though she still looked pale and worn-out from her illness.

Elise was thrilled for her. Haley's handbag design business, HA! was taking off, she was passionately committed to the success of ROOTS and she was deeply in love with Marlon Cates, who loved her right back.

She deserved all those wonderful things and more after giving up her dreams early in order to take care of her younger siblings after her single mother's untimely death.

Elise wouldn't have begrudged her any of it and she refused to feel even a tiny niggle of envy that everything seemed to be coming together so perfectly for Haley when Elise's life seemed like such a tangled mess.

"What you're doing here is a good thing, Haley. It's been really cool to be a part of it this week, in my small way."

"Not small." Haley squeezed her arm with affection. "You know we would have had to cancel the whole thing if you hadn't stepped in to save the day. I can't begin to tell you how much I appreciate it."

"I had help," Elise said. "Your hardworking volunteers plus those amazing kids."

"They are, aren't they? Amazing, I mean. I think I

get more out of associating with them than the other way around."

She looked at the clock suddenly. "And speaking of the kids, they're going to be here any minute now. You're staying, right? I won't let you leave, not after all your hard work."

Elise nodded. "I brought some party clothes to change into so I didn't have to go back to the ranch to change."

"See, that's why you always were the smartest girl I know."

Ha, Elise thought as she headed for the ROOTS women's restroom. If she were as smart as Haley thought, she would have stayed far away from Matt Cates the moment she spied him at The Hitching Post the other night. Instead, she had let her life become more and more entwined with his and now here she was fighting down completely inappropriate anticipation at the likely possibility that he would come to the party.

Not that he would be thrilled to see her. The last time she had seen him, the anger in his eyes that she had believed he was two-timing his fiancée by kissing Elise would have melted every inch of snow on the whole road out front.

She hadn't seen him in four days, since that tense scene here. His outrage still seemed unfair. If he was telling the truth—and she still hadn't managed to completely convince herself of that, despite every instinct that urged her to believe him—he and Christine Mayhew *wanted* people to think they were engaged, right?

Or at least one particular person, Christine's ex-boyfriend.

For him to be angry with Elise for believing the rumors they had started themselves seemed wrong, somehow.

She changed quickly, out of jeans and a hooded sweatshirt into a pair of black slacks and a shimmery white blouse, sheer at the neck and sleeves, then sighed as she replaced the utilitarian small hoops she'd put in her ears that morning with her favorite chunky, dangly crystals.

Why did it matter if Matt was upset with her? Engaged or not, her reasons for stopping their kiss the other night at Clifton's Pride remained. Nothing had changed since Monday. If anything, things were more tangled than ever now that Jack and Betty Castro were returning to Thunder Canyon for the holidays.

She thought of the phone call she had received the night before from Betty and her stomach quivered with nerves.

Betty and Jack were back in Montana, staying with friends in Billings. Betty had sounded desperately eager for Elise to join them for dinner on Sunday. She knew they genuinely wanted to get to know her, to forge whatever relationship they could with her.

Elise had always considered herself a nice person. She tried to treat people with decency and respect. But the Castros' continued overtures made her want to saddle up one of the Clifton's Pride horses and ride fast and hard into the mountains to hide out somewhere she wouldn't be found for days.

Her reaction was ridiculous, she knew, and rather shameful. The Castros weren't trying to hurt her. They only wanted to become acquainted with the child who had been taken from them by circumstances beyond anyone's control.

After she applied a new coat of mascara, Elise gazed in the mirror at the face she had seen looking back for twenty-six years. She had inherited her cheekbones, her eyes, the curve of her mouth from Betty and Jack. Didn't she owe it to them to at least be cordial?

She had two brothers she didn't know, an entire family history to learn. She couldn't keep avoiding them, hoping this whole tangled mess would just sort itself out. It was time to face her angst.

But not tonight. This was a Christmas party and she wouldn't ruin it for the teens that Haley helped.

The first guests had started to arrive by the time Elise finished changing her clothes and makeup. Haley had started playing some holiday music and Elise could see a group of teens already taking to the small dance floor they had set up.

She could see Haley's siblings, Austin and Angie, as well as many of the volunteers and teens she had become acquainted with the past week, including CJ McFarlane, Roy Robbins and Ryan Chilton.

Marlon was helping Haley fiddle with the speakers.

And Matt. Her insides did a long, slow roll when she spotted him filling glasses with punch at the refreshments table.

He looked dark and rugged and absolutely gorgeous in a dark green sweater, tan slacks and boots.

He wasn't alone, Haley suddenly realized. Next to him was the lovely brunette she recognized from the restaurant the other night, though that seemed a lifetime ago.

Christine Mayhew.

They were talking and laughing but she had to admit they looked more friendly than romantic. Was it possible he was telling the truth? She wanted to believe him. The last three days she hadn't heard any more rumors about any engagement—but she hadn't heard anything about it being a sham, either.

Haley suddenly grabbed her arm, distracting her from any more pointless wondering. "Help! I can't find the MP3 player I spent hours loading with a Christmas dance mix while I was sick," Haley wailed. "Have you seen it?"

"Is it your pink one? I think I saw it on the table in the back room. Let me go see if I can find it."

She supposed it wasn't a very good sign when she couldn't wait to leave a party not three minutes after she showed up. She hurried to the other room and emerged a moment later with the MP3 player in her hand.

Haley hugged her. "You're a lifesaver! We would have had to listen to 'Jingle Bell Rock' all night."

"Oh, horrors!"

Her friend laughed and headed back to Marlon and the sound system. Elise was just about to go talk to Austin and Angie when she saw Christine Mayhew heading in her direction.

The other woman was indeed beautiful, tall and curvy. Elise felt about twelve years old in contrast.

She wasn't at all prepared when Christine gave her a warm, friendly smile. "You're Elise Clifton, right?"

"Yes," she admitted warily.

"I'm Christine Mayhew. Matt's told me a lot about you."

"Has he?"

Christine's smile was warm and open and not the slightest bit jealous. "I have to tell you, I've never seen him like this about any other woman."

She stared. "Like…what?"

"Nothing. Sorry. Forget I said anything." Christine sent an amused look over her shoulder to where Matt was watching them intently. "I'm on a very important mission here tonight."

"Oh?"

"I'm under strict orders to convince you beyond a sliver of doubt that Matt and I are not engaged."

Elise cast a quick look at Matt then shifted her gaze away. She knew perfectly well she shouldn't have this little fizz of happiness welling up inside at the word.

"Matt is a great guy," Christine went on. "Don't get me wrong. I care about him and always will. But there won't be any wedding bells ringing for the two of us. We're friends, that's all. I swear it."

What was she supposed to say in response? *I'm really happy to hear that* didn't seem quite appropriate under the circumstances.

"He was doing me a favor," the other woman said firmly.

"Why are you telling me this?"

"Matt asked me to. He told me he explained it all to you but you still had some doubts."

"What about your ex-boyfriend?"

Christine shrugged. "Word on the street is that he's started dating someone else recently. I can only hope she turns out to be a keeper for him so he'll take my number off his speed dial."

She paused and studied Elise until she could feel her face heat in another of those blasted blushes. "Can I give you some advice?"

"Okay," she said slowly.

"I've been friends with Matt for a while now and as I said, I've never seen him like this over any woman." Christine gave her a careful smile. "I think you're more important to him than even he wants to admit."

Elise shot him another look. Though he was busy talking to his twin brother, he must have felt the weight of her stare because he shifted his attention to her. For a moment they stared at each other and the crowd, the decorations, the music all seemed to fade.

"Matt is a great guy. When he finally falls for a woman, I have a feeling he will move heaven and earth to make her feel happy and safe and loved."

Elise drew in a shaky breath. She didn't know what to say. She did know she shouldn't be fighting this powerful yearning to be that woman.

"Pretending to be his girlfriend these last few months has been great fun," Christine added, her glittery earrings reflecting the Christmas lights from the tree. "I can only imagine being the real thing would be a million times better."

With that parting shot, she walked away, leaving Elise floundering for a response.

For the next hour, she carefully avoided Matt as she circulated among the party guests and helped Haley with hostess duties. She knew she owed him an apology for ever doubting him but the middle of a noisy, festive party full of teenagers didn't quite seem the proper venue.

She was in the kitchen preparing another plate of appetizers when she finally couldn't avoid him any longer.

He walked in and something unreadable flashed in his gaze when he spotted her there. "I'm under orders from Haley to see if there are any more of those cheesy cream puff thingies in here."

"A few. I was just about to carry them out."

"Here, I can take them." She handed him the tray but instead of heading back out to the party, he stood in the doorway.

"It's a great party, Elise. Haley's giving you all the credit."

"Not true," she protested. "She had already laid all the groundwork. I only had to finalize a few details."

"Well, you did a great job. Everyone seems to be having a wonderful time, from the kids to their parents to the volunteers. And I know fundraising wasn't the intent of the party but Haley said donations have been pouring in."

She could barely focus on anything but Christine's words. *I've never seen him like this about another woman.*

She had to be wrong. He was treating her just like

he treated everyone else. Maybe even on the cold side of the politeness thermostat.

"More donations are always good."

He gave a short laugh and set the plate of appetizers back down on the counter. "Yeah, they are. Haley has done wonders with a small amount of money. Who knows what she can accomplish when her funds increase?"

He paused and gave her a careful look. "So do you want to tell me why you sound like I just told you somebody injected botulism into the cream puff thingies?"

She blinked, then flushed. "I'm happy about the donations. I just...I...I owe you an apology."

"I guess you've talked to Christine."

She sighed. "She was only corroborating what I already knew. I believed you that day you came here to ROOTS and explained about your sham engagement."

He winced. "It was never supposed to go that far, I swear it. I didn't expect anyone else to hear about it. I'm sorry you were caught up in it. The whole thing was stupid."

Christine was right, Elise realized. Matt was a good man. When he gave his heart, he would give it completely. He would never betray the woman he loved for some thrill *du jour*.

He couldn't be more different than her first boyfriend.

She drew in a deep breath, her pulse racing. "Christine basically told me I would be crazy if I didn't...give things with you a chance."

He gazed down at her but said nothing for several

long moments. The party sounds were muted in here, just a throb of bass, and she could swear she heard her heart beating in her ears, keeping time to the music.

"Are you going to listen to her?" he finally asked.

She swallowed hard and realized just where they were both standing—under one of the many clumps of mistletoe the kids had hung for the party.

"I'm thinking about it," she murmured, then without giving herself time to second-guess, she rose on tiptoes and brushed his mouth with hers.

He froze for just a moment, his mouth firm and delicious against hers, and then he made a low sound in his throat and kissed her back with a slow and aching gentleness.

Both of them kept their eyes open and she was hypnotized by the deep brown of his eyes as he stared back at her, unsmiling.

In that instant, she made a decision, what felt like a monumental one to her.

She eased away and gave him a tentative smile. "Would you like to go to Billings Sunday with me to have dinner with my...with Jack and Betty Castro?"

He looked as if he hadn't quite heard her right. "You want me to go with you while you have dinner with your birth parents?"

She nodded, feeling edgy and foolish and wondering if she was crazy to even ask. "To be honest, I think I could use a friend on my side there. But more than that, I really would like to...spend time with you. If you want to, anyway. I thought it would give us a little time to talk, on the way there and back."

She sounded like a complete idiot. Why couldn't she be smart and sophisticated, someone like Christine?

But Matt didn't seem to mind. His eyes were warm and he seemed to know exactly how difficult she had found it to ask him.

"That sounds terrific. Really terrific, as long as you're sure the Castros won't mind if I tag along."

"I don't think they will."

"Great. It's a date."

A date. She did a little mental gulp but it was too late to back down now.

"We'd better get these appetizers in there before those teenage boys start eating the popcorn strings I worked so hard on."

"Good idea."

He grabbed the plate and they headed back into the reception area.

Christine was sitting at a table talking to Erika Traub and a very pregnant Holly Clifton. She smiled when she saw them emerge from the kitchen together but Elise was painfully aware of a few speculative looks zinging between the two of them and Christine.

When news started to filter out of Matt's "breakup" with Christine, speculation was bound to fly that perhaps Elise was the cause of it. The thought of being the subject of more gossip filled her with dread and for a moment she was tempted to tell Matt to forget about everything.

No. She was tougher than that. She could withstand gossip. Hadn't she been doing it since her father's murder?

Matt smiled at her and she resolved to forget about everything for the rest of the night, to simply enjoy the party.

It was long past time she found a little holiday spirit.

Chapter Ten

"What was your favorite subject in school?"

Elise took a sip from her water glass at the elegant restaurant in Billings, doing her best to handle what felt very much like an interrogation. Beside her, Matt nudged his knee against hers and out of the corner of her gaze, she took great comfort from his supportive smile.

"Um, English," she finally answered. "I've always loved to read. Working in a bookstore is a dream come true."

That was apparently the perfect thing to say to a high school teacher. Betty's eyes warmed and her smile widened. "You come by that naturally, my dear. Women on my side of the family have always been big readers.

My mother, my aunts. All of us. They're all dying to meet you, by the way."

Oh, mercy. Elise hadn't given much thought to extended relatives she might have to meet. Aunts, uncles, cousins. Just the thought of it had her snatching up her water glass again and gulping it like she had just run a marathon through the Mojave.

Under the table, she felt Matt's leg nudge her knee again. He was doing it on purpose, she knew, offering her whatever physical comfort she could take from his touch.

"So Jack, tell me about being a police officer in San Diego. Harbor police, isn't it?" Matt asked as smoothly as the attorney he might have become, finessing a witness. "You probably deal with some really fascinating cases. What were you working on just before you came out to Montana?"

"My partner and I are trying to nail a money launderer working with the Mexican cartels. It's mostly legwork but we've had some close calls."

With Matt's subtle encouragement, all through their entrées Jack told stories about his work while Betty added her own perspective about what life was like being married to a police officer.

Elise liked both of them. They seemed to be a genuinely nice couple who loved each other and their family. That was one of the toughest things about everything that had happened. If circumstances had been different, she would very much have enjoyed the chance to get to know them.

Jack was just like the delicious cheese rolls they

served at the restaurant…crusty on the outside but warm and gooey at heart. Betty was smart and funny with a deep streak of kindness Elise had already sensed.

They seemed great, two people she instinctively wanted to know better. But everyone just seemed to expect so much of her.

Maybe it was only her. Erin didn't seem to be having the same trouble adjusting to everything. From the moment Erin met Helen and Grant, she seemed to instantly love them and had melded into the fiber of their family with apparent ease, with none of this stiff awkwardness Elise felt around her birth parents.

Elise knew she couldn't love them as parents and probably never would. Helen and John were her parents and no amount of DNA testing would ever change that, just as Matt kept trying to tell her. She just wished she could relax and become more comfortable with Jack and Betty's eagerness to be part of her life.

She just had to try harder, she told herself. "How long will you be staying in Montana?" she asked at the next conversational lull.

Betty and Jack exchanged a look. "We don't have to be back for work until after the New Year," Betty said.

"We actually wanted to talk to you about that," Jack added.

Her nerves suddenly tightened. "Oh?"

"Erin tells us you've left your job at that bookstore here in Billings to spend some time in Thunder Canyon with your mother and brother."

"I'm not sure if that's a permanent leave or not. I guess you could say I'm on sabbatical."

Jack and Betty exchanged another look, then Betty reached across the table and gripped Elise's hand in hers. Her birth mother's fingers were long and slender, just like hers, Elise thought.

"I know we've mentioned this in passing before but we wanted to make more of a formal offer. We would really love you to come stay with us for a while."

Elise felt a lump rise in her throat at their hopeful faces and she didn't know how to respond.

Betty squeezed her fingers. "We have tons of room now. It's just the two of us, since your brothers…" She faltered a little and looked at Jack for help, then cleared her throat. "Since our sons are both back east now."

Elise had never lived anywhere but Montana. The idea of moving to California wasn't without some appeal, she had to admit, but beneath the table, Matt's long leg tensed next to hers and a muscle flexed in his jaw—reminding her of a very big reason she wasn't sure she wanted to leave Montana just now.

The Castros seemed to sense her hesitation.

"Don't worry about answering now," Jack said in that gruff tone she was beginning to recognize was characteristic for him when his emotions were involved. "You just think about it over the holidays. And you know, maybe you might enjoy just coming down for a couple weeks and testing the waters a bit."

"Which are lovely, by the way," Betty added. "The waters, I mean. Beach, sunshine, perfect weather."

"Beats scraping six inches of snow off your car every morning during a Montana winter," Jack said.

"I can see where it would." She managed a smile, more than a little charmed by this taciturn police officer.

She thought of her father, strong and honorable and handsome, always willing to listen to her troubles and offer her advice. She had desperately missed having a father in her life during her formative teenage years, when everything from boys to school to her future seemed so confusing. Grant had tried to fill a paternal role in her life, but an older brother's advice wasn't quite the same as a father's.

"I'll think about it," she promised them now, aware of Matt's continued tension beside her.

The conversation shifted to foods she enjoyed and stories about her childhood. By the time they finished dessert, some of the tautness in her shoulders had eased.

She was suddenly glad she had come—and immensely grateful to Matt for being so willing to step up and join them as her support system.

"Thank you for coming all the way to Billings just for dinner," Jack said after he'd picked up the check. "We would have been happy to come to Thunder Canyon, you know. We're going to be there anyway in a few days."

"I know. That's what Betty said when we discussed arrangements over the phone. But I really didn't mind coming here."

Actually, she had been the one to suggest they meet in Billings—she just hadn't told the Castros why—that she wanted to avoid all the prying eyes in Thunder Canyon and those who would be sure to gossip about Elise meeting up with her birth parents for dinner.

Since the Castros mentioned they planned to stay with friends in Billings before coming to Thunder Canyon in time for Christmas, she had jumped at the opportunity to meet them in relatively neutral territory.

"This was lovely," Betty said while they were finding their coats.

"It was." Elise shivered a little when Matt's fingers brushed her hair as he helped her into her coat.

"We'll see you again while we're here," Betty said. "Your mother invited us out to the ranch for Christmas Eve, then called back to say you were all going to a big party at some new lodge and we were invited to that as well."

Helen hadn't mentioned she had invited the Castros to Connor McFarlane's lodge opening.

"Everyone in town is talking about it," Elise said. "Matt and his father actually built it."

"It will be good to see some of our old Thunder Canyon friends," Jack said.

A few hours ago, Elise might have dreaded the idea of facing them again in a few days. Now she didn't find it nearly as overwhelming. She was making progress, she thought. Baby steps still made up forward motion, right?

"Have a safe journey back to town, my dear," Betty said. She wrapped Elise in a lavender-scented hug. When she pulled away, Elise was disconcerted to see tears in her eyes. She was more surprised when Jack also wrapped his arms around her.

"You think about what we said, about coming down to San Diego. We would sure love having you there."

"I will," she promised.

Matt took her hand when they left the restaurant. The sky was a starless matte black and the air carried the smell of impending snow.

Matt held the door of his pickup open for her. Acting completely on impulse, Elise brushed her lips along his jawline. "Thank you so much for coming with me tonight. It means the world to me. I'm not sure I could have made it through without you."

He shook his head and kissed her forehead. "You did fine, El. Great, in fact. I could barely tell you were nervous."

She eased back onto the seat while he walked around to the driver's side. When he climbed inside and started the truck, he immediately turned the heater on high to take away the chill.

"They seem like nice people," he said.

"They are." She closed her eyes and rotated her neck to ease some of the strain of the evening. "I think I suddenly realized tonight that letting them into my life and maybe my heart isn't really a betrayal of my family."

He gripped her fingers in his. "Of course it's not. There's room enough in there for everybody."

Including tall, dark-eyed cowboys with sexy smiles.

Elise shivered a little, suddenly stunned by how very quickly Matt had become such an important part of her life.

Despite the poor timing and the general emotional uproar in her life, she was falling in love with him. Real love, not some girlish infatuation. Each moment she spent with him, those ties binding her heart to him tugged a little more tightly.

She ought to be terrified, but somehow all she could manage for now was a little flare of panic, quickly squelched.

"I hate to ask after you've already been so wonderful to come all this way with me just for a steak…"

"A great steak. And wonderful company," he corrected.

She smiled. "Right. But I forgot one of my mother's Christmas presents at our house here in Billings. I bought it months ago and hid it in the back of the closet. Somehow I overlooked it when I was packing for the move to Thunder Canyon. The house is only a few blocks from here. Do you mind if we stop there before we head back?"

"Not at all."

She gave him directions and a few moments later they drove down the wide, tidy street where she and her mother had lived for more than a decade.

Neighbors along their street had always enthusiastically celebrated the holidays. Every house had decorations of some sort—from a couple of those big inflatable snow globe thingies to the discreet colored bulbs the sweet, elderly Mrs. Hoopes in the little house on the corner left up year-round.

By contrast, the small brick house she shared with her mother looked dark and cheerless against the dank sky, even though a few of the windows gleamed with the lights they had set on timers to avoid announcing to the world the house was empty.

They should have at least put up a Christmas tree before they left for Thunder Canyon. Neither of them had thought of it in all the craziness of discovering the mix-up at Thunder Canyon Hospital twenty-six years ago.

"So do you think you'll go to San Diego with the Castros?" Matt asked after he put the pickup in gear in the driveway of her house.

She shot him a quick look. Though his tone was casual, his brown eyes watched her intently. Her mind flashed back to that stunning kiss beneath the mistletoe, to the soft, tender peace that had wrapped around them like holiday ribbons.

"I need to give it more thought. I certainly wouldn't mind escaping the cold this winter but there are…other reasons I'm not sure I want to leave Thunder Canyon right now."

The silence seemed to seethe between them and she could feel her cheeks burn from more than just the pickup's heater. She reached for the door handle, needing to escape the finely wrought tension inside the cab.

"It should only take me a moment to find the gift in my closet."

"I'll come with you," he said.

"If you want, I'm sure I can find some cocoa or something before we start out back to Thunder Canyon."

"Sounds great."

He opened the door for her then took her elbow to

help her through the snow. She and her mother had paid a neighbor boy to keep the walks clear and it looked as if he was keeping up with his responsibility. Still, Matt didn't let go and she was grateful for his warmth as he helped her up the steps to the small porch.

Inside, the house had that expectant feeling of a place that hadn't seen human interaction in a few weeks. The air was musty and still and a thin layer of dust that would make her mother crazy if she saw it had already begun to settle on everything.

Matt flipped on more lights, taking an obvious interest in the comfortable chic decor Helen favored.

Though small, the house had always seemed warm and bright to Elise, especially after the oppressive darkness that had descended on Clifton's Pride after her father's murder.

"Nice," Matt said.

She smiled as she untwisted her scarf and set it on the usual spot atop the console table in the entry.

"I think it became a haven of sorts for both of us after my father died. Grant was busy with his own life by then, so my mother and I just had each other. We made a pretty good life here."

"You didn't want to go off on your own?"

She shrugged. "I moved into an apartment for a year or so while I was in college but it seemed silly to pay rent when my mother and I have always had a great relationship and never seemed to get in each other's way."

She paused and gestured to the living room. "Go ahead and make yourself comfortable. It will only take me a minute to grab my mom's present and then I'll see what I've got in the kitchen."

"Why don't I do a walk-through of the house, check the pilot lights on the furnace and water heater, the pipes, that sort of thing?"

She smiled a little. Wasn't that just like him, to think about those sorts of guy details that probably wouldn't have occurred to her? "Thanks. Good thinking," she answered, then headed down the hall to her bedroom.

Her room was icy and she took a moment to flip on the gas fireplace for an instant warm-up. After she pulled her desk chair over to her closet, she climbed up to dig in the back recesses of her top shelf for the handcrafted necklace and earring set she had purchased for her mother at a summer art fair and then promptly forgotten about until the other day.

After she returned the chair to her desk, her gaze landed on a framed picture that had sat there so long it had become a usually overlooked part of the landscape.

She picked it up, the glass frame cold and heavy in her hands. The picture had been taken at Clifton's Pride a few weeks before her father's death. If she remembered correctly, one of her aunts had taken it near the horse paddock and it featured all of them—John, Helen, Grant and her, looking skinny and small with blond braids and a little freckled nose.

She looked absolutely nothing like the rest of her family. Everything was different—the shape of her eyes, the tilt of her nose. How had they all missed the signs for all these years?

She was a changeling, an interloper.

Her thumb traced John Clifton's strong, smiling features, frozen forever in her memory just like this. Raw emotions bubbled up in her throat, clogging her breath. She missed him so dearly.

What would he have to say about this whole mess? She couldn't even begin to guess. Then she thought of Jack Castro and his gruff eagerness to be part of her life.

It was too much. The stress of the evening, her conflicted feelings, everything. She sagged onto her desk chair and clutched the photograph to her chest, fighting tears and memories and this gaping sense of loss.

Some time later, she heard Matt walking down the hall and hurriedly swiped at her stupid tears.

"Everything looks like it's running just fine," he said. "I nudged the thermostat up a little bit while we're here. Remind me to turn it back down when we go."

His voice trailed off as he entered the room and Elise winced. Why did he always have to see her at her worst? She felt like she had been an emotional mess since the moment she bumped into him at The Hitching Post.

He crossed to her quickly, his eyes dark with concern. "What's the matter? What happened?"

She gave a resigned sigh and held out the picture. "I thought I was doing so much better about everything tonight at dinner. Coming to terms with…all of it. I had a good time with Jack and Betty. They're very nice people, people I think I could grow to care about. Then I saw this picture of my family…the family I've always known as mine…and I just feel like I've lost something somehow."

"Oh, sweetheart. Come here."

He pulled her into his arms and she hitched in a breath, feeling foolish and weepy and deeply grateful.

"This is so stupid." She sniffled. "I'm such a mess."

"Anyone else would be in the same situation. You've had the rug yanked out from under you again, just like it was when your father was killed."

She stared at him, stunned that he could so clearly understand something she hadn't even put together in her own head. She felt as if she were reliving those terrible days of loss and uncertainty all over again. "That's it exactly! I'm not sure how to go on now that everything has suddenly changed."

"You're doing fine, Elise. Give yourself some credit."

His faith in her warmed a cold place deep inside. "Thanks, Matt. You must be so sick of me and my maunderings.

Yes. Exactly! She felt as if she were reliving those terrible days of loss and uncertainty all over again as she struggled to adapt to her changing situation.

"I don't know what that word means," he admitted with a soft smile. "But I'm not sick of you. I could never be sick of you, Elise."

His arms tightened around her and with a sense of inevitability, she lifted her mouth to his. When his lips slanted over hers lightly, the whole twisting, crazy emotional snarl inside her seemed to settle.

The kiss was slow and tender, and she closed her eyes and savored it.

"Thank you," she murmured after a long moment. "I don't know what I would have done without you here tonight, both earlier and just now."

"You would have made it through," he replied. "You're much tougher than you seem to think, El."

"When you say that, you make me want to believe it."

He kissed her, his arms a warm comfort around her. "I remember after your dad died, watching how you coped with everything you'd been hit with. I thought then what a strong person you were. I could tell you were hurting, but you survived it. I always admired that about you."

She was quiet for a long moment, her feelings for him a thick, solid weight in her chest, and then she stood on tiptoe again and kissed him, telling him with her mouth and her hands the feelings she was afraid to voice.

He pulled her against him and deepened the kiss and they stood wrapped together for long moments while the flame from her gas fireplace flickered and danced and tiny snow pellets hissed against the windows.

She wanted to be with him. The yearning blossomed inside her, fierce and powerful. She felt as if everything the last few weeks—okay, for years, if she were honest—had been leading them to this moment.

A low, sultry heat simmered between them and she could taste the change in his kiss, from tenderness to something more, something rich and sensual and delicious.

She pressed against him, tangling her fingers in his hair, stealing sensuous delight through the slide of her tongue along his.

He made no move to capitalize on the convenient queen-size bed behind them so Elise decided she would just have to take matters into her own hands. She eased down and pulled him along with her.

He made a low, sexy sound in his throat and stretched along beside her, his body hard and powerful. She could feel the heat of him scorching her, his tightly leashed strength, and for one crazy moment she couldn't believe this was really happening, that she was really here with Matt Cates.

Somewhere in her room amid the collected detritus of her childhood—maybe in a box of keepsakes under her bed?—was the diary she'd kept in elementary and junior high school, where she had poured out all her silly angst about him.

Why wouldn't he notice her?

He sat with that silly, brainless Jamie Fletcher at lunchtime.

He smiled and joked with her while they were standing in line for the drinking fountain.

She wondered how he would react if he knew about her girlhood crush. Would he be mortified or amused?

She didn't care. Not right now, with his arms around her. This was so much more wonderful than anything she could have imagined back then.

His mouth trailed down her throat, his breath warm on her skin. Everything inside her seemed to sigh. If she had even an inkling back then how magical kissing Matt could be, she would have gladly tripped through the hallway every single day at school, if that was the only way to make him notice her.

His mouth slid just below the loose cowl of her sweater, and she shivered, aching for his touch.

"We'd probably better stop," he murmured.

"Why?"

His gaze met hers, clear reluctance there. "We've still got a long drive back to Thunder Canyon tonight."

"It's snowing," she pointed out in what she thought was a particularly reasonable argument. "Let's just stay here for the night. We can head back in the morning, can't we?"

He sat up and drew in a ragged breath, his eyes dark and hot. "I really don't think that's a great idea, Elise. In case you haven't noticed, I can't seem to keep my hands off you."

She could see his arousal in that slumberous look he wore, hear it in his ragged breathing. He wanted her, just as much as she wanted him, and the realization left her feeling sexy and feminine and powerful.

She hadn't experienced that particular heady mix of emotions very often in her life and she decided to revel in it.

"I don't want you to. Keep your hands off me, I mean. In case *you* haven't noticed, I happen to like your hands on me."

He closed his eyes on a rough-sounding sigh. "Elise—"

"Spend the night here with me, Matt. I want you to."

Chapter Eleven

Her low words sizzled through him, rich and potent, with a hell of a kick. Just like Christmas eggnog. He stared at her, slender and delicate and lovely, and he wanted her with a fierce hunger.

It would be so very easy to take what she was offering, to kiss her and touch her until they were both crazy with need.

But he thought of her tangled emotional state, the stresses weighing on her for the last few weeks and knew he couldn't take advantage of her like that, as much as he ached to taste the passion he sensed brimming just under the surface.

His entire strategy since that night at The Hitching Post had been one of patience. He intended to give her plenty of time to come to terms with everything that had happened the last few weeks with her family—and with the possibility of a deepening relationship between the two of them.

She was throwing that plan all to hell.

He wanted to devour her right now, just cover her body with his, slide beneath that silky-soft comforter on her bed and spend the night wrapped together while the snow clicked against the window and the world outside this room ceased to matter.

He wanted that so intensely he could barely hang on to a coherent thought, but he did his best, knowing this was too important for him to screw it up.

"I'm not sure this is the right time," he began valiantly.

She smiled that soft, reckless smile again and he wondered a little wildly what had happened to his sweet Elise and how this sexy seductress had taken her place.

Not that he was complaining or anything.

"This is the perfect time," she murmured, leaning into him. "I want to be with you. I want it more than I can tell you."

He closed his eyes, praying he could do the right thing here. Finally, he rose and stood beside the bed. When he spoke, his voice was low and tinged with sadness.

"I wish you were saying that because you meant it and not just because you want to forget everything for a little while."

She stared at him for a long moment and then she gave a low, throaty laugh. "Is that what you think this is?"

She rose until only a few inches separated them. He could feel the heat of her, smell the delicious raspberries-and-cream scent. She splayed her fingers against his chest and he could swear she would scorch through the material of his shirt.

"You're wrong, Matt. So wrong. I've wondered how it would be with you since I was old enough to even understand about the difference between men and women. You've never noticed me as anything but sweet little Elise." She sighed. "I guess it's confession time. My thoughts about you have always been anything but sweet."

She smiled again then leaned in to kiss him, her mouth soft and delicious, and he was lost.

This probably wasn't the smartest thing he had ever done but right now he didn't care. The only thing that mattered was Elise and the heartstopping promise of her kiss.

His body was yelling at him to rush, to rip off clothing and surge inside her fast and hard but he drew in a shaky breath and sought control. Not that way, not with Elise—at least not this time.

He felt as if he'd been handed a precious gift all wrapped up in pretty paper, and he wanted to savor every moment of discovering its secrets.

Without lifting his mouth from hers, he lowered them both to the bed again. Her breasts brushed against his chest and her thighs shifted on either side of one of his legs. He propped most of his weight on one elbow, worried a little about crushing her, but she wrapped her arms around him, nestling against him as if she wanted to be nowhere else in the world than right here with him.

"You tell me if you decide you've changed your mind," he ordered against his mouth. "I can't guarantee I'll like it, but I'll stop."

"I can take care of myself, you know," she said with that same enticing smile. "You can stop watching out for me now."

"Never," he said hoarsely.

He deepened the kiss, licking and tasting and exploring her mouth until he couldn't think straight. She tasted so good, sweetly delicious, and he couldn't seem to slake his hunger.

He wanted—needed—more. He slid his fingers beneath her sweater to the small of her back, and his insides trembled at the sensuous contrast of her soft skin against hard, calloused fingers that had driven a few too many nails.

"My hands are too rough," he murmured. "I don't want to hurt you."

"Never," she repeated his words earlier and eased into his touch.

They kissed for a long time, until she sat up a little and reached to pull the edges of her sweater over her head, leaving her in only a lacy red bra that barely cupped her lush little breasts and instantly ratcheted his temperature up about a thousand degrees.

He gulped. "Um. Wow."

She laughed. "I like sexy lingerie. It's a quirk, I know. I guess you'll just have to decide if you can accept it."

"It's going to be tough," he growled, "but I can prob-ably manage."

He unbuttoned his own shirt and pulled it off, aware of her eyes watching every moment and the hot tendrils of hunger coiling through him. He knew he'd been at-tracted to her before, but he never expected this sort of wild, ferocious heat.

She spread a hand over his chest and made a sexy little sound in her throat and then she toppled him back-ward on the bed and kissed him, her honey-blond hair a silky, sensuous veil around them.

How the hell had he overlooked her all these years? What was he thinking, always considering her just a sweet kid he needed to watch out for? A smart guy would have seen the sexy woman inside all that sweet-ness and would have jumped at any chance to be with her like this much sooner. He felt like he'd wasted far too much time as it was and didn't want to squander another moment.

She was everything he had ever wanted, all those nebulous things he hadn't admitted, even to himself. Even as they kissed and touched, he was aware of that edge of uncertainty around them. Her life was in chaos right now—as she'd said, she wasn't in a good place for a relationship. Though he knew it would be difficult, especially after tonight, he would just have to dig deep for patience.

He could wait. For now he had this, he had her, and he wasn't about to waste time worrying about all those uncertainties.

He slid his hands to the sides of her breasts above

the lace of her bra and she hitched in a breath, her stomach muscles contracting. "Oh, yes. Perfect," she murmured.

"Not yet," he said with a lopsided grin. "But heading there."

He was wrong. This was sheer heaven.

Elise felt powerful, sensual. He carefully flipped her back onto the pillow and danced his thumbs over her curves, then pushed one of her bra cups away before lowering his mouth.

She gasped aloud and gripped his head tightly, arching against him and holding him in place while he tasted and explored one and then the other.

With one hand, she slid her fingers through his hair, with the other she explored all that tantalizing skin stretched across his strong back.

The years of construction work had hardened him. He wasn't bulky but every inch was tightly leashed muscle and she wanted to taste all of it. She pressed a kiss to the muscles that corded between his neck and his shoulder and knew the exultant power of feeling his tremble of reaction.

Despite the fact that he was here, in her arms, in her bed, this still didn't seem real. She was afraid she would wake up and he would be gone.

She was almost more afraid that she would wake up and he would be right here, all those hard muscles and tender concern shoving their way into her defenseless heart.

"I care about you, Elise," Matt murmured after they

had removed the rest of their clothing, after their bodies were entwined and all that hard strength surrounded her. "I want you to know, this is important to me. *You're* important to me."

His words seemed to sneak through whatever was left of her paltry defenses to nestle in next to her heart. As much as they scared her, in a weird sort of way they managed to calm her more.

She *was* in love with him. This wasn't infatuation or friendship with benefits but something she had never known before.

Maybe that's why she had been fighting her feelings so hard. She wasn't sure she was strong enough to survive the sort of heartache Matt could leave behind.

She thought of Grant and Stephanie, how deeply they loved each other. They only had to walk into a room together and you could feel it snap in the air like ions whirling just before an electrical storm.

Marlon and Haley shared the same sort of love and everyone could see it.

She supposed she had always expected that when she finally fell in love it would be a soft and easy sort of thing, like settling in near the fireplace with a good book—even as some part of her had yearned for exactly this sort of wild, consuming passion.

"You're important to me, too," she confessed, her voice low. She wasn't going to worry about heartbreak. Not now. For now, she only wanted to focus on this moment, this man, the incredible heat and wonder of being in his arms.

He gripped her hands in his and kissed her as he

entered her with one powerful surge. Oh, yes. Now it was perfect. Her body shifted and settled to accommodate him and she wanted to lie here beneath him for the next week or two, just savoring this rare and beautiful connection between them.

"Elise," he murmured. "My sweet Elise."

She loved the sound of her name spoken in that rough-edged voice, the heat in his eyes as he kissed her.

She clutched his back as he surged inside her, every muscle shivering with delight. She felt as if she were like that eagle in the needlepoint they had bought for Haley, as if she were soaring and circling on currents of air with widespread wings, climbing higher and higher toward the sun. And then he kissed her, his mouth fierce and demanding, and reached a hand between their bodies, to the heat and ache at her core, and she climaxed in one mad, crazy instant that left her gasping and arching against him needing more and more.

When she glided back to earth, she found him watching her out of those hot, hungry, dark eyes.

"That was just about the sexiest thing I've ever seen," he said on a growl, then he kissed her fiercely and she held him while he found his own release.

After he had taken care of the condom—even in this, he protected her—Matt slid back into bed and pulled her close, nestling her against all his heat and strength. "You matter to me," he said again.

The snow continued to beat against the window and the sky looked dark and menacing, but here they were safe together. With her cheek resting on his chest, she listened to his strong, steady heartbeat in her ear and thought about love and fear, fantasy and reality and the strange twistings of fate, until she fell asleep.

For the first time in his life, Matt found himself reluctant to return to Thunder Canyon.

Usually he loved driving through town, that first glimpse of the mountains, the sense of homecoming, of belonging in a beautiful place.

Not today. Climbing out of Elise's bed in the predawn hours was just about the hardest thing he ever had to do. Unfortunately, though he would like to forget everything and stay right here, he had obligations waiting for him, the last few finishing details to the McFarlane Lodge, and knew they needed to make an early start.

Okay, he hadn't minded the early start—especially when he woke with a soft, sleepy Elise in his arms. She had kissed him, her body warm and pliant, and they had pleasured each other while dawn stretched across the sky.

He would have liked to think the incredible night and morning they spent in each other's arms could magically solve all the issues between them.

Unfortunately, reality wasn't always so cooperative. With each mile that he drove closer to Thunder Canyon, she seemed to pull away from him, until it was all he could do not to jerk the pickup around and head back to Billings.

Though she continued to make small talk with him—about the weather, about the Christmas gifts she was giving her family, about the things she had enjoyed at her job at the bookstore—she seemed distant, distracted.

Her words would sometimes trail off in the middle of a sentence and he would shift his attention from the road for a moment, to find her gazing absently out the window.

Finally, when they were only a mile outside the Thunder Canyon town boundaries, he knew he had to do something to try yanking her back toward him.

"Connor McFarlane's lodge is nearly finished," he said. "We should be wrapping it up today."

"I've heard it's beautiful. Haley said your dad gave her a tour and she can't stop talking about all the luxurious details."

"McFarlane's throwing a big party on Christmas Eve, inviting most of the town."

"Yes. My mother and Grant are planning on going. Remember, the Castros said they were going, too."

"That's right. I forgot we talked about it last night at dinner." He grabbed her hand and squeezed her fingers. "I guess I've been a little distracted."

He loved watching that little blush steal over her features. He had a feeling he would never tire of it.

"You and your father should certainly be the guests of honor for all the hard work you've put into the place."

He shrugged. "Like you said about the ROOTS party the other night, it was a team effort. But watching people enjoy a place you've built is a gratifying experience."

His hands tightened on the steering wheel. Nerves curled in his gut, something that didn't sit well with him.

"Listen, I want to take a date to the party. Specifically, you."

Her eyes widened and he didn't miss the barely perceptible clenching of her fingers in his.

"Matt, I'm not sure I'm ready for that."

He gave her a long look across the width of the cab. "Funny. I would have thought last night proved you were."

She sighed. "Everyone in town is already whispering that I'm the reason you broke your engagement to Christine. Yesterday morning before you and I left for Billings, I went to the grocery store with Steph and three people stopped her to ask if it was true the wedding was off. None of them would meet my gaze and I could practically feel the disapproval radiating off them. The two of us showing up together at the McFarlane Christmas party would certainly add considerable fuel to that rumor."

There she went, trying to find excuses again. Just how hard was a guy supposed to work before he gave a cause up as lost?

He thought about the connection they had forged together the night before, the sweet peace they had shared, and he was angry, suddenly, that she seemed willing to give that up without a fight.

"Who the hell cares about a little gossip? You and I both know it's not true and so does Christine. What else matters?"

She huffed out a breath. "That's easy for you to say. You've never cared about gossip. Good grief, you and

Marlon spent your lifetime raising as much trouble as you could, gossip be hanged."

He acknowledged some truth to that, but those days seemed far away.

"I'm not like you," she went on. "I hate finding myself the center of attention—and I feel like I haven't been standing anywhere else since the day Erin Castro showed up in Thunder Canyon."

She paused and pulled her fingers away from his. "When my father was murdered, I know everyone talked about me all the time. I could feel the conversation stop. Nobody talked to me about his murder except my few close friends. Haley, mostly, since Steph was in a pretty dark place with her dad's murder, too."

She sighed. "With everyone else, I felt like I had entered some kind of social black hole. I know they were kids and probably didn't have the skills to deal with such a rough thing. Nobody knew what to say, I guess, so it was easier to ignore me. But it still hurt, especially because I know everyone said plenty behind my back."

"I always talked to you," he said curtly, sick of her excuses and the whole damn situation. "*Always*. And I never let anybody say anything hurtful about you or your family, at least when I was in earshot."

He could feel her gaze on him. He shifted his attention from the road long enough to see her features soften. She reached a hand out and touched his thigh.

"You always did," she agreed. "You've been riding to my rescue since we were kids, haven't you?"

He couldn't have this conversation while he was

driving, he decided. Since they were close to Clifton's Pride, he steered onto the shoulder and put the truck in gear so he could safely face her.

"Because I care about you, Elise. I always have. I convinced myself you were just a sweet girl, maybe a little naive, who needed somebody to watch her back. And then you showed up in town again and I realized my feelings for you ran much, much deeper."

She drew in a shaky breath. "I care about you, too, Matt. Last night was…well, you know what it was. I don't want to screw this up. But I don't have the greatest track record with relationships and I'm so afraid."

"You think I'm not? You scare the hell out of me, Elise."

She gazed out the window at a magpie scavenging for berries on the stark, bare crimson dogwood branches along the ice-crusted creek. "I'm not bringing my best self to this," she finally said. "I don't think I can right now."

Those nerves in his gut coiled more tightly. "So instead of giving me the chance to show you I can be patient, you want to push me away, just as you've been doing since you came back to town."

"I don't know. Maybe." She sighed. "I told you I was a mess, Matt."

"I guess you have to decide what's more important to you. A little pointless gossip." He took a chance and reached for her hand, then drew her cool fingers to his mouth. "Or the way we feel about each other."

She narrowed her gaze at him. "Not fair."

He grinned and put the pickup in gear to drive the

rest of the way to the ranch house. "Whoever said I was fair?"

When they reached Clifton's Pride, he could already see a few signs of life, though the day was just starting: A ranch hand hauling a bucket of something, a light on in the kitchen, the rumble of a tractor probably hauling hay bales out to hungry cattle in some distant, snow-covered pasture.

He moved around to open her door before she could climb out and helped her down from the high truck. "I'll swing by before the party. I really hope you'll be here."

She sighed. "You're not going to give up, are you?"

"I walked away from law school without a backward look and haven't regretted it for a moment. But something tells me if I gave up on you as easily as I did that, it would haunt me for the rest of my life."

Chapter Twelve

"Here we go."

Matt parked his pickup in front of the sprawling Mc-Farlane Lodge and Elise could do nothing but stare.

"Wow! It's gorgeous!"

The house was everything people in town had said, soaring and majestic like the mountains around it. Constructed of log and stone, it seemed part of the landscape, as if it had grown here amid the boulders like the Douglas fir and spruce surrounding it.

"We worked with a log home company out of Helena on the structure but Cates did all the work inside."

"I'm sure it's even more beautiful there than it is from the outside."

"You ready to go see?"

She gazed at Matt across the width of his truck. He

must have showered and shaved just before he picked her up at Clifton's Pride. His brown hair appeared freshly combed, his jaw smooth, and all through the drive here the scent of his sexy soap or aftershave or whatever it was had been driving her crazy.

He wore a dressy black leather bomber-style jacket over a tan twill shirt that made him look rugged and masculine, darkly dangerous.

He looked like the sort of man who could take on dragons. Or at least a house full of curious friends.

"Yes. I think I am."

"I'm really glad you came with me," he said as he opened the door for her.

She had to admit, she had waffled back and forth all week long. Some part of her would have liked to stay back at Clifton's Pride—and not simply because of the potential for wagging tongues.

Since her father's murder, Christmas Eve had become one of her least-favorite days of the year. She didn't miss the irony. Like most kids, she had always loved the holidays when she was a girl. Her father had loved the season, too, and she had many wonderful, vivid memories of her girlhood: Christmas caroling, wrapping gifts, sneaking baskets of gifts and food onto needy porches.

If the weather wasn't too snowy, every Christmas Eve her dad would saddle horses for her and Grant and the three of them would take a long, snowy ride into the mountains while Helen stayed back at the ranch putting the finishing touches to their Christmas Eve dinner.

They were wondrous times for a girl, filled with

laughter and excitement and breathless anticipation. After his death, all the joy and magic of the holidays seemed to die with him. Helen had tried to make an effort, but over the years Elise had come to the point where she wanted to just forget the whole day.

She'd even come to dread it, finding it too much of a struggle to pretend to be bright and cheerful when she wasn't.

As they walked up the winding pathway to the house, Elise tried to tamp down her nerves. She was so tired of this wild tangle of emotions. She wanted to just enjoy herself today, to focus on family and friends.

And Matt, the man who had become so very important to her.

Now, on the porch of the home he had built, she looked around at the fine-crafted details. The outdoor lighting looked like something out of a museum and the massive front door was hand-carved, a sculpted, twisted design of a tree with curving branches.

She couldn't resist touching the polished wood. "Wow. This is really exquisite, Matt. Beyond anything I expected."

He looked pleased at her praise and that fragile tenderness fluttered in her chest.

She had missed him this week. Both of them had been preoccupied with family obligations and he was busy with the beginning stages of a new Cates Construction project. She had only seen him once, when he had picked her up two nights earlier for a quiet dinner at his house.

Afterward, they had bundled up and gone for a chilly

walk through the darkened streets of town with his chocolate Lab bounding through the snowdrifts ahead of
them. Though they didn't encounter a moose this time
as they had in Bozeman, walking hand in hand through
the snowy streets in the moonlight had been sweet and
peaceful.

He had kissed her when he took her back to Clifton's
Pride but not with the heat and passion she wanted.
Rather, he had exhibited remarkable—albeit frustrat-
ing—restraint and had limited their embrace to a few
brief moments.

She pulled her fingers away from the door and slipped
them through his. "It's really stunning, Matt. I'm very
impressed."

"Come and see the rest."

He pushed open the door and they were instantly
assaulted by noise—shrieking children, jazzy holiday
music playing through hidden speakers, laughter and
the low, chattering hum of a dozen conversations.

She knew just about everyone. Her mother was talk-
ing with Steph's mother and Judy Johnson, owner of the
Clip N' Curl. In another seating group, she spied Holly
Clifton talking with Erika and Shandie Traub.

A few people looked up at their entrance and Elise
thought she saw a few raised eyebrows, but she told
herself she didn't care. Matt was right, a little gossip
wouldn't hurt her.

They hadn't made it two steps inside when suddenly
Christine Mayhew hurried over to them, her arms outstretched. To Elise's shock, Christine pulled her into a
warm hug, laughing and talking about something one

of the children had just said. She hugged Matt next and then looped an arm through Elise's.

Elise saw confusion on more than a few faces. She was confused, too, since she had barely met Christine but the woman was acting as if they were best friends.

Christine talked with them for several moments before excusing herself. "There's Tori. I need to ask her who did that incredible oil painting in the master bedroom."

Before she walked away, she gave Matt a sidelong smile. "Unless you think that wasn't sufficient to prove to everyone in town you didn't wrench out my poor little heart and drive over it with your backhoe, you beast."

He grinned. "That ought to do it. Thanks, Chris."

"Anytime," she said with another hug to Elise before she sauntered away.

"So that was all a setup?" Elise asked.

He shrugged, trying and failing to look innocent. "I figured the best way to shut off the gossip valve in a hurry was to show that this is not some torrid love triangle. Looks like it worked."

Oh, she was in serious trouble. That tenderness zinged through her again and she was immeasurably touched that he would make the effort to keep her out of the spotlight.

She should have expected it. He *was* her self-appointed protector, wasn't he? Apparently that covered everything from schoolyard bullies to social scandals.

She couldn't resist smiling at him. "You're a very sweet man, Matt," she murmured.

His brown-eyed gaze met hers and everything inside

her sighed at the warm light there. "Guys don't like to be called sweet, El," he said with a mock growl.

She checked to make sure they were out of earshot of others at the party, then she spoke in a voice pitched low so only he could hear. "Okay. How about this. When you do thoughtful little things like that, I find it incredibly sexy. Even better than that thing you do with your tongue in my ear."

He gave a rough laugh. "Cut it out or I'll be dragging you out of the party before we even say hello to our hosts."

As much as the idea of that appealed to her right now, she knew this party was important to him. He had worked hard to create a showplace for Connor McFarlane and was justified in being pleased with his efforts.

"I want to see the house. Will you give me a private tour? Show me all the secret corners and out-of-the-way closets?"

He sent her a dark look but grabbed her hand and led her up the staircase. On the way, he pointed out details like the hand-peeled banister and the imported light fixtures.

He kept up a running commentary as he led her from room to room. Though she wouldn't have thought she could find a discussion on the challenges of post-and-beam construction fascinating, he made it interesting and she admired the obvious care Cates Construction had put into the work.

In one of the bedrooms, he started discussing the relative merits of using alder or black walnut. He was so impassioned about it, she couldn't help herself, she wrapped her arms around his neck and pulled his mouth down to hers.

For an instant, he only stared at her and then he closed the door firmly, leaning against it so no one could interrupt them while he kissed her properly, as she had been wanting him to do since the moment he picked her up.

That sweet peace fluttered through her as he kissed her, the sense of rightness and home and everything wonderful. She held him close, heat churning through her and her emotions a thick, tangled clog in her throat.

By the time he eased away, both of them were breathing raggedly.

"You're killing me, Elise. Everyone in town is downstairs and all I want to do is lock that door and forget the rest of the world exists. Hell, look at me! I can't even leave this room until I'm a little more…under control."

She glanced down at his obvious arousal and smiled, thoroughly enjoying herself. "Well, then, I guess you'll just have to tell me more about exactly why black walnut is so vastly superior for its hardness and durability."

He stayed a safe distance away for several moments while Elise wandered through the bedroom and its attached bathroom, admiring all the thoughtful little luxuries in the design. Finally, he determined he could face polite company again.

When they left the room and walked down the stairs sometime later, Elise could sense something momentous happening. Excitement seemed to coil through the lodge like the silvery garlands on the tree.

"What's going on?" Matt asked the first people he saw standing at the bottom of the stairway—his brother Mitchell and sister-in-law Lizbeth.

"The craziest thing." Lizbeth's lovely features glowed. "Connor and Tori are getting married."

Matt frowned. "Haven't we all known that for months?"

"No, I mean right now. They decided on the spur of the moment that this was the perfect time to tie the knot, while all their friends and family are already here and everyone is celebrating. We're having a wedding in just a few moments! Won't that just make Christmas Eve perfect?"

"Oh, how wonderful," Elise exclaimed.

"Tori already has her dress and veil. Knowing her fashion sense, it's going to be gorgeous," Lizbeth said.

"What can I do to help?" Elise asked.

"I think everything is nearly ready. Tori's upstairs with Allaire getting dressed. I think Shandie's doing her hair."

"I'll help set up the chairs," Matt said.

For the next half hour the lodge was filled with a flurry of activity as the residents of Thunder Canyon rallied to help organize the last-minute wedding. Flowers and greenery were snatched from the elegant decorations for bouquets and corsages, slim white candles were gathered from various locations around the house and arranged along the mantel and someone shifted the music on the sound system from holiday carols to sweetly romantic songs.

Matt and his brothers and some of the other men

had dragged every available chair into the huge great room and arranged them in rows, all facing the twenty-foot Christmas tree and the sweeping mountain views beyond from the floor-to-ceiling windows.

Now, Elise sat beside him while soft, romantic music played. He reached for her hand as Connor and his teen-age son CJ walked up to stand near the Christmas tree. Connor looked handsome and successful in a gray de-signer suit that set off his distinctive auburn hair.

Everyone rose when Tori appeared at the top of the curved half timber staircase on the arm of her father, Dr. Sherwood Jones, with her best friend Allaire Traub and CJ's friend Jerilyn Doolin as her attendants.

She looked breathtaking, in an off-the-shoulder, three-quarter-length dress. Shandie had worked won-ders with her strawberry-blond hair and it was coiled atop her head in a style both elegant and romantic.

While everyone admired the lovely bride, Elise found her attention shifting to Connor McFarlane, waiting near the windows. Something fragile and sweet tugged in her heart when she witnessed the soft light in his eyes as Tori glided down the stairs with her arm tucked through her father's.

The two of them radiated happiness and Elise wasn't the only one dabbing away tears as she listened to their heartfelt vows and saw their obvious joy in each other.

After the ceremony, Connor brought out magnums of champagne and everyone lifted flutes in a toast to the glowing couple. When several toasts had been offered, Connor nudged Marlon. "You know, we're all set for a wedding now. Everybody's here. Trust me, you could save yourself a lot of trouble if you just took care of things now and tied the knot."

"A lovely offer—thanks," Haley said with a smile. "But I have my heart set on a spring wedding."

"Have you set a date?" Elise asked.

Marlon and Haley exchanged glances. "Yes," Haley answered. "Finally. We decided last night on April 11, if we can put it together that soon."

Tori hugged her. "If we could throw mine together in half an hour, I think a few months should be plenty of time."

"You'll still be my maid of honor, won't you?" Haley asked Elise.

Would she be in Thunder Canyon for the wedding? Elise had no idea what the future held, but she decided she would do whatever it took to help Haley have the most beautiful wedding in Thunder Canyon history. She deserved a wonderful happy ending of her own.

"You couldn't keep me away," she answered with a hug.

"I don't think you're going to be the only ones hearing wedding bells in the near future," Connor said with a gesture toward Erin Castro and Dillon Traub.

They stood in a group with Elise's mother and Grant and Stephanie. Erin and Corey held hands and even from here, Elise could sense the bond between them.

Everyone around her was getting married. She swallowed hard with a careful look at Matt, who had left their group to talk to his father and a few other men.

He looked strong and gorgeous and everything inside her seemed to sigh whenever she saw him. She wanted what it seemed everyone else around them had found but she was so afraid to dream about forever, especially right now when everything felt so topsy-turvy.

Mindful of the hazards of overindulging—hadn't she learned *that* particular lesson painfully well?—she took only a tiny sip of her champagne while she listened to the ebb and flow of conversation around her.

Out of the corner of her gaze, she spied Grant and Stephanie approaching Erin's group. As she watched, her brother slipped an arm around his newly discovered sister's shoulder and guided her to a couple of Thunder Canyon old-timers who must not have had the chance to meet her yet.

The champagne took on a bitter taste and suddenly the room felt close and airless.

Suddenly she thought of what Matt had said the other day, that there was room in her heart for everyone. She was definitely discovering that. She was already coming to care for the Castros. Didn't the same hold true? Just because her family had embraced Erin didn't mean they were pushing her away at the same time.

She let out a shaky breath. She had been acting like a spoiled brat, she realized. She wanted something—her life back, the one she'd known before Erin discovered the hospital mistake. Since she could no longer have it, instead of reacting with dignity and grace and looking for the good in the situation, she felt like she'd been throwing a pissy temper tantrum since Thanksgiving.

How had anybody been able to stand her?

As she gazed out the window, through the trees she saw a wide glimmer of white not far away from

McFarlane Lodge. Silver Stallion Lake, she realized. Because of the way the road curved, she hadn't realized it was so close.

She glanced around the crowded room at everyone celebrating weddings and engagements and Christmas and then looked back at the lake, a favorite spot of locals. The idea of clearing her head was suddenly immensely appealing. Since she didn't think anyone would miss her for a few moments, she headed for the room where they had hung their coats earlier.

A moment later, she slipped out the lovely sculpted door and into the lightly falling snow.

"No, I'm not joking," Bo Clifton, Elise's cousin and the town's new mayor-elect gave Matt's father a solemn look. "Completely serious. I know it's hard to believe but I just got the phone call from the sheriff that they've arrested him."

"Who's under arrest?" Matt asked, overhearing just the tail end of the conversation as he approached them.

"Arthur Swinton," Frank said, eyes wide and shocked.

His father hadn't been a fan of the mayor whom Bo was supposed to be replacing after the new year. He considered him a prosy old windbag, but he seemed as shocked as Matt that the man had been arrested.

"What are the charges?" Matt asked.

"Multiple counts of embezzlement and fraud of public funds," Bo said, his features grim. "You know how the town budget has been struggling so much for the last few years and revenue seems to have dwindled to a trickle? Well, it turns out the soft economy is only partly responsible. Arthur Swinton has been dipping his fat little fingers into the city's coffers, maybe for years."

"I always knew he was difficult to work with," Frank said with disgust. "Always making us jump through ridiculous hoops when it came to building permits and zoning regulations. I just never imagined he was crooked."

"I did," Grant Clifton said. "Everything makes sense now. I never could figure out where the redevelopment tax incentives we'd been promised to expand the resort had disappeared to. Now I know."

"We'll get everything straightened out," Bo promised them all. "I'm pushing hard for the swearing in to be held on New Year's Day so I can start cleaning up this mess and get this town back on track."

Grant clapped him on the shoulder. "Whatever you need, Bo, we'll help. I've been talking with Corey and Dillon Traub and we've got big plans for the resort."

"The Traubs are partnering with Caleb Douglas and Justin Caldwell?" Matt asked, surprised.

"That's the plan," Grant said. "They're looking for another investment and see nothing but good things for Thunder Canyon and the resort in the future. We're talking a major expansion here."

He paused and smiled at the Cateses. "You know, we're going to need a reliable construction company. Cates is at the top of that list."

Pride surged through Matt. His father had built a solid reputation in Thunder Canyon and he knew his work the last few years had only added to that, but his professional satisfaction was tempered by plenty of uncertainty.

Part of him rejoiced at the idea of the revitalization of Thunder Canyon and the role Cates Construction might play in that. But the other part was all tangled up with a woman who didn't even know if she wanted to be anywhere near the town he loved.

News of the mayor's arrest had spread through the party and several people approached Bo for more details. While the man was busy explaining everything he knew about the charges against Swinton, Frank pulled Matt aside.

"You think we can handle a big project like Grant and the Traubs have in mind?" Frank asked. "We might need to add to the crew."

"I'm not sure," Matt admitted.

His father stared. "What do you mean, you're not sure? Wrong answer, son. You're supposed to say, 'Sure, Dad. I got this. We can handle anything.'"

On a professional level, Matt knew the company could handle any challenge that came its way. Hadn't they proved it the last few months by bringing in this job for Connor McFarlane quickly and efficiently?

When it came to his tangled, complicated relationship with Elise, he wasn't sure of anything.

"Dad, I need to be up-front with you," he finally said. "Since we talked last week about me taking over the company, a lot has changed." He paused. "More than a lot. *Everything* has changed."

Concern furrowed his father's brow and Matt squirmed under his scrutiny.

"Let's go where we can talk in private," Frank said gruffly, leading the way through French doors to one of several covered decks off the back of the house.

The deck was warmed by an outdoor gas fireplace, flames dancing and weaving as they pushed away the heavy, expectant cold of an impending storm.

"What do you mean?" Frank said after Matt closed the doors behind him. "What's changed?"

He looked down at the town he loved and was surprised at the ache in his chest. "I might be leaving Thunder Canyon," he said quietly.

Frank stared at him and Matt saw a host of emotions cross those expressive brown eyes, ending with resignation.

"It's Elise Clifton, isn't it?" he asked.

He shoved his hands in his pocket. "How did you... Why would you say that?"

His father shook his head. "I knew the moment I saw you two come in together. You've got that look in your eyes, the one I've seen all three of your brothers wear. Guess I shouldn't be so surprised."

Did he really want to be lumped in with his love-struck brothers? He thought about it for a moment, then gave a slight smile. "Yeah, that about sums it up," he answered.

"Doesn't mean you have to up and leave. Your brothers seem to be happy enough sticking around," Frank said.

"You know I love Thunder Canyon, Dad. If I could figure out a way, I would in a minute. But Elise hasn't been back in a long time. Things here haven't been easy for her. She has some pretty dark memories."

His father was silent for a moment, watching the flakes drift down in the gathering twilight. "She has reason, I suppose. Poor thing. I guess you and she will have to figure out your own path."

"We're working on it. To be honest, it's a hell of a lot more rocky than I expected."

His father nudged him with his shoulder. "The best views always come after a long, hard climb. Don't worry, you'll figure things out. She's not stupid, our Elise."

"Not in the slightest. But she has a lot of things to work through."

"You know your help has been invaluable at the company the last few years," his father said gruffly. "But I'll figure out how to get along without you if I have to."

"Thanks, Dad." He was fiercely grateful, suddenly, for his parents and the support and love they had always showered upon him and his brothers.

"You coming back inside to join the party?" Frank asked.

"In a minute. Think I'll watch the storm come in for a moment."

Sure enough, the snow already seemed a little heavier than it had when they walked onto the deck and those gray-edged clouds looked plump and full.

After his father left, Matt watched the trees twist and curl with the increasing wind. He could see downtown from here, cheerful and bright against the gathering darkness and felt another pang of regret. He would love to live here the rest of his life, to raise children, to help build the town and leave a legacy for those children. He could imagine many more Christmases spent here, filled with joy and laughter, friends and family.

But with something lost, something infinitely more precious could be found.

He was thinking about choices and growth and the future when he spied a slender figure bundled up in a red peacoat heading through the trees. He narrowed his gaze. He knew that coat. He had hung it himself when he and Elise had arrived.

Where was she going? The only thing in the direction of that trail was Silver Stallion Lake.

Of course. Crazy woman. Didn't she know it was dangerous to wander away on her own with that kind of storm brewing? Not to mention, with the above-freezing weather they'd had the last few days, more snow was bound to make the snowpack unstable and avalanche-prone.

All his protective instincts rattled around inside him. No way was he going to stand by while she put herself in possible danger. He hurried back inside the house and found his own coat quickly then headed outside to follow her trail in the gathering gloom.

The trail toward Silver Stallion Lake crossed the narrow road that ended in the box canyon where Connor had built his home. Some distance away toward town, Matt could see a huge cornice of snow blown by the wind now covering the peak at the canyon's edge.

He frowned. Add a few more inches on it and he could easily imagine the danger of a snowslide could potentially be high.

He would have to warn Connor when he returned to the house. But first, he needed to find Elise and make sure she was safe.

He walked quickly through the pines down a deer trail. The snow was soft and light for now and the air smelled of pine and winter. As he expected, he found her at the small lake, surrounded by pines and the pale ghostly skeletons of the winter-bare aspens.

In the few moments' head start she had, she must have unearthed a pair of skates from the small structure on the edge of the lake that was kept stocked with such things for locals' use. She sat on a log bench tying the skate. When she finished, she stood and glided out gracefully onto the ice.

Though he was aware of the need for haste and caution with the storm blowing in, he couldn't resist watching her from his concealed spot in the trees. She looked free and relaxed as she whirled and danced.

He thought of his father's words. He was lovestruck, just as his brothers. The realization should have scared him, sent him hurrying away. Instead, he was aware of a sweet, fragile tenderness.

He loved Elise. No matter what, he loved her. Nothing else mattered. She was everything he had ever wanted, the only thing he needed. If she wanted to move away from Thunder Canyon, he would do it. Hell, he would go live in a hut in Borneo if it meant he could have Elise with him.

He finally emerged from the trees and made his way down the trail toward the bank of the frozen lake.

She toed to a stop when she spotted him and stood waiting as he carefully moved across the ice.

A thin trail of tears had left a mark down her cheeks and his heart ached for her. "Oh, sweetheart. Are you okay?" he asked.

She smiled and it took a few beats for him to realize what seemed so different about her. Despite the tear stains, she looked relaxed, happy.

At peace.

"My dad used to bring me to the lake all the time when I was a little girl. I had completely forgotten how much I love it here. It always seemed to me when I was little that the mountains appear to cup this valley like comforting hands. That sounds silly, doesn't it?"

"Not to me."

"I can see my dad clear as day, holding my hands and towing me along the ice while I slipped and slid and tried to find my skate legs for the first few moments. I wasn't the most graceful kid, as you might recall. I was so clumsy everywhere else but when I skated, it seemed like I forgot that."

He pictured her as a little girl, small and slender for her age, running so fast she often stumbled as she tried to keep up with all the other kids. He could visualize her father, too, strong and handsome, a man everyone in town had admired and respected.

Learning she wasn't genetically John Clifton's child must feel to her as if she had lost her father all over again. He couldn't even imagine how difficult it must be for her.

He wanted to comfort her, to say something magical

that would make her pain disappear. He couldn't think of any words so he reached out and gripped her mittens in his own gloves.

"Is this the way he did it?" he asked and began walking backward, pulling her across the ice.

"Be careful. You're going to fall," she warned.

His heart was a sweet, heavy ache in his chest. "I'm counting on you to catch me, Elise."

Her gaze locked with his, emotions churning there. Despite the party still in full swing back at the McFarlane Lodge, despite the storm hovering just out of view, despite all the turmoil, he wouldn't have traded this moment for anything.

Just the two of them in the quiet hush of a miraculous Christmas Eve.

After a few passes across the lake, he stopped in the middle of the ice and with a sense of destiny, he pulled her into his arms and kissed her.

Her mouth was cold against his but she sighed and wrapped her mittened hands around his waist, leaning into him.

The kiss was slow and lovely. Perfect for the evening and the moment.

"You should know something," he murmured against her mouth. "I told my dad just now that I might not be taking over Cates Construction after all."

She eased away from him, her expression perplexed. "Why? I thought you loved being a builder. Are you thinking of going back to law school?"

"No. I do love the work. But I figured I can do the

same thing anywhere. Billings. Bozeman. Even San Diego if that's where you decide you want to go."

He brushed his mouth over hers. His heart seemed to pound loudly in his ears. This was a risk he had never taken with a woman before—never *wanted* to take. With her, it was right. He knew it deep in his bones.

"I love you, Elise," he murmured.

She drew away from him sharply and nearly stumbled backward on the ice. Her hands flailed a little before she caught her balance. "You…what?"

He saw shock and disbelief and something else, a tiny spark of something bright and joyful that filled him with hope.

"I love you," he repeated firmly. "If you're not happy in Thunder Canyon because of the memories or your dad or what's happened with your family or whatever, I won't try to convince you to stay. I would never do that to you."

He moved forward to take her hands in his again while the fat flakes landed in her lashes, on her cheeks, in her hair. He pulled her across the ice into his arms again and kissed the corner of her mouth.

"You don't have to stay in Thunder Canyon, Elise. But I'm not about to let you go somewhere else without me."

She closed her eyes for a long moment. When she opened them, that tiny sliver of hope he had seen had been replaced by sadness.

"You can't love me, Matt."

"Why not?"

She didn't answer, only pulled her hands away from him and headed across the ice, her movements no longer full of grace and beauty but abrupt, forceful, each stroke digging into the ice.

He followed after her as she sat down on the log to remove the ice skates. "Don't tell me how I feel, Elise. I've never been in love before but I know exactly what this is. I'm crazy about you."

"How can you be?" she asked, her voice bitter. "I'm such a mess and you seem to have borne the brunt of it these last few weeks."

He heard the despair in her voice, that sadness that had seemed such a part of her since she had come back.

But he had also seen that moment of joy in her eyes. He had tasted the heat of her kiss and sensed the suppressed emotions behind it.

She cared about him. They had something special here and he wasn't about to let her throw it away because of some misguided idea that she didn't belong here.

If he ever thought he might have had the skills to be persuasive in a courtroom, now would probably be a really good time to prove it.

He sat beside her on the fallen log, remembering when he and some buddies had dragged it over to the edge of the lake a few years back.

"You asked me how I can love you," he said quietly. "A better question would be, how can I not? Yes, you've had a rough few weeks. But no matter what you think, all I've seen is a woman facing a hard situation with strength and courage."

She flashed him a look, then returned to unlacing her skate. He hoped she was listening. All he could do was try.

"Despite your own turmoil," he went on, "you've reached out to everyone else in town. Just look at what you did for Haley last week and how hard you worked to make Christmas great for some needy kids at ROOTS, despite your own ambivalence about the holidays?"

"Haley's my friend. I did it to help her."

"I saw you with all those kids, Elise. You can tell yourself you were only helping Haley but I saw how excited you were to give them all their gift bags—the bags you spent hours preparing. And the Castros. You were so great with them at dinner, patiently answering all their questions about your childhood even though I saw how difficult it was for you to be there."

"You helped me get through that. I'm not sure I could have done it on my own."

"You could have," he assured her. "But don't you think it's significant that you asked me to come with you? That you turned to me for help when you needed it?"

He reached for her hand and brought it to his mouth. "I love you, Elise. No matter how much you've been fighting it, I know you have feelings for me, too. I want a future with you, no matter where and what shape that future might take."

Chapter Thirteen

Elise listened to his words, low and fervent amid the snowflakes fluttering down, and that tiny, fragile joy curled through her again.

This couldn't be real. She couldn't really be sitting on the banks of Silver Stallion Lake with Matt Cates declaring his love for her. Things like this didn't happen to girls next door like her. Any moment now, she was going to wake up and discover this was only some surreal dream brought on by too much eggnog.

But now, if it were a dream, she wouldn't feel the wet snow in her hair, the cold of the ice seeping through her boots.

"I love you, Elise," Matt murmured one more time. "You trusted me out on that ice not to let you fall, just as I trusted you. Don't you think we can trust each other about this?"

She stared at him as the snow fell heavier, until his features were hazy, indistinct.

She didn't need to see him. She knew every line, every angle of his face.

She loved him.

The precious truth of it slid through her, filling and healing every battered aching corner of her heart.

She loved him—and she suddenly knew that if she threw this chance away, she would be the craziest woman who had ever come out of Thunder Canyon.

She gave a tiny, bubbling little laugh, unable to contain so much happiness inside.

"You're right. You're so very right."

"Elise—"

"I love you, Matt. I have loved you most of my life, if you want the truth. Those days when we were in school and you were always watching out for me, keeping me safe—you were my hero, Matt. Everything I ever dreamed about."

He made a low sound of disbelief and for some reason, that made her laugh again. She was so happy, she wanted to shout it to the trees, to spin around and around on the ice like she was a fearless, clumsy six-year-old again.

She took off her mittens then reached for his hands and slid his glove off so she could raise his warm hand to her cold cheek.

She held his hand there against her skin. "I had no

idea back then how you would ride to my rescue again, Matt. You saved me."

"No, I didn't. You would have come through."

"Maybe. But I feel like I was falling through that ice, floundering in the cold, and you reached a hand in and yanked me back to light and warmth again. Thank you for that and for…giving me back myself."

She smiled tremulously. "I love you."

He stared at her and she saw heat and wonder and she thought she might even see the sheen of tears there. "Are you sure you don't have dreams of being an attorney? That's quite a closing argument."

"No, thank you." She smiled.

He kissed her there amid the falling snow and she tasted a sweet tenderness and the promise of a beautiful future.

Her father would have approved, she thought. He would have been delighted she found someone who could make her so very happy, who could pick her up when she stumbled, brush her off, and give her a chance to soar across life like she skated across Silver Stallion Lake.

They kissed softly for a long time, love wrapping them tightly together against the elements.

Finally, he drew away from her. "We're going to freeze to death if we stay here much longer. Do you think you're ready to go back?"

She slid her hand into his, loving his heat and the solid strength of him. "No," she answered. "But I think I'm ready to go forward."

He smiled and kissed the tip of her nose then led the way through the storm.

* * *

The snow was falling in earnest by the time they made it back to the lodge. A good four inches had fallen, Elise realized. Not enough to make driving impossible for Montanans used to inclement weather, but certainly enough to make it challenging.

She saw that several vehicles that had been parked out front earlier were gone. Probably families with young children, returning to their own homes for their own holiday traditions—hanging stockings, telling stories, setting out cookies for Santa.

It was Christmas. Anticipation nudged her like an old, familiar friend. Christmas, a time of hope and renewal, of miracles and second chances.

"Come home with me and spend Christmas Eve, Elise," Matt said just before they pushed open that beautiful door to Connor and Tori's home. "Will you?"

Through the windows, she could see her family inside. Both of her families. Her mother was chatting with the Castros and they all looked so happy together.

They wanted her to be happy with them, she realized. No one had been pushing her to the outside. She was the one who had refused all their efforts, the outstretched hands waiting to pull her toward them.

They would be sorry if she wasn't with them on Christmas Eve but there would be other years. This year, she wanted to be with Matt and she knew her entire crazy, complicated family would understand.

She smiled at him. "I just need to tell my mother so she doesn't worry," Elise said. She pushed open the door but before she could go inside, a huge rumbling roared above the sounds of the party coming from inside.

"What on earth?" she gasped, grabbing his shoulder.

"Avalanche," he said grimly. "Look."

Perhaps a quarter mile away down the road, she watched a vast, unrelenting sweep of snow tear away and pour down the mountain, breaking trees and moving boulders in its destructive path.

When it stopped, the only road back to town was completely covered with several feet of snow and debris.

Elise was still processing the shock of the slide as the other guests rushed out onto the wide porch.

"What the hell was that?" Connor McFarlane, still in his wedding suit, looked around. "It sounded like a hurricane."

"A slide blocked the road," Matt said. "I saw the cornice earlier and it looked unstable. I was going to warn you but got…distracted. I'm guessing all this heavy wet snow must have shifted the base enough to send the whole thing tumbling down."

"Did you see what happened? Is anybody down there?" Bo Clifton pushed his way through the crowd. "Do I need to call out search and rescue?"

"I don't think so. I didn't see anyone," Matt said. "A car had just driven through but they were a half mile down the road already when the snow came down."

"We'd better go check it out," Matt's brother Marshall said.

Several men hurried to find coats.

"By the looks of it, it's going to take several hours to dig out the road," Matt warned Connor.

"You mean we're stuck here?" someone said. "But it's Christmas Eve!"

"Oh, dear." Helen and Betty Castro exchanged distressed looks.

"I'm sorry about this." Connor immediately stepped in to take charge, as he was so good at doing. "We have plenty of food and blankets. It will be fun. We'll have a good, old-fashioned Christmas Eve."

He was being remarkably decent about sharing his wedding night with half the town, Elise thought. His words and his calm manner seemed to galvanize those remaining at the lodge into action. Immediately, people went in search of blankets and pillows and the party took on an even more festive air.

Elise was helping Haley organize an impromptu holiday classic film festival in the lodge's elaborate media room for some of the disgruntled teens when she suddenly became aware of Erin standing in the doorway, watching her with a wary expression.

"Do you guys need any help in here?"

She studied the other woman and was ashamed of herself for her small-minded jealousy of the last few weeks. None of this was Erin's fault and she had tried several times to forge a friendship. Elise had been the one pushing her away.

"Actually, I think Haley's got everything under control. I was just about to go to the kitchen and see if I can make popcorn. Want to join me?"

Erin looked surprised at the invitation but gratified.

Together, they unearthed several bags of microwave popcorn in the elaborate kitchen and stuck one in each of the pair of gleaming appliances.

They talked casually for a few moments, until Erin suddenly blurted out, "I don't want your life, you know."

Elise stared at the other woman. "I'm sorry. What?"

Erin pushed a strand of blond hair out of her face. "I know you've been struggling to deal with what happened twenty-six years ago. I just wanted to let you know I'm sorry you've been hurt by everything. I never expected... well, what happened. I'm sure you probably would have preferred if I'd never come to Thunder Canyon looking for answers."

Elise traced the events of the last month. She thought of how her life would have been different if she had never come back to Thunder Canyon. She probably never would have reconnected with this place and the people who had been so important to her once.

Through the kitchen doorway, she heard Jack Castro's gruff laugh and she thought of how kind and loving Erin's parents were and of the two brothers she had scarcely met.

And Matt.

If Erin hadn't come to Thunder Canyon to dig into the secrets of her past and discovered that fateful mistake, Elise would never have reconnected with Matt. She never would have discovered that sometimes silly girlish dreams could come true.

That secret joy shivered through her again, the love she would no longer deny, and on impulse she hugged

Erin. The other woman froze for just a moment before Erin returned her embrace.

"I've always wanted a sister," Elise said. "In a weird sort of way, it almost feels like we were twins separated at birth."

Erin laughed. "Oh, please! Not twins. Isn't our past twisted and tangled enough?"

She laughed. "Good point."

Before she could say anything else, a thin, nervous voice interrupted them.

"Excuse me, have you seen Bo?"

She turned and found Holly Pritchett Clifton, her cousin's lovely new wife.

"I think he's down assessing the avalanche with some of the other men to figure out how to dig out the road," she answered. "Is everything okay?'

"Um, not really." She gave a nervous-sounding laugh. "We're stranded here with no way into town on Christmas Eve in the middle of a blizzard."

"I know," Erin said. "Things couldn't get much crazier, right?"

Holly gave that nervous laugh. "Want to bet? I think my water just broke."

"What is taking so long?" Erica Rodriguez Traub exclaimed. "I swear, I wasn't this nervous when my own baby was born."

The entire temporary population of McFarlane Lodge seemed to be on edge, gathered in the great room while upstairs in a hastily arranged delivery room, Holly was attended by Drs. Marshall Cates and Dillon Traub—and, of course, Bo.

As the hours ticked away, everyone stranded at McFarlane Lodge hovered in a state of excitement, even the teens who emerged from the media room every once in a while to check the status of the delivery.

And then, finally, at ten minutes to midnight, a thin, high cry wailed through the house. Everyone in the great room raised up a huge cheer.

A few moments later, Marshall emerged onto the landing. He looked disheveled and tired but Elise saw the quiet satisfaction in his eyes.

"It's a boy. Mother and baby—and mayor—are all doing fine."

"Good thing we've got plenty of champagne," Grant said, breaking out another magnum.

Elise declined to drink as she kept a careful eye out the window. Down below through the snowy darkness, she could see lights moving at the avalanche site.

Once it had been determined that the threat of more snowslides had passed, Matt had hiked down the mountain through the storm for one of the Cates Construction backhoes to begin digging out the avalanche.

Elise hated thinking about him out there in the cold, but she wasn't at all surprised. That was the man she loved, strong and dependable, always willing to help out those in need.

She was still watching sometime later when she spied those lights approaching the house and a few moments later, a bundled figure walked up the porch. Soon after,

Matt walked inside and started stomping off snow in the entryway.

Her heart a sweet, heavy ache in her chest, Elise hurried to him and threw her arms around his neck, not caring at all who might be watching. She kissed him with fierce emotion and he responded with gratifying enthusiasm.

"What was that about?" he murmured after a few moments. "Not that I'm complaining."

"It's after midnight. Merry Christmas, Matt."

She helped him out of his wet gear and found hot cocoa for him. She would have thought he would want to stay right next to the fire, but he grabbed her hand and a blanket and headed out to the protected covered porch, where the gas fireplace still sent out its warmth.

He sank onto a cushioned lounger out there and pulled her onto his lap, wrapping them both in a heavy blanket until they were snug and cozy.

He kissed her deeply then, his mouth firm and demanding, and she clutched him tightly, shaken by the emotions churning through her. She longed for a little more privacy so they could make love but she knew she could be content to be with him like this, hearts and bodies entwined beneath the blanket.

The storm was lifting. Outside their safe shelter, Elise could see tiny scattered stars glimmering through the clouds.

She sighed, resting her cheek against his broad, muscled chest, his heartbeat in her ear.

"I don't want to leave," she murmured.

He gave a rough-sounding laugh. "I don't think we

can sleep out here. Even with the gas fireplace and the blankets and your considerable body heat, I'm afraid we'll freeze."

She tilted her head to study his features. "I don't mean right here, tonight, though this is pretty wonderful. I meant...I don't want to leave Thunder Canyon."

His arms tightened around her and he shifted so he could meet her gaze, his brown eyes intent and hopeful. "Are you sure? You don't like it here."

Her hair brushed his chin as she shook her head. "Not true. Part of me has always loved it here. And tonight while you were down clearing the road and we were up here waiting for Holly to have her baby, I...I can't explain it, but I was part of something. Something bigger than me, bigger than any of us."

She smiled. "It was wonderful. Really wonderful. Everyone was so concerned about each other and I realized how very much I have missed that in my life, being part of a community. I have enjoyed living in Billings but it's never felt like home. Thunder Canyon is home and it always has been. I want to stay."

His arms tightened again and he kissed her with a new intensity, his eyes filled with emotion. He had been willing to leave the town he loved for her, and his willingness to make that sacrifice meant all the more to her now, when she could see how very much her words meant to him.

"What will you do?"

"I thought I would see if Haley needs more permanent help at ROOTS. I was also thinking about opening a bookstore. Somewhere roomy and welcoming, with plump couches for people to stretch out in."

"It sounds wonderful, El." He nuzzled her neck. "I know a good builder who might be willing to give you a good deal."

"I may take you up on that."

"What about San Diego and the Castros?"

She shrugged. "Maybe I can go spend a few weeks with them once everything settles down a little."

He was quiet for a long moment. When he spoke, his tone was one of studied casualness as his fingers traced the skin at the small of her back, just below her sweater

"You know, San Diego would be a great honeymoon destination."

She stared at him, her heart pounding. "Honeymoon?"

"Maybe not next week or even next month, but that's what I want. I figured it would only be fair to warn you."

She gave a disbelieving laugh, even as her heart continued to pound. Marriage. With Matt Cates. A future with his teasing smiles and tender kisses, with that strong sense of honor and goodness. A future with him watching out for her—and then transferring that strong protective streak to any children they might have.

She pictured Holly and Bo and the tiny baby they both loved. She could easily picture a little dark-haired version of Matt chasing after them, riding in the backhoe with him, skating across Silver Stallion Lake.

A few snowflakes blew into their cozy shelter and

one landed at his temple. She kissed him there, letting the cold melt against her mouth.

"Now," she murmured. "Now everything is perfect. I love you, Matt. Merry Christmas."

And as he held her, more stars peeked out through the clouds to glitter above the quiet peace of Thunder Canyon.

* * * * *

A sneaky peek at next month...

Cherish™

ROMANCE TO MELT THE HEART EVERY TIME

My wish list for next month's titles...

In stores from 18th November 2011:

❏ Firefighter Under the Mistletoe – Melissa McClone

& A Marine for Christmas – Beth Andrews

❏ Unwrapping the Playboy – Marie Ferrarella

& The Playboy's Gift – Teresa Carpenter

❏ Christmas in Cold Creek – RaeAnne Thayne

In stores from 2nd December 2011:

❏ Expecting the Boss's Baby – Christine Rimmer

& Twins Under His Tree – Karen Rose Smith

❏ Snowbound with Her Hero – Rebecca Winters

Available at WHSmith, Tesco, Asda, Eason, Amazon and Apple

Just can't wait?

Visit us Online

You can buy our books online a month before they hit the shops! **www.millsandboon.co.uk**

1111/23